Jack's little daughter
needs a mother...

...So do Steed's
orphaned nephews!

Jack and Steed. They were
parents without partners—but
look what they've fallen into!

The
Parent
Trap

**Emma Goldrick** was born and raised in Puerto Rico, where she met and married her husband Bob, a career military man. Thirty years and four children later they retired and took up nursing and teaching. In 1980 they turned to collaborative writing. After sixty years of living in over half the world, and a full year of studying Mills & Boon® style, their first submission was accepted. Between them they have written over 40 books and have sold over 22 million copies worldwide. Goldrick hobbies include grandchildren, flower gardens, reading and travel. Sadly, in 1996, Bob Goldrick passed away. Emma continues to write in his memory.

> "Emma Goldrick's light humorous touch combines delectable characters giving readers a wonderful lasting impression."
> —*Romantic Times*

**Helen Brooks** lives in Northamptonshire and is married with three children. As she is a committed Christian, busy housewife and mother, her spare time is at a premium but her hobbies include reading, swimming, gardening and walking her two energetic, inquisitive and very endearing young dogs. Her long-cherished aspiration to write became a reality when she put pen to paper on reaching the age of forty, and sent the result off to Mills & Boon. Since then, Helen has written 25 novels and has currently sold over 3 million copies of her books, which have been translated into more than 12 languages.

> "Helen Brooks pens a superb story with rich characters, sparkling interplay and a riveting emotional conflict."
> —*Romantic Times*

# The Parent Trap

LOVEABLE
KATIE LOVEWELL

*by*

EMMA GOLDRICK

THE DEVIL YOU KNOW

*by*

HELEN BROOKS

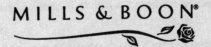

MILLS & BOON®

MILLS & BOON and MILLS & BOON with the Rose Device
are registered trademarks of the publisher.
Harlequin Mills & Boon Limited,
Eton House, 18-24 Paradise Road, Richmond, Surrey, TW9 1SR

*Loveable Katie Lovewell* and *The Devil You Know* were first published in
separate, single volumes by Mills & Boon Limited.
*Loveable Katie Lovewell* in 1991 and *The Devil You Know* in 1992

*Loveable Katie Lovewell* © Emma Goldrick 1991
*The Devil You Know* © Helen Brooks 1992

ISBN 0 263 80661 8

05-9712

Printed and bound in Great Britain
by Caledonian Book Manufacturing Ltd, Glasgow

# LOVEABLE
# KATIE LOVEWELL
*by*
EMMA GOLDRICK

To my great-niece,
little Katie Clark,
whose determination and
lovely red hair will
some day knock 'em all dead.

# CHAPTER ONE

KATIE LOVEWELL was the girl who fell asleep on the day of her father's funeral and woke up nine months later wondering what had happened to her life. Oh, not asleep as in the fairy-tales, waiting for Prince Charming to come and do his thing. Rather she fell into a daze, in which she ate and slept and worked—and did other things—without understanding or feeling the world that swirled around her. But on the day she woke up everything changed.

Kate could not for the life of her remember why she had come to the party, except that she needed the money. The old mansion, set low on the flank of Massanutten Mountain above the South Fork of the Shenandoah River, was full to overflowing with guests, most of whom were strangers to her. Or she to them. Mrs Fessenden's invitation had at first seemed like a challenge. A chance to pin Peter down among his own kind. And now she was doing her best to avoid him, and everyone else. They were just not her sort of people.

When the crowd finally migrated from the swimming pool out at the back, swirling like muddy water towards the two open bars in the ballroom, she saw it as a chance to think things through again, and slipped around the veranda and down to the now-empty pool area. Her feet were tired. A full morning at the pre-kindergarten had left her worn, flat, like a bottle of Coke left open too long. The two hours in the courthouse hadn't helped, either.

She settled herself gently into one of the lounge chairs, smoothing her navy knee-length skirt around her carefully, fluffing up the double row of ruffles that centred her white blouse. One more mark of distinction. She had come directly from the district court. Everyone else at the party wore jeans or bikinis or ragged shorts. It never ceased to amaze her how much the rich paid to look poor! Her eyes casually monitored the pair of cardinals settling into their spring routine in the ash trees. The smell of magnolias was almost overpowering. Virginia was coming out of its cloak of winter, flourishing. The noise above her, in the house, was muted by the garden that separated them, and the birds spoke valiantly of another summer to come. She closed her eyes, pulled out the pins that locked her long straw-coloured hair at her neck, and leaned back to think it through one more time.

'Are you the child-minder?' A tiny voice, almost at her elbow. Kate's eyes snapped open. Looking directly into her green eyes was a pair of childish blue ones, and a little girl, hesitant, unsure. An unruly mop of brown hair, a round pleasant face, a very short body—and a smile which came slowly, sweet enough to tear your heart out.

'Child-minder? Do you know some child who needs minding?' And a broad smile of sharing welcome. It was hard not to welcome such a little thing. Eight years old, perhaps? There were gaps between her teeth.

'I—my dad said there was a child-minder, while he— oh, here he comes now!' It almost seemed as if the little girl snapped to attention, shoulders back, eyes suddenly neutral. Katie stretched around to see. The man thundering down the path looked ominous. Big, powerful—not too tall, but tall enough. Black hair, black eyes, a Roman nose, and a three-piece suit. She smiled, and twisted at the engagement ring on her finger.

'You there—what's your name?' A gentle baritone, not at all in keeping with the eyes.

'Me?'

'Well, I don't mean Nora. So that only leaves you.'

'I guess it does, doesn't it? I'm Kate.'

'Kate, I want you to watch Nora for a few minutes. It shouldn't take long to find Fessenden and settle my business. OK?' The frown had disappeared, along with the promise of murder and mayhem. A pleasant smile replaced it, to match the little girl's, with the same result. It had been a long time since she had been assaulted from two directions with charisma. A nice feeling, that. So I'm a child-minder, she whispered to herself. Why not? It's the thing I do best!

'I'd be glad to watch—Nora?' The little girl smiled and moved closer to her chair. Her little hand slid along the arm of the lounger until it slipped under Kate's elbow, and there it stuck. The man nodded his head. He looked ten years younger than he had while thundering down the path. Another smile, equally divided between the two of them, and he turned around and rumbled up the path towards the house again.

'Wow!' Katie chuckled.

'Yeah, well, that's what all the women say,' the child offered solemnly. And then with great pride. 'That's my dad.'

'Wow,' Kate repeated whimsically. 'Does he have a name?'

'Him? I told you. His name is Dad.'

'Yes, I see. Very appropriate, too. And what might your name be?'

'My name is Lenora—but nobody calls me that except the principal at the school when she's mad at me. Everyone else calls me Nora.'

And how about that! Kate chuckled to herself. All plainspoken, but leaving no doubt that the poor principal had had to deal with 'Lenora' on more than one occasion. Such a gentle creature to be hiding a small devil within.

'Well, Nora, my name is Katie, or Kathleen. How about that for a name?'

'Katie? I don't know anybody else by that name.'

'No wonder,' she returned wryly, feeling the bite of her own problems. 'There's not much of it going around these days.'

'You're pretty, Katie.'

'You must have some sort of problem with your eyes, Nora. I'm too big—much too big.'

'My dad likes big girls.'

'So that makes me pretty?'

'What else?'

'OK,' Katie laughed. 'So I'm pretty. But let's keep it for our secret, shall we? Look at those lovely birds.' The child responded with enthusiasm, but quietly. Only a hiss of exhaled breath disturbed the area as the pair of cardinals chirped at each other and the world.

It was the flurry in the grass at the bottom of the hill that alarmed them both. A quail, nesting in the taller uncut grass, was disturbed, and shot into the air, its wings beating a warning to all the wildlife around it. The warning spread through the scattered trees and a flock of sparrows took wing, wheeling away from the country estate in the direction of an adjacent farm.

'What is it?' the little girl asked, squeezing back against the lounger and Katie's arm.

'I don't know. Something's coming up the hill.' Kate swung to her feet, herded the child behind her, and gradually backed in the direction of the old apple tree a dozen feet away from the pool area. She was doing her best to remain cool and calm, in order not to alarm the child. When she heard the baying she knew.

'Try a little tree-climbing, Nora,' she said brightly. The child made an objection, which was overlooked as Katie swung her up into the safety of the lower branches. 'Can you skedaddle up higher?' she asked cheerfully.

'Sure,' Nora returned. 'Easy.' And set about giving a demonstration. Kate turned back to look down the hill. It was just what she had suspected. Some drunken fool had released the gates on the pen that held the two guard dogs, and they were coursing up the hill in wide sweeps, searching.

It was hard to keep her cool. She could still vividly remember the day when she and her little Border Collie, Shep, had come walking through those woods on the other side of the creek. The guard dogs had been loose that day, too, and Shep had given her life so that her mistress could escape. She swept the scene in front of her, with no idea how much like steel her green eyes looked under pressure. And then back to the little girl, who had managed to scramble two branches higher into the foliage of the apple tree.

'That's the way to do it,' Katie called up at the child. Her own hands wrapped themselves around the lower branch of the tree, a sturdy limb some six feet from the ground. With the agility that came from practice she swung herself up into the safety of the tree. Even at that the dogs were almost on her as she pulled her heels up. The two of them, unmuzzled as well as loose, lunged upwards on their hind legs, snarling a challenge, baying.

'They look terribly mean,' Nora called down anxiously. 'They can't climb trees?' The 'I hope' was not announced, but understood.

'No, they can't climb trees,' Kate said. It was all false-face. Her heart was in her mouth as she glared down at the two jumping dogs, and they glared back at her. But the child would suffer if frightened, and that *must* not happen. The secret corner of her heart, which treasured children beyond anything, would just not let it happen. Perhaps a scream for help? She discarded the thought at once. Nora would be more frightened by screaming than by actions.

Luckily the scream was not necessary. The baying of the dogs themselves served as the alarm. Up the hill from behind them the burly figure of the gardener and dog-keeper came struggling through the grass. Evvie Hamilton. A friend of her father's, and a man of long acquaintance, armed only with the ultra-sound whistle and a pair of leashes. He must have blown the whistle, because the two dogs' ears came up, and both heads turned over their shoulders. Katie relaxed, and gave some attention to herself.

Her neat skirt was rucked up around her waist, there was a conspicuous run in her tights, one button had snapped off her blouse, and her hair had come down in a golden mass. She checked out the girl, who seemed to have suffered no damage, and started to make emergency repairs to her own person. It was then that she heard the other roar from up the hill, in the direction of the house. The outraged male, she chuckled to herself. Nora's father, bounding down the hillside with a croquet mallet in one hand, roaring defiance at the dogs and at the world.

The animals themselves were totally confused. A moving human with a weapon represented the one challenge they had been trained to attack, but the relentless whistle behind them ordered recall. Slowly, one step at a time, they retreated downhill, their snarling heads turned in the direction of the new attack.

The pressure off, Kate relaxed against her tree trunk and laughed. Her husky, throaty gurgle tickled the child's fancy. She began to giggle. The racing man, ten feet or more from the tree, heard them both, and slowed to a stop. The dogs continued their retreat until finally they backed right into Hamilton's legs and were quickly leashed. 'You OK, Mr Lee?' the keeper called.

'Out of breath,' Nora's father returned, waving a hand. 'But I suppose I'll live.' He was strolling now, over to the bole of the tree, and looking up. 'Lovely. Are you two planning to roost up there all day?'

Katie struggled vainly with her skirts, her face blush-red. It was extremely difficult to be modest when perched in a tall tree wearing a short skirt. She had blown her entire image, and that for the *second* time in one day!

'If you've finished leering you might help us down,' she suggested coldly.

'I was just about to suggest that. Lovely—er—legs.' He held out both hands. 'Come on, just jump.'

'And you're going to catch me?' It was beginning to be enjoyable. She struggled to keep a straight face. She stood at five feet eleven, and when her comfortable one hundred and forty pounds landed on him there would be some sort of splash indeed! From her position above him it was difficult to see just how tall he was, but his foreshortened head, clustered in short black curls, looked extremely—attractive? And that wasn't a word she had used for a man in the last several days.

'Well, come on,' he repeated. She shrugged her shoulders, and swung her feet around off the branch, disarraying her skirt even further. His eyes seemed to widen as a big grin flashed across his face. She used both hands to lift her bottom up off the branch, and slid down on top of him. His hands grabbed at her just under her arms, and managed to slow her progression, but not enough to avoid catastrophe. She heard him mutter 'What the hell' under his breath, and they both hit the ground, he on the bottom.

Somehow or other she found herself sitting on his stomach, his arms wound round her, his hands half-supporting her breasts. That second shock was almost as bad as the first. She struggled with his fingers unsuccessfully.

'Lady, maybe if you could get off me,' he offered in a very mournful voice. But the pressure of his fingers on the underside of her breasts said otherwise. She broke away with a violent wiggle, landed on her knees, and glared at him.

'Hey,' he complained as he rose to his knees. 'Don't glare at me. I'm the white knight, aren't I?'

'I don't know,' she spat at him. 'Sexist, and racist too? There's only one kind of white knight around here. They wear sheets and hide their faces. Look at me!'

It was hard not to cry. The only thing that held her back was her mother's oft-repeated admonition, 'big girls don't cry!' And when you had grown to be as big a girl as Kate had that rule was added to all the rest of a growing list of taboos that 'big girls' don't do. You didn't cry. She didn't. You didn't hit men in the face, not matter how much you would like to. She didn't. But you did stand up and glare at them. That was allowed. She did.

The surprise was mutual. He clambered to his feet at the same time, and there they were, hardly six inches apart. And my eyes are staring at his Adam's apple, she told herself in awe. She tilted her head back to glare up at him, but the glare failed. Along with her father's name she had inherited her mother's Irish wit. 'You'd be a lot taller if you didn't have so much of you bent under for feet,' she said pertly.

'You're not such a shrimp yourself,' he admitted cautiously.

'Hey, don't I get to come down out of the tree?' the child above them asked.

'Your leg is bleeding,' he told Kate. Both his hands were resting comfortably in the indentations of her hips, and he was looking her over inch by inch.

'I believe so,' she said, sighing, not moving her eyes for a minute from his face. There was some—attraction—there, but what it was she could not define. And so she drank her fill of him.

'Hey, you two!' Nora had scrambled down to the lowest branches of the tree. 'I can't jump from here without help.' Both heads below her turned slowly upwards. The child was grinning at them. They grinned back. It seemed almost as if space had been crossed after a long voyage, and they were reunited as a family.

'If you don't let go of her you can't catch me,' the child giggled.

'I—you wouldn't mind waiting just a minute?' His hands were moving restlessly within a circle of inches at Kate's hips. She caught her breath, not knowing what he might do next, nor what she would do in return. Whatever effect it was having on him, she knew deep down in her that the score was morality zero, excitement ten at that moment.

He did what she least expected. He bent over slightly, kissed her forehead gently, then raised his hands in his daughter's direction. The child whooped, threw herself down off the limb, and was caught safely high in his arms. It seemed to be a game they played often. Kate felt the doors close in her face as they shut her out. She had known them only thirty minutes, and she felt bereft.

Kate managed to rearrange her blouse, and then bent over to check her leg. A twig from the branch had ripped through her tights and scraped a three-inch long shallow gash in her skin. The bleeding had almost stopped, and the hurting had begun. But that was another thing big girls didn't do—they didn't admit to hurt and pain. So she didn't.

'Daddy, her name is Kathleen, and she saved my life.' Nora, flashing her golden-brown curls in the air around her father's face.

'I don't know how she did it,' he answered. 'She just reached up and put you on that branch?'

'Yup.'

'But that thing is six feet above the ground, and you're going on fifty pounds, little bit.' He shook his head in disbelief.

'The dogs were running at us,' Kate explained as she brushed herself down. 'That adds considerable adrenalin to the system.'

'Here, let me help.' He set his daughter carefully down on the ground, spun Kate round at the shoulders, and began vigorously to brush her clear of leaf and clinging twiglets. It was not the lightest of brushings.

'I—I think you'd better not go any further,' she suggested as his hands reached her hips again.

'I—perhaps you're right,' he sighed, disappointment plain on his face.

'I can do the lower bits,' the child broke in, and began to pick more foliage off the lower segment of Kate's skirt.

'My name is Lee.' He offered a hand and watched approvingly as her own hand, by no means small, slid into his.

'Of the famous Virginia Lees?' The smile was back on her face.

'Not hardly,' he chuckled. 'The family name was Leslovicíz when my grandfather came over. The Immigration inspectors told him the country wasn't big enough for a lot of names like that, so we became Lee.'

Her own smile was cut off abruptly. From up on the hill behind them Mrs Fessenden was calling imperiously, 'Kate! We're about to eat, Kathleen!'

'Duty calls.' She sighed, struggling to get her own hand back.

'Duty?' he asked. 'Come on, now. You can't be one of the servants in this mausoleum!'

'Not exactly,' she told him as she managed to break away and took a couple of limping steps up the hill. 'I'm not exactly part of the crowd, and not exactly *not* part of the crowd, if you follow me.'

'Well, I don't,' he snapped. For a moment she hesitated, unwilling to walk away from the warmth, but she needed the money. Mrs Fessenden called again shrilly. New money, Katie told herself, married into an old name. Mr Fessenden—he called himself Colonel Fessenden for no apparent reason—had left to his wife the pursuit of society while he did obscure things and made a great deal more money. Kate's leg bothered her. She limped a step or two up the path, to find a strong arm at her elbow.

'Mr Lee?'

'John, actually. My friends call me Jack.'

'I—I do thank you. I need the help.'

'And hate like hell to admit it?'

'I suppose. It's a family trait.'

'Family? How many? Where?'

'I—nobody,' she sighed as she struggled upwards. The pain was diminishing by each step, but she was not about to tell him, and lose the warmth of that arm. 'There's nobody left but me.'

'I don't even know your last name.'

'Yes.'

'Aren't you about to tell me?'

'I—only if you promise you won't laugh.'

'I promise. With a family name like mine, why should I laugh? I'll never laugh at you, Kate.'

'But we've only—just met.' And why is it that it's so important to say? she asked herself. Where did all this warmth, this comfort come from? I've had a lot of friends, but none of them made me feel like this.

'We've known each other for centuries,' he laughed. 'I met you when you were Nefertiti. Remember?'

'Oh, lord, are you one of those reincarnation people?'

'No, but you're getting maudlin about time,' he returned . That chuckle hid behind every word of his, and it built up her excitement. 'Don't you feel we've known each other for a long time?'

'I—yes,' she admitted. 'But surely not Nefertiti.'

'I just made that up.' His hand tightened at her elbow, and the sun seemed to have acquired a rainbow of delight, which was quickly punctured.

'We're waiting, Kathleen,' Mrs Fessenden fussed. Patience was not the woman's finest attribute. Kate stumbled at the doorstep.

'There's no rush,' Jack interrupted. 'Kate's been injured by those damn dogs of yours. She needs a few minutes to clean up. Look at her leg!'

'But my guests are starting already, and I *always* have her perform while we eat!'

'You're lucky she doesn't sock you with a half-million-dollar lawsuit,' he told her grimly. 'Where's the nearest bathroom?'

Mrs Fessenden drew back in alarm. Half a million dollars was a major amount, even to the *nouveau riche*. She recognised the threat, and *lawsuit* was a word right at the top of her vocabulary. 'Kathleen? Surely Kate wouldn't sue me because some——'

'Some idiot——' he prompted.

'Because one of my—guests—accidentally let the dogs loose?'

'The bathroom,' Jack interrupted again. 'I'll consult with my client.' Mrs Fessenden turned a peculiar shade of purple, and waved a weak hand down the hall.

'I'm your client?' Katie was struggling to contain the giggles.

'My daddy's the best lawyer in the Newnited States.' Nora had panted up behind them to join in the conversation.

'United,' he corrected absent-mindedly.

'Yeah. Like I said.'

'Sit over there, Miss—you never did tell me.'

'Lovewell,' she sighed. 'And don't you dare laugh.'

'It's not the least bit funny,' he agreed. 'Lovewell.' He enunciated it as if he were tasting it. And was happy with the result. 'Now, even a place like this must have a first-aid kit.' He slammed his way through the three wall cabinets until he found what he wanted. 'You'd better let me help you off with those tights.'

'I——' Alarm bells went off in her head. Thirty minutes was hardly long enough to know anyone before letting them help you off with your tights. Especially when you wore them *under* your briefs. No indeed! She slapped his hands away and stepped back.

'I think...I could get them off by myself—if you would kindly step outside,' she managed.

That huge grin was back again. 'Spoilsport! Nora, you stay here with Kate, and call me if she gets in any trouble, right?'

'Right, Daddy.'

She hurried, fumbled, and consequently took longer than one might have expected before she nodded to the little girl, who promptly called her father back in.

'Put your leg up here,' he ordered as he slid a small footstool in her direction. 'That's a lovely leg, don't you think so, Nora?' And the conversation went on between father and child, ignoring Kate completely, as he gently washed the injured area, pat-dried it, and applied a soothing lotion.

'Now there it is,' he finally announced. 'You won't need a bandage.'

'I thought you were a lawyer, not a doctor?' she asked.

'I am, but I'm also a jack-of-all-trades.'

'John,' his daughter prompted. 'John of whatever you said.'

The man stood up, towering over both of them, both eyes fixed on Kathleen's face. She felt the impact of it. 'How would you like to have a smart-alecky daughter like that one?' he questioned. 'My name is John.' He said it lightly, but there was a tremendous weight of importance behind the words. She could feel it, and nervously licked her lips, not quite sure what to say.

'Nora would make somebody a wonderful daughter,' she finally admitted.

'Well, *my* momma don't think so,' the child snapped. A frown covered the little face.

'That's enough, Nora,' her father chided, and tried to change the subject. 'Now I don't know what it is that you do, but as long as it isn't ballet dancing I guess you're ready for it, Miss Lovewell.'

Miss Lovewell. The camaraderie was gone, along with her first name. Withdrawal symptoms? Or something to do with Nora's mother—who was presumably his wife? Kate stood up carefully and tested her leg. It was stiff, but strong enough to support her. 'Thank you for your help, Mr Lee.' She offered her right hand, only to find him ignoring it as he grabbed for her left.

'An engagement ring?' A peremptory tone, distant, chilled, as if he were cross-examining some witness or other. She looked down at her hand in surprise. In all the excitement she had forgotten completely about Peter.

'Yes,' she said sadly. 'But I won't be wearing it for very long. Just as soon as I get through with this job I'm going to find him. And then I'm afraid it will be all over.'

'Oh, wow,' Nora said softly, stepping aside to watch them both glare at each other. A knock at the door interrupted the tension.

Mrs Fessenden had sent a maid this time. A scrawny local girl of sixteen, trying to help support her family. 'Excuse me.' Kate tried to step round him and get to the door.

'Excuse *me*,' he offered. 'And thank you for saving my daughter. It was very brave of you.'

'I wasn't very brave,' Kate muttered. 'I was scared to death.'

'Ah, but big girls don't scare easily,' he chuckled as he stepped aside.

'A lot *you* know,' she muttered as she sidled out the half-opened door. 'Goodbye, Nora. It was nice to meet you.'

'And my daddy too?'

Katie looked down at the little pleading face, and, not understanding the question, managed to create a tiny smile. 'And your daddy too,' she assured, and hurried out towards the ballroom as fast as her legs could carry her.

Buffet tables had been set up all along the east wall of the huge room. Some of the guests were already wandering down the line, filling plates. The others, the younger crowd, were still clustered around the ornate bar at the far end. And I remember when I danced here, Kate told herself fiercely. When I was a member of the set, and never dreamed things could be different. So young, and such a fool! She made her way over into the corner, where a grand piano sat partly hidden from the rest of the room by potted palms and flowers.

She had brought no music with her, but needed none. It was all part of the Fessenden approach. Pile the classics on top of snobbery, and everyone would applaud. As now. Katie massaged her fingers, positioned the stool, and began to play from memory. Something moving, to begin with. Excerpts from Stravinsky's *Firebird*. And then into softer tone-poems. Smetana's *Die Moldau*, Ravel's *Bolero*, Chabrier's *Espana*, the *Sorcerer's Apprentice* by Dukas, and finally Debussy's classic *Afternoon of a Faun*. A neatly packaged thirty minutes, served up much like the chicken in aspic on the table. A spattering of applause broke the final silence, and suddenly Kathleen became aware she had company.

'I had to find a place to leave Nora,' he said. 'So this is what you do. And very nice, too. But why here?'

'Because I need the money,' she snapped, disturbed by being forced out of her music. It was a hiding place to which she had resorted many times since her mother had died, four years before.

'You could be a concert pianist,' he nagged idly.

'I could starve to death, too,' she returned bitterly. 'Why don't you go away?'

'I'm imposing on you?' A stiff and quick response.

'I don't know. I've got something to do.'

'I'll help you.'

'No.' She held up her hand in a stop-sign gesture. 'No. It's something I have to do for myself.' No, it's something I don't *want* to do, but I must. Nobody can do it for me. How could I convince anyone that this big, strapping girl was petrified by relationships? That even after what had happened today she was uncertain, confused, doubting?

'Then I'll wait.'

'Suit yourself,' she sighed, unwilling to argue further. 'You're a nice man. Don't get yourself involved with me.'

'You're some sort of pariah?'

'You can read about it in tomorrow's paper.' She dropped the lid over the keys, rested her hands there for just a moment, then took a deep breath and got up. The guests had finished snacking, and were starting to mill around. She had only to listen to find her target. Peter Lester was larger than life, and noisier too. His baritone bellow could be heard above everything. Strange, it had always been so, but this was the first time she had noticed. He was in the corner, next to the bar.

Kate tugged at her blouse and skirt, took the time to check up on her hair again, and then stalked on trembling legs the length of the ballroom. Peter and his friends. All alike. They were members of the hunt set, and dressed the type. They were also a bunch of complete bores, and sounded like it. And I've known *that* for months, she belaboured herself. Years, in fact. So why has it suddenly become so apparent—so unavoidable? How did I ever become engaged to Peter? She knew the answer. She was lonely, and, in the beginning, he had been kind. But that was not the sort of answer she wanted, so she pushed it to the back of her mind. The crowd parted. They had been discussing real estate and some new 'in' thing they knew about. Something about her facial expression, or her tall, solid figure, perhaps, caused them to move just that slight distance to create a path for her.

Peter's back was to her. He was busy murmuring some secret to his hangers-on. They were all grinning in expectation of the punch line—to her surprise it didn't seem to be a bawdy tale. She tapped him on the shoulder, and he turned round.

'Oh, Katie! I thought you would want to rest after all that wonderful music.'

'Don't fuss me, Peter. You never heard a note. I was watching you. We need to talk, you and I.'

'You make life sound so grim, my dear. These are all my friends. You can talk here.'

'Not here.' Peter, somewhat lubricated at three in the afternoon, was beginning to feel the atmosphere that the rest of his friends had already sensed. They faded away, like wavelets running back down the beach.

'Please, Peter,' she begged, tugging at his arm.

'Oh, all right,' he muttered. He set his half-empty glass down roughly on the bar, and started out up the side of the ballroom, dragging her beside him. His narrow face was set, angry. He used his free hand to brush the long blond hair out of his eyes. Yesterday she had admired that motion; today it frightened her. But big girls don't get frightened. Oh, Mama, if only you knew what you've done to me, she sighed to herself. Payment is required, and the bill falls due every day!

At the end of the ballroom there was a corridor connecting to the main house. Peter went to the second door to the left, and threw it open. 'In here,' he muttered. 'There's not much chance of any of this crowd coming to the library. I'm not sure any of them can read.'

Another thing I hadn't noticed, she lectured herself. He's always so cynical. Always casting himself as so superior. What a fool I've been!

'Well?' The door closed behind them, Peter went directly to the little disc in the centre of the floor. As with practically every room in the house, a decanter and glasses stood there. He poured himself a half-glass of brandy, and swilled it down in three quick gulps.

'Peter——' She hesitated. He was scowling at her as he slumped into the chair. Why, he doesn't even like me! The thought pierced her. I was going to marry him, and he doesn't even like me! It was too late for that.

'Peter—the—the police came to the house at midday. I——' She had his attention. There was a twisted smile at the corner of his mouth as he looked up at her.

'There was no work at the library,' she struggled on, 'so I came home early—and—the lock on the door was broken. I don't understand. And then the policeman came. A deputy sheriff.'

'And?'

'And he said something about my rights, and asked me a lot of questions about—it was marijuana, Peter. How did marijuana get into my house? Only you and I have keys.' The last part of the sentence trailed off into a mutter. Peter was laughing at her.

'You, Peter? Is that why you wanted a key? You?'

'Well, what do you know?' he chuckled. 'The lady finally caught on. Yes, Kate, me. What a lovely name. I knew you were the one just as soon as I heard your name.' He reached out for the brandy decanter again, and splashed his glass full. 'So what did you tell them?'

'Me? I—I didn't know anything. What could I tell them? They said—they made me go down to the court-house, Peter, and yelled at me and—but I didn't know anything, did I?'

'You'd have to be blind not to know something,' he laughed. Strange, she told herself, I always thought it was a boisterous laugh, but it's not. It's coarse—unfeeling.

'So what do you want from me?'

'Peter—they said—I—the court, tomorrow. I have to go, they said. They released me without bail because—because of my father. And tomorrow—you have to come with me, Peter, and tell them it's not my fault. You *have* to!'

'I don't think I've got the time,' he chuckled, sipping at his glass. 'I have this—er—appointment over in Front Royal.'

'You mean with the woman you've been keeping over there?'

'Hey, you really do surprise me. How did you know about Evelyn?'

'I've known for months,' she sighed. 'I—I thought it was something men did before they got married.' It was hard not to sound bitter. Terribly bitter, with a pent-up rage, not against Peter, but against the whole male world.

'Well, you wanted to play reluctant spinster. That's a funny gag for a hulking woman over twenty-five. You didn't expect me to be celibate until you got around to putting out, did you?'

'I suspect not.' She leaned forward over the desk, saving up emotional strength for the labour that had to follow. 'I think you had better have your ring back,' she sighed. It was only a tiny diamond, but she had treasured it for all the months of their engagement. 'You won't come to court with me?'

'Of course I won't,' he snapped. 'How stupid do you think I am?'

There was one spark of fire left in her. 'No, I understand, Peter. There's only one stupid one among the two of us, isn't there? What was it you really wanted? My house?'

'Bingo,' he laughed. 'You finally made the connection. A fine house, out of sight, right on the county border, good access roads. Everything just right.' He picked up the ring and toyed with it. 'Would you believe how sentimental I am? This was my mother's. I'm glad to get it back.'

'Then I must be glad for you. Now, if I may have my key?'

'Which one?' he laughed. He reached into his pocket and pulled out a set of three keys, all identical.

'You had it copied!' The last wisp of control fled as Katie banged the top of the desk with her balled fists. 'You had it copied!'

'Twenty-five times,' he laughed, struggling up from the chair. He staggered, and the chair fell over, masking the noise of the door opening behind them. 'Everybody

in our group has a copy,' he laughed. 'You've had your
nose to the grindstone so much every day that we've had
a regular ball for weeks. Oh, Katie, you're some kind
of landlord, let me tell you!'

She stood stiffly up, back straight, head erect, fists
clenched at her sides. If only I could hit him, she
screamed at herself. But big girls don't do that! So
instead she stood rigid, trembling, repressing even the
screams that tore at her throat, the tears that trembled
on her eyelids.

But the objection didn't seem to apply to *big men*.
John Lee appeared behind her, stalking the man behind
the desk. One of his big hands snatched Peter up by the
scruff of his neck. The other moved in a short, straight
line directly to the side of Peter's jaw, made a vicious
cracking sound as it hit, and Peter flew backwards over
the upset chair, bouncing along the floor until he ended
up against the bookcases on the far side of the room.

'Creep!' the big, quiet voice commented to her. She
opened her eyes. Two arms were extended in her
direction. She walked into them, up against the solid
frame of Jack Lee. The arms closed around her, and,
despite all the dictums of her childhood, the tall slim
girl let loose the tears, sobbing, almost childlike, against
the soft sweater. 'Oh, God, what am I going to do?' she
wailed.

'Everything will be all right,' he said softly, stroking
her hair. 'Everything will be all right.' And somehow she
almost believed it.

# CHAPTER TWO

JACK LEE held Kate long enough for the tears to dry. Peter Lester was stirring on the floor, but just barely. Jack walked over and nudged him gently with the toe of his shoe. 'Just make sure that neither you or any of your crowd go near this girl again,' he said quietly. It was a quiet demand, yet full of threat, and the man on the floor understood. But there was something in Peter's look which seemed to indicate more trouble to come.

Jack came back to Kate and wrapped her up in his arms again. The pair of them watched as her former fiancé sidled to the door, paused as if to say something, then scuttled from the room. 'A real creep, Kate. I don't understand why a pretty lady like you would be engaged to such a—to him.'

'I don't either,' she said tiredly, nestling just the slightest bit against him. 'It's been a confusing year. First Papa died, and then I discovered there wasn't any money. And everyone I thought was a friend turned out not to be. So when Peter came along I was so lonely, and he— damn! I don't want to talk about that right now.'

'It's all right, Nefertiti,' he comforted. 'Here now. Buck up your courage. Nora's in the kitchen, being stuffed with brownies if I guess rightly. Let's go.'

They went out into the corridor and back to the same bathroom which they had first used. Kate bathed her eyes hastily, doing away with most of the visible signs of her outburst, then started to fix her hair.

'You always seem to be doing that,' Jack chuckled, as he trapped both her hands in his. 'Leave it down. I like it that way.'

'I'll bet you do,' she said wryly. 'If it were all curly, the way yours is, I'd understand. Well—all right—just for now.' And that's the way it has to be, she thought. I'll do him a favour in return for the one he's done me. After all, we probably won't meet again. Strangers just don't stay in Stanfield. I wish I knew...

'John?' He turned around and looked attentive. 'Where do you live?'

'In a motel right this minute,' he said. 'My daughter and I are gypsying it, looking for a place to settle down. We've been around here for three days. It looks to be a nice area. What do you think?'

'I——' His hand was under her arm, urging her towards the kitchen. 'I've lived here all my life. It's nice, but—well, it's a farming centre, and you know how badly off the farmers are these days. To make money from grain you have to have a lot of acreage. Poultry is doing well. Tobacco is continually under the gun. Congress could remove the subsidies any day. And the peanut crop is—lord, they've still got half of last year's crop in storage. The only thing that's holding up is apples, you know.'

Why am I babbling so? she thought. He's a lawyer. What the devil does he care about apples? She looked up at him, and wished she had really been Nefertiti.

He tucked an arm under her elbow again, and moved her in the direction of the kitchen. Nora was at the big butcher-block table, chewing on freshly made chocolate-chip cookies. 'So I made a mistake in brand,' he chuckled. 'Come on, little bit. We have to take the lady home.'

'That's nice,' his daughter managed, mouth stuffed with the crisp cookies.

'You don't have to take me home,' Katie interjected. 'It's way on the other side of Stanfield, and I have my bike out back.'

'Don't you listen, Mr Lee.' Mrs Milligan, the chief cook and bottle-washer, had been eavesdropping shamelessly. 'It's eight miles and more down the valley. How that girl ever manages I'm darned if I know. Works her fool head off, she does.'

'But I can't just leave my bike here,' she protested weakly.

'You don't hafta,' Nora interrupted. 'We got a rack on the car, don't we, Dad?'

'Indeed we do,' he laughed. The hand was at her elbow again, moving her off dead centre.

'Don't forget your envelope,' Mrs Milligan called after them as they opened the screen door at the back of the house. Kate flashed her a smile of thanks, and took the little white envelope stuck in the rack just inside the door. He looked at her, curiosity running rampant across his strong face.

'Money,' she said pertly. 'One mustn't mix money with the social life, you know. So I get my filthy lucre at the back door in a plain unmarked envelope. Half an hour of music, fifty dollars. I don't do half as well at the pre-kindergarten.' She could not suppress the wistfulness in the last part of that statement. She loved her music. It had been a great deal of her life. But if push came to shove, children would win out over music any day now. But how did you explain that to a stranger—and a man, at that—without giving him some crazy ideas? She shrugged her shoulders, and let him urge her on.

His car turned out to be a Cadillac. What else? It seemed almost to be blasphemy, strapping her twenty-year-old bicycle on to the back bumper. 'It looks just a little out of place,' she sighed, as he ushered her into the front seat.

'The car?' he queried. 'Well, it's last year's model. We can't all be millionaires.' He sounded hurt. She hurried to patch over the misunderstanding, only to see that ridiculous twinkle in his eyes.

'I hope you're having fun out of us country cousins,' she snapped stiffly. She turned her head away from him to avoid his open stare.

'You're no relative of mine,' he returned. He gunned the motor and swung out on to the old country road. They went through Stanfield in a hurry, then turned south to follow the county road behind Dickey Ridge, parallel to Route 340. She stared at the old, familiar terrain, counted crows in flight, studied budding laurel trees high on the mountain—anything to avoid looking at him. Behind them, Nora maintained an unusual silence for a child.

'Here,' Kate said after a few minutes. He slowed, and took the turn into her drive. The old house had never looked better. The sun was already low over the mountain, to the west, and the shadows hid the dilapidation.

'Well, I do declare,' he said in an imitation drawl. 'Massa lives high on the hog. Where are the slave quarters?'

'Don't be impertinent,' she snapped. 'You sound like a Yankee. And the slave quarters were all behind the house. General Sheridan burned them all down in 1864. He was a Yankee, I recollect.'

'Well, don't blame me,' he chuckled. 'My family was still in Yugoslavia then. Is this still Warren County?'

'Yes,' she sighed. 'All this. What are you doing?' He was out of the car and around its front before she recognised what was going on. It was the first time a man had held a car door for her in many a day. She stuttered an apology, which he waved aside.

'We had to get your bike off,' he said. 'Nora, come help Kate get her machine unbuckled.' And with that he wandered off towards the house.

'Well, I'll be——'

'You'll be what?' the little girl prompted.

'I—I don't know what I'll be,' Kathleen giggled. 'Didn't I hear him say he was going to help me with the bike? And then he walked off?'

'Fathers are like that,' the child responded very maturely. 'I think that's what they call in school having short attention span. You think so?'

'How would I know, love? He's your dad, not mine. What do we do now?'

'Well, you hold the frame while I unbuckle this snap-fitting here.' And the bicycle came off the complicated mount without a bit of trouble. By that time Jack had wandered back.

'Smashed your lock,' he said. There was a contented sound in his voice, as if a smashed lock was a welcome challenge. 'Where's the nearest hardware store?'

Kate was tired. It came over her suddenly, an emotional tiredness which had drained all her batteries. She longed for a place to sit down, and the porch was closest. 'Down there.' She waved generally southward. 'Bentonville.' Her legs managed the short distance to the porch, and she thumped herself down on the second step.

He came over and squatted down in front of her, taking her pale face between his hands. 'Tired? Too much for you? Do you think you can survive for a few minutes?' And then, without waiting for an answer, he stood up again. 'Nora, you stay here with Miss Lovewell while I go get us a new lock for her door.'

The child showed that odd maturity again, coming over to sit beside Kate, putting a small arm around her waist, nodding with understanding. The father trotted back to the car, and kicked up a few pebbles as he returned to the road.

'That's a strange man,' Katie said as they watched the brake-lights on the car sparkle for a second at the corner. She looked down at the girl. 'And you're a strange one, too, aren't you, Lenora?'

'Who, me?' The child returned a gamine grin, and whipped a crumpled cookie out of the pocket of her denims. 'Want a cookie?'

Kate glanced at the wreck of the cookie and shuddered. 'I—I don't think so. I'm not very hungry.'

'That's the trouble,' the child insisted. 'You didn't eat no lunch——'

'Any lunch,' Kate corrected.

'Any lunch. And you need some coal in your burner. Well, that's what Dad says.'

'And if Dad says, it must be right?'

'Why, of course!'

For whatever reason, Kathleen found herself munching on the cookie, her eyes trained on the hills. The ball that was the sun sat just on the tip of the Massanuttens, flashing red and yellow and russet.

'There's a lot of mountains around here,' Nora offered after a few minutes of silence.

'Indeed there are. But not where you come from?'

'We come from Washington. DC that is. As far as I
know there ain't no——'

'Aren't any.'

'Yeah—there aren't any mountains in Washington.
Just statues and senators. Dad says they're both alike—
the statues and the senators, I mean. If the senators don't
keep moving people begin to think they're statues. I
didn't like it there at all. You can breathe better out here.'

'Yes, that's true.' They both took an exaggerated
breath. It *was* nice in the valley. There was the blossom-
smell of the laurel high on the mountain, the sweet, heavy
scent of unturned earth, and the laughter of the river as
it ran in front of the house. Another moment of silence.
What better chance? Kate asked herself. A dirty trick,
picking on the kid, but how else do I learn? *He* obviously isn't going to give me the time of day unless it
suits him! 'Does your mother like it around these parts,
Nora?'

'Huh!' A disgusted grunt. 'How would I know?'

'Well—you must know *something*——'

'Yeah, sure. When I was one years old she ran away.
I ain't never seen her since. And don't tell me I can't
say ain't, 'cause I can!'

'I—I wasn't going to.' And that's a red-faced lie, she
thought. It's so darn automatic, after working at the
school, to correct everyone's English. What a stupid idea.
And now Nora needed soothing.

'You don't seem to have suffered from it,' she
suggested. 'Look what a lovely child you've turned out
to be!'

'That's not what they said at the school,' the girl announced grimly. 'That's why we had to—that's why we
moved out of Washington. Daddy says they were all a

bunch of—oops. He told me never to use those words at all. Never.'

'Wow!' And another silence. 'Want to see over my house?'

'It's all your house? Yes, I'd like to see it.' The pair of them stood up, joined hands by mutual consent, and walked into the big house. They were on the third floor when the horn sounded outside, heralding Jack Lee's return. Nora clattered down the stairs to meet him, throwing herself at him desperately as if he had been gone on an exploration to Mars.

'And Daddy, would you believe it, they have fourteen bedrooms! Fourteen! Of course lots of them are little, up on the top floor, for the servants, you know, but the rest are somethin', believe me.'

'Oh, I believe you, princess,' he chuckled. He set down his packages by the front door, stripped off his jacket, and looked around. 'An electric outlet?'

'Over here.' He plugged in an electric drill, and began at once.

'Had to buy a drill, too,' he explained as he kept his head down in the work. 'Didn't bring a single tool with me. Fourteen bedrooms, huh? How many baths?'

'I don't remember,' Nora laughed. 'I was so busy counting beds and things. Some of the rooms don't have nothing in them.'

'Fourteen bedrooms, and only four baths,' Kate interjected. 'Everybody needs to sleep. Not everybody has to take a bath—well, not all at the same time.'

He stopped work to look up at her. 'Don't be apologetic,' he advised. 'Four baths is plenty—depending on how many people there are to bathe.'

She refused the gambit, and after a minute or two he went back to work. By five o'clock, he had removed the old broken lock, replacing it with a new deadbolt affair, which he carefully explained. 'It looks as if the old one was put on years ago,' he commented.

'Yes,' she said with a perfectly serious face. 'Right after General Sheridan burned down the slave-quarters.' He shook his head slowly, and she was unable to repress the giggles.

'She's funnin' you, Dad,' Nora broke in.

'I can see that. Why do you suppose she would do that?'

'Because I think she likes you.'

'Do you think so? Shall I ask her?'

'It must be a ball of fun living in a house with you two,' Kate commented dourly. 'A pair of comedians, no less. I thank you for fixing my door.'

'And what do you suppose she means by that, Nora?'

'I think she wants us to check the door from the outside, that's what.'

'Well!' He stood up, gathering his tools together. 'I can take a hint. I suppose she expects us to sweep up all this sawdust, too?'

'No, she doesn't.' Kate barely managed the words. Giggles were getting in the way. 'She's more than capable of sweeping up a few bits and pieces. And I really *do* thank you—and not just for fixing my door, either.'

'You know what you ought to do, Daddy?'

'No, what?'

'You ought to kiss her.'

'You think that would be a good idea? Why don't you tote these things out to the car for me.' The child hefted the bag, and started for the door.

'No—I—take your father with you,' Kate pleaded.

'Go ahead, Nora.'

Kate backed away from him slowly. He followed. The grin he wore seemed to cover his whole face. The curly black hair, disarranged during his work, crowded down over his forehead. The dark, dark eyes positively sparkled. The widespread lips revealed a firm line of teeth that seemed to get bigger and bigger the closer he came, until she could see nothing but the gleam of his eyes, the sparkle of his teeth. His head bent over, hovered, poised, and dived at her lips.

It was like a whisper of a promise. A momentary contact that left a taste of sweetness behind. 'Katie?' he murmured. She was too busy to answer. Too busy wrapping her hands around his neck, pulling his head down to repeat that magic touch. He seemed to hold back for a second, and then joined in. The second touch was not that fluttery promise, but a warm moist meeting of two souls. It lasted until Kate ran out of oxygen; their lips parted reluctantly, and for a moment or two he stood there, looking down at her enigmatically.

'Are you sure you don't have something else to tell me?'

'I—no,' she stuttered, not even remembering what he might be talking about.

'Then I guess I'd better go,' he said. His arms unfolded and released her. She took a half-step backwards, nervously rearranging her blouse, which didn't require any attention at all.

'I'd guess you'd better,' she said softly. 'It was—nice meeting you. Perhaps we might run into each other some other day?' Did I make that too much of a pleading? Or is this goodbye? I don't want to say goodbye. Not to you!

'Oh, I'm sure we'll be seeing each other,' he returned. He squeezed her waist with both hands, then turned on his heel and made off. She followed him to the door, standing with it open, watching, as he strode down to the car, climbed in, and drove off. From the passenger side a little hand waved at her. She returned the salute, and then watched. Watched for another ten minutes, staring at the empty road, and the settling dust which his tyres had kicked up. Just staring.

Fourteen bedrooms, four baths, six family rooms of various sizes, one huge kitchen, and one occupant. The thought hit her in the face as she closed the door behind her, shutting out the world, and locking her into her own private corner. One large house, two hundred and forty acres of land, and not a penny of income, save what she could pick up from odd jobs. As she straggled back to the kitchen it was hard to keep the tears from her eyes.

How the place had bustled when she was young! Life had danced. Her beautiful mother had been the core of local society—until the accident that killed her. And after that her father—her pillar—had turned inward, neglecting everything, until lung cancer ended everything.

'I'm sorry, Miss Lovewell,' the family lawyer had said on the day of the funeral. Harry Bledsoe, in his late sixties, a dry stick of a man who had managed to stir a compassion for the young woman in front of him. 'By the terms of the will you inherit the house, the land— and just enough money to pay the inheritance tax.'

'But Mr Bledsoe, there was my mother's money——'

'All gone, my dear. It was illegal for your father to touch it, but he *was* your guardian. And he spent it all.'

'I—but what can I do?'

'Kate, there's only one answer. You have to sell the place. It's a bad time to sell farm land, but the house might bring something reasonable.'

'I—I can't just make a decision like that.' The lawyer was surprised to see the tears. He felt just like half the world did. Big girls just *didn't* cry. Spartans, they were supposed to be, able to bear anything.

'There's time,' he offered tentatively. 'The will must be probated, accounts settled, taxes recomputed. I doubt if it can be done in nine months. You have that much time.'

'But then you'd advise me to sell?'

'Yes.'

And now there was only a month left. Thirty days of April. She had done her best, but, untrained in the available jobs, she had not succeeded. A part-time librarian, a teacher's aide at the kindergarten, a part-time musician. In a world full of well-trained specialists there was hardly room for the partially trained. And the best she had come up with was to sell out, take what money resulted, and go back to Richmond for training. In something. What a life goal that would be. Training, in *something*!

It was a question she took to bed with her every night. A problem she awoke to face, still unsolved, every morning. As she puttered through the mechanics of a simple supper it bothered her as she worked.

She was on the stairs at nine o'clock, on her way up for a bath, when three cars drove up into the drive, their headlights bouncing off the old house, and their horns blaring away. Somebody tried the front door, then pounded on it. I should have got a dog, she told herself grimly. Two dogs. The pounding continued. There was an old shotgun in her father's den. Solidly rusted, with no cartridges to fit, but it *looked* impressive. She fetched it, and made her way to the door.

The pounding continued. She leaned against the inside of the door, resting her head on the solid oak panel, and prayed that they would go away. Instead the noise-level grew; somebody was singing 'Shenandoah' very much off key. Others were trying to help. The door rattled as a weight was thrown against it from the outside. It was useless just to stand, hoping. She fastened the safety-chain, turned the deadbolt key, and opened it.

Peter Lester was on the doorstep. 'Well, it's about time,' he announced. 'My key won't fit. Open up, Katie. We've come to have a party.'

'You're drunk,' she answered disgustedly.

'Not yet. But I will be. Open up.' He turned around and yelled to the crowd in the cars. 'Come on up. We'll have a big time. I've got an awful lot of girl up here!'

The roar of laughter snapped Katie out of her stupor. There were eight of them. Enough to make big problems. Enough to do a great deal of damage. She flicked on the porch lights, then thrust the muzzle of the shotgun through the partially opened door.

'Peter, can you see what this is?'

'Why, I do believe it's a shotgun,' he crowed. 'Is it real?'

'Try touching it,' she suggested.

He stretched out a finger and laid it on the cold gun-metal muzzle. 'Why, I do believe it is. So what, Kate? You couldn't hurt a flea.'

'If you want to think so,' she said softly. 'Remember today, Peter? You broke our engagement, and got me arrested. Remember that? And now you've come up to my house after dark and threatened me.'

'Me? I haven't threatened you.' The bluster had gone out of him as the hole in the muzzle of the gun tracked the middle of his stomach.

'Oh, yes, you did, Peter,' she continued, trying to fill her words with steel. 'You threatened me. That's what I'll tell the sheriff, you know.'

'But I'll tell him differently,' the man said uneasily.

'There. You did it again,' she chuckled. 'You threatened me again. And how could you tell the sheriff anything, Peter, after I've blown your stomach away?' She moved one hand to the breach of the gun and thumbed at the hammers. One of them moved with a deadly click. It was enough. The man she had planned to marry backed slowly and quietly down the stairs, climbed back into his car, and slammed the door.

Peter leaned his head out of the car window. 'But I'll be back,' he yelled. 'I'll be back.' The rest of his crew had become strangely silent. They followed as he drove away.

Totally drained now, Kate slammed the door shut, affixed the deadbolt lock, stood the shotgun up in the corner by the door, and for the first time in her life toured the entire house, making sure all the doors and windows were closed and locked.

There was barely enough hot water for her bath. The water-heater and the furnace itself needed replacement. She sank into the tub, immersed herself thoroughly in the last of her bubble-bath, and did her best to relax. It was hard to do. 'I'll be back,' Peter had yelled. And he surely would. She knew enough about him to realise he had a mean streak ten miles long and remembered a grudge better than an elephant could.

'So how come you planned to marry him, dummy?' she asked the empty room. And had no answer. Because

I've been in a daze since Dad died? Because I'm a misfit in this crazy world. The world is made for little people. If David and Goliath were battling right in front of me now, I'd cheer for the giant! At least *that* brought a little grin to her face. It gave her the courage to look into the mirror and not reject what she saw.

'You could have lovely hair if you brushed it,' she told herself very firmly, and proceeded to do just that. In the end it looked less like straw and more like thin-spun gold, falling down over her breasts, reminding her. She slipped her flannel nightgown over her head reluctantly, wanting for one more minute to stand foolishly nude before the mirror, and dream.

The bed was warm. When the furnace had packed up she'd had enough money for an electric blanket. It served well. She dived into its warmth, coiled up on her side, and day-dreamed. Lenora Lee. What a lovely child. I could go for a kid like that. Who are you kidding, Kate Lovewell? That's not the Lee that draws your attention! Jack Lee. What a lovely face. I wonder how many thousand women he's kissed like that? I wouldn't care how long the line was if I were the last! I wonder how it would be if he were here right now, right here?

She had read a great many books about the subject, but had no practical experience. So it was no wonder that as she fell asleep she was blushing.

# CHAPTER THREE

THE next day Kathleen woke up to an early morning haze. A cloud had settled on the valley. Only the tops of the mountains projected high into the sunshine. It would soon burn off. Kate was not one of those who woke up laggardly. With her it was instant awareness and eagerness to be about the day. But for this one morning it was a pleasure to lay abed.

She stretched to her limit, toes touching the old ornate footboard, hands flat against the headboard. There was a sensuous feeling to it all—a feeling of renewal. All her separate muscles made report as she squirmed in the warm bed, and their message was *happiness*. It was as if, suddenly, the past year had been completely excised from her memory, making her once again the cheerful, sensible girl she had always been.

But the clock haunted her. It was an old pendulum time-piece whose face registered to within the minute, but whose chimes were always ringing two hours ahead. And at the moment it was sounding a false 'nine-o'clock.' She slid out from under the blankets, shivered in the slight chill of early spring, and made a dash for the bathroom.

You have a part to play today, she told her mirror image. You have to convince Judge Pettibone that you're still the solemn, sincere Katie who he has known for all your years.

The weatherman had predicted a warm day, despite the morning chill. So a neat shirtwaister, dark brown,

44

with low shoes—the judge was a small man himself. A little flash of colour at the throat—the pale yellow scarf her mother had chosen for her. And hair, brushed for its full hundred strokes, then braided—and put up? No. Left hanging behind her, halfway down her back. No make-up. The judge was seventy years old. Well, perhaps a little light lip-gloss. A touch of perfume, a jacket in case the weather predictors were wrong, and down for a cup of coffee and two pieces of toast.

She had been summoned to the court for ten o'clock, the first case on the docket. It took almost that long to prepare herself and then pedal the old bicycle the distance into town.

Stanfield was one of the really old towns in the valley, with narrow streets, houses set back from the pavements, trees lining the main streets—both of them. Industry was seeping into the valley. Up north at Winchester, over at Harper Ferry. Even a few miles away, at Front Royal. But not yet to Stanfield. A brick court house, built before the war between the states, was set on the top of a small hill, with full lawns surrounding it, a few shaded trees, and a monument. A commemoration to T.J. Jackson and his foot cavalry who had camped on that lawn one night in 1862. General 'Stonewall' Jackson, that was.

A bleary-eyed bailiff met her at the door of the district courtroom, and ushered her to a front seat, conspicuously alone. Three or four other people huddled in corners, waiting for cases to be called.

She settled into her seat, and felt the gloom of the old building descend on to her shoulders. The bench was as old as the building. Lord knew how many women had sat right here and felt the same, she thought. Keep your spirits up. Smile! It was a hard order to fill.

The door at the back of the chamber opened, and Judge Pettibone, complete in black robes, came in. The bailiff chanted an unrecognisable litany, culminating in 'All Rise.' The rustle throughout the room caught her by surprise. She turned around quickly. While she was dreaming, the place had filled. A flash-bulb went off in her face. She blinked her eyes, and turned to the front again. The judge sat down in his easy-chair, settled himself, and banged the gavel. Everyone sat down. Katie followed suit.

Judge Pettibone fumbled through a handful of papers his clerk had set before him, and cleared his throat. 'In the case of the Commonwealth of Virginia versus Katie Rosalie Lovewell, an arraignment. Mr Prosecutor?'

'The state is ready, your honour.'

'And Little Rosie—er—Miss Lovewell?' She looked up, startled. He had always called her Little Rosie, ever since the day she had topped him, on her tenth birthday. 'You have no lawyer, Kate?'

'I—no, your honour. I—I don't have the money for a lawyer.'

The judge sighed. 'You understand, this is not a trial. This is an opportunity for the state to demonstrate sufficient evidence to make a trial necessary. But it is an important step in law. You need a lawyer. Shall I appoint a public defender?'

'I—I really don't——'

'She has an attorney.' A pleasant baritone voice from the back of the court. She didn't need to turn around. It was Jack Lee. She hunched herself down into her jacket-collar. If there was any single thing she *did not* want this man to know, this was it. And here he was. My lawyer? God. I not only need a lawyer, I need a keeper!

'Er—Mr Lee, is it?' Judge Pettibone was having trouble with his bifocals. He took them off and wiped them with a handkerchief. 'We don't often have such well-known attorneys in our area. You are licensed to practise in Virginia, Mr Lee?'

'I am.' He ambled down the aisle, briefcase in hand, and squeezed on to the bench next to Katie.

'Miss Lovewell, is Mr Lee acceptable to you in this case?'

I ought to be happy, she told herself, as she huddled miserably in the seat. I ought to—cry. Why him, lord? She made a stab at her eyes. He leaned over. 'You're supposed to smile and say yes, and look very, very confident,' he whispered.

'I—it's very hard to do,' she managed to mumble. The judge was waiting patiently. 'Yes,' she announced.

'My client and I need a moment or two to confer, your honour.'

'Of course. Take what time you need.' The gavel thumped, and the judge went back to his paper-shuffling. Across the room the local prosecutor, Tom Gerney, glared at the defence, and then shrugged his shoulders. Jack leaned closer to Katie, dropping one arm on the bench behind her.

'Nora tells me that thirteen of your fourteen bedrooms are dusty,' he whispered.

'Well, I can't be everywhere at once,' she returned defensively, startled by the turn of conversation.

'So you could have one of the servants dust?'

'I don't have any servants,' she whispered stormily. 'Just me.'

'You mean you spent the night alone in that monster of a house? Suppose somebody came?'

'Somebody did,' she snapped loudly, and then blushed as everyone in the court turned in her direction. She dropped back down to a whisper. 'How am I going to get out of this horrible situation?'

'Don't worry about a thing,' he chuckled, patting his briefcase.

'Yes, that's what John Brown's lawyer told him just before they took him away,' she replied sharply. 'What have you got in that valise, papers?'

'Who was it?'

'Who was what?'

'Who was it that came in the dead of night? Lester?'

'I—yes. I sent him away.'

'Just like that?'

'No—not just like .that. It took a little doing. I—I threatened him.'

'The talk around town is that Katie Lovewell is a big, soft-hearted girl who wouldn't hurt a fly.'

'You shouldn't listen to gossip. I've hurt a lot of flies in my day. But I—I'm afraid he might come back again.' That in a tiny whisper that faded away into silence almost before it was completed.

'I don't think so. He can't walk around much with a broken leg.'

'You—you broke his leg?'

'Not yet. I'm a great psychic, though, and I see a terrible accident about to happen to Peter Lester.'

'I—I——'

'You don't approve of violence?'

'I thought all lawyers obey the law! What's in the valise?'

'All lawyers do,' he whispered sternly. 'Me, I'm a Yugoslavian shyster.'

'Oh, my.' And then, for want of something else to say, she repeated her question. 'What's in the valise?'

'Four sandwiches,' he whispered, moving closer to her ear. 'Nora made them this morning. You can have your choice of bacon and egg, or egg and bacon.'

'I—I don't understand!' But she did. The devil was gleaming at her out of those dark eyes of his, and the corner of his mouth was flicking back and forth the tiniest bit.

'That's just what I need,' he chuckled softly. 'A confused client. Now, all you have to do is keep your mouth shut—unless I stab you in the rib like this.' He demonstrated by tickling her just under her lowest rib. She jumped, wondering how he knew her sensitivity at just that particular spot.

'And when I do that,' he said very urbanely, 'you look the judge straight in the eye and say "yes, sir". Got it?'

Katie was beginning to regain her composure, her light-heartedness. She could not see how this mess would be straightened out, but this certainly was the man to do it. Still, he needed taking down a peg. 'Is it all right if I say "yes, sir, Uncle Victor"?' she asked primly.

'Oh, my,' he laughed. 'So that's how it is!' The gavel thudded on the judge's desk.

'Your honour.' He stood up. She looked up at him, wondering why it was that her world seemed so much more secure. 'We are prepared.' The old judge peered at them both, then took off his glasses again and wiped them nervously.

'You agree, Katie?'

'Yes, sir,' she whispered, and blushed again as Jack dropped into the seat beside her and tickled her. 'Yes, sir,' she repeated, as loudly and firmly as she could. The judge smiled at her, rapped the gavel, and sat back. 'Mr Prosecutor?'

Tom Gerney, the prosecutor, got up from his chair like a whale coming to the surface for oxygen. 'The state has one witness, your honour, and some material evidence, which indicates that the defendant is guilty of possession for sale of a Class Three substance—namely, marijuana. I call Deputy Paine, of the county sheriff's office.'

'I know him,' Katie whispered to her attorney as the young man was sworn in. 'He's a terrible dancer. Awful.'

'That won't have much impression on his police work,' he advised. 'Tell me something interesting.'

'Well, he likes to use his muscles. You know, the strong-arm type. He sees himself as another John Wayne. I'll bet he broke my door lock.'

'Now that's interesting,' her counsel chuckled.

'And so he was speeding, and I chased him,' the deputy was saying. 'And he pulled up in front of this house and ran in and locked the door behind him.'

'This house was that of the defendant?'

'Well, sure. Everybody knows where the Lovewells live.'

'So go on, please.'

'So he wouldn't come out. I went around the house trying all the windows, and I figured I had to go in through the front door, you see. So I did. I kicked the door open, and there he was. Jeff Filmore. A cousin of the Lester family, your honour.'

'I know,' the judge sighed. The point had just broken on his doodling pencil. 'Please go on.'

'Well, anyways, there he was, and right on the table in the hall was this little plastic bag of leaf. So I gave him a citation for speeding, and a lecture, and I brought this here bag back to the station.' The young man smiled, as if the recitation had been harder than the arrest.

'And chemical analysis of the contents of the bag, your honour, indicates it to be marijuana. Shall we produce the technician, your honour?'

'Mr Lee?'

'No, your honour. The defence wants to save the county as much money as it can. We'll stipulate that the bag is filled with marijuana. Or anything else the prosecution wants to call it.' The judge's gavel thumped a time or two. 'None of that,' the old man cautioned.

'Then that's our case,' Mr Gerney concluded. 'The house belongs to the defendant. The marijuana was found in the house. There is enough evidence to bring the matter to trial.' He moved back towards his desk in the well of the court. The young deputy started to get up, but stopped as Jack Lee came over to the stand.

'You know, your honour,' he said conversationally, 'I do believe we might save the county even more if I might ask a question or two?'

'Most unusual,' the prosecutor mumbled.

'But it has a nice ring to it,' Judge Pettibone conceded. 'Go ahead, Mr Lee.'

'Well, now, Deputy——?'

'Paine,' the young man offered nervously. There was something authoritative about this big wheel from the nation's capital.

'Yes—Deputy Paine. You were chasing this young man—Mr Filmore, I believe—on a speeding charge?'

'Yes. Eighty miles an hour, he was doing, right up Main Street.'

'And if you caught him you were going to arrest him?'

'Oh, no. A traffic citation, and a good lecture. Unless he was drunk. Which he wasn't. Scared, but not drunk.'

'So, he had committed a misdemeanour. Not a felony. Just a misdemeanour; if it *was* a crime, it was a very tiny one. Now, tell me again about breaking down the door.'

The young policeman fingered his too-tight collar, and thought for a moment. And then his face lit up. 'Well, sir,' he said. 'I was in, like, hot pursuit. That's what we call it in——'

'I know.' Jack smiled back at him. 'Go ahead.'

'Well, as I said, I was in hot pursuit of a criminal, and he hid behind a locked door, so I broke in.'

'And of course you had a search warrant in your pocket?'

'Now why would I carry somethin' like that around?'

'You mean that you really had no suspicions about the contents of the house *before* you broke down the door?'

'Why, of course not. I told you. It's the Lovewell house. I didn't have any suspicions.'

'Of course not. You were in hot pursuit.'

'Well, yes. We can break in any place where there's a criminal we're chasing.'

'And this Filmore fellow. He had a key, did he?'

The deputy stammered. 'To tell the truth he had two keys. I brung them to court if you want to——'

'Ah, yes. Of course. I don't think we need to see the keys in this case, Deputy. Now, you broke in—smashed the door lock, to be honest about it? Unfortunately there wasn't any criminal inside the house, was there, Deputy Paine? All you intended was to give a traffic ticket. That's not exactly a criminal offence in itself. So you didn't *see* a felony being committed. All you saw was a misdemeanour. Too bad.' The young deputy sagged back in the witness chair, his mouth hanging open.

Lee turned to the judge, who was busy inspecting his fingernails. 'Your honour will recognise, of course, that in the case we have before us the officer had no legal right to break down the door, and therefore whatever he may have found inside cannot be considered in evidence against my client. I move for dismissal of the charges.'

'Granted.' The gavel banged before Lee had finished the sentence. 'Case dismissed. Go home, Rosalie.'

'But your honour——' Gerney was struggling up out of his chair again, but the judge had gone. Katie stood up, startled, confused. Her lawyer had gone over to the prosecutor's desk.

'Strange, isn't it?' he said loudly enough for the few reporters to hear. 'Filmore is in the house with the drug, but it's my client, who wasn't even home at the time, who gets arrested. Whatever happened to Filmore?'

'He offered to turn state's evidence, for immunity under *this* charge,' Gerney muttered.

'Stupid,' Lee returned gruffly. 'Even a second-year law student could see the hole in it. I wouldn't want to see my client suffer from any further harassment. Not any.' He was tapping the table in front of the prosecutor's nose with one heavy finger, to emphasise the words.

'Now then, Katie, about this other matter.' He came smiling back across the courtroom, and took her elbow.

'Y—you mean I'm free? That's it?' she stuttered. 'I don't have to—to go to jail?'

'You don't get to pass GO either,' he chuckled. 'Or collect two hundred dollars. Stupid case.'

'But—but I'm not found guilty? Or not guilty either?'

'I'm afraid that's the way the cookie crumbles.' She could read the sympathy in his eyes, but was determined not to be a public watering-pot. In private, maybe—but not in public. She tilted her head back, squared her shoulders, and marched out of the courtroom beside him as if she hadn't a care in the world.

'Miss Lovewell,' one of the two reporters interrupted, just as they reached the door.

'My client has nothing to say.' Lee did not exactly push the man aside, but just flowed over the space where he had been standing. 'My client and I are considering suing a few people in this town.' And by that time they were on the pavement, and there was the Cadillac, standing in a 'No Standing' zone.

'No parking ticket?' she ventured as he closed his door behind him.

'Not a chance,' he laughed. 'God smiles on the daring. Or something like that. Now, I want you to know how valuable those sandwiches are. Did you ever try to keep house in a motel? Nora's not too happy about it, and we have to stay in this area for a little more time. I just don't know what we'll do.'

She looked at him thoughtfully. 'You must have been a ham actor at one time or another,' she prodded. 'That's a terrible act you're putting on. This is where you turn on the weepies, and pray for a roof to put over your only child's head—she is your only child, isn't she?'

'Yes. Do go on.'

'And how terrible it is to be cast out in the snow without kith or kin or——'

'Well, it's cloudy over the mountain. That *might* be snow.'

'Hah! In April we don't have snow in Virginia. It's in the State Constitution.'

'My mistake. You have lovely hands for such a big girl.'

'If you say that again I'll *hit* you.'

'Say what?'

'Big girl,' she simpered. 'I'm damn sick and tired of being a *big girl*!'

'It's all relative,' he laughed, and drew her over beside him. 'There. You don't look too big. Not to me. Try the head on the shoulder bit.' It was a nice offer. She gave it a try. It was a very good fit, her head on his shoulder. Very comfortable. She closed her eyes for a moment, and when she woke up they were parked in front of the motel, his shoulder was gone, and he and Nora were carrying suitcases out of the double room.

'Oh, that's so nice of you,' Nora yelled. 'I couldn't of stood that motel another night. Not one more night. Thank you, Katie!' The 'thank you' was accompanied by a very large, wet kiss from the back seat. 'You're wonderful!'

'Yes, I am, aren't I?' Katie returned, trying to fight her way out of the morass. 'What am I wonderful for?'

'For inviting us to stay in some of your fourteen bedrooms,' the child said gleefully. 'Can I have one at the top?'

'Now we mustn't hurry Miss Lovewell,' her father interrupted. 'She has a great deal on her mind, and I'm sure she's forgotten a thing or two. Run back and check the room, Nora. We wouldn't want to leave anything behind.'

Katie watched the little girl skip as she headed back to the room, and then turned to examine the father. He stood her inquisitorial inspection with pure innocence written all over her face. 'I did invite you, did I?' she asked.

'I think Nora had the right idea.' He was into the front seat beside her before she could formulate her thoughts. Both arms came around her shoulders, tugging her in his general direction. She put up her hands to maintain her private space.

'Just a darn minute!' she protested. 'I need to know what's going on here, counsellor. Just when was it that I invited you and your daughter to move in with me?'

'Why, just before you fell asleep,' he said meekly. 'I was telling you that——'

'Yes, I remember that part. You were telling me a sad, sad story about Nora being penned up in a motel room. That I remember.'

'Well, she *thinks* you invited her, and I'd hate to see her disappointed, wouldn't you?'

'Darn you. It's all a put-on, isn't it? Why me?'

'Because,' he sighed, and added a little tug to the pressure of his arms. Her resistance collapsed immediately. In fact, she helped a little by sliding along the seat until they were thigh to thigh. And then, in one little helpless shrug, she collapsed across his lap, pinned between his chest and the steering-wheel, while he nibbled on her ear deliciously.

'That's why,' he said softly a few minutes later. 'I wish you wouldn't wear earrings. They take all the fun out of ear-nibbling.'

'Do they really?' she returned vaguely. It had been such a pleasant minute. One hand was already up unfastening her little gold studs when a thought hit her.

'That child is taking a long time just to check a couple of rooms.'

'You sound very suspicious.'

'Well, I can't help it. That's the sort of woman I am. You're very confusing, Mr Lee—Jack. I—I don't know what to make of anything at all. Yesterday I was—well, it was pretty terrible. And now all of a sudden you've got me twirling around in circles. Where *is* your daughter? And why do you have that silly grin on your face?'

'The grin is pure enjoyment,' he chuckled. 'I need to keep you confused, lady. As for my daughter, she's waiting for this.' His hand fumbled with the ring on the steering-wheel, and a deep-throated horn sounded. Almost at once Nora popped out the door and ran for the car.

'It *is* all right?' Jack asked softly.

'Of course it is,' she returned gently. 'But you didn't have to go through all this con-game. I would have done it for *Nora* in any case.'

'Hey, how about that? Just for Nora.' His injured innocence was too much to stand. She burst into giggles.

'Is this some game you and your daughter play very often?'

'Nope. This is the first performance.' He turned the key, and the big motor sprung into life.

'The act could use a little more polish,' she said primly, and then, to emphasise the point, moved to the far side of the seat. 'Why don't you sit up front here, Nora, between your dad and I?'

The invitation was accepted with alacrity. The child wiggled her way over the back of the seat and plumped herself down between the two of them, her hair flying, and her smile glowing. It just matched the brilliance of the sun, breaking through the valley haze at last. 'And just where do you propose we go to eat these sandwiches, Mr Lee?'

'Oh, me, back to Mr Lee?'

'Don't eat the sandwiches,' Nora whispered in her ear.

'I have remarkably good hearing,' her father interjected.

'For a man your age,' the girl returned, giggling. 'That's what Grandma always said.'

Katie was caught on the horns of a dilemma. She wanted to know about the sandwiches because her stomach was growling. But even more she wanted to know about 'Grandma'. Or anything and everything about this crazy family beside her. Family. How's that for a nice word? My daughter and I—and—him? Dreamer! As usual, her thoughts crossed on separate tracks and she lost the point she was trying to make. 'Does your grandmother like sandwiches?' she asked.

'Not these sandwiches,' Nora hissed at her. 'He bought them two nights ago at a fast food place on the road! Ptomaine Heaven, I think it was.'

'You mean your father lied to me?' Katie over-emphasised the dramatic. The phrase came out sounding like a line from the ancient thriller, *East Lynne*.

'Never,' her father interrupted. 'Truth also lies in the eye of the beholder, and is subject to a certain amount of—manipulation.'

'What he means is——' Nora started off.

'I know what he means,' Katie laughed.

'And no, her grandmother doesn't exactly care for sandwiches,' he added. 'Does that take care of everything?'

'Everything but my stomach and my job,' she sighed. 'I think I'd better check the job first. The kindergarten is next to the Presbyterian church, and the library is just around the corner. Could you drive me there and drop me off? I'll only be a minute. This is my day off from both, but I don't know when either of them wants me tomorrow.'

'And then?' He looked at her over his daughter's head. That little suspicion—that doubt—was in his eyes again.

What did it remind her of? Papa, with his fishing line in the creek, and not really sure he had hooked his fish?

She gulped at the thought. 'And then——' she stuttered. 'Then I think we can all go home and I'll make us a lunch—and—and we'll see.'

'Free lunch, Pop,' the little girl squealed. 'Cooked by somebody who really knows how to cook! You do, don't you, Katie?'

'Cook? Oh, yes, that's one of my few talents. Nothing fancy, mind you.'

'Thank heaven,' the child bubbled. 'Daddy can't cook for a nickel, and neither can Grandma, and every time she fires a—oh my, I wasn't supposed to mention that, was I? Oh, Katie, you are going to be the salvation of our family. Is that the right word, Dad?'

'That's the right word, love. The very right word. Is this the church?'

'I'll just be a minute,' Katie bubbled. It was contagious, being with this crazy pair. What was the name of that fellow you were going to marry? Don't remember, do you? Good for you, girl, you're finally getting a little sense. You've mourned the best part of a year, and now it's time to get about the world's business!

In the event, it took less time than even she had thought, and she came out of the building with a very sober face.

'Oh-oh,' Jack murmured as he came around the car to help her in. 'Now what?'

'I—I lost my job,' she mumbled. 'They—the Board fired me.'

'For what reason?'

'You know,' she sighed. 'Because I wasn't found not guilty. Drugs and kids don't mix, I guess. But I need that job. I *need* it.'

'Right now what you need is a good meal,' he commanded. 'To hell with the school—and the library, too.' The car spurted forward, giving her hardly time to fasten her seatbelt. The little girl between them moved closer to her.

'Daddy only talks like that when he's mad,' she whispered. 'Look at his eyebrows and his eyelashes.' Katie peeped out of the corner of her eyes. Their driver was concentrating on something. The road, perhaps. His eyebrows were perfectly straight, his lashes half closed, and his lips were moving.

'That's a sure sign?' she whispered back.

'Sure sign,' the little girl agreed. 'Somebody around here is gonna get in a lot of trouble—real soon.'

'I hope it's not me.'

'Oh, it's not you. He likes you. He likes you a whole lot. So do I.'

'That's nice.' Katie picked up one of the little hands and squeezed it. 'I—I like you, too. But I think two of the three of us are plumb crazy.'

'Maybe all three,' the man slouched behind the wheel contributed. He drove on for another few minutes, his lips twitching like fury. And then, almost as if he was talking to himself, 'That was a very silly case. Why did they charge you rather than Filmore? They had nothing at all to connect you with the case——'

'Except that he was in my house,' Katie interjected.

'Not important,' he continued. 'They would have to connect you to him or you to the drugs...or do you suppose that was what Filmore offered them? To connect you to the drugs?'

'But I never—I don't think I've met this Filmore boy more than once in my whole life.'

'Funny, isn't it?' he repeated. 'It almost seemed that the prosecutor and the deputy were out to get you, by any means, while the judge was all on your side of things. How does that come about?'

'The old and the new,' she told him. 'The judge isn't really my uncle, but he and my family, and, oh, about forty per cent of the people in the village, we've all been here for centuries, so to speak. On the other hand there are new people—folks who've just moved into the area, like the Fessendens and the prosecutor and the Lesters—and the sheriff is new, too. Late-comers. New money, that sort of thing. They're trying to take over the town, and the old order is resisting. But I don't know what they'd want with me. I'm just a very small cog in the wheel around here, you know.'

He drove on for another few minutes, and then started muttering again. 'But you have something,' he stated. 'You have that fine house and all those acres around it. Now who would want your house—or your acres?'

'Nobody that I know of,' she sighed. 'I've been trying to—I've been debating about selling, but there aren't a lot of buyers in these parts. What are you thinking?'

'Nothing much,' he commented as they came up on the house. 'But there's an old Roman instruction in curious cases like this. *Cui bono?*' He nodded his head and left the Latin phrase hanging there, as if she certainly ought to know what it meant. And I'm darned if I'm going to embarrass myself by admitting my ignorance, she told herself firmly.

Nora came to her pride's aid. 'What's that mean, Dad?' the little girl asked. 'Cui watchamacallit?'

'*Cui bono?*' her father repeated in very satisfied tones. 'Who profits from it?'

# CHAPTER FOUR

'LOVELY,' Jack said warmly, pushing his chair back. He was looking at the ruins of what once had been lunch. Thick slices of rare roast beef, warmed with her special gravy recipe, baked potatoes from her only extravagance—a fine Microwave unit—spinach out of the freezer, and a tossed salad.

'You didn't care for the salad?' she asked tentatively.

'Well, you were eating it, so I thought not to crowd you,' he chuckled. 'To tell the truth I'm basically a meat and potato man. That's a hard thing to be, living in Washington, and eating out all the time.'

'Yeah,' Nora complained. 'While I had to stay home with Grandma and eat that *French* stuff.' Her tone indicated that French cooking had come out last in the cuisine race. And then she confirmed it. 'I like peanut butter and jelly.' The child looked over at her begging to have the delicacy produced instantly.

'Next time,' Kate half promised. 'But you have to eat some vegetables.'

'Daddy doesn't.'

'But he will. Honestly he will.'

Her father failed to look enthusiastic about the whole idea. In fact he shook his head negatively until he read Katie's frown, and suddenly became interested in the left-over apple pie.

'You don't see much of this in the big city,' he remarked.

'Well, there's plenty in the valley,' she said, doing her best to restrain laughter. 'You can have any kind of pie you want in these parts, as long as it's apple. Now why don't you two scoot and select which bedroom you want, while I wash up the dishes?'

'That shouldn't take long. Nora and I will help.' The pair of them stood up simultaneously, and began to pile dishes in the dish-washing machine in the corner of the big kitchen. Another relic from the good old days. And I have to spoil their fun!

'I regret to tell the pair of you that the dish-washer doesn't work.' She walked over behind them. Jack immediately had his head into the insides.

'Doesn't work?' It was some sort of rhetorical statement, not a question. He checked the power cord, re-seating it into the plug in the wall, closed the lid, and pressed the start button. 'Everything seems to work fine, lady.'

'Did I tell you my dad is a great fixer?' Nora was trying to make some sort of point. 'He's terrible handy to have around the house.' What's this child trying to do to me—to us? Katie asked herself. And because she was afraid she knew the answer she blushed and closed her ears.

'I don't see a thing wrong with it,' he repeated. Katie shook her head wryly. A crazy pair.

'Test the water,' she suggested. He looked at her, puzzled, then lifted up the lid and dipped a finger into the barrel of the washer.

'Nothing wrong with the water,' he reported. His daughter tugged at his shirt.

'It's supposed to be hot,' she offered in a conspiratorial whisper.

'Oh, hot! There's something wrong with the hot water?'

'There's nothing wrong with it,' Kate said primly. 'There just isn't any.'

'Ah.' His whole face lighted up, like Sherlock Holmes hot on the trail. 'Tell me about it.'

'Tell you about it? I—I have to think about that. Why don't you two go select your bedrooms while I do the dishes and think?'

'Nora, do you get the idea that she's trying to get rid of us?'

'Yup. We better go.'

'Oh, and there's no heat,' she told them. 'So if you take a bedroom up on the third floor it's pretty cold up there.'

'No hot water, no heat?' he probed. She made a face at him.

'This isn't a hotel, you know.'

'C'mon, Dad. Don't tease.'

'Why, baby—what a thing to say about your dad!'

The little girl stamped her foot. 'Don't tease, Dad. I don't want this one to get away!' Her father considered for a moment, and then a broad grin spread across his face. 'What a lovely thought,' he mused. 'You are indeed your father's daughter.' They tumbled out of the kitchen together, leaving a completely confused woman behind them.

For some time after that, while she heated a pan of water and struggled with the dishes, Katie could hear the pair of them racing around upstairs. The house was solidly built, but a hundred and fifty years of hard usage had warped a floor plank here and there, and sounds reverberated in every direction. Carpets, that's what I need. Carpets, a new roof, a new furnace, enough money to pay off all the bills. And there are only twenty-nine days left in April.

On any other day this past year that last thought would have thrown her into a panic, but now there was too much happiness around for her to be down for more than a minute or two. And then there was only one pair of footsteps upstairs, and some heavy body was climbing down into the cellar. Where I haven't been in ages, she reminded herself. Dad always had a man who came for things in the cellar.

'And if you were of any use to yourself,' she lectured aloud, 'you would have found out about things in the cellar, instead of floating around trying to be a social butterfly, without a penny to fly on!'

'Wow!' Nora said from the door. 'You're a butterfly? Pretty big for a butterfly.'

'Snooping?' she returned, but in a friendly tone.

'That's the only way to learn anything,' the girl said. 'Can I help?'

'Well—yes. What else does your father like to eat besides roast beef?'

'Good-looking girls,' Jack Lee said from out in the hall. 'I have to go back to that hardware store for a control valve and a length of pipe and a couple of new nipples.'

'Do you really?' Katie was not about to take the ultimate step and ask what and why.

'Go away,' his daughter instructed him. 'This is woman-talk.'

'I should be so lucky,' he laughed. 'Between the pair of you I suspect there isn't enough knowledge about woman-talk to put in a thimble.' Katie had a blockbuster of a comment to throw at him, but before she could get her tongue in gear he was gone. So she stuck it out at his disappearing back.

Nora picked up the dish-cloth to wipe, looking the industrious well-trained little girl. Which she might be, but having a father like that—well, who knows? 'Katie, do you have a boyfriend?'

'I—no, I guess not. I didn't get all the gravy spots off that dish. Let me have it back.'

'This one? I meant—you don't have no attractions at all.'

'*Any* attractions, dear. Any. We don't say *no*.'

'No, I suppose we don't. I'm glad.'

'Why? Because that's the last of the dishes? Now, what do you think your father would like for tonight?'

'Peanut butter and jelly?'

'I doubt that. How about fish? I've got a nice fillet of haddock. You like fish?'

'Sure.' A very subdued answer. The sort one gets from children who were trying very hard to maintain good relations without poisoning themselves.

'And three kinds of vegetables?' A malicious jab at a poor, undeserving child! It's her father you're aiming at, not Nora!

'I don't care. Like Daddy says, I can take them or leave them alone. Mostly leave them alone.'

'This isn't getting us anywhere,' Katie laughed. 'Come on, help me find the sheets and things and get the beds made.'

It was a surprise to find that Nora hadn't chosen the small bedroom at the top of the house. Instead she had picked the room next to Katie's, separated by a shared bathroom. 'And your dad?'

There was a large familiar grin on the child's face as she turned in the other direction. 'This one.' She threw open the door of the bedroom directly across the hall, the big master bedroom which took up almost half of the south wing.

'Why do you suppose he picked this one, Nora?'

'Because the bed's so big, that's why. Where are the sheets?'

It took almost an hour to find everything, all carefully put away in camphor balls, and needing a little airing that time would not allow.

By that time Jack was back, roaring up to the house in a cloud of dust. The two girls went downstairs to greet him, but he had already plunged into the cellar, and was banging on miscellaneous pipes, making odd noises, cursing a time or two, and, at last, giving himself a cheer.

'Hey, up there,' he yelled up the stairs. 'Turn one of the thermostats up to seventy degrees.' Katie went back into the living-room and performed the simple adjustment. There was a clanking and groaning from the cellar, things started, motors ran, and the lawyer sauntered up the stairs. His face was smeared on one side with soot, both hands and arms were filthy, but he was grinning that great big grin.

'You fixed something?'

'Dad fixes everything,' Nora said indignantly. 'Only in Grandma's house she won't let him.'

He gave the child a warning glance, and she covered her mouth with her hand.

'A prophet without honour?' Katie was finding it hard not to smile back at him, and this was a serious time. 'What was the problem?'

'The feed-pipe from your oil-tank broke. You have a safety-valve that shut down and turned everything off. All I had to do was replace the pipe and the safety-valve, clean up the mess, and there we are. Your hot-water tank is a part of your furnace. A real old installation. You should have called a plumber. How come you didn't?'

'It's not that easy,' she sighed. 'It's a long trip from town, and plumbers keep office hours these days.' And then, much more softly, 'And they don't come when they know they can't get paid.'

'Money?'

'I—yes. But there was more than that. After all, it was getting to be spring, and I didn't know about the hot water, and there's only—well. There just isn't much time left, and——'

'Hey, now. You've been doing fine all day. No more tears. Want to tell me about it?'

She shook her head. 'I—I have to start the dinner.'

He pulled her over to the sofa and sat her down. 'You'd be a lot better off if you told me about it,' he said softly. One of his arms came around her shoulders. Nora had quietly effaced herself. He tilted Katie's chin up in the right direction. And if he kisses me I'll blow all to pieces, she told herself. All to pieces. His mouth came down gently in her direction. She steeled herself, hoping that she had enough strength to stay afloat during the encounter. But just as she decided she hadn't, and could therefore surrender with honour, there was a tremendous series of banging noises from all over the house. The living-room rocked with the noise, and then with the echoes. The whole house seemed to shake on its foundation.

Nora came rushing back into the room, frightened. Her father reluctantly disengaged himself, and stood up. His lips were moving silently.

'Daddy?'

'Nothing to worry about,' he sighed. 'Hot-water radiators?'

'Yes,' Katie told him. 'One in every room. Two in the dining-room and the study. Twenty-two rooms. What's the matter?'

'Oh, lord,' he returned. 'I had to drain the hot-water pipes before I could solder a new section in. And when you turn on the water again there's a great deal of air in the pipes. Every single one of those radiators had a petcock on the top to let air out. And that's what we have to do, go around the house and let the air out of each one of the radiators. Mount up, troops.'

'I've got to fix the dinner,' Katie interjected hastily.

'I don't know what a petcock is,' Nora added dolefully. He looked at them both sternly.

'Desertion in the face of the enemy,' he charged, then grinned, and dashed out of the room to do his duty.

'Did you get kissed, Katie?' the child asked as she watched her father take off on the run.

'No, darn it.' Well, it was an honest answer, she told herself. I really was prepared for total surrender. 'Come on, kid, let's go wrestle with the fish.'

The rest of the afternoon was slow and lazy, as Katie and Nora got better acquainted in the kitchen, and Jack Lee dashed around the house like a cavalry trooper riding to the rescue. At four o'clock everything seemed to slow down to a stop. The two girls went out to the front stoop and sat down, to be joined shortly by Nora's wide-smiling father. 'Best afternoon I've had in months,' he boasted as he took a pull at the can of beer in his hand.

'We *do* have glasses,' Katie said mildly.

'Never touch the things,' he chuckled. 'I like this. How about you, baby?'

'I'm not a baby,' Nora returned with considerable dignity. 'It's all wonderful.' She gestured out in front of her, to the westward, where the long flat top of

Massanutten held the sun up in the sky, and then behind them, where the Blue Ridge and Mount Marshall towered. 'I sure do like this place, Dad. We oughta stay in a town like this.' It was a soft, wistful appeal. Kate slipped an arm around the little girl's thin shoulders and offered comfort in a light squeeze. The child shifted her weight and fell back against Kate's breast—and sighed contentedly.

'Don't ham it up,' her father warned. 'It's all very nice. All of it. And only what—sixty miles from Washington?'

'Just about. But the roads don't exactly go straight from here to there. They tend to slant northward, towards Winchester.'

'Is that a fact?' he mused. Little emotions were coursing over his face, as if he had just found another piece of a puzzle. And then he stood up. 'Almost three hours to sunset?' he enquired.

'About that. Seven o'clock more or less is when we lose the sun.' The clock in the living-room took that as a cue and bonged off six loud chimes.

'Good lord.' Jack jumped up as if there was some rush to life, then looked at his wristwatch. 'Your darn clock is two hours fast,' he commented.

'No,' she countered. 'My darn clock is exactly on time. But the darn . . . bonger—it's off. What's the problem?'

He grinned and settled back against the solid post that held up the roof of the veranda. 'I suspect we might have visitors tonight, ladies. One last attempt to scare you off, Miss Katie.'

'You'll never make a southern accent,' she laughed. 'Oh, the dinner!' She jumped up and ran for the kitchen. He came along behind her. Nora remained on the stair-step, trying to identify the flocks of birds that wheeled overhead.

'So you don't care for my Rhett Butler impersonation?'

'Not without a great deal more practice,' she teased. 'Most of the strong dialects in the United States are fading away—within the big cities, that is. Sooner or later, my professors always said, there will be a standard American spoken in these United States.'

'Your professors?'

'You didn't think it possible?' she laughed as she checked the oven's heat and slid the tray of fillets in. 'I was a student at the University of Virginia for two and a quarter years. I hardly believe it myself. Nobody could be as stupid as I've been these last nine months. Everything seems to be falling to pieces around my head, and I don't know why!' She turned back to him and stood there, hands on hips. 'Why, Mr—er—Jack? Why?'

'Well, I hardly know what's happened, so I can't tell you all the "whys",' he said softly. 'You have to confide in me, Kate. Talk it all out.'

Her hands were busy with the salad. The rice was bubbling nicely. Her mind wandered off through the months. He was a good man, this Jack Lee. That's what Papa would have called him. A good man. You could almost say it was written on his shirt-collar. So why not tell him? Perhaps not everything, but something.

'We were a happy family,' she sighed. 'My dad had money—family money. My mother had some, too. But they loved each other so much there wasn't room for me.' She paused and grimaced at the memory.

'And we had this farm. Two hundred and forty acres, with twenty acres under tobacco allocations. You know about that?'

'A federal subsidy.' He nodded his head. 'Worth its weight in gold. You can lease the rights out to other farmers.'

'No,' she said angrily. 'No.' He shrugged his shoulders. 'So then tell me about it.'

'We—my mother died four years ago,' she continued. 'It was an accident. Can you imagine that? She was run down by a car out on the county road.' And I'm not going to cry, she told herself fiercely. I've cried all I'm going to! 'She never told me she loved me, and I never told her—I loved her, and suddenly it was all too late, and she was gone.' His head snapped up. She had not meant to say it aloud—it just came out. She crammed her fist into her mouth as if to shut off the flow of words. But he was not about to let her escape.

He crossed that invisible boundary that she maintained as her private territory, and hugged her. The warmth was her undoing. The fist came loose and the words tumbled out. 'They wanted a boy,' she mumbled. 'Or maybe a nice, cuddly little girl, like Mama. And I wasn't either of those things. So they put up with me—but left me outside their little circle. I was the cuckoo in the nest. I tried so hard to be like Mama, but she was only five feet two, with dark black hair. And Dad, he was only five feet seven. They—just didn't know what to make of me.'

'And how did you cope?'

'I—I just sort of tried to shrink, but I was too awkward. So Dad tried his best to make me into a boy. But after I—after my twelfth birthday that didn't work, so they sent me off to school. That's the way it went. Home for a week, then off to some other school or camp—until Mama died.'

'And then?'

'And then Papa went to pieces. He really needed me, you know. So I came home, but he—when Mama died he lost all his interests. Except gambling. He never lost that. And then, nine months ago, he died. He died of lung cancer. The first thing I did after the funeral was to go out and have that entire tobacco allotment plowed under. Twenty acres of tobacco. I replaced it with soy beans. I don't ever intend to grow that—that weed again. No matter how badly I need the money!'

'Well,' he said cautiously. 'Well, well.'

And that's how interesting my life story is, she told herself bitterly. Well, well. He can't think of a thing to say. Look at him, his brows all furrowed, his eyes blank. He's a hundred miles away. I wonder where his wife is?

She paid for her own wanderings. Not looking where she was moving, her hands landed on the hot edge of the fish-tray. Her scream was more of disgust than pain. The pan teetered in the mouth of the open oven, and then fell on the floor. Upside-down, of course, her mind confirmed. Her burnt fingers had gone to her mouth, just meeting the tears rolling down her cheeks. 'I—I don't know what I'm doing,' she quavered, and then bit off the words. They weren't really necessary. Anyone could see she had lost her marbles.

'I do,' he said, gathering her up like a bundle of laundry and hustling her over to the sink. The cool water was a blessing.

'I—I'm all right. It was only a little burn. You could put me down—please?'

His face was so close to hers it filled her whole horizon. Late afternoon, she thought, and he already needs another shave. I wonder if he would have a curly beard? There was a scent about him, too—a scent of man, untainted by after-shave and perfumes. Real man. Why am I so alive to his every move?

'You really need to keep that finger out of the kitchen for a while,' he said as he let her feet slip slowly towards the floor. Katie had the feeling of *déjà vu*. She slid down the length of him, just as she had while in the apple tree, feeling the strength, the purpose, the wild sexuality of him. Her face was as red as her two fingers when she stood on her own feet and readjusted her clothing. He was still standing close—too close for comfort. He isn't doing anything, her conscience yelled at her. He's just standing there! Wild sexuality? Where did you get that crazy idea?

It was her own desperate need to break the tension that caused her to move away. Her feet went slowly, leadenly. 'Oh, my, the dinner!' she exclaimed, her voice cracking under the strain. 'The dinner's ruined.'

'We couldn't just pick it up and wash it off?' he enquired from behind her. Which made her miss the laughter in his eyes.

'No, of course not,' she almost shouted at him. 'What sort of a—housekeeper do you think I am?' She scurried over to the oven and began to restore a little order. To her *mind*, not to the floor and oven. What sort of a *housewife* do you think I am? That was the phrase that she had swallowed down, almost choking on it. What's wrong with your words, Katie Lovewell? What is it?

You've been asleep for nine months, and now every time this man comes around there are rockets going off in your stupid head!

'Hey, let me do that before you really mess things up.' His big hands picked her up from her knees and set her aside as if she were about his daughter's size. 'Nora!' The bellow was loud enough to be heard in Front Royal—

or Winchester! The child came running in, a big smile on her face.

'Nora, our landlady has burned her hand. Scoot up to the bathroom and see if you can find some Solarcane to put on her fingers.'

'In *our* bathroom,' Katie added. The girl dimpled and ran. The father took hold of both of Katie's elbows and backed her into one of the kitchen chairs.

'Sit there,' he ordered, and began to clear up the mess for himself.

'Bossy,' she muttered under her breath.

'You'd better believe it.' He chuckled as he worked. 'If Nora and I were out camping we'd just brush this fish off and have at it. Where the devil is the garbage can?'

'I—I haven't swept the floor in a week,' she mumbled.

'Is that so?' There was a big lint ball in the dust-pan he had found behind the door. The pain in her fingers had become small potatoes.

'Are you laughing at me?'

'Not in the least,' he commiserated. 'I wouldn't dream of laughing at a lady in pain.'

'Then how come it sounds so strange when you say it?'

'Must be my Slavic accent,' he suggested. But he turned his back as he said it, then Nora erupted into the kitchen with the tube of balm, and her chance to get back at him had passed.

'So what will we have for dinner?' she asked the pair of them as they cleaned and polished her kitchen far beyond the need created by the dropped fish.

'I've been gaining a little weight lately,' he said. That solemn tone again. The lawyer-tone, she told herself grimly. As if his next question would be, 'And when did you stop beating your wife?'

'So perhaps it wouldn't hurt us all to fast?' she asked. 'We—we could always go out to eat. There are two nice little restaurants in Stanfield... my treat.' And I haven't the slightest idea where I'd get the money, she thought. My credit card's exhausted, and I haven't a—good lord, of course I have! There's the fifty-dollar bill I got from Mrs Fessenden! Her face brightened visibly as the suggestion became a real possibility.

'You know, Katie, you have a wonderful face,' Jack said. Her head came up suspiciously, as it always did when someone tried to pay her a compliment. And then he stepped on her ego. 'Anyone can read just what you're thinking by watching your face!'

She did her best to school herself. Calm dignity, her mind recited. Calm dignity. Or hit him one! He must have seen *that* thought too—he stepped back a pace or two, grinning.

'In any event, we can't go tonight.' He looked down to check his wristwatch. 'I'm expecting company.'

'I could make the dinner,' Nora interjected. Katie looked down at her, surprised. Eight years old? I can make the dinner? And her father doesn't seem to be the least put out by it all.

'Good idea,' he commented. 'I've some things to see to outside. Katie, one of the things you should know is that there's only room for one cook at a time in the kitchen. So you go putter around upstairs while Nora makes a spread for us. Right?'

'Now you tell me,' she grumbled. 'If it hadn't been for you haunting my kitchen we wouldn't be in this mess.' He and his daughter both grinned at her, and he gave her the big finger pointing at the kitchen door, the way a baseball umpire indicated a player or manager who'd been thrown out of the game. The ridiculousness of the whole affair seeped up into Katie's front brain cells. She shrugged her shoulders at them, and walked off.

There was always something to do in such a big house, of course, but her good intentions all went down the drain when she went into her bathroom and found that the hot water gushed and steamed on application. More to hide her transgression than anything else she locked herself into the bathroom, filled the tub, and took her first leisurely soak in many a day.

She was back downstairs by six, urged on by a call from Nora. The table in the kitchen was set for three; her 'tenants' were waiting for her. Jack stood up and held her chair for her. It was something she was not accustomed to. She sank into it like a duchess, prepared for almost anything except the peanut butter sandwich in the centre of her plate. She looked up at them both. That calm stare came back to her from their separate eyes. A look of challenge, anticipation, laughter. And I can play the game, she told herself, squaring her shoulders and sitting back deep in the chair.

'Lovely,' she said. 'Chunky? I always like chunky peanut butter.'

'Well, now,' Nora confessed. And then more brightly, 'But it's got apple butter in it, too.' There was a little anxiety in the statement.

'That's fine,' she giggled. 'I—apple is the Holy Word in these parts. I just love apple butter!' The little girl chortled and relaxed. The dinner went on, with more conversation than consumption.

'And there's seconds of everything,' Nora added as her father pushed back his chair and began to stack the dishes.

'No—no, thank you.' The child had come round to Kate's chair, expectantly. 'I don't think I can eat another morsel.' Without thinking about it at all, her arm went around the child's shoulders and enveloped her in a warm hug. It felt so comforting—and yet so ordinary. It was something that *ought* to be done, she told herself.

They adjourned to the front porch, bringing their coffee-cups with them. The western sky was bright with promise for the morrow. '"Red skies at night, sailors' delight",' she quoted.

'Sailors? Around these parts?'

'Well, we have more rivers than we know what to do with,' she staunchly defended. 'And plenty of lakes and things. You don't have to be on the ocean to be a sailor, you know.'

'Of course not.' He had gone into that absent-minded shell again. A sudden and complete transition. After a few minutes of silence he asked, 'Any lakes on your property?'

'Why, no. Why do you ask?'

'Nothing really. I suppose your land runs in back of the house?'

She shook her head in the gathering dusk. 'No, of course not. It's all in front of us. It runs right up to Route 340.'

'Ah.' The conversation died. The little girl was yawning.

'What time do you go to bed, Nora?'

'At eight o'clock—sometimes nine. Whenever Dad— when we can be together.' The living-room clock struck eleven behind them.

'Then it's time for bed,' Katie said. 'Can I take you up?'

'And tell me a story?'

'And tell you a story.'

'My dad can't tell stories for beans.'

'That's difficult to believe,' Katie chuckled. 'I thought *all* lawyers were good at telling stories. But yes, I know a story or two. I'm a librarian.'

He always seemed to catch the tail-end of statements. 'How did you get to be a librarian?' he asked. And looked as if he really wanted to know.

'At the university,' she returned. 'I majored in Library Science. Come on, Nora.'

'Just a minute.' He held up his hand, his head cocked in a listening position. 'I want the house to look just the way it did when you were alone,' he finally said, in a soft, firm voice. 'No more lights than usual, Katie. And make it a long story. Don't come down until I call you. Got it?'

'I——' She wanted to argue, but there was something about the way he was standing, half crouched, intense, that stopped her. And then she noticed something else. His car was gone from in front of the house, and it looked almost as if someone had swept up its tracks in the dirt of the drive. But perhaps that's an illusion, she told herself as she clutched at Nora's hand and tugged her up. Maybe it's just too dark. She turned around to say something else to Jack, but he was gone.

Child-bathing was a new experience. Katie knew all about children outside their homes. How they reacted in crowds, what needed to be done to keep a child-group active in a constructive direction. But this one-on-one in a bathtub was something entirely new, and enjoyable. The girl was a delight. With her share of tiny scars, freckles, and a mole right in the small of her back, she was animation and life in the water.

'Hey, *I've* already had a bath,' Katie protested for the tenth time as more than a little water splashed up at her. 'What a lovely mole, Nora.'

'Oh, that old thing!' The girl twisted and turned, trying to observe. 'That's a family thing. Grandma has one, and you should see Daddy's. His is a little lower than mine, though.'

I should see Daddy's mole? That will be the day! Katie was giggling as she held up the big bath-towel and the little girl stepped out on to the bath-mat.

'Why do you turn all red like that?' The girl was staring at her face, her lips puckered in a need to know. All of which increased Katie's coloration.

'It's—it's the steam,' she stuttered. 'The bathroom's warm, and I'm not used to it.'

'Yeah, well, how about that story?'

She looked like a doll in the long cotton nightgown. 'I have a nightgown just like that,' Katie told the girl as she dried the long blonde hair with a vigorous application of towelling. 'Even to the little red rosebuds on the shoulders.'

'My dad bought it for me,' Nora returned. 'Story time?'

'In my bed,' Katie suggested. 'Your father said not to put on any lights in unusual places.' The little girl squeaked in delight and wiggled by, out into the bedroom. The big bed became a trampoline as she bounced three times, high in the air, and then collapsed.

'That bed's pretty old,' Katie advised as she stripped down the covers and managed to trap the little nymph. 'It could collapse, you know.'

'Aw, it can hold me,' Nora returned. 'I'm only nine.'

'Nine? I thought you were—it doesn't matter. Now, have you ever heard the story of the Four Bears?'

'That's Three Bears,' the child returned. 'Once upon a time——'

'Well, in *my* story it's Four Bears,' Katie said, tucking the sheets up around those bony shoulders. 'Do you want to hear it or not?'

'Well, of course I do.' The child settled herself against the pillows, and the story began. They had hardly progressed to the point where the Four Bears were chasing Rod Red Hood around the kitchen table, when the cars came.

The motors were like a dose of reality in a pleasant world of fantasy. Katie held a cautionary finger across the child's lips, then went over to the window and peeped out from behind the protection of the lace curtain. A bright moon lit the front yard. The cars—three of them—looked ominous in the silvery light of the moon. Three cars, one with the front doors open. And a banging on the front door.

'I want to talk to you, Katie,' a voice yelled up. 'I know you're up there.'

'Yeah, we just want to talk,' another voice commented from the cars, and a gale of laughter followed. The door shook in its sills as the knocks became blows. 'Katie! You'd better let us in, lady.'

'Yeah, lady!' Again the laughter from the other vehicles. And then a greater surprise. From out of the darkness behind them a bull-horn cleared its mechanical throat.

'All right, you people in the cars. We've got you surrounded. If anyone makes a wrong move, we shoot!'

Kate, her heart in her mouth, fumbled her way back to the bed. The little girl was laughing. 'That's only Daddy playing cops and robbers,' she giggled.

'Well——' Katie could find nothing to say. She sank down on to the bed, holding hands with the child, and drawing courage from the little girl! That was when the shots began.

It wasn't a single shot, but rather a fusillade that rocked the area, and brought screams from the passengers in the cars. The sounds seemed to be coming from the front of the house, and then from both sides. The yells from the group in front of the house were confused. Whoever had been standing on the porch made a mad dash back to his vehicle. Motors roared, and the three automobiles sprayed dust and gravel as their tyres spun, caught, and roared out on to the highway.

'Oh, my God,' Katie half screamed. 'Your father!' She was all the way down the stairs before the import of what she was doing sank through her confused mind. I hate guns and shooting. I'm afraid of bullets! So what am I doing running like this? Because of him?

The argument served only to blind her further to what was going on. She slammed open the front door with anxious haste, and took the first three steps down off the veranda like a world-class sprinter. There was no need to go further.

Jack came strolling up out of the dark, that broad grin on his face, trailing a handful of something in one hand. Those big arms opened, snatched her up off the ground, whirled her around, and hugged her close.

'I don't think that particular crowd will be back, ever,' he chortled just before he kissed her. The world, already confused, crumpled into little pieces. She hung in his arms like a huge rag-doll, unable to associate time and place and sensation, and unwilling to try. All the universe applauded. When he released her she staggered, her legs unable to support her. He rectified the problem.

'Did I scare *you*?' he asked. She could see the worried look on his face. For me, that worry, she told herself. God help me, he worries about *me*!

'It's you I'm worried about,' she yelled at him, suddenly angry. 'You—you might have been killed out there! You have to take more care, because——' Because if you don't, I'll never be able to glue myself back together again. Never! Her mind prepared the words, but her tongue was unwilling to release them.

'You——'

'Hey,' he said, alarmed at her confusion. 'There were only five of them.'

'It wasn't the *them*,' she screamed at him. 'You could have been hurt badly—with all those—who was it out there with——?' The words stuck in her throat. She threw herself hungrily at him, hanging on desperately around his neck while her lips did their best to devour him. He was startled at first, but then caught the spirit of the game, and joined in. They didn't break until, out of breath, they heard Nora at the upstairs window.

'If you two keep that up all night I'll never hear the end of my story,' the little girl yelled down.

'Yeah, story,' her father panted.

'You could have been shot!' Katie repeated breathlessly.

'Me?' The look on his face was pure astonishment. 'Not with these.' He held up the string of fire-crackers in her face. 'Half the damn things didn't even go off. I'm never going to buy fire-crackers in Maryland again. Never again!'

'Fire-crackers,' she gasped. 'Why, you——'

'Uh-uh, Katie Lovewell,' he said as he held both her hands to protect himself. 'Southern ladies don't use words like that!'

'I never said a word,' she gasped as she struggled to free herself.

'No, but you were thinking them!'

And I was, she told herself as the struggle ceased. And it was for sure. Darn the man!

He was standing close, and in the light of the early moon she could see the planes and shadows of his rugged face. And his heavy black eyebrows. Black, except for the tiny tuft over the centre of each eye—a tiny white tuft that went straight up, almost like the Devil's horns in medieval paintings. An omen, she asked herself? Am I dealing with Beelzebub himself, or just a facsimile?

A look of complete frustration settled on his face as she giggled at her own imagination!

# CHAPTER FIVE

ON THE next bright morning Kate did the one thing she hardly ever did. She slept late. The morning sun was already high over the Blue Ridge. A clock was booming—eleven times. Her mind filtered the sound, translated, and spurred her up out of the warm bed.

She bounced up and over to the half-opened window, and inhaled the mixture of sweetness and bird-song. For some reason it seemed wonderful to be alive on this particular morning. She made a quick stab at her usual exercises, but as she moved through the graceful drill her mind recalled the previous night, and her mood changed. The nerve of that man!

There was hot water at the shower-head. She revelled in it, working up her anger as hard as she worked up a lather. When her conscience forced her out of the shower she was ready to assault the world.

Ghengis Khan, she told herself grimly as she threw on a T-shirt and wrap-around skirt. That's what he's going to think I am when I get through with him. Imagine the nerve of that man! He had no right to frighten me so! Katie started for the stairs, but had second thoughts. Just because you mean to chew him up and spit him out doesn't mean you shouldn't look nice.

So back to her dressing-table, the silver-mounted brushes that had been her father's last gift to her, and a massive attack on her tumbled hair. I really ought to get it cut, she sighed, but knew she never would. Under the brush-strokes order was restored. She fastened it into a pony-tail with a little pink ribbon. It made her look young, and she wanted to be young this day. Young and angry. Anything else would be overdoing it. I'm only going to breakfast with the man! And that was the crusher—breakfast with the man. Just to be on the safe side she added the tiniest dab of perfume. Barely a touch.

Her slippers were the slide-in style. The heels bumped on each step as she clattered down to the kitchen. The two Lees were there already, the father staring into his second mug of coffee, the little girl finishing up her scrambled eggs with such enthusiasm.

'Oh-oh,' Nora said. Her father looked up. 'Storm warning,' the girl told him as she snatched up her glass of orange juice and faded out of the line of fire. Katie jerked a chair out from under the table and threw herself into it with reckless abandon.

'Well?' She stared at him with daggers in her eyes.

'Well, what?' A cautious approach, as he felt his way.

'Well, what did the child mean by all that mumbo-jumbo?'

'That—ah—sailor talk? You're a sailor, aren't you?'

'You know darn well I'm not! What did she mean?'

He squirmed a little, then set his mug down and tried to out-stare her. It didn't work; her anger quotient was already set too high.

'So all right,' he sighed. 'It means small boat warning, storm signal. To us sailors, of course. I thought you were a sailor.'

'I'm not a sailor,' she snapped. 'I'm just a big dumb country girl who has fallen among thieves. How *dare* you?'

'How dare I what?'

'How dare you frighten me half to death last night with your darn fire-crackers. How dare you let me think

you were in the midst of all that shooting. How dare
you!'

'Fallen among thieves? I'm a lawyer.'

'Same thing!'

'Well!' He dragged the word out. It almost served to
take him around the table, where he snatched up both
her hands just as she attempted to club him with one
open palm. 'So you really care? I thought I'd be a month
getting you to that point!'

'What in the world are you babbling about? Of course
I care. I mean I would——' I mean my mouth has gotten
me dead into a possum-trap, fool! 'I mean I care about
any human being caught in a terrible situation. How did
I know there wasn't a Libyan hit-man out there in the
dark, looking for you? How could I——?'

'You needn't cry.' One of his fingers trapped the falling
globe of a tear. He pulled her up out of her chair. She
came willingly, moving forward into the warmth, the
protection that she had dreamed about all the restless
long night.

'I-I'm not crying,' she stammered.

'Of course not. Something in your eye, no doubt.'

'Yes.' Yes, yes, yes. I've got you in my eye! What a
nerve you've got, insinuating yourself into my house,
into my life, and making me—making me feel again.
How dare you?

'I don't have a clean handkerchief.' His voice was deep
and soothing. She cried herself out, making a mess of
his linen shirt-front, and not caring. When the storm
passed she leaned back to look up at at him.

'I was worried.'

'I know.' A feeling of regret there, and a promise.
'Sometimes I don't think ahead.'

'Like a little boy,' she stated flatly.

'Just so. I may never grow up.'

You don't have to on my account, she wanted to scream at him. I like you the way you are! But she was having trouble with words again. His lock of hair had fallen down over one eye. She stretched a finger out and flipped it back. There was a delightful look on his face. One that...

'Katie? There's somebody on the telephone who wants to speak to you.' Nora sidled halfway into the kitchen, giving her father an apologetic shrug. 'I had to answer the phone, didn't I?'

'Not necessarily,' he grumbled. Katie struggled just enough to break free. It was not something she *wanted* to do, it was something she *had* to do. You can hardly stand nose to nose with the child's father under her very eyes, can you? She can't help but be offended for her mother's sake!

The pair of them watched as she stalked out of the room. 'How come I always come in and find you kissing her?' Nora asked.

'I didn't get that far,' her father complained. 'How come when I'm trying to kiss her you always walk in?'

'I should knock, huh?'

'No, love.' He swept her up in his arms and hugged her mightily. 'Not at all. You're the first woman in my heart.'

'Hah!' his daughter said. She had learned a great deal in her few years.

'Why is it, baby, that you keep trying to marry me off to every woman I bring home?'

'Grandma keeps telling me to do that. "Spur him on", she keeps saying.'

'Hey, they're only girlfriends.'

'You don't need a girlfriend. You got me.'

'So?'

'I need a mother. Grandma keeps saying so. And you're not much of a chooser. I like this one a lot.'

'I—think maybe I do too, love. Where is she?'

They found Kate in the living-room, slumped in a straight-backed chair by the telephone-table, staring blankly out of the window.

'Katie?' Jack walked across the room quietly. For such a big man he moved like a cat. 'Katie?'

She jerked her head around, looking as if she had travelled a million miles since she'd left the kitchen. There was a glisten of moisture in her eyes.

'I—I'm sorry. Did you say something?'

He put both his hands on her shoulders. 'What is it?'

She waved him off, unwilling to discuss the problem. He insisted, bending down to one knee beside her and cradling her face between his hands. 'What?'

'Everything—I don't know,' she said dully. 'I just can't understand. Everything seems to be falling apart. The library called. They've suspended me. Now I don't have a job at all, no money coming in, and hardly any time left. I—I don't understand.'

'Any time to what?'

'I—I don't want to talk about it. Why is all this happening to me? Why did those—people—why did they come last night? Why was I arrested? What—I can't even hold a part-time job in a town library, and that's the only discipline in which I've been trained. What am I going to do when I have to sell the farm?'

'You didn't mention that before,' he said solemnly. 'Selling the farm, I mean. Hey, now.' He pulled her head over towards him and kissed each of her leaking eyes. 'For a girl who doesn't cry much you surely do get your eyelids wet.'

'Why, Jack? Just tell me why?'

'Come over here with me,' he sighed, and, without waiting for her approval, picked her up off the chair and carried her to the couch. She settled back in its corner, then leaned towards him as he joined her. Her head fell on to his shoulder as if it were her natural place. He moved a couple of times to find the comfort-point, his arm around her shoulders, the other hand holding both of hers, resting in her lap.

'Nora,' he called.

'I know,' the little girl said from the protection of the doorway. 'Go take a walk, Nora. Don't be snoopy. Nora. Well, Nora knows when she's not wanted.'

'And thank God for that,' he muttered into Katie's hair. 'Now, little lady. You have to sell the farm?'

'Yes.' She sniffled a couple of times. I'm not crying! I'm not! 'Papa—gambled. When the—he left everything to me, but there wasn't anything to leave. Does that make any sense? They've been probating the will. You know about that sort of thing?'

'I know.'

'At the end of this month they have to settle up the estate.'

'Who is *they*?'

'Papa's lawyer. Mr Bledsoe. Of Bledsoe & Gerney.'

'That's a familiar name. Gerney. The prosecutor, wasn't he?'

'I—I hadn't thought. It's such a small district. Prosecuting is only a part-time job.'

'Bledsoe & Gerney, huh? There can't be much call for a *pair* of lawyers in Stanfield.'

'I guess not. They go to Winchester, Front Royal, Staunton—places like that. And they have a real estate thing going... What's the matter?'

Jack snapped to attention, and, since his arm was behind her, the movement had thrown her up against him, hard. His lips were pursing in and out. And then he settled back down again. 'Nothing's wrong,' he said quietly. 'Just a cramp in my leg.'

She looked at him suspiciously. People with cramps in their legs usually massaged the leg, or jumped up, or something of that nature. Not this one. But he *was* very adept at concocting a story.

'Go on, please. You were saying that they were settling up, and by the end of the month——?'

'Mr Bledsoe said that without a doubt the debts would exceed the assets, and so—well, you know how badly things are going with small farms. Who would want to buy a farm these days? Maybe I might make enough to cover the debts, but then—this old house is a monster, but it's all the home I've ever had!'

'That's how you see your problem? You have to sell the farm?'

'Why, yes, what else is there?' She sat up to look at him. He was wrestling with a problem again. She could see it all on his face. Not what the problem was, but rather that he was struggling with it.

'I don't know,' he said finally. 'But I intend to find out. In the meantime...' Again that pursing of lips, that far-seeing stare in his eye, the tip of his tongue coming out to moisten his upper lip.

'In the meantime,' he said forcefully, smiling at her, 'I find that I've more business to do in these parts than I had thought. How about this? I need a place for Nora and me to camp out, and some adult supervision for her while I'm busy. Suppose, Miss Lovewell, that I hire both you and your house for the next couple of weeks? How would that suit?'

'I—I'd be glad to help,' she returned, using a finger to dry her eyes again. 'But I couldn't take any money for it. It would be out of friendship.'

'Nonsense,' he chuckled. 'Friendship doesn't stock the freezer, or pay for the oil for the furnace, nor compensate for having my very own librarian on hand. All that takes money.' He named a very sizeable amount that made her head spin, and then he sat there and watched her response. She hesitated, fighting with her own devils for a minute or two before capitulating.

'I—I think I could compromise my principles for a— that's a lot of money!'

'Think nothing of it,' he chuckled grandly. 'I'll find a way to get my money's worth. Now then, aren't there woman things to be done around here while I get about my business?' He stood up, offering her both hands. She accepted gladly, and was towed to her feet in the grand manner.

'I'm—every time I talk to you my troubles seem less important,' she sighed. Perhaps he'll kiss me now? It would be such a wonderful ending to a terrible story! But he had something else in mind.

'What about laundry service?' he asked. It threw Katie completely off-centre.

'Laundry?'

'Yes. I can see I didn't bring enough handkerchiefs with me to survive in this house. Out you go. I have to make a telephone call. All lawyers are born with a telephone stuck in their ear.'

He offered a playful little pat at her derrière as she walked out the door. His daughter poked her head in as soon as Katie disappeared into the kitchen.

'Everything OK?' she asked anxiously.

'Everything's fine,' he reported. He was whistling tunelessly as he dialled a long-distance number.

'Who you calling?'

'I'm calling Uncle Vanya. Children should be seen and not heard. Why don't you go try to make a few points with our landlady?'

'Uncle Vanya? Why do we need a detective?'

'That's for me to know and you to find out,' he laughed. His eyes were full of teasing love as he watched his daughter fidget in the doorway. The number was ringing. He waved the child away.

She stuck her tongue out at him. 'And don't think I won't find out,' she said very firmly, and headed for the kitchen.

Katie was at the kitchen stove concocting her belated breakfast when Nora came in. She was feeling much better. Unburdening helps, she thought. He can't do a thing, I'm sure, but it helps to talk. And he has such a lovely shoulder to lean on.

'Having breakfast again?'

'I'm having breakfast period,' Katie commented. 'I'm a big girl. I need to stoke my furnace regularly.'

'You don't think you'll get fat? My aunt Helen always worries about getting fat.'

'Never gave it a thought. Join me?' It was just a touch of guilty conscience. After all, she had contracted to house and feed them both, and the child looked as if she needed feeding up. Nora pulled up a chair, which seemed to signal acceptance.

'Eggs, bacon, milk?'

'Yes, ma'am.'

'My, you're a polite one. Do you have a lot of aunts and uncles?'

'Ten thousand. Well—maybe not that many. We have a bunch of relatives. All in my dad's family. Do you know my uncle Vanya?'

'No, I can't say that I do. Toast, too? I meant to make biscuits, but I must have over-slept. I almost never do that.'

'You must be a very clever lady. You don't have any children?'

'Why, no, Nora. I'm not married.'

'But you're very clever—and beautiful. You *could* be married if you wanted to.'

'Why, thank you! What a nice thing to say.'

'You don't want to?'

'Oh—I guess I want to,' Kate mused. 'Most girls think about marriage. I *almost* did get to the altar, you know, but it went sour.'

'But you still want to?'

'Why are you so insistent, Nora? Yes, I suppose I want to, but a girl has to be asked, you know. I can't just pick out a good-looking man and grab him and drag him to the church.'

'You could if you picked a little one,' the child giggled. 'I'm glad you—this is lovely milk.'

And that's a quick switch of subject, Kate chuckled to herself. This one is her father's child. No doubt about that. And what's good for the goose is——

'Nora, how is it that you and your father came to this area?'

The little girl looked up at her without guile. 'Oh, we were bound for Staunton, for a vacation...'

'Vacation? Aren't all the schools in session at this time of year?'

'Well——' There followed a very great hesitation, then the child's smile vanished. 'Not mine,' she said. 'I go—

I went—to a private school, and there was—well, somebody suggested why don't I go for a vacation...?'

Katie found it hard not to grin at the sincere little face which was finding it so hard to keep its own secrets. 'And who was the somebody that suggested such a thing?'

'I think it was Sister Mary, the principal.'

'Ah. And then what happened?'

'And then Grandma yelled at me in Croatian, and Daddy, he yelled back at her, and he just filled up the car with things, and we started for Staunton.'

'But why did you stop in Stanfield?'

'You wouldn't believe. It was late at night, and dark and all, and we got a flat tyre right in front of the Highway Motel, and that was it!'

'You mean your dad picked this area out because of a flat tyre?'

'Yup. Do you think you'll make biscuits tomorrow?'

'And if she does, will you wash the pans?' Nora ducked away as her father came in behind her and ruffled her hair gently. He allowed no time for an answer.

'What's to see in this area, Katie? I've got some things in hand, and I think we ought to tour some of the places of interest.'

'Of course,' she agreed. 'I'll lay out something simple for dinner—how about steaks and chips? There are a million historical sites within a fifty-mile radius of the house. The valley was one of the great battlefields of the war between the states, you know. Very educational.'

'Yeah, battlefields,' Nora groaned. 'Is that all? More statues?'

'No.' Katie shifted horses in mid-stream. 'We could go down to the Caverns and hear the music.'

'Caverns? That's more like it,' the two of them chimed in.

So they put things in order, and motored in style down the Pike to Luray, then turned west on the New Market Road until they came to the Cavern parking lot, not yet crowded with the tourists that would inundate the place come high summer.

A smiling guide led their small group through the railed walkways that connected the several chambers, stopping long enough for them to hear a recitation by the Stalacpine Organ, a huge and complex arrangement that made music by striking the natural stalactites with rubber-tipped hammers. Well-lit and well patronised, the Luray Caverns were but one of the many hollows under the earth formed by years of water activity among the soft limestone rocks.

It was cool underground, cool and damp, and they were all pleased to come out into the sunshine again and make their way back to the big house. Katie felt a tug at her heart as they drove up to it; Jack was more pragmatic.

'That side gutter needs fixing!' he exclaimed. 'And don't let me forget to get at that darn clock.'

'You leave my clock alone,' Katie insisted. 'It's been that way all my life. I wouldn't know how to tell time if you fixed the thing.'

'And the back door is warped,' Nora reported.

'Great!' He grinned as he escorted them to the door, and then disappeared, a man with a mission that he loved. An hour later, while the two girls were working on the dinner, he was still banging busily on the back door. 'See what I mean?' his daughter commented wryly. 'He just loves fixing things. If we stay long enough your house will be completely overhauled. That's my daddy.'

When the front doorbell rang at about four o'clock Nora ran to attend to it, and was back in a second. 'He says he's Colonel Fessenden,' the child reported. 'He don't got——'

'Doesn't have,' Katie corrected.

'Even librarians do that?' the girl asked, and then plunged back into her report. 'He doesn't have a uniform or anything, so I left him in the front room.'

'Oh, dear,' Katie sighed. 'He's a very important man in these parts. And I look a mess!'

'Not a real colonel, is he? I seen plenty of colonels in Washington. They're not all *that* important—and you look nice just the way you are. Go talk to him. I'll finish the potatoes.'

'I will,' Katie promised as she pulled off her apron and hung it on the hook by the kitchen door. 'But first tell me how you became such a well-trained girl, love?'

Nora ducked her head and turned away to hide her mobile face. 'I don't suppose you know my grandmother?'

'No, I don't suppose I do, but I remember my *own*. Like that, is she?'

'Like that,' Nora returned solemnly. 'Lift that bar, tote that barr'l. Little girls should be seen and not heard. Like that. You'd better hurry. The colonel won't want to be kept waiting.'

'It's only an honorary title,' Katie called over her shoulder as she left the kitchen, and so missed the look of relief that swept over the girl's square little face.

'Ah, Katie.' The colonel had been poking around the almost-empty room, fingering her mother's collectables on the shelf beside the fireplace. He was a tiny martinet of a man, barely five feet four, with a moustache out of proportion to his face, and hardly a hair on the top of his head. 'I remember your mother kept this room full of furniture.'

'Yes, well, times have changed,' Katie responded. 'Have a chair, Colonel. And some refreshment. Tea?'

'Brandy would be better,' he replied. He inspected the dusty couch, and decided to stand. Katie went to the sideboard for a drink, and brought it to him. Colonel Fessenden. He and his family had moved into the district some few years earlier. What he did for a living was still obscure. What his wife did was try to take over the social leadership of the community.

'I'm sorry I missed you at our party,' he drawled. He sipped at the brandy in one hand while the other brushed a minuscule speck of dust from the lapel of his sports coat. 'You seemed to disappear.'

'Your dogs tried to eat me,' she said. 'I began to feel I wasn't welcome. Did you want something specific, Colonel?' He hadn't earned the title, and she hated to use it on him, but why fight city hall? There were still two or three *real* colonels in the district, with records that demanded respect.

'Not really.' Fessenden possessed a very deep voice for such a little man. 'I was passing, and remembered I had a small duty to perform.'

'Duty?' Katie was puzzled by the phrase. Before her father's death the colonel had shown a great deal of respect for her; not since. What duty could he have towards her?

'Er—yes. Duty,' he repeated as he finished off the brandy. 'I understand you are forced to sell your farm, Katie. That's a terrible thing, but it happens to us all now and again.'

'Does it?' she responded bleakly. His sharp little nose flashed around in her direction.

'And so I wanted you to know I would be happy to buy it from you, my dear. Take the load off your back, so to speak.' He reached into his pocket for a calling-card, on the back of which he pencilled in some figures. 'At about that level, should you be interested.'

Katie took a quick look. The house alone was worth as much as the colonel was offering for both house and farm. She managed to get her face under command. Her 'poker-face,' her father always called it. And it's too bad that Dad didn't have a poker-face, she thought as she tapped the card against her fingernail. I wish I knew with whom he gambled.

'I'll consider it,' she told the colonel. 'I—have to contact my advisors, you know. I don't know a great deal about land prices.'

'Advisors?' The colonel's ears perked up. 'You have advisors?'

'Oh, yes,' she told him. 'I'll let you know, Colonel. And I do thank you for your offer.' She was walking towards the front door, and her visitor had no option but to follow. As she closed the front screen-door behind him, he turned back to her.

'Don't be too long about it,' he said. 'Prices change quickly in the real estate business, and I'd hate to have your property go to public auction.'

'I understand,' she said. 'And thank you again.' The little man stumped down the steps and headed for his Cadillac, leaving Katie at the door, still tapping her fingernail with the card. And why would he want to buy my farm? she asked herself as she watched. He doesn't farm. He has enough land for his—mansion. Why would he think his price might be acceptable? Is he trying to buffalo me? And just how do you suppose he knew that I had to sell? And why am I so darned suspicious of everyone and everything? She was still pondering the question when she went back to the kitchen.

They were all tired that night. Nora went to bed early, without protest. The Tale of the Four Bears had now progressed to another crisis, and the little girl fell asleep with a smile on her face. 'Good story,' Jack whispered as he came in for the tail-end of the tale. 'Can't wait to hear the ending myself. Who wrote it?'

'Shakespeare,' she giggled, leading him by the hand out of the room and down the stairs.

'Shall we *set* a spell on the porch?'

'You really *are* a Yankee, aren't you?' she challenged. 'People around here don't talk like that at all.'

'You bet,' he chuckled. 'I come from the north. North Croatia, that's my family background.'

He seemed to do it without thinking, dropping his arms around her shoulders as they went outside and sank down on the top step. Twilight was on them, and Kate shivered. Not from the cool wind; her sweater took care of that. It was his arm, resting solidly as if it owned the place. And his hand, casually toying with the ends of her hair, with the lobe of her ear as he talked.

He was talking about Tennessee, where he had travelled often, but the words passed right over her head. She was busy forming fantasy, filling her mind with a million miles of him, from the tiny inch he was offering. When he pulled her back against his chest she went willingly, and her contented sigh gave the whole show away. She dreamed until the first stars came out, and would have continued, but his arm had dropped lower, around her waist, and those wandering fingers were playing strange tricks with her mind. She snapped back to attention, moving uneasily as his hand wandered up to her breast. The movement stopped, but the hand remained in place.

'What?' he asked softly.

'I—we won't be able to do this much after the next two weeks,' she stuttered. 'Mosquitoes, and things that squeak in the night.'

'That's not the problem,' he said, squelching her movement as well as her speech. He spoke softly, but there was iron in his tone as well as his arm.

'I—I don't know what you mean,' she sighed. He laughed and turned her around to face him.

'This is the problem,' he answered. He pulled her slowly up against his hard frame, giving her plenty of opportunity to object. The idea never crossed her mind—at that moment, that was. When he offered his lips, brooding over her in the darkness, she made the very tiniest of objections, and then hauled down her flag. It was a repetition of the last time he had kissed her, but this time there was more comfort than passion. When he broke away she whimpered in protest, and pulled his head down again to taste of the wild honey.

Jack laughed, a triumphant male laugh, and bent to her. This time the warmth was swallowed by fire, the comfort by wild passion as he probed her sensitive mouth with his tongue, stroked her back with one hand, and tangled his other in the depths of her hair. When he broke off this time it was only to stand up, sweep her up in his arms, and start for the door.

Her breath and her conscience caught up to her at the same time, just as he fumbled to open the screen-door. 'What—where are we going?' she gasped.

'Upstairs,' he chuckled. 'I'm too old for sparking on the front stairs when there are plenty of comfortable beds to be had.'

She put out her hand and snatched at the latch. He came to a sudden stop. 'What's the matter?' he asked.

'I—I'm too young for playing games in your bed,' she said. The words came out in all their bitterness. She didn't *want* to say them. She wanted so very much for him to sweep her up the stairs without a single word being said, and accepting what was bound to come after. But having verbalised it, he had made it cheap. The kind of thing that high-school girls did behind the barn. It was too much for a girl with her narrow upbringing. Too much the sort of thing she could expect from men like Peter.

'Come off it,' he snorted.

'Put me down,' she snapped. 'I may be your landlady, but I'm not your resident——'

'Good God!' he interrupted as he set her feet gently down on the floor of the porch. 'You've never done this sort of thing before?' He did not sound bitter. Disappointed—certainly regretful, but not bitter. She backed away from him, trying to hide her face—her too easily read face.

'Is that what you really mean, Katie?'

'What would your wife say?' she countered, fumbling the words over her tongue. She regretted it as soon as it was said, but regrets were possible; recall was not. In the darkness it was impossible to see his reaction, but her fingers told her that his face had turned to stone. He stood for a moment, then turned on his heel and went into the house, leaving her standing there alone.

Katie turned back to the rail, took three steadying breaths, and glared unseeing out into the distance. The smell of pine filled her nostrils. In the distance, up in the National Park, the lonely sound of a loon echoed in the air. Feeling just as lonely as the bird, she clutched at the rail and let her foolish tears run again. It was a full hour later before she was able to pull herself together and go up to her own bed.

# CHAPTER SIX

AN HOUR after Jack left Katie managed to stumble up the stairs into her own bedroom. She bypassed her bath, dropping her clothes as they came off, in little piles on the floor. Neglecting even her nightgown, she dived under the covers, huddled up in a little ball, and cried. The pillows bore mute evidence of the agony. Why? Why? Because he has a wife? She wanted to believe that to be the reason why she'd rejected him. Wanted to, but couldn't. 'I don't give a darn about your wife,' she whispered into the darkness.

Then why is it? Am I so crazy, so mixed up about my parents? So wanting to be loved—by anyone? Surely not anyone. There had been more than one groping boy in her life. They had all left her feeling just a little bit— dirty. So why now, with *this* man, so suddenly? Just a touch, and she had caught fire. If he had carried her one more step further she would have gone up like a balloon, without hope of salvation. So then it's me, not him. Is that right, girl?

Me. Brought up in the narrowest of ruts—con- ditioned to act and react, but not to think. When they all preached at me 'Bad girls do it, nice girls don't' it had all been a rote reaction. Of *course* that was the right way to act. 'Nice girls don't.' And I laughed because it was so easy not to. I never did realise how terribly hard it could be, until tonight, to continue to be a 'nice girl.' I'm beginning to hate the sound of the words. There I was, until today, saving myself—for what? A twenty-five-year-old virgin, and as proud of my stupidity as any fool could be. Can love be that proud? And on that note, by light of earliest dawn, Kate finally fell into an exhausted sleep.

The next three nights were almost frigid. Inside the house, not outside. The state of Virginia hurried towards summer. In fact it provided a magnificent pyrotechnic display, the first major thunderstorm of the year. But inside the house it might as well have been January. Katie found herself tiptoeing around the house, doing her best to avoid Jack, at the same time sharing a growing relationship with Nora.

'Dad blew it, huh?' the little girl exclaimed one day, as they worked in the kitchen on a shepherds pie.

'I don't know what you mean. Make sure there's plenty of flour on the board before you try to roll the crust.'

'Grandma says he's not very patient. It gets him in a lot of trouble. He's got a short fuse. At least, that's what Grandma says.'

'I'd rather not talk about your father.'

'Isn't that something? That's what *he* said this morning. You two are a funny pair.'

'If you mean your father and I, we're—we're not a pair at all!' And we ought to be! What good does it do to go to bed alone and cry into your pillow all night? I was scared, that's all, not stricken by some darn morality. If he had given me more warning maybe I could have adjusted. I could have thought up some nice line like 'your bed or mine?' Or something like that. Instead I jumped like a jack-rabbit and kept running! Despite the preachments, God didn't intend me to be a virgin for the rest of my life! It's the only game in the world where you can only get experience by—by experiencing it. That's a stupid way to put it, but there it is.

'Hey!'

Katie finally felt the hand tugging at her skirt, the raised little voice. 'I'm sorry, I must have been miles away. What did you say, Nora?'

'I said, shall I put the pies in the oven now?'

'I—let me inspect the top crust. Yes, that looks good.'

'And then I said——'

The front door opened, and footsteps echoed. Katie cocked an ear. 'Yes? You said?'

'And then I said if you mean to duck out on Dad you'd better start now, but it's already too late, because——' The little girl squealed in excitement, and ran to the opening kitchen door, yelling, 'Uncle Vanya!'

Katie waited in the background while the family greetings were exhausted. Uncle Vanya, with Jack Lee hovering in the background. Uncle was the most *ordinary* man Katie had ever seen. About five feet eight, neat brown hair, a sharp nose—only his eyes, dark and gleaming with intelligence, reminded her of Jack. He wore a suit of some neutral colour. When she turned to check on the oven it amazed her to discover she couldn't remember what colour it was. Uncle Vanya.

When introduced, he displayed a courtly old-world manner, bowing over her hand, smiling up at her. 'Yes,' he said in a perfectly innocuous American accent. 'Just as my sister described.'

'Vanya is *my* uncle,' Jack explained. 'My mother's brother.'

She made him welcome. It wasn't hard. Everything pleased him; he was ready to talk about anything in the world, from the price of apples to the Pittsburgh Steelers. So the atmosphere in the house lightened, and by dinnertime they were all friends again.

'But I never did hear what you do for a living,' she asked as they gathered in the living-room for coffee.

'Uncle Vanya's the World's Greatest Detective,' Nora announced proudly.

'Retired,' the man added, and suddenly Katie recognised that his hair was white, not brown, and there were wrinkles on his forehead. When she said so, he laughed.

'The art of being a good detective,' he lectured, 'is to be so ordinary that people pay you no attention at all. Turn around, please.' He waited until her back was to him. 'Now,' he continued, 'describe me, please.' And for the life of her she was unable to do so. She turned back again, shrugging her shoulders, laughing.

'As you said, John,' the older man said, 'she is so lovely when she smiles.'

It was pure nerves that made her spill the coffee as she filled Jack's mug. Nora brought a paper towel, and Uncle Vanya changed the subject, but it took Katie more than a minute or two to restore her cool.

'I don't think you can do any detecting in this area,' she said after a time. 'Stanfield is such a small town. Even an ordinary-looking stranger would still be a stranger!'

'So we practise the art of deception,' the old man chuckled. 'I have a partner. He sets up in the town now. A big brash red-headed Irishman. He will go everyplace, make all sorts of noises, be so abrasive, you see, as a decoy. And behind his cover I will go softly as a mouse— and things will happen.'

'But—I don't know what it is you're detecting.'

'You,' the old man chuckled. 'You are what I am detecting. And now I must be going. I will not come back, you understand, until the case is settled. If by some accident you should meet me in public you must not acknowledge that you know me. Goodnight, beautiful lady. Be good to my useless nephew.' This time he went the whole way, bowing and kissing her hand at the door. When he went out it seemed that he took the fresh air with him into the darkness.

Nora was too excited that night to go to bed on time. It took almost an extra hour of story-telling to settle her down. When the child's eyes finally closed, Katie sat by the bed for another five minutes, trying to make up her mind. It was a useless exercise. She had already decided what she wanted to do—and really just needed to acquire the courage to go and do it. On her way to the doing she detoured by her own room, added a touch of lip-gloss, a patina of rouge, and just the veriest fragment of mascara. After all, courage came in many kinds of packages, and package-decorating was an Old Dominion custom.

Jack was out on the porch, cloaked by night, when she came downstairs. She went silently to his side, dropping down on the top step just a few inches from him. His massive head turned to acknowledge her, and then went back to studying whatever it was that had attracted his attention. She wanted to blurt out what she had to say, but hadn't 'the gumption', as they said in those parts. After all, you couldn't—not after three days of cold silence—plumb down beside a man and say... well, you couldn't, that's all there was to that. So she sat and shared his silence.

It might have been fifteen minutes later that he stirred. 'Fascinating, those lights on the mountain. They move like fireflies. I thought the mountain-top was deserted.'

'Not entirely,' she said softly. 'It's part of a National Forest. There are those who come and go up there all the time. It's a marvellous view.' A pause. 'I liked your uncle Vanya very much.'

'And he liked you, Katie. But then, you're a hard girl *not* to like. With a little luck, and Vanya's suspicious nose, we'll find some answers to those questions of yours.' He stared off into the distance again. A curtain of stars was unveiled as high-altitude winds blew clouds away. The scent of the valley, loaded with apple blossoms and laurel, filled their nostrils. He sighed, a deep, gusty sigh.

'Katie, I'm sorry that——'

'Jack, I'm sorry——'

Their apologies both started at the same moment, and both stopped. He looked at her. She could see his teeth sparkling by starlight as he grinned. 'Ladies first.'

'No. You.'

'OK. Katie, I wanted you to know I'm sorry about that affair the other night. I had no right to assume what I did, and——'

Her hand on his sleeve stopped him. 'I think perhaps you *had* the right,' she said glumly. 'I—I wouldn't want you to think I was playing games—playing hard to get, Jack. It was just that it so surprised me that I really was flustered. If I had had any idea what I was doing I wouldn't have been so darn—I wouldn't have said anything like what I *did* say. I was *acting* like some—some idiot. Why shouldn't you think that of me?'

'Nonsense.' Both those strong hands were on her shoulders again. 'Don't you ever say things like that about yourself again.' A triple-shake left her in no doubt about his anger. '*I* know you aren't, and *you* know you aren't, and that will be the last time I hear that from you!'

There didn't seem to be anything else to say except 'yes sir'. She tried it out. It earned her another shake.

'I'm not your uncle,' he snapped. 'Never mind the *sir* business.'

'The thought never crossed my mind,' she gasped, 'that you might be my uncle.' My lover, yes, but not my uncle. Never that, Jack Lee!

That was the right answer, apparently. He urged her to lean in his direction, directing gently with one hand. She turned, resting in his lap and the curve of his right arm, looking up at him, wishing. The kiss came slowly. A feather-touch, a circular gliding motion, and then a gentle sealing. His left hand stroked her cheek, then trailed down her willing frame to rest in the little hollow between waist and hip. Like a huge fly-wheel building up to speed she could feel passion accelerate. She reached for the open neck of his shirt and buried her hand inside against the smooth rock of his chest. Something in the back of her mind, some guardian, kept whispering 'hurry'. Her inability to know how or in what direction to do the hurrying infuriated her. She whimpered. He moved his head and stared down at her.

'Wow,' Jack said. 'The other night—what was it that set you off?'

She struggled to get a grip on her runaway emotions. They were hard to rein in—almost impossible. He waited patiently.

'I don't know how to talk about it,' she moaned. 'It wasn't just—I wanted—there was your wife to consider!' She offered it as a diversion, only to have him snap it up angrily.

'Oh, my God!' His hand came back up to her cheek, then threaded through her hair. She could feel his fingers quiver as they explored the hollow behind her ear. He was thinking of something, and his hands moved without purpose. Then he pulled her up to a sitting position, and gently set her back on the step.

'I don't know where you get your information,' he said remotely.

'I—Nora told me.'

'I see. Now that's something *I* don't like to talk about,' he said. 'But I'll tell you anyway. I don't have a wife. Six months after Nora was born Helen packed up, cleaned out both our bank accounts, and deserted us. We haven't seen her since. Two years ago I divorced her. It wasn't a happy time for any of us, and I don't suppose she ran off because I was the perfect husband. But that's the way it is. Does that make you feel better?'

'Oh, yes, yes—very much so. I mean, I'm sorry about you and your wife, but——'

'But there's something else?'

'I—yes. There's something else.' She ducked her head away from him, her fists clenched. Only the pain of her own fingernails biting into her palms kept her from screaming everything out into the night.

'What?' He was staring at the side of her head, and used a finger to turn her chin back in his direction. His voice was cold. 'Now here's where you tell me that nice girls never have done it with strangers?'

'No!' she screamed at him, unable to contain her frustrations. 'Damn you!' She beat on his shoulders with her fists. He stopped the attack by grabbing both her fists in one of his hands.

'So what is it, then?' he asked.

She took a deep sobbing breath. 'It's because this nice girl has never done it with anybody at all,' she mumbled.

'What!'

'You heard me.'

'My God! Whoever would have thought...?' he mused. 'All the way up into the Blue Ridge, and I find——'

'I know,' she said bitterly. 'A twenty-five-year-old virgin. I was always proud of the fact, and now it's become an almost intolerable burden to me.'

'That's not what I was going to say,' he returned. 'You prize yourself too lowly. I was going to say I've come all the way up the Blue Ridge and found honesty and an old-fashioned thing called virtue. And being a typical Washingtonian I don't know what to make out of either one of them!'

'Don't build it up into too big a thing,' she sighed, moving that additional inch away. 'Things don't seem as black or white as they did yesterday. I'm very mixed up. I don't know what's come over me. I didn't mean to tell you anything like that. I wish you would forget it all.'

'Everything?'

'I—yes, everything.'

'You're not going to ask me to relieve you of this "intolerable burden"?'

'No.'

'Have I insulted you?'

'No.'

'Then come back over here where you belong.'

'Yes,' she sighed again, and barely nipped off the 'sir' that tried to follow. Back in the cradle of his arms she luxuriated in the feel and scent and sound of him, his heart beating steadily in the ear she pressed against his chest, his chin resting among the wind-blown tendrils of her hair. It *was* where she belonged.

'We have a lot of problems, you and I,' he half whispered, his lips moving down close to her ear. 'And when we get them resolved, lady, we're going to come back to this "burden" of yours.'

Kate stirred uneasily in his arms, making a vague protest. He subdued her with an ounce of extra pressure. 'Please don't talk like that,' she moaned. 'Am I not going to have anything to say about it?' She waited breathlessly for his answer.

'Not much,' was the laconic reply. 'I'm what you might call the dominating macho man, love.'

She shivered at the threat and the promise. Her education almost led her to go into battle over the subject again; her inherited instincts cut off both the words and the thought. She huddled closer, not willing to be separated from him. 'And what do we do until then?'

'And until then,' he laughed, 'we're going to live dangerously.' His roaming hands gave description to what he meant.


It rained all that night, and was still drizzling the next morning. The two Lee faces at her breakfast table were glum, to say the least, although they improved considerably when Katie provided hot blueberry pancakes with maple syrup. Well, *almost* maple syrup. And, after stacking all the dishes in the refurbished dish-washer, Jack gave them both a big smile.

'Time for us to have a council of war,' he announced. 'Coffee in the library, in ten minutes.'

His daughter glared at him. 'I s'pose I'm gonna disappear, am I?'

'Not at all,' he assured the child. 'We're a team, us three. But you can have cocoa instead of coffee.' They both turned to look at Katie.

'And I suppose I'm going to make the coffee and wait on you hand and foot?' she enquired, allowing a little sarcasm to creep in.

'No,' he returned. 'I'll make the coffee.'

'He makes terrible coffee,' his daughter commented. 'Grandmother told me that. It'll poison you.'

'Nora!'

'Well, it will,' the child insisted. Katie pulled the girl over to her side.

'That bad, huh? Then I suppose I'll have to make it just to stay alive?'

'But you don't have to wait on me hand and foot,' Jack interjected. How can he make himself sound so serious when his eyes are laughing? Katie asked herself. 'Hand is all right,' he continued, 'but we don't need foot-waiting.' And then he cocked his head to one side and offered her the most appealing look she had seen in years.

'All right, all right,' she gasped, unable to restrain the laughter. 'I know a good con-game when I see it. Coffee in the library in ten minutes.'

They were both waiting for her some twenty minutes later as she pushed the trolley into the room. 'I thought maybe a little more toast—and I found a couple of croissants left over. And Nora will pour.'

'Me?' the girl said, just a half-second before her father said the same thing.

'You,' Katie assured her. 'Girls have to learn things like that, and now's a good time to practise.' She moved around the heavy table and took a chair across from Jack.

'Have I been missing something?' he mused, as his daughter performed faultlessly.

'No, but Lenora might have,' Katie told him softly. 'She's growing fast. She needs——'

'I need a mother,' the child interrupted. 'And the sooner the better!'

A quick, deep silence. And then, 'Well, I do,' Nora repeated. 'You've always told me to speak up about 'portant things!'

Katie ducked her head to hide the blush that crowded into her cheeks. Jack Lee seemed to have been overcome by something which choked him. He took a sip at his coffee-mug to clear his throat.

'Now, to business,' he finally said as his daughter glared at him.

'Daddy——?'

'We'll talk about that together some other time,' he offered blandly. 'Right now we have to take care of Katie's problem. One problem at a time, that's my motto.'

'Never do today what you can put off until tomorrow. That's your motto,' his daughter grumbled as she slid back in her chair and folded her arms. Good lord, Katie thought. Was I ever so smart when I was her age? This girl thinks like a twenty-year old. I'd love to say something about the matter under dispute, but I just don't dare!

Jack Lee rapped on the table a couple of times with the top of his ball-point pen. 'Item,' he said, making a note on the big yellow pad in front of him. 'During the last year things have changed immensely for the Lovewell family, right?'

Katie nodded. Nora glared.

'For example, your father took up gambling.'

'I wouldn't say it quite that way,' Katie interjected. 'He was always a gambler, but never as bad as——'

'Yes.' He made another note. 'You have to gamble someplace, with someone. In a small town like this, where? With whom?'

'I don't know,' Katie admitted. 'He just went—out. As far as I know there aren't any gambling casinos in the valley.'

Jack tapped his pen a couple of times, his lips pursed. 'Most gambling is cash only,' he said thoughtfully. 'But, if he was gambling to excess, there might be a time when he needed cheques, or credit cards, or—you wouldn't have your father's cheque-book around?'

'In the bottom drawer of that desk,' she replied, pointing to the ancient roll-top construction that stood in the corner. 'You want me to——'

'Yes, but not just at this second,' he told her. And then broke off the puzzled look on his face and smiled at her. It was like the sun coming up all over again. Katie could feel the pleasure spreading through her body.

'So...' he continued, tucking the smile away somewhere out of sight. 'Your father begins to gamble heavily. Things go from bad to worse, and we come to the day that we met you at the Fessenden place. Let's go over that part again.' He made a couple more check-marks on his pad. 'You are invited to——'

'Hired to,' Katie interrupted. 'I wasn't there as a guest.'

'OK, hired to.' Another two marks on his pad. 'And while you're working up steam somehow or another the guard-dogs get loose. How often before has that happened?'

'Never, to my knowledge.' Katie could feel a tension building up inside her. She plucked ineffectually at a loose thread in her skirt.

'But that happens on the day that idiot Filmore runs by a sheriff's car and gets caught by what is probably the dumbest deputy in the county—in your house.'

'True.'

'We heard the deputy say *he* got in by forcing the door. How do you suppose Filmore got in?'

'I'm afraid he had a key,' Katie murmured. 'Peter— I gave him a key, and he had twenty-five copies made. Everybody in his crowd had one! I get so mad when I think of it! And why couldn't I think of it before then? I'm probably a great match for that deputy sheriff of yours.'

'He's not mine yet,' Jack said. 'But he will be. Believe me, he will be. Now, suppose we stop right at that point. And what do we have?'

'I haven't the slightest idea,' Katie returned. Nora squirmed in her chair and waved her hand for attention. Her father nodded in her direction.

'Somebody's trying to scare Katie off,' she said.

'Scare Katie?' He nodded again. 'Possibly. Scare her to what? Run away?'

'She wouldn't do that,' the child observed.

'I think you're right. Scare her to do what else? Sell the farm?'

'But——' It was a ridiculous thought, but somehow Katie couldn't get the words to come out. 'Don't be silly,' she finally managed. Both of them stared at her. 'I was already going to have to sell the farm. It wasn't exactly a secret, you know.'

'But perhaps not just at this moment,' Jack suggested.

Katie struggled to her feet. 'What are you saying? That there's some secret little conspiracy going on? That the town is plotting to get rid of me?'

'Not exactly the town,' he told her. 'That's what we'll have to find out. Did those dogs get loose by accident? Did this Filmore kid just "happen" to be speeding by your house? Was the marijuana just a coincidence? Now there are a few questions to start off with. And our time limit is—is what, Katie?'

'Three weeks,' she murmured. 'That's when I *have* to have the money to settle the estate.' She paced the room a couple of times. 'I think this whole thing is rubbish. My family have lived in this town for centuries.'

'But not everyone in town can say the same,' he cautioned her. 'But that's enough talking for the moment. Right now I'm due in court.'

'In court, Daddy? Is this when somebody's gonna get a zinger?'

'Several somebodies,' Jack returned, and that smile was back. 'Katie Lovewell strikes back!'

'She does?' A trembling in her legs forced Katie to reach for support. Jack Lee was the only thing available. She grabbed on to him as if her life depended on it.

'She does,' Jack said, chuckling. 'The kindergarten where you worked is a private outfit, and a knockover. We're filing civil suit against them this afternoon. I think they'll run for cover the minute they hear.'

'On what grounds?' Katie asked.

'Oh, I'll think of that on the way to the court-house,' he said. 'Civil rights? Anti-feminism? Defamation of character? No, we can't use that one. That's the one you're suing the sheriff on.'

'I am?'

'You am. Give us a kiss, ducks. I need a little courage. You're also seeking an injunction against the library for discrimination. Those librarians are hard to handle.' Katie was so completely bedazzled that it hardly seemed worth the bother of trying to avoid his kiss, even though his daughter was standing there, admiring. He enveloped her like her own individual cyclone, whirling her up into the clouds, thoroughly disconcerting her mind, and then dropping her and rushing for the door.

Katie turned slowly and stared at Nora. 'Your father,' she said solemnly through dry, trembling lips, 'is a man of violent passions.'

'I ain't sure what that means.' The girl reflected for a moment. 'If you mean he's a sort of wild one, yeah! That's what Grandma always keeps saying. You know, most of the other women he kisses sort of hang on and come up laughing. Maybe you take the whole thing too seriously. Do you think?'

And that's the prize thought, Katie Lovewell thought. I'm taking instruction from a nine-year old child on how to kiss her father! And maybe it's not a bad idea. I'm not doing too well all by myself, am I? But there was an after-thought, one that had a tinge of bitterness to it. 'You mean he kisses a lot of women?'

'I couldn't count high enough,' Nora responded. 'I'm only in the fourth grade, you know.'

# CHAPTER SEVEN

KATHLEEN rode her bicycle into town the next morning. There was a horde of little things to be done among the few stores in Stanfield, and Jack had gone off with his daughter in tow. An old-fashioned town, Stanfield, like any of the ten thousand you might see throughout the rural south. Main Street went north and south, forming the western border of Court House Square. The white-pillared baptist church occupied one corner. The episcopal church sat on the opposite side of the diamond in all dignity. The methodist church sat back from the street demurely, surrounded by its own grove of oaks. And the court house commanded all of the north side. A stately row of maple trees surrounded and sheltered the square. At least half the trees had been there to see General Jackson as he had driven his foot-cavalry up the valley during the war between the states.

As Katie came out of the pharmacy with a handful of parcels she ran into Evvie Hamilton, the man who controlled the dogs on the Fessenden estate. It was too good an opportunity to miss. 'Day off, Evvie?'

'Half-day,' he drawled. 'Miz Fessenden don't go much for full days off. Ain't seen you around much, lately.'

'Busy,' she admitted. 'Care to take a cup of coffee with me?'

'Don't mind if I do,' he agreed, and led her down the block to the Stanfield Coffee Shoppe. They found an empty table in the corner, and ordered.

'Miss your dad, I do.' Evvie sipped at his mug. He was a man who would never see sixty again, with a fringe of white hair, and one missing tooth right in the middle of his weather-beaten grin.

'I do myself,' she answered. 'But we have to get on with living, don't we? How are the dogs?'

'Funny. You're the third one to ask me that in the last three days.' He managed another sip. 'You'd think it was a big thing, that with the dogs. The sheriff's deputy asked me that very question. Well, no, that ain't right. He *told* me that the gate lock must of been broke.'

'The deputy?'

'Strange, ain't it? Him and Miz Fessenden, they makin' out like a pair of bandits when the colonel's not around. Can't quite imagine that. She's hunting high society, and he's lower than a raccoon's belly, but well, it ain't my business to talk.'

'So that was it,' Katie murmured. 'The lock was broken.'

'Well, now, I didn't rightly say that, Miss Katie. The *deputy* said the lock was broke. I looked at it that same day. Wasn't nothin' wrong with the lock, 'cept somebody unlocked it. Miz Fessenden gave me a line of chatter about broken locks the next day, so I went back to check. And what do you know?' He grinned at her across the table. 'There was a new lock on the gate, and the old one done completely disappeared! Now how's that for a mystery?'

'It surely is something,' she agreed, but was hard put to keep her mind on the conversation. Someone had unlocked the gate. Why? Who? Katie was unable to sit still. She just *had* to move. Making a quick excuse, she left the shop and went out into the sunshine. One of the old men playing chequers across the square waved to her. She waved back, and stepped out into the street. As she remembered it later the first sound was that of a motor accelerating. The screech of brakes came later, almost too late. She barely turned her head in the direction of the noise before the heavy truck skidded. The left front corner of the bumper caught her in the thigh as she tried to move out of the way, and tossed her back on to the pavement, where she collected a crowd in a hurry.

'Are you hurt, Katie?' She managed to focus on the face leaning over her. It was the driver of the truck, Peter Lester. With her vision blurred it was hard to see the expression on his face.

'Only my pride,' she muttered as she managed to sit up.

'You walked right out in front of me,' Lester insisted. 'You all saw, didn't you?'

A couple of younger men in the crowd made agreeing noises, but there was a background argument. 'Didn't see you really try to stop,' Evvie Hamilton said.

'You want to watch what you say, old man,' Lester warned. 'You've got no call going around making accusations. Accidents happen. Sometimes they're God's warning.'

There was a bustle at the edge of the crowd, and Jack Lee appeared at Katie's side. He dropped to one knee to examine her. He was all business, running his hands over her legs, checking the bruises on the side of her head. 'Nothing terribly bad,' he murmured as he supported her back. 'But we'll get you to the hospital just the same. One of you people call the ambulance.'

Katie's head was whirling. The bruises hurt, but still everything seemed to be so funny, sounded so hollow.

Except for Jack. She leaned back into the warm comfort of him and giggled. 'We don't have an ambulance.'

'All right, love,' he comforted her. 'That's a little concussion you've got there, I'll bet. I'll drive you to the hospital.'

'And we don't have one of those, either,' she sighed. 'You have to go over to Front Royal to find a hospital. Or down to Dr Franklin's clinic at Luray.'

'Oh, brother!' she heard him mutter, but the words were indistinct. And in a moment Nora was with him. 'Hold on to her while I get the car,' he told the girl. Katie felt the change of arms as the child settled down beside her. There were other hands to help; Katie felt the need to keep her eyes closed. But she heard everything that was said.

'Run over my girl, did you?' Jack Lee, talking to somebody. *At* somebody, for a fact. Katie, who hated violence, shuddered and shut her eyes.

'It was an accident,' Peter Lester blustered. There was a tremor of fear in his voice, which made Katie feel ever so much better. 'Anybody can tell you it was an accident.'

'Accidents don't happen to *my* girl.' There was a satisfying thud and a gasp from the crowd. Katie decided to make the sacrifice, and opened one eye. Peter Lester was sitting in the middle of the pavement. There was something wrong with his very handsome nose. Jack Lee leaned over and pulled him back up to his feet, then casually brushed him down and straightened the younger man's shirt-collar.

'Accidents *never* happen to my girl,' Jack said in a low, warning voice. 'Got that? *Never* happen to my girl.'

'I—I've got it,' Peter said.

'Good. I like a quick learner.' With which Jack gave
him a little push, and Peter was back sitting on the kerb
again with blood running out from between his fingers.

'I'll get the car,' Jack continued in a casual voice. 'You
folks watch over my girl?'

'I don't know what you're making such a big fuss about,'
Katie grumbled. The trip to the clinic had exhausted the
rest of the day, and all that Dr Franklin had had to say
was, 'Go home, keep off your feet, take two of these,
and call me in the morning.'

'Even the doctor said it was only a little bruising,'
Katie complained. '*I'm* the one who got hit, and you're
going around with a sore head, like some bear caught
at the beehive! Why in the world would Peter Lester want
to run me down? Everything you turn to seems to be
some deep conspiracy. For God's sake, it was only trivial
accident. I didn't look where I was walking.'

'He also said it might be a concussion,' he muttered
as he stamped back and forth in the living-room. And
wearing my carpet to the nub, she thought as she watched
his feet, not daring to watch his face. The whole idea
seemed worth a giggle. She tried it out tentatively as she
shifted her weight on the couch.

'It's not funny,' he snapped as he whirled round and
stomped over directly in front of her. She looked up at
the furious face he wore, and then that crumpled, he
dropped to his knees, and gathered her up as gently as
if she were a Ming vase. 'My girl doesn't have accidents,' he muttered in her ear. 'Damn you. You've got
to be more careful, woman!'

'Everybody has accidents,' she murmured. One of
those huge hands of his stroked through her hair. Well,

it's one way of getting attention around here, she told herself, and again the giggle escaped.

He set her back into the depths of the couch, and carefully rearranged the pillows behind her. She relaxed against them with a sigh of relief. It *had* been a strenuous day. Jack Lee settled back on his haunches. Even in that position he was nose to nose with her. Nora came in from the kitchen, carrying a glass beaded with frost.

'Lemonade,' the girl offered as she handed over the glass, and then took a quick look at her father. 'Lecture time,' she giggled, and made for the door before his glare caught up with her.

'The voice of experience?' Katie held the glass to her lips, not to sip, but to have something between herself and this—man.

'You'd better believe it,' he muttered. 'That's all I need. Another female as sharp-tongued as my daughter. Why me, lord?'

'I don't know,' she mused. 'Been to church lately?'

'And that,' he growled as he rose to his full length, 'will be enough of that. Listen up, lady.'

I should stand and bow, Katie told herself. And probably kiss his foot. But being the patient gave her *some* rights, so she merely nodded. He began his little speech; she heard not a word. There was something attractive about how his chin bobbed as he emphasised his words. How his eyes gleamed darkly, how the tip of his right ear seemed to wiggle on occasion. How that black curl fell down across his forehead when he gestured—and he did a great deal of that. A woman, she told herself, would find it terribly difficult not to succumb to his blatant masculinity. Aren't I? And then the silence rang in her ears. She brought herself back to reality, startled by the quiet.

'Well?' Hands on hips, legs slightly apart, he towered over her the way the Colossus might have towered over the harbour at Rhodes, controlling her every entry-point, every thought. And she had no idea which sheet of music he was singing from.

'Perhaps,' she muttered.

He exploded. 'Perhaps! What the devil does *that* mean, woman?'

'Perhaps you'd better repeat a little of that,' she sighed. 'Like everything after "Listen up".'

For a moment he looked as if he might be ready to explode. Katie shivered and pulled back to the depths of the sofa. And even as she moved his red face smoothed, his eyes shifted from storm to twinkle, and the corners of his mouth turned up. When he laughed it was with raucous enthusiasm, with what her father used to describe as a two-county laugh.

'Didn't hear a word, huh?'

'I—was busy thinking,' she admitted, and then ducked her head. 'Did I miss a lot?'

'Not really,' he returned. 'Katie Lovewell, I've been looking for a woman like you for years!'

'Well, I've been right here all the time,' she told him wistfully. There was a touch of sadness in the words, too. She wished he had looked *faster*, or come sooner. She had wasted so much time looking around among unsatisfactory men! And he had had the colossal nerve to marry another woman! But then if he hadn't there wouldn't be Nora, would there? And she loved the practical little girl almost as much as she loved her father. So, filled with vague pains and strong pleasures, she said nothing. Even when he leaned over and added a massive hug to all her problems. And barely an hour later, prohibiting any further interesting developments, Uncle Vanya arrived.

'You couldn't find a better Croation meal this side of the ocean,' the old man said some time later as he carefully wiped his moustache and set his spoon down. 'Your mother teaches you to do this, John?'

'Me,' Nora interjected. 'Grandmother taught *me*. Papa can hardly boil water, and Katie is too tender to cook.'

'Too tender don't need cooking,' the old man chuckled. 'But I hear about the accident, lovely lady.'

'Accident, hell!' Jack commented. They all turned to stare at him.

'Ah, you may be right.' Uncle Vanya nodded his head in agreement.

'Right there on the square in broad daylight?' Katie shook her head doggedly. 'Not possible. And Peter Lester, for heaven's sake? Why in the world would Peter do something like that?'

'For the normal reasons,' the old man said slowly. 'For vengeance, for profit. One or the other, or maybe both?'

'You can cross out vengeance,' Katie retorted. 'He was never in love with me. There'd be no reason for vengeance. And I don't have anything that he could profit from. Look around you. Does this old house indicate a profit motive?'

'As it stands, no,' Jack said. There seemed to be signals flashing across the table from him to his uncle, signals that they both understood. 'And maybe it isn't the house, but the land it stands on.'

'Hah!' She shook her head at their ignorance. 'I can't even give it away. Are you suggesting there's oil on the land, or something?'

'Nora,' Jack said. 'Why don't you clear the table while your Uncle and I have a talk with Katie—in the living-room.'

The little girl turned to Katie and shrugged her shoulders. 'See what I mean? Little pitchers, and all like that. I suppose I have to wash the dishes, too?'

'I'll come and help after a while,' Jack promised. 'Now then, Miss Lovewell—isn't that a grand name, Uncle Vanya? Come on, now.' And before she could catch her breath Katie was up in the air again, swung up in his arms as if she were a five-pound sack of flour rather than a hundred and forty pounds of full-grown woman, and headed for the living-room. If it were not for the pain in her thigh she might have enjoyed the whole thing. Especially where the weight of her rested on his right arm, which came around her back and anchored a hand barely an inch below the swell of her attentive breast. But how could you tell a man you hardly knew, whose daughter was staring after them, that she wouldn't object if he got a better hand-hold?

So when he carefully folded her on to the living-room sofa and re-worked the pillows to her satisfaction she was almost purring. And when Uncle Vanya made the coffee and brought it out she had almost forgotten her pains and aches, and *was* purring like a contented cat. And then Jack poured cold water all over her parade.

'You've heard of the East Coast Megalopolis?' he casually enquired. Katie fumbled for a moment. Not because she didn't know, but rather because her mind was deep-diving on another track entirely.

'You mean that prediction that because the cities are expanding so rapidly that pretty soon there'll be just one metropolis, stretching from Boston to Washington? But that's a twenty-first century concern.'

'All the way to Richmond, Virginia,' he corrected. 'And it's already started to happen. Some of the largest construction companies in Washington are looking farther afield right now, trying to find a nice sizeable trace worth developing for luxury housing. The only thing that limits their search is access.'

'I can see that, but what does it have to do with me?'

'As the crow flies from Washington, Miss Lovewell,' he announced pompously, 'where is there a nice un-developed valley area with plenty of land available, good water, lovely view, moderate climate?'

'Am I supposed to guess?' she asked weakly.

'And if you substitute helicopter service instead of the crow flying?'

'You don't mean—here? In our valley? Along the South Fork?'

'Here,' he said amiably. 'In your valley. And only a half-hour from Washington by helicopter. Along the South Fork of the Shenandoah.'

'Well, I'll be tongue-tied and dipped in goose-grease!' she muttered. 'Here?'

'Here. To be exact, *right* here, lovely lady,' Uncle Vanya interrupted. 'This farm, this house, this land. The planning has been going on for months, and the word evidently has leaked out. In fact, the major consortium was planning to bid on the land in about thirty days.'

Jack came over to the couch and perched on its arm, one warm hand ruffling her hair. 'And so you see,' he said in a soft, solemn voice, 'why there are a select few in the valley hoping to acquire the Lovewell farm very quickly?'

'B-but——' she stuttered.

'And why,' Uncle Vanya added, 'that same select group would like to scare you off, get you to move?'

'Quickly,' Jack chimed in. They both stared at her, waiting for an answer which did not come. Jack's hand continued its warm seeking within the massive fold of her hair, mesmerising her.

'Katie?'

'I don't understand, really,' she said. 'There's one group in Washington that wants to build in this area? Then why would someone in the valley want me to move out?'

'Because——' and now his voice was harsh '—the local sharks haven't the skill or the capital to develop the area themselves, but if they can get their hands on title to the land they can hold up the people in Washington, and make a killing. And all they have to do is get Miss Katie Lovewell to sell out to them. How's that for a profit motive?'

She shook her head at him. 'Not my friends,' she murmured. 'My family has lived here forever. Nobody would do anything like that for——'

'They're not *all* your friends. Come on, Katie, don't walk around with blinkers on. Has anyone offered for the land?'

'My lawyers,' she offered. 'They—really didn't want the land, they just wanted to help me pay off my dad's debts.'

'Sure they did.' Both men grinned at her. Almost like a pair of sharks, she told herself, but then they're the good guys. Aren't they?

'And then there was Colonel Fessenden,' she added.

'And what do we know about the good colonel?' Uncle Vanya asked.

'He owns a nice estate, but not enough land for a major development,' Jack retorted.

'And those dogs of his didn't get loose by accident,' Katie said apologetically. 'Somebody tampered with the lock on their kennel-run.'

Both men looked at her, startled. 'Tampered with the lock?'

'Well, Evvie said the lock had been——' Her voice fell an octave, as she almost whispered '——unlocked.'

Jack Lee muttered something in Croatian, and smashed one of his fists into his other palm. Uncle Vanya made soothing noises. Nora poked her head around the kitchen door to listen, and then suddenly disappeared.

'What is it?' Katie stared at both men, and at Nora's disappearing back. 'I——'

'My nephew,' Uncle Vanya said. 'He lives like the—fire-cracker? That is the word? Any little problem and he blows the head off? My apologies. It is hard to believe he is the lawyer in the family, no?'

'I believe,' Katie said quickly. 'Anything he says, I believe.'

Uncle Vanya struck his forehead with an open palm. 'Quick,' he admonished his nephew. 'Take the lady. Go north to Front Royal, where is a good church, and marry her before she recovers. Or maybe go south instead. In Staunton they got such a grand mental clinic!'

And by that time Jack had recovered his aplomb. 'The name of the game is conspiracy,' he said. 'Katie becomes the target suddenly, the day of her piano recital at the Fessendens'. Some amateur cop tries to involve her in a drug episode. Then someone sets the dogs loose. The next day she goes into court——'

'And if you hadn't appeared they would have chopped me up into hamburger,' she interrupted. Jack nodded and smiled at her. A brief smile. It flashed in her direction like a lighthouse beam, and then was gone.

If Katie had been more mobile she might have changed course towards that lighthouse, but her muscles were too bruised, her head ached, and the telephone rang. And a moment later Nora came into the room.

'What?' Jack asked. Nora shrugged her shoulders.

'A man called, on the telephone,' she said.

'What man?'

'He didn't say,' the little girl responded. 'He just said to tell Vanya that it's going down the day after tomorrow.'

'And that's all?'

'That's all we need,' Uncle Vanya said. 'We have to go, John. Right now. We've got a lot of things to get done before dawn.'

'But hell, I can't leave Kathleen alone here! Who knows what'll happen?'

'Who knows what won't happen?' Vanya snapped. 'There is Lenora. She could stay?'

'Not good enough,' Jack returned. 'Not good enough. By Satan and all his devils, why now? We need another——' He stopped in mid-sentence and stared at his uncle. They both ruminated and then looked at Nora.

The little girl's smile collapsed. 'Oh, no,' she said, sighing.

'Oh, yes,' her father said. At which all three of the Lees stepped into the adjoining room, leaving Kate all alone among her daydreams.

It was more than an hour later when a solemn little Nora came back to the sitting-room, and coughed. Katie, who had been up to her ears in dreams about apple blossoms and organ music, came to with a start. 'Nora? Where's your father?'

'They're both gone,' the little girl reported. Something was bothering the child. She was standing in front of the sofa, using the toe of one shoe to scratch the back of the other leg, and occasionally swiping at her eyes with a dry knuckle. 'They left about an hour ago. Dad said—not to worry, that he'd be back for sure. Uncle Vanya didn't say nothin'.'

'Well, isn't that curious?' Kate was still struggling out of the fog of her dream.

'Men!' Nora stabbed at her eyes again. 'It ain't curious, it's downright aggravatin'. But I suppose all men are like that?' She looked up at Kate, who had managed to struggle to her feet.

And how in the world would I know about 'all men'? Kate asked herself. Those lovely eyes were glued to her, and an answer must be provided. Kate took a deep breath, and crossed the fingers on her right hand, behind her back. 'Yes, it's the sort of thing most men might do,' she said. 'There's no need for us to worry? Who the devil does your father think he is, telling us not to worry. We'll worry or not as we wish, that's what we'll do. Men don't own the world, even though they think they do! They've made a terrible mess about everything. It's time we women took over the reins!'

'That's great,' Nora said gleefully. 'That man needs somebody to set him down now and again——' And then, somewhat more subdued, 'Only I ain't got the nerve. You're gonna do wonders for this family.'

Yes, I certainly am, Kate thought. If only I get an invitation to join, and if Jack and I learn how to get along with each other, and if—— What about Grandmother, who, according to Nora, rules the roost? 'I'm not sure I have the nerve, either, Nora. But with the two of us together I think we could handle things. And now, little bit, don't you think it's time for both of us to get to bed?'

\* \* \*

The night seemed to have thirty-six hours. Nora, whose room was separated from Kate's by a shared bath, pleaded to have the connecting doors open. Kate sat by the little girl's bed, pushing her fantasy tale of the Four Bears to its furthest point. Nora tossed and turned and finally crossed over into dreamland at about ten o'clock.

Kate went off to bed herself, after a careful quiet shower. As she patted herself dry she looked over her shoulder into the huge mirror opposite the tub. No doubt about it, she told herself grimly, if life continues on like this I'm going to be black and blue and yellow for the rest of my life. She powdered those places she could reach, and went gingerly to bed herself.

It was not exactly a toss-and-turn night. It was more like a toss-and-squirm night. Every time she tried to turn over her scratches and bruises reminded her of reality. And every time she managed to drop off she was dominated by a strange nightmare, the one where she was being chased by the two slavering dogs who were getting close enough to bite. And then Jack appeared out of the darkness, the dogs stopped while he patted them and gave them a cheerful 'well done, boys', and then he commanded the dogs to continue their attack. Over the dogs' muzzles Jack's face seemed to expand and his perfect white teeth turned into yellow fangs, moving closer and closer—and then Kate woke up, shivering and perspiring in the cool breeze coming in through her open window.

At about three in the morning Kate had had enough. She slid carefully out of bed, and went downstairs. The house was old; it creaked in the night winds. Kate had known this for years. Nevertheless, coming downstairs now, with all her thoughts scrambling themselves, she jumped at every squeak, winced at every slam or bang as the wind wrestled in the shingles. By the time she had finished warming a mug of chocolate she was a nervous wreck.

She warmed her hands on the outside of the mug, picked up a blanket from the sofa, and then hobbled outside to the steps, where she huddled up against the stair-post and peered out into the shadows. Shadows because the moon had sprinkled the area with a tiny bit of light, and the sweet smell of lilacs floated on the breeze. She set the mug aside for a moment, and wrapped herself up in the light blanket. It provided just enough warmth to make her comfortable. She picked up the mug again, nursed on the warm, sweet drink, and dreamed.

Jack Lee. What a strange and complicated man. He could fix 'everything' with his hands and almost anything else with his mind. He was not, perhaps, the most handsome man in the world, being just a little too imperious for all of that. He had a beautiful daughter. And a line of blarney that would astonish the Sphinx. And I love him very much! Kate grinned at that last statement. It was all true, and she might as well admit it, for all the good that it did. She wrapped her hands around her knees and rocked back and forth for a moment. The morning star was rising at just that moment. It stood like a beacon, almost alone in the dawn sky. But I was never Nefertiti, she told herself, and the thought saddened her.

'Couldn't sleep neither?' A soft, lovely voice. Katie turned her head slightly. There were two bare feet balancing themselves on the top stair beside her. Nora, in her cotton granny nightgown, white with red rosebuds scattered from its high neck to its low hem. The little girl looked pale in the breaking dawn, as if she knew something that frightened her.

'Set a spell?' Kate patted the stairs beside her. Nora sank down, and Katie shared the blanket with her as the pair of them huddled side by side.

'You *do* love my dad?'

'Hard to believe, but I do. Honest Injun.'

'Me too.' A moment of silence. 'I'm scared. There's somethin' mean goin' on in this town.'

'But what?' Kate shifted slightly so that she could keep the girl in her direct line of sight.

'I don't know *what*. I just now *is*! That don't make much sense, does it?'

'Doesn't,' Kate corrected automatically. 'That *doesn't* make sense.' Another pause while the pair of them reflected. 'On the other hand——' Kate looked down at the beautiful head of hair beside her as she unwound one arm from under the blanket and wrapped it around Nora. 'On the other hand, it *does* make sense, if you follow me.'

'Yeah.' A hand crept into Kate's. 'It's too bad. I wish—you'd make one heck of a mother, Katie Lovewell!'

'Oh? I don't get a chance to play in the game? Something your dad said?'

Nora blushed. 'I—I just snooped,' she said. 'He told——'

'He who?'

'Daddy, of course. He told Uncle Vanya that you were too good for the likes of him.'

'Ah.' Kate shifted again. Her damaged bottom was complaining about sitting still too long on a hard wooden step.

'Well, I don't mean you should quit,' Nora protested. 'It's worth a chance, ain't it?'

'I'm not likely to quit,' Kate said. 'I never even got started. I probably am too good for him, but you know, Nora, there are more women than men in this world. It doesn't come out even no matter what we'd like. And that being the case, even though I *am* too good for him, I'm going to get him anyway!'

'Now I'm glad to hear that,' Nora said, sighing. She leaned over and rested her entire weight on Kate's shoulder. 'I'm in your corner, you know.'

Another pair of smiles was exchanged, and then there was silence until the pre-dawn expanded itself into the tiny noises that together heralded the day. Not the roosters; they never seemed to know what time it was. But rather the rustle of bluebirds and robins as they swung out into the country, looking for both the early and the late worm. And the chorus of tree-frogs, punctured faintly by the barking of some dog halfway over in the next county. And a low-pitched rumble, far distant in the sky.

'What do you suppose that is?' Nora asked sleepily.

'Airplane,' Kate said. 'Sometimes they cross the valley, but hardly at *this* hour. Maybe some amateur pilot who's lost his way?'

'Anything could happen,' Nora sighed. The pair of them searched the dawn sky as the noise became louder. And louder. And louder.

'What in the world...?' Katie yelled as the blue and white helicopter took a turn around the open garden in front of them, and then came to a halt not more than twenty-five feet from the steps before cutting its motor.

'Oh, my!' Nora gasped. The little girl has better eyes than me, Kate thought as she tried to blink away the dust raised by the whirling blades.

'Oh, my goodness,' Nora said. She shook herself out of the blanket and went running down the stairs, barefoot, and dressed only in her nightgown. Kate, who was hardly a bit better off as far as dress was concerned, tightened the blanket around her and wished she was ten miles away. Something even stranger was happening. Nora halted her rush halfway between the stairs and the helicopter as the side-door of the machine opened, and the co-pilot climbed down and turned to assist the passenger to disembark.

And, in the middle of a spring morning in the 1990s, the little girl who was too advanced for her age gathered her nightgown together in both hands and curtsied.

The old woman was dressed in black, except for the string of pearls around her neck. A long black dress that fitted her rotund little form to a nicety, and reached down to within inches of her high-topped boots, with a flash of white lace at the high collar and wrists. Her white hair was arranged in a neat chignon, with not a hair out of place despite the helicopter's wind. Little Nora ran across the space that separated them, and bowed to kiss the extended hand. It was a small enough ceremony. Very impressive, whatever it means, Kate told herself as she gradually rose, doing her best to wrap the blanket more carefully around her. Nora, a few feet away, broke out into a wide smile at something the old woman said, and managed to kiss the cheek proffered before they turned and started the stately march towards the stairs, chattering away.

They came to a halt at the bottom of the stairs. Kate, not knowing what to say, offered something between a half-bow and a nod of the head, and then added a somewhat tentative smile.

Nora broke out into a gale of giggles, which lasted just long enough for the lady to nudge her and say reprovingly, 'Lenora!' The little girl stifled her laughter, pushed and shoved at her face until it was solemnity itself, and said, 'Grandmother, may I present Miss Kathleen Lovewell?' The closely cropped white curls nodded gently. 'Katie,' the girl continued, 'My great-grandmother, Eleana Nostrova Evanov, of the House of Karageorgeovic.'

Oh, God, Kate muttered under her breath. What do I do now?

# CHAPTER EIGHT

'AND so you see,' the little white-haired lady said as she sipped at her cup of tea, 'it isn't all that difficult to understand. Pay attention now. We of the elder generations have been so accustomed to all the old-world courtesies. The House of Karageorgeovic has long since been wiped out of existence. Except for me. Most of the royal houses of Europe have also vanished into convents, prisons, poverty. Me, I am different. My grandfather had the foresight to feel the wind of revolution rising, so he packed us all up and brought us to America. Did you know the Karageorgeovic family once ruled the kingdom of Serbia?'

The old lady smiled at Katie's astonished look. 'But of course you would not know. Why, even the kingdom of Serbia has disappeared. And that's why I insist that the children of my family practise the amenities—in memoriam, you might say. And you can tell your friends, my dear. It might do something for your reputation to know you are consorting with a former princess. If it hadn't been for the disappearance of the Serbian kingdom, and the wilfulness of the House, I—yes, me— would be the pretender to the throne! Are you impressed?' Another gamine grin ran across her unwrinkled face. 'Don't be *too* impressed, my dear. As it is, I am just the grandmother of the Lee family. Now, let me see, what should you call me—do you have a grandmother of your own?'

'No,' Katie said. 'Not a one.'

'Then,' the matriarch said as she squared her little shoulders and assumed an almost imperial stance, 'you shall call me Grandmother also. Is it not so?'

'But I——'

The old lady held up a hand. 'No, no, Kathleen. No humble gratitude. My grandson has told me all about you, and all about his plans.'

Well, then why the devil didn't he tell *me*? Katie grumbled to herself. Or is this the way one becomes a member of the House of Serbia? By royal fiat? If that— if that man ever shows up again I'm going to show him a few favourite tricks of my Cherokee ancestors—and they certainly have a longer history than Serbia!

'B-But I thought he was Croatian,' she managed to stammer.

'Well, to my shame,' Grandmother said placidly, 'there was none of the Serbian royalty left, and I had celebrated my eighteenth birthday with no one in sight, so I was forced to undertake a marriage somewhat below my station in life—yes, to a Croatian, whose only possession in the world was my deep and abiding love. How I miss that man! And my grandson is a fine example of the result. The blood must be mixed from time to time or it grows thin, no?'

'Now I'm completely lost,' Katie admitted. 'John is your son?'

'Grandson, my dear.'

'And Nora is your——?'

'Granddaughter. Ah, I see. You think a woman of my position wishes to be somebody with a great-granddaughter? And then Nora marries young—it is a trait in my family—and presently I am a great-great-grandmother? Bah! A woman has her pride, is it not so? Grandmother is as far as I go! So they are all my grand—whatever. You must humour an old woman. Would you believe that I am...seventy-five?'

I would believe, Kate told herself very solemnly, eighty-five. Or even ninety. But she managed a smile, and said, 'I find it hard to believe, Grandmother. Have some more cookies?'

'It might not be good for my figure,' said the little round creature. But she reached for the plate, and Kate could see that self-same twinkle that starred her grandson's eyes from time to time.

'Kate—I mean Miss Kathleen—is a whale of a good cook,' Nora said. 'Won't it be great to have someone in the house who knows how to cook?'

'A lovely idea,' her grandmother replied, sighing. 'You know, little one, when I was your age, before the First World War, we actually had six cooks and one chef in our home. But where the devil is that boy? Kathleen?'

'I'm afraid I don't know.' Kate shook her head and ducked away from the matriarch's discerning eye. 'Last night—he just went away. He didn't say goodbye, he just went away. And his uncle Vanya with him.'

'Ah, Vanya—another rascal, that one. But not even a goodbye at all?'

'Not a word.' Kate looked at Nora, hoping for support. The little girl shrugged her shoulders. 'Not a word,' Kate repeated. 'There was a telephone call, and he took a message, and that's all I know.' Her head drooped like a tattered flower, and there were almost tears. But I won't cry, she told herself. Not for me, not for him, not for anything!

'Hmmm,' the princess pondered. 'Vanya was in Washington last night. In fact he brought me word then.'

Nora jumped in before Kate could, to her terrible shame, make a fool out of herself over that man. 'What was the message?' Nora asked excitedly.

'Why, nothing much, my dear. It was that I was needed urgently in Virginia to—er—baby-sit two little girls, was the way it came out. And so I had the maids pack, and the helicopter ordered up, and here I am.'

A helicopter instead of a coach and four, Katie sighed to herself. Even if he asked me, how could I fit into a family like this? As the Irish scrub-woman? And what would they say if they knew I was one quarter Cherokee, from the Western Nation? Where *is* that man?

Nora started to add something to the conversation when the telephone rang. In the two-horse race Nora won, but only because Kate was still hobbling from the damage to her structure. 'It's for you,' Nora said as she handed over the instrument. The child looked as if someone had stolen her last lollipop.

'It's not my fault.' Nora would have nothing of *anyone's* apology. Katie took up the handset. 'Hello?'

'Hello. Miss Lovewell? This is Colonel Fessenden.'

I'm going to get rid of this telephone, Kate told herself. The only people who call me are the ones I don't want to have call me! And they all want to tell me something that I don't care to know! 'Yes, Colonel?'

'Miss Lovewell—Katie. I find myself running foolish errands for my wife. Is her lawyer there at your house?'

'Her lawyer? I'm afraid I don't know the man, Colonel.'

'Oh? I was sure you did. My wife—oh, well, it isn't important. If he should come by, please tell him that the auction will be held tomorrow morning.'

'Well, I'd be glad to deliver the message,' Kate said quietly, 'if only I knew who he was.'

'Why, Mr Lee, of course. I was sure you——'

Whatever else the colonel had to say was never recorded. Katie Lovewell, at the end of her rope, gave a great sigh, dropped the telephone, and slid gracefully down on to the living-room rug in a dead faint.

'Well, it wasn't my fault,' Nora muttered for the third time. 'Whoever heard of a girl fainting?' Katie opened one eye. She was stretched out on the rug beside the couch with a pillow under her head and a blanket spread neatly over her.

'Why, in my day girls did that all the time,' Grandmother contributed. 'And Kathleen did it very well. Neatness, you know. One cannot just faint away and fall down. One must be—*chic*?'

'I never fainted in my life,' Katie interjected weakly, to no good purpose.

'She did it nicely, I'll give her that,' Nora agreed. 'I wonder if she could do it better with a little more practice? Are you sure we can't pick her up and put her on the couch?'

'I'm sure,' the matriarch said. 'You are a very small person, Lenora, and I am too. Besides, a royalty does not become a beast of burden.'

'I *never* faint,' Kate repeated. 'I never——'

'I hear you, child. There's no need to be abusive about it. You never faint. So climb up and lie down on the couch. We both of us couldn't pick you up.'

The telephone rang again, just as Kate settled back on the couch. Nora ran for the instrument as Grandmother tucked another pillow behind Kate's back. 'It's for Kate again,' Nora reported, stretching the flexible cord over to the couch.

'I can get up to do that,' Kate said. No matter what Serbian matriarchs did, Virginia women answered the telephone standing up. She staggered to her feet, and then promptly fell over again. 'But I'll make an exception for now,' she said much more humbly.

'Lie back,' Grandmother insisted before she would let Kate hold the telephone. 'Put your head a little higher on this pillow. There, that looks rather well. Now go ahead. I'm sure it's good news!'

'Yes, I'm sure it must be.' Kate reached for the instrument, almost convinced by the two smiling faces. 'Hello,' she offered, and listened, then quietly passed the telephone back to Nora, and stared out of the window across those beautiful acres that the Lovewells had owned for almost two hundred years.

'Kate?' Nora shook her shoulder gently. 'Katie?'

'Kathleen?' Grandmother Lee knelt by the couch, a worried look on her usually placid and unfurrowed face.

'Katie!' Nora's panic-stricken voice rose a half-octave.

Katie Lovewell waved a hand vaguely in their direction. 'The sheriff's office,' she muttered in a deadly undertone. 'I must have gotten the days wrong. They have fore-closed on the farm, and will auction it off tomorrow,' Kate sighed, but held back the tears.

Nora groaned a protest as she threw her arms around Kate. 'They can't do that,' she sobbed. 'Can they?'

'You bet your last dinar they can't,' Grandmother said firmly.

It was an altogether different group that gathered around the kitchen table after dinner. With just one or two determined words the last representative of the House of Karageorgeovic had changed from a sweet, dod-dering old lady to a lioness protecting her young. Two long-distance telephone calls had brought help. Four husky young men arrived by helicopter at about six-

thirty, each holding the leash on a fit and ferocious
Doberman pinscher. Grandmother provided instructions at high speed. All four men grinned, as if they were
looking forward to some exercise, and then the house
settled down.

'You know,' Grandmother said at about eight o'clock,
'our family operates a service agency, with our own
detectives, lawyers, and so forth.'

'And Grandmother is the head of it all,' Nora interjected. 'Really, Kate, you can't win at stud-poker if you
smile every time you get an ace.'

'It's true, then,' Kate answered mournfully. 'I have
fallen among mountebanks and thieves.'

'Not quite true,' Grandmother said as she studied her
hand carefully. 'It's just that not *all* royalty escapes with
the country's treasury. My grandfather was too busy with
a certain—well, with someone when the crash came, but
we managed to escape with a considerable amount of
money to... and no, little miss Lenora—it was not the
Treasury of Serbia. That had already been spent. So we
escaped with money and our wits to support us. And
consider, when our earliest ancestor Tsar Boris the First
ascended the throne he had really been only a bandit
chief. Listen.'

'I don't hear anything,' Kate replied after a quiet
moment.

'Of course you don't,' Grandmother said. 'That's what
I meant. There's no sound. No dogs coughing, no wind
blowing—unusual. Nora, you run up to bed now.'

'But Grand——'

'Lenora!' The little girl hopped up as if someone had
applied a hot iron to her foot. She stood perfectly still
until she had mastered all her objections, and then
curtsied and ran for the stairs.

'Most old-fashioned,' her grandmother mused as she watched the child. 'She grows like a weed. The old courtesies help keep her in hand. Now then, child——' Kate hobbled around the table to help the old woman rise. They each took a look at the other, and both giggled. 'The blind leading the blind,' Grandmother said. 'Now then, your instructions. There are only two people who can steal past our dogs, and I am one of them. Ergo, someone is outside who the dogs know very well.'

The matriarch chuckled to herself, and took Kate's arm. 'I should have brought a cane,' she said. 'But that's what pride does to one. Now, little one——' Kate, who topped the old lady by a good six inches, stifled another laugh. The old lady tapped her wrist; just a little pat, it looked to be, but the fingers snapped like the end of a bull-whip. 'We must remember our manners, child. Er— what was I saying?'

'Now, little one,' Kate reminded her as she rubbed her sore wrist.

'Yes. Now, little one, this intruder must be coming to see you. And you will obviously prefer to see him alone. So you may help me up the stairs and see that I get settled, after which you shall come down again and set yourself—ah, on that big stuffed rocking-chair—that would be best, and wait for him.'

'And wait for him?' Kate was beginning to feel like fresh bait for the lions at the colosseum. 'Wait for him who? What shall I do if——?'

'You'll think of something,' Grandmother said gently. 'Do what comes naturally. Within reason, of course,' she added judiciously.

Kate, feeling as thoroughly over-directed as any movie star might, almost swallowed her tongue. But she finally mastered herself, offered her arm again, and carried out the instructions.

Back downstairs by nine o'clock, she curled herself up in the indicated chair, and tried to settle down, to no avail. Someone who knew all the dogs as well as—Grandmother? It was her first use of the title, and she felt somewhat embarrassed. Someone who would want to see her? Someone whom she would like to see alone? She shook her head. There's no doubt about it, she told herself, ever since I first met this Lee family I've lost at least half my marbles. But if it *is* who I think it is I don't want to meet him dressed in these crummy trousers and this apron.

Which is why the loveable Miss Lovewell was just hobbling down the stairs fifteen minutes later, dressed in her one long sheer yellow nightgown with the matching peignoir over it, only to find the intruder had already broken in. And to demonstrate his brass he had put out the living-room lights and was rocking gently back and forth in *her* chair.

'Well,' Kate grumbled as she stopped in the doorway. 'You've got your nerve!'

'C'mon, Kate,' the voice she knew so well said. 'I've had a hard day.'

'*You've* had a hard day! Say listen, you rotten little—big—Croatian, you don't have any idea of what *hard* really is!'

'Now what?' The words seemed to float on some moving current in the darkness. 'You sound as if you might possibly be angry with me.'

'You'd better believe it,' she said in fury. 'You disappear off the face of the earth just as all my enemies seem to be gathering to do me in. And not a word of explanation!'

'It just *seems* that way, Kate. Come over here.'

'Not on your ever-loving life,' she snapped. 'If you want I'll get a kitchen-knife and *then* I'll come over there!'

'Now Kate.' She heard the chair squeak as he stood up. Apprehensively she drew back into the shadowed doorway, her mouth suddenly parched.

'Don't come near me. Not another step nearer!' She stepped back into the kitchen, and found a convenient broom-handle. 'I'll brain you if——'

'You couldn't,' he said. His voice was hypnotic, as dark as the world from which he spoke. 'You know you couldn't, Kate Lovewell.'

'Don't kid yourself,' she snarled, squeezing the broom-handle with all her strength.

'*I'm* not the one who's kidding,' he said. 'Love arms, and disarms. You love me, Kathleen, and you know it. Come over here.'

'I don't,' she sobbed. 'I don't, do you hear me? I'm no puppet whose strings you can pull. Go on back to Serbia, why don't you, and haunt a castle?'

'That's Transylvania you're thinking of. And a very distant relative known as Vlad the Impaler.' A dry chuckle enveloped her. 'There's no use fighting it, Kate. Come to me.'

'I will not,' Kate said fiercely, but even as she said it her feet were moving reluctantly in his direction. 'I will not!'

'You will, Kate. Because you want to. Come!'

'You must think me mad or stupid or something,' she muttered. Her feet were still moving. No matter how often she commanded them to stop, they moved.

'I think you're beautiful,' he whispered. Only the whisper was necessary. She was already within touching distance, and his arms closed around her and drew her that last few inches. 'You are beautiful,' he repeated as he tilted her chin up and sealed her mouth with his lips. 'Beautiful, lovely, loveable.'

She managed to turn her head away, and raised one hand to cover his mouth. 'Don't tell me what you don't mean,' she said, sighing. 'Maybe I do love you, damn you, but I don't *like* you! Leave me——'

But he was not about to leave her alone. Gently, but as firmly as a closing vice, he trapped both her hands against her body. She made an inarticulate protest. He freed one of his arms; it went around her shoulders with the hand planted squarely in the middle of her back. The fire and temptation of him warmed her through the thin linen of her nightgown, and then suddenly it was not warmth but searing torture as his fingers traced circles in the middle of her back and then walked down to her hips.

'Don't,' she muttered. 'I don't——'

'Love isn't cold porcelain,' he interrupted. 'It's fire and emotion and wildness.' And as he talked he turned her slightly, and his hand came around to tempt and touch the tip of her breast. 'See that?'

She didn't *see*. At the veriest touch she felt the surge of energy flash through her system as her breast grew hard and the bronze nipple stood to attention. Her body shivered uncontrollably, and it was the shaking that *he* felt. He laughed, almost gloated, as his hand brushed aside both peignoir and nightgown and cupped the fullness of her.

'Don't,' she protested weakly as her head spun and her reason was shaken by the violence of her own reaction. He laughed again as he swept her up in his arms and fumbled through the darkness in the direction of the couch. As if he were far away she heard him curse as he stumbled over a foot-stool, and then he dropped her gently on to the massive couch.

For a moment she felt coldness as his body moved away from hers, and then he was back, warmer than before. She knew without touching him that his shirt was gone and her nightgown was being swept aside. His tongue laved her nipple; his teeth nibbled. She moaned again, writhing and squirming as, just for an instant, she felt the sharp prickling of hair as some not-quite-shaven segment of his chin scraped across her breast. Her whole body shook as his lips chased a kiss down over her stomach, past her navel, and then back up to seize her lips again.

She gasped as the muscles of her loins contracted. He stole her tongue and plundered her mouth, and then drew back for a moment and chuckled. It was a tactical mistake. There was just enough of silence and chill and fear to plunge her back into logic. 'Don't,' she said more firmly.

'You don't mean that,' he murmured as he renewed his attack. 'I knew you couldn't help yourself.'

It was enough, and more. With a burst of her muscular self she broke free from him and pushed his head away. A cool breeze bathed her, adding to her strength. 'I said no.'

He froze in position in the darkness for just a moment, and then one finger explored her cold face and neck. All her trembling had ceased. Anger had replaced passion. 'You really *do* mean it, don't you?' he mused. 'I can't believe it!'

'Believe it,' she growled at him. 'Get off me, you— damn Croatian!'

'A-ha,' he grunted. 'My grandmother is here.'

'And all your rotten ancestors,' she snarled. 'Get off me!' He moved. Slowly, regrettably, puzzled, but he moved.

Kate swung herself up to her feet, and fumbled with her nightgown. 'Love is not enough?' he taunted from a safe distance.

'That isn't love,' she snapped. 'That's plain, downright lust.'

'They're both part of the same thing,' he said, sighing. 'Love without lust is only an imitation. You don't need another friend, you need a lover.'

'As it happens,' she said coldly, 'I don't need either one. When I do I'll put an advertisement in the local papers. And at its end the ad will say, "No Croatians need apply".'

'Wow,' he said. 'What did I do wrong?'

'It all depends on your definition of wrong,' she replied. 'Although I admire your grandmother, I think the house of Karageorgeovic must have been a collection of pirates. You knew, of course, that the sheriff plans to auction off my farm tomorrow?'

'Tomorrow? I thought not until the day after.'

'A falling out among thieves,' she commented acidly. 'You probably deserve it.'

'What the hell are you talking about now?' he muttered. His big hand closed on her shoulders and gave her a good shake, enough to rattle her brain-pan around.

'You know what I'm talking about, Mr Lee. Just suppose you tell me the truth one time. Are you or are you not Colonel Fessenden's lawyer?'

Deep in darkness, she could see nothing of him except his shadow, but Kate would have sworn that he muttered something along the lines of 'Oh, my God!'

'Well? Have you had enough time to think up a good lie?'

'I wouldn't lie to you, Kate.'

'Ha! That's all you've ever done since we met. Answer the question; are you Colonel Fessenden's lawyer?'

'Well——' She could feel his hesitation. 'No, I'm not. Not exactly,' he replied.

'And just what does that mean?'

'That means that the colonel is just what he seems— a noisy busy-body without enough sense to organise a scam like this.'

'So——' Kate felt the light of inspiration. The colonel was a bumbling busy-body? So who else was there to organise any kind of a crooked scheme, and require the best lawyer in the 'Newnited States,' as Nora told it? The recollection brought a little chuckle, but no relief.

'No, of course not,' she said. 'You're Mrs Fessenden's lawyer, aren't you?'

'Yes, so all right,' he muttered. 'I'm Mrs Fessenden's lawyer. But it's not what you think, Kate.'

'No, I'm sure it isn't,' she said. 'I'm sure all these little additions are your own idea. Setting yourself up in my house to keep up to all my defences, trying your best to turn me into your kept woman—your private whore. God, I hate you.'

'Kate?'

'Look, by tomorrow night you'll have it all and I'll have nothing. I hope you get someone in here to take care of Nora, so she——' A sudden jolt of comprehension struck Kate at just that moment. And it was just like the damned opinionated man! 'Ah,' she said. 'That's why your grandmother arrived so suddenly. To take Nora out of this mess! I should have seen it all. It was all there in black and white, written large on the wall, and dumb

Katie Lovewell—trusting Katie Lovewell—she couldn't see past the tip of her nose. All right, Mr Lee, I know the pattern now. It's almost twelve o'clock. Please get yourself off my property. At least I'm entitled to one last night's sleep in the old homestead.'

'Kate, I——'

'Just get out,' she said wearily. 'Get out. Now. And if I don't see you again in this century I'll count myself lucky!' Kate wheeled around, her back to him, to block out the tears. And when she had cleared her eyes enough she turned back slowly. He was gone.

She stumbled on the stairs, not because of the tears, of course, but because of her sore leg. But when she fell into bed the tears really came—in bucketfuls. When she woke up in the morning her sheets were all crumpled and wet, and Nora lay beside her, holding her hand tightly as if the little girl feared she was losing something precious.

Kate managed to drag herself downstairs by about ten o'clock. Grandmother Lee was standing at the foot of the stairs, beaming up at her. As soon as she saw Kate's disgruntled appearance her own smile vanished. 'Your leg still hurts, child?'

'Among other things,' Kate said glumly. The little grandmother took her arm and escorted her out into the kitchen. Nora was busy at the stove, making a stack of pancakes. She looked up at Kate, and then ducked her head without saying a word.

'Good morning, Nora.'

The child brightened visibly. 'Oh, we're still speaking?'

'Why, of course we are, love.'

'In spite of the dirty tricks my dad has been playing?'

'In spite of,' Kate said, and walked over for her daily hug. 'See? Children are not responsible for the deficiencies of their parents.'

'Well, I'm glad to hear that, whatever that means, 'cause my dad, he struck out completely last night.'

'Ah. It sounds as if some little pitchers were sticking noses in,' Grandmother commented. 'Is this why the volunteering to make breakfast is?'

'No such thing,' Nora said suddenly, but she ducked her head again.

'So just where were you when you heard?' Kate said casually.

'Oh, just at the foot of the stairs...darn you, Kate, you're worse than a mother! I wasn't going to tell you that.'

'I've been practising,' Kate teased. 'I can see that mothering is not all that easy.'

'Then you—he——' It was a time for honesty.

'No, sweet. There is no "you and he" any more. You were right. Your father struck out last night.' Kate slumped into her chair at the table, and dabbed at her own eyes. It was going to be hard, learning to live without Jack—and his daughter; but there it was. The three of them started to eat as if their forks were moving to the tempo of the *Funeral March*.

The meal was topped off by a knock at the door. One of the guards, complete with dog, came in. 'What is it, Wroclau?' Grandmother asked.

'A deputy from the sheriff's office,' Wroclau reported pleasantly. 'My dog didn't like him, which seemed to be a nice thing at the time. He made a large number of noises about what he was empowered to do, so I thought you might wish to deal with him.'

'Indeed I would,' Grandmother Lee said. 'Come in, young man. Come in, and tell us your troubles.'

'Deputy Sheriff Paine,' Kate murmured as Paine came warily to the table. His shiny new uniform was dusty, the corner of his highly polished boots bore the marks of fangs. Altogether Deputy Paine looked as if he would have been happier elsewhere. He edged forward towards a chair. The dog close behind him growled. The deputy jumped up as if he had been bitten, and stood at attention.

'Well?' Grandmother had assumed her regal attitude. Paine edged another inch or two away.

'I have this order,' he muttered. 'An auction of everything on the farm, land and goods and all.'

'I see. Then perhaps you could show me this—order?'

'I don't have to do that!' For a minute the town bully flared up, and went down as quickly as the dog came up to his feet and bared his teeth. 'I mean, I'm not supposed to show a court order to every Tom, Dick, and Harry.'

'No, of course not, but how about every Kathleen?' Kate interjected. 'Since I'm the owner who's being dispossessed, surely I get to see the order?'

'Mr Bledsoe, he told me I wasn't to show it to anybody,' the deputy muttered.

'Ah. Mr Bledsoe? A lawyer?' Paine nodded his head, and then cringed as the dog sniffed around his heel. 'Then perhaps we can expect that you want something else?' The deputy gave an affirmative nod.

'Wroclau,' Grandmother Lee ordered, 'bring in another one of the dogs, would you please? Mr Paine seems somewhat uncooperative.' The words were enough. Paine, looking as if the words hurt him, hurriedly said, 'Mr Bledsoe wanted me to sort out the best

equipment and set it aside for himself when he comes
to the auction.'

'And when will that be?' The Princess of Serbia had
dissolved into somebody's kindly grandmother. The
deputy took a deep breath, as if breathing had not been
a common thing in his life lately.

'They're coming today, right after one o'clock,' he
gobbled. 'Listen, I'd better go——'

'Perhaps we should hear more about all this,'
Grandmother said sweetly. 'Sheriffs' auctions have to be
advertised. There has to be a legal time for inspection
before——'

'Please, Grandmother——' Kate put one hand on the
old lady's arm. 'I know you're doing all this for me,
and I appreciate it, but——'

'But you wanna give it up, Kate?' Nora looked over
the table grimly. 'All your past, and all your future, and
you just want to give it up?'

'It doesn't seem to matter,' Kate said. Her deep sigh
told the entire story. 'There's no sense in battling for
another day, or hour. I'll miss all my past, little love,
but I don't have any future. Let it go.'

She slumped back down into her chair, hands in her
lap, a look of resignation on her face. Grandmother Lee
pursed her lips as she thought. And then a quick gleam
of enjoyment sparked from her eyes. Nora, who was
about to protest again, received a short snappy sit-down.

'Well, in that case, Deputy Paine,' Nora's grandmother said, 'I guess we will not try to stand in your
way. An auction of all the land and equipment, beginning
at one o'clock today?'

'Yes, ma'am,' Deputy Paine said. 'Can I go now?'
They all watched as Mr Wroclau escorted the still-shaking
official over to the door and out on to the steps. For a

moment silence reigned. Up until Nora said, 'I don't believe it, Kate. I never thought you was a quitter.'

'Were a quitter,' her grandmother corrected her absent-mindedly. 'Were a quitter.' A pause for further consideration. 'Now Nora, you go call in all our young men. Have them leave the dogs on station. And then I'll—— No, I hate to use that instrument of torture. No, after you call the men in, you make a telephone call to your Uncle Vanya. Here is his address.' She handed the girl a crumpled piece of paper.

'What do I tell him?' Nora looked perplexed. 'I didn't know he was in Front Royal.'

'That's *two* questions, young lady. He's in Front Royal because I told him to go there.'

'And what is the message?'

'Why, tell him to come here.' And then, anticipating another question, 'Because I want him here.'

'Yes, ma'am.' The little girl left the table and rushed for the door, stopping only when her grandmother cleared her throat loudly. At which noise Nora skidded to a stop, turned, and offered the briefest curtsy the world had ever seen.

'She'll do.' Grandmother Lee smiled with some satisfaction. 'And so will you, loveable Kate Lovewell. Now——'

'Me?' Kate's spirit was so low she would have had to look up to see a snake's belly pass by.

'You,' Grandmother Lee said. 'You have size and shape and beauty, but you need a little more instruction in chicanery. And that we will begin immediately. I'd like to kill that grandson of mine. Where was I?'

'You'd like to kill that—you can't do that!'

'Of course I can't,' the regal charmer said. 'I'm saving that for you, no? Now, here's what we shall do.' And she explained it all slowly and carefully, until even Kate started to chuckle.

# CHAPTER NINE

THE auctioneer arrived just after lunch. He was a professional from outside Luray. 'Jake Weathers,' he introduced himself. 'Friend of your father's I was, little lady. Your dad and me was at school together. Best of friends, as I remember. Up till the time he married *my* girlfriend. Lovely lady, your ma. And now you have to sell out?'

'I'm afraid so,' Kate said. Little lady? His must be a memory that stretches way back! 'I—don't understand any of this, but my lawyer said that it's——'

'Bledsoe? A snake in the grass,' Weathers interrupted emphatically. 'And this be your...grandmother?'

'Absolutely right.' Not the matriarch this time, but somebody's hill-country granny. She came out and stood beside Kate, putting an arm around the girl's slender waist. 'This is a public auction? You wouldn't mind if a few of us bid—on the smaller things, of course?'

'Don't mind a'tall,' he said. 'As you say, a public auction. But, let me tell you, the craziest auction I've ever seen. Only gave me twenty-four hours' advance notice, they did. If it wasn't for the fact the place is run down, I'd think...' He paused in mid-sentence, and chewed on the wooden toothpick that seemed to be perpetually in his mouth.

'You'd think?' Grandmother Lee prodded.

'I'd think this was as phoney as a three-dollar bill,' he opined. 'Got to have a crowd to make a successful auction. Ain't seen nothin' but the little newspaper ad from up Front Royal away. That's a long way from here. Folks like to be able to drive around, look things over before they bid. And you know sumpin' strange? According to this equipment list they give me, you ain't got enough stuff around to farm one acre.'

'That's the way of it when somebody has to hurry,' Grandmother said. 'Perhaps we could help? We still have three or four hands available. They might check your list against what's in the barns? Or maybe the rest of the equipment is—how do you say——? Ah, Vanya! May I present my oldest son, Vanya, Mr Weathers?' Uncle Vanya was playing some part—Kate was not quite sure which one. The old plantation owner? He was dressed in a three-piece white suit, with a flower in his lapel. A wide-brimmed black hat covered his bald spot.

'Folks call me Jake, ma'am. Vanya?' Two hands, almost as big and tough as each other, met in a shake. 'Vanya? Ain't heard that kind of name before in these parts. You a foreigner?'

'I guess you might say that,' Uncle Vanya said. 'What made you suspect?'

'Easy. In Virginia people talk *real* English.'

'Of course,' Grandmother chuckled. 'Everything outside Virginia is foreign.'

'You jus' bet,' Jake laughed. 'You been to one of them la-de-dah schools, I suspect.'

'Hit it right on the head,' Uncle Vanya admitted. 'Graduated from one of those back-country schools called Balliol. Heard of it, have you?'

'Might have,' Jack said. 'Somewheres up north?'

'Can't fool you,' Vanya said, chuckling. 'Say, look, instead of all this searching around, why don't you give me the list, and I'll have the equipment brought out in the sunshine? Be easier to handle that way.'

'That's my son,' Grandmother Lee interjected proudly. 'Always was brighter than the average Karageorgeovic.'

'Well, look here,' Jake commented. 'Here comes the crowd.'

As crowds went, this one wasn't much. Two patrol-cars from the Sheriff's department. One limousine containing Mrs Fessenden and a man sitting back in the corner, almost invisible. One car each for Bledsoe and for Gerney, the legal team, and a car for the bank representative. 'Although I don't know why he would come,' Kate whispered. 'Our house mortgage was paid off in 1884. I've got the framed receipt hanging on the wall in the living-room.'

'Shush. I think we're about to begin.'

Jake's name was accurate. He was a weather-beaten and somewhat bent mountain-man. In normal conversation his voice was a raspy whisper that seemed almost ready to give out. But when he climbed up on the seat of the buggy that Grandmother's guards had just wheeled out, and started his chant, he could be heard for half a mile around.

Mrs Fessenden came round the front of the limousine, heading for a position at the front. Kate barely caught the disgusted look on the woman's face, and then shrank back to the side of the buggy. The man behind Mrs Fessenden was Jack Lee. Bile rose in Katie's throat, bile and anger and fear and—good heavens, could it still be love? She followed his every move as he came up behind his client, and began to whisper in her ear. Somehow all the sounds around her faded. Everything had turned into a silent movie, but only for a moment.

'No, I don't think I can do that,' Jake was saying. 'Got everything orderly on my list, and that's the way I mean to sell it.'

'I don't want to stand around while you sell off this junk,' Mrs Fessenden wailed.

'Junk?' Jake looked back at his list. 'Says here this junk is worth nigh on to seventy thousand dollars. Got a reserve figure, at that. Prices can't go below the reserve, and there ain't nobody but the present owner can waive the reserve price. And that is Ms Lovewell.'

Somebody was breathing excitedly in Kate's ear. 'Waive it,' Vanya said. 'Waive everything.'

'I waive the reserve figures on everything,' Kate yelled, and then wondered why she had done so. It pleased Grandmother. It pleased Uncle Vanya. It almost seemed, from this distance, that even Jack Lee was smiling, pleased. What have I done wrong now? Kate asked herself. Something stupid, no doubt about that!

Jake went back to his high-speed chant, asking for the first bid on the buggy. 'Twenty-five,' Uncle Vanya called.

'That's the way,' Jake encouraged him. 'Twenty-five hundred dollars.' His little hammer slammed on the back of the seat. 'Who'll give me twenty-six?'

'You've got that wrong,' Vanya yelled. 'That's twenty-five cents.'

It looked for a minute as if Jake had swallowed his toothpick. 'Twenty-five cents for this fine antique buggy? It's worth fifty dollars as a museum piece. Who'll give me twenty-six?'

Kate peered around the side of the buggy. All the participants had gathered in a tiny crowd. All four of Grandmother's guards were stationed at strategic points surrounding them. Each guard had brought his Doberman from wherever they had been hidden.

The dogs were impatient, and had to be restrained. Despite the leashes the animals were sniffing at shoes, giving warning growls.

'That'll do it,' Kate whispered to Grandmother Lee.
'Mr Bledsoe is chairman of the museum. He's bound
to——'

'Twenty-five dollars,' Bledsoe yelled.

'Ah, that's better,' Jake crowed. 'Now we're going.
Mr—Bledsoe, you bid twenty-five dollars?' There was
a loud silence from the centre of the crowd. Kate had
to stretch up on tiptoes to see what was going on.
Grandmother Lee was too short to see at all, and it
aggravated her. Lawyer Bledsoe was having trouble, too.
The moment he announced his bid one of the Dobermans
raced towards him, stood at practically no distance away,
and growled. A moment later a second dog came racing
through the crowd, his own handler barely able to keep
up on the leash. The guards said something under their
breath to Bledsoe; the dogs said something under their
breath to the lawyer. Something on the order of 'Make
another bid and I'll tear your throat out'. Or so Bledsoe
seemed to interpret it.

'Not me,' he bleated. 'Not me. I'm not bidding, just
clearing my throat.'

'Well, in that case,' Jake Weathers concluded mournfully, 'I got one bid on this fine buggy, twenty-five cents.
Who'll make it thirty? Twenty-five, going once, going
twice . . . sold to the gentleman with the moustache.' His
little hammer bounded off the buggy seat, and it seemed
that everyone sighed. Uncle Vanya brushed at his tiny
moustache, and grinned at his mother. Who promptly
grinned back.

The afternoon moved slowly forward. Jake Weathers
worked his way up through the longest pile of junk
anyone could wish for. Several times Vanya and his
mother would bid against each other, driving the price
up a penny or two at each call. Mrs Fessenden stirred

her anger, and made long complaint, after which one of
the guards was sent off for a chair. The auction dragged
on.

But Jack Lee never said a word. Kate kept herself
behind the buggy, glancing from Grandmother to Jack,
working herself up into a frenzy. There was only one
interruption. At about three o'clock in the afternoon
Nora came out on to the porch. The little girl watched
for perhaps ten minutes, then stomped across the grass
to stand in front of her father, both hands on her hips,
a mutinous scowl on her face. She said something to
him, something very short. He gave a one-word reply.
Nora shrugged her shoulders, then kicked her father in
the shin with one of her sharp-pointed shoes. He shifted
his weight to the other foot, and made some indis-
tinguishable retort, but Nora had already left.

Jack Weathers halted the auction. All the audience
was watching the girl, anyway. She walked straight across
to Kate, gave her an affectionate hug, and turned to her
uncle. Her voice was loud enough to be heard throughout
the crowd. 'Uncle Vanya, I wanna get a divorce from
my father. Can you help me?'

A buzz of conversation rustled through the crowd.
Her uncle bent down on one knee and conducted a quiet
conference with his niece. Kate exhaled. She had been
holding her breath for what seemed like hours. But Uncle
Vanya, she knew, would be both direct and patient with
the girl. Can you divorce your parents? Kate asked
herself. And select someone else? What a great idea!

'Well, now, that's all the odds and ends of things,'
Jake said. 'Why don't we get this auction on the road?
The next item on the list is one house, and two barns.
We'll sell them off as a unit. Who'll bid—ten thousand
dollars?'

'Ten thousand dollars,' Mrs Fessenden shouted.

'Ten thousand dollars. I have ten thousand. Eleven thousand?'

Mrs Fessenden stood up and glared around her. The guards and the dogs made no attempt to interfere. Grandmother Lee, who had been sitting on the buggy seat, took Vanya's arm and stood up. All eyes turned in her direction. She coughed, looked around with the most gentle of expressions on her face, and said, 'Five hundred thousand dollars.' And quietly sat down again.

The silence was so loud and long that it must have been heard as far away as Richmond. Deep, deadly silence! Mrs Fessenden seemed to waver, and grabbed at the nearest arm to keep herself upright. Jack Lee's arm, Kate noted. I hope he gets leprosy from it. Or worse, shingles! I wish it was me, holding on there like a mustard plaster!

'I don't think she's got twenty cents,' Mrs Fessenden yelled. A car drove up behind her, a middle-aged Buick, with the colonel at the wheel. The dapper colonel crawled out, looking neither dapper nor young. He hurried over to his wife. 'I demand she show she's got the money,' his wife was yelling. Jack Weathers pounded his gavel for silence. Colonel Fessenden whispered something in his wife's ear. She seemed staggered by whatever it was she had been told. The dominating scowl on her face fled before an attack of fright. She turned pale, and collapsed in her chair again. Another car drove up.

'Well, ma'am,' Jake said. 'You got that kinda money?'

'I have a few pennies,' Grandmother Lee said. 'Four or five bank drafts, each for fifty thousand dollars.' She fumbled around in her massive leather pocketbook, and came out with a handful of papers. 'I always like to carry a little pin-money with me. Would that be enough?'

'Lady, was you wantin' to bid on the State House that would be enough.' Jake's interest in his toothpick suddenly seemed to desert him. He struggled for a minute. 'I got five hundred thousand,' he chanted, slamming down on his little hammer. 'Do I hear six?'

A third car drove up. Altogether now, Kate thought, we've attracted six state troopers, the county sheriff himself, and two or three miscellaneous dark-suited men whom she could not identify. And, while Colonel Fessenden did his best to comfort his weeping wife, Jack Lee walked over to the sheriff, standing by the auctioneer, and they conferred. It seemed that Jack was doing the speaking, the sheriff was doing the nodding, and Jake Weathers, once every thirty seconds was saying either 'You don't say? or 'Well, I'll be dinged!'

The two lawyers, Bledsoe and Gerney, trying to appear like casual passers-by, began to slide out of the middle of the crowd, only to find themselves confronted by two very large policemen. 'Don't be in a hurry,' the legal beagles were told. 'There's plenty of entertainment to come.'

Sheriff Baker climbed up on the buggy, and called for attention. 'For those who don't know,' he announced, 'I am the county sheriff. It is my special pleasure to announce to you that this auction is illegal, and is hereby cancelled.' The several spectators began to fade away. 'No, don't rush off,' the sheriff said.

'I have here in my pocket some bench warrants. If you young men over there would arrest Mrs Fessenden—that lady behind all the tears in that chair. Ma'am, you are under arrest, charged with conspiracy to defraud. Along with these two lawyers over here. Got them? That's nice, what you young people can do. Take them in to Stanfield, and lock them up until Judge Pettibone can get around to them.' The sheriff stopped to check off a couple more names on his list of wants and warrants.

'And now you there—with the dog—yes, you. You're standing right next to Deputy Sheriff Paine, for whom I have a warrant charging malfeasance in office, possession of a controlled substance, and possession with intent to sell a controlled substance. I have some more warrants for him, but that ought to do. Yes, sir—you might use his own handcuffs on him. That seems right and proper. And if you will put him in my car over there I'll take him along after a time.'

'And what about Colonel Fessenden?' Uncle Vanya asked. 'I have a terrible suspicion about men who become colonels without ever being in the military service.'

'Wull, as best me and the FBI are concerned,' the sheriff mused, 'there's only two charges against the colonel. One is for keeping dogs without a licence——'

'And the other?' Grandmother Lee queried.

'Well, ma'am. The other ain't really a charge. He's been consorting with a known criminal—to wit, Mrs Fessenden, but the Commonwealth of Virginia cannot legally prosecute him for stupidity. You can leave now, Colonel.' The sheriff carefully climbed down from the buggy. 'Arthritis,' he commented as he reached out for a helping hand.

'Hey, just wait a minute,' Katie yelled. Everyone stopped in place. 'You're letting the worst one of them get away. Him.' She pointed her finger dead at Jack Lee. 'The mastermind of the bunch!'

All those separate people, going in their several directions, stopped for a moment to take in her accusation, and they all began to laugh. The sheriff roared so much that he had to fumble for the chair that Mrs Fessenden had been using, into which he collapsed.

Everybody was laughing, except for Jack Lee and Kate Lovewell; Jack, looking as if he was about to commit murder, was walking angrily in her direction.

Kate, having been born of no stupid parents, hesitated for a second or two, and then took off for the hills behind the barn! In a matter of seconds her mind triumphed over her damaged leg. From a fitful hobble she worked her way up to gazelle speed. And besides, she told herself, in desperation, I know the land, and he's a damn foreigner!

'So, I've finally caught you!' Tackled her, for a fact. Tackled her as she broke out of the trees and tried to make it across the hay-loft north of the house.

'You'd better look out,' Kate yelled at him as she rolled over, sat up, and started to brush debris from her hair. 'The sheriff isn't too far away. I can scream like you've never heard before. They'd lock you up for a hundred years, here in Virginia. Folks around here don't put up with——'

'With what?' he interrupted, his face as grim as the executioner's.

'Attempted rape,' she muttered, her mind too far-gone for sensible thinking. But then, having caught her breath, she put her intelligence to work. 'Assault and battery,' she added to the list. 'Look, my elbow's bleeding!'

'Damned if that's true,' he said. 'That's my nose and my blood. What do you have to say to that?'

'Fraud,' she said belligerently.

'Fraud? How do you figure fraud?'

'Kissing with intent to deceive,' she muttered. 'Turn me loose, you damn Croatian bas——'

'No. That's not true.' He sat up beside her and shook her, not too gently. 'My mother and father were married for two years before I was born. Want to try again?'

'Consorting with the enemy,' she blustered. 'Conspiracy to defraud.' She used both sets of knuckles to clear the tears from her eyes. 'Don't you think I saw what you were up to? Don't you think I believe what the colonel told me? I wasn't born yesterday, Mr Lee. You were Mrs Fessenden's lawyer long before you became mine.' She stopped for another deep breath. Accusing and loving, all at the same time, required a great deal more energy than she was prepared for. 'And that, I'm sure, is malpractice, Mr Lee. Wait'll I call up the county bar association. I'll bet you could be debarred——'

'It's not like de-horning cattle,' he interrupted. 'You mean I could be disbarred!'

'Just another one of your legal technicalities,' she muttered, and the thought turned on her tears almost automatically.

'Don't cry, for God's sake. That's not fair. Enough is enough. I'd think you'd be happy as a clam to see me disbarred. Thrown out of work. Putting my daughter on welfare. Shaming my grandmother's fair name?'

'Oh, God,' she wailed, and the drip of tears turned into a waterfall.

'Oh, God? You wouldn't want to see me ruined?'

'About *you* I don't care a darn,' she managed. 'But Grandmother and Nora, that's a different story! *You* they could put away for years and years, and it would never stir a tear. What are you doing?'

'I'm addressing the first charge,' he murmured. Suddenly they were both sitting up, facing in opposite directions, and his arms were around her, pulling her over to lean against him.

It was close to six o'clock, and a cool wind was starting to blow up the valley. But his touch, his envelopment cut off the chill. She relaxed against his warm chest, relaxed her muscles, let her whole weight fall on his arms and against his shoulder. One of his hands came up and brushed her hair out of her eyes. She stared at him, a rabbit hypnotised by a hawk. 'What——?' she managed to whisper.

'Kissing with intent to defraud,' he said softly. Her mouth half opened to protest, and he sealed her up with his lips. Warmth and moisture, an insistent pressure as his tongue penetrated her mouth and set his mark on her. Kate struggled for a microsecond, and then collapsed into the enjoyment of it. His one hand stroked her hair gently; the other held her in his kissing-trap. He could have done *that* with two fingers, she told herself wildly as she came to life.

There was a need running wild in her mind. A need to be closer, to explore, but her position, sitting beside him on the grass, was not helpful. She managed to wiggle her way up and into his lap. 'Oh, Jack,' she murmured during that second or two while her mouth was clear of him.

And now he was not holding *her* at all. Her own hands had come up around his neck, her body turned slightly so that she pressed against the steel of his chest, her tongue seeking, finding.

'Oh, Jack,' somebody sighed. His free hand was at her waist, exploring the hem of her blouse. Slipping under it to rest for a moment on the soft bulge of her hip, and then wandering up, tantalising, towards the swell of her unfettered breast. And then everything came to a halt.

She cried out for a moment against the loss of warmth, the cessation of wild sensations. He was pushing her slightly away from him. 'Oh, no,' she pleaded.

'Oh, yes,' he corrected. 'Kissing with intent to defraud?'

'No.' A tremendous sigh shook her body. He felt it more than she did. 'No,' she said. 'Not guilty.' And then a pause as she struggled for control. 'Why did this happen to me? I've been a nice girl for years and years, and now look at me! I love you, Jack Lee, even if you're the most dangerous uncaught bandit east of the Mississippi. Why me, God?'

'That's a good start,' he commented as he helped her up to her feet. 'Now, if I can get you back to the house we'll see if we can sort this whole thing out.'

Kate looked down at the crushed grass, the soft and perfect nest they had shared for too short a time. 'Maybe we'd better wait until the sheriff leaves the house,' she suggested. 'I wouldn't want you arrested before you do this major miracle—explaining all this away, I mean!' Maybe we could wait out here as long as tomorrow, hoping it won't rain? Hayfields are famous in history for use in this sort of... I wish I knew what you really call it. Queen Victoria certainly ruined a large and interesting part of the language!

'No stalling,' he said, interrupting her wonderful little daydream. 'Back to the house. My grandmother doesn't approve of an unmarried couple doing things in a hayfield.'

'What things?' she challenged.

'Those things that both you and I are thinking about doing if we don't get up and out of here,' he told her as he snatched up her hand and started off in the general direction of the house. Kate Lovewell dreamed all the way home.

'You're supposed to carry her, Daddy.' Nora stamped her foot in disgust. They were all gathered around the dining-room table—Grandmother Lee, Uncle Vanya, and Nora. But when Kate tried to move away from the feast which Nora had prepared her leg was so stiff that she could not move it.

'You can see she's hurt,' Nora insisted. 'She wasn't that bad off when you chased her into the trees.'

'How lucky I am to have such an observant child,' Jack said sarcastically. 'And if I pick her up I'll have a strained back. You don't seem to have any idea how much the lady weighs!'

'Don't bother,' Kate growled. 'I'd crawl before I'd let that man lay a hand on me. On my hands and knees I'd crawl!'

'Everybody clear out of the way,' Jack announced. 'We're about to——'

At the head of the table the little old lady, dressed in starchy black with white Belgian lace running from here to forever, tapped twice with her spoon against her glass. The little tinkle brought the entire discussion to a close. With a dozen well-chosen Serbo-Croatian words one could almost see the diadem resting within the crown of her white hair. Her son Vanya gasped. 'Mama!' he cautioned. Her grandson John shut his mouth carefully, as if afraid he might break the hinge of his jaw. Her great-granddaughter Nora covered her mouth with both her hands to keep the giggles from leaking through. And without any further debate Jack came over to the table, carefully turned Kate's chair, lifted her out of it, and carried her through to the living-room, where he deposited her oh, so gently on the sofa. He took a step backwards to admire his work, grinning, but another spurt of Croatian wiped the grin away.

'Now?' he asked. 'She's been insulting me all day.'

'So would I,' his grandmother said. 'Now!'

The last gentle word cracked like the tip of a bull-whip. As big a man as he was, Kate could see him flinch. He came back to the couch, reached down for her hand, and treasured it. 'My grandmother,' he said, 'instructs me to tell you how sorry I am to have been such a stupid——' He stopped, and glanced across at the matriarch. She nodded her head in a commanding gesture. He turned back to Kate again. She shifted uneasily, trying to move an additional inch away from him. But he looked so—loveable that she lost her sense of fear. 'Where was I?' he asked.

'Sorry that you were such a stupid,' Kate suggested very meekly.

'Yes. That I have been such a stupid jackass.' And then he treasured her hand in his once more, and bent over and kissed its palm. There was silence from the group, and then a round of applause. Under cover of the noise he leaned closer and whispered, 'Actually, she didn't say jackass, but the word she *did* use was...untranslatable.'

'Eating humble pie?' She was whispering, as he had been on that last exchange. 'Now you're going to tell me that your grandmother is queen of the roost, and you're a downtrodden beat-upon male!'

'I couldn't have said it better myself,' he said, with all his usual cockiness. 'Now, Uncle Vanya, why don't you tell the young lady about my exploits?'

'It wouldn't do to be caught blowing your own horn? Well, all right. Actually, Miss Lovewell—er—are you actually going to marry this big oaf?'

'I . . . haven't been asked,' Kate retorted.

'Well then, Katie,' he said, chuckling. 'We operate a corporate business. My mother is the financial whizz, I do all the detecting, and my nephew here does all the thinking. So it didn't take us long to see what the focal point of the problem was—is? Sometimes I have trouble with the little English words still. So; the new development in this area will undoubtedly start right where your farm is. And the person who knew this, besides the developer, was Mrs Fessenden. Who, by the way, is the brains in her family. The two lawyers were working at the legal aspects, the deputy sheriff responded more simply to money.'

'But why couldn't the information have leaked out from the developer?' Kate asked.

'Later,' Vanya replied. 'Later.' He scratched the tip of his nose, replaced his glasses, and continued. 'So the first step was to get your father into a mess about money. The answer again was money. A gambling operation was set up, in which your father was the only—er—'

'Pigeon,' Jack furnished.

'Yes, pigeon,' Vanya said. 'Now your father was very distracted at the time. The death of your mother, I presume. In any event they took him for a great deal of money. Peter Lester was the kingpin of this affair. And he has agreed to testify to that concern.'

'Peter?' Out of the corner of her eye Kate could see the quick frown that flashed across Jack's face at the happy sound. Kate used both her hands to trap Jack's. 'I only thought it was—you know—righting a wrong he had done us, confessing and all that. I'm sure God would erase a few of the black spots on his character.'

'Yes, I'm sure He will,' Vanya agreed. 'Just as soon as poor Peter's broken jaw heals.'

'Oh, my,' Kate offered. Out of the corner of her eyes he could see Jack turning his hand over so that she couldn't see the back of it, and his bruised knuckles.

'Well, anyway,' Vanya continued, 'the major problem was getting the evidence, the warrants—all that paperwork that the law requires. So when we discovered that the foreclosure had been declared, and the auction scheduled, why, my nephew John volunteered to act as the decoy to delay them. He went over and volunteered to be Mrs Fessenden's advisor.'

'Only Grandma had already figured out how to slow things down,' Nora said gleefully. 'If you really wanna know where all the scheming comes from, there it is.' She pointed dramatically across the room at the matriarch.

'Damn it,' Jack said mournfully, '*I* was supposed to be the hero of this, and you've blown the works, Miss Nora Lee.'

'So then you were busy behind the scenes gathering all this evidence, and stuff like that,' Kate mused. He was wearing a terribly shifty look, so she took a wild guess. 'That didn't include wining and dining the lady?'

'Of course it did,' Jack responded. 'Don't you ever read any spy and detective stories?'

'Yes, I read a number of them,' Kate said as she shifted her gaze to the blanket he had thrown over her, and began picking at one of the loose threads. 'And the thing that bothers me is that the macho hero spends a great deal of his time with the villainess in a horizontal position!'

'Luckily no member of the House of Karageorgeovic would ever consider doing things like that,' Grandmother interrupted. 'And another thing that will make you happy, Katie. In Virginia gambling is illegal, except when conducted in a state-licensed place of business. And since your father's gambling was conducted in Mrs Fessenden's house no debts accrued from such action may be collected. With a smart lawyer I think you could recover, oh—Jack?'

'Anything's possible,' Jack Lee told her. 'Anything from twenty-five dollars to two hundred and fifty thousand. How's that grab you?'

'Oh, lord, that sounds fine,' Kate said, excited. 'I can have the rest of the house fixed up and painted, and put the land to some use, to keep those pirates from Washington from turning the valley into a...' Her voice trailed off as she noticed that nobody in the room except herself was smiling.

Uncle Vanya put his hands in his pockets and began to whistle dolefully. Nora backed up until she bumped into her father, and then looked up at him with a worried look on her face. 'Papa, is that going to spoil everything?'

'I think, at this point,' the matriarch said, 'we had best leave everything in my son's hands. Vanya?'

'I have the car. I think I'll start back to Washington now,' he said. 'I could send the helicopter down for you in the morning?'

'A very excellent idea,' Grandmother agreed. 'And for now, considering how late it is and how much we've done, I would suggest that you and I, Lenora, go to bed.'

'I don't wanna,' the little girl snapped. 'Everybody's had all their questions asked, and there wasn't none of them as important——'

'Weren't,' her father interrupted.

'Weren't none of them important as mine, and why should I have to go off to bed before I find out if——?'

'Go to bed, child,' her father commanded. 'You're not the only one who wants that answer. Git!'

And so goodbyes were said, cheeks were kissed, Vanya disappeared, and in a moment the smooth sound of his limousine motor could be heard. Nora stood for a moment at the foot of the stairs, and then, with her great grandmother's hand on her shoulder for support, laboured up the stairs, chattering away like a finch in the nest at daybreak.

'And that,' Jack Lee said, 'leaves only one question to be answered.'

'No, that's not true,' Kate said. 'I have a question.' She moved over to make room for him to sit on the porch.

'In all this weaving and boxing, Mr Lee, we kept bouncing around the question about how did Mrs Fessenden find out about the land business?'

'I don't know,' he lied. She pressed him. 'Well,' he finally admitted, 'we employ only Serbs and Croatians in our office. One of them sold us out. His name? Karageorgeovic, of course.'

'Reverting to type, was he?' she said, chortling. The corner of his mouth kept twitching. She didn't pursue *that* problem, because she wanted to have some small advantage over him in the years to come. Fifty years or more. The Karageorgeovic family seems to be long-lived, doesn't it? It was a good question, so she asked.

'Lord, no!' he exclaimed, startled by the change of subject. 'The Karageorgeovic family was a race of scallywags who fast-talked their way on to the throne of Serbia, and then married into the rest of the Slavic kingdoms. They seldom lived long. Assassination was a great form of entertainment back in the good old days. No, the only members of the family that turned out to be long-lived were those who took refuge in America.'

Kate looked up at him, pursing her lips. So we'll live together for fifty years if I don't assassinate him sooner, she thought. What a lovely idea.

He was staring at her, wondering what was to come next. So she went on. 'Back to this development, and all those people you trust implicitly. Who is it that *owns* all this development, in whom you have such absolute trust?'

Jack Lee got up from the couch, and moved away to the open front door. 'There'll be a beautiful moon tonight,' he said. 'Now that I think of it, this would be a wonderful place to raise a family.'

'No doubt. The name, please. Who owns this development company?'

'Me,' he said glumly. 'Just me.'

# CHAPTER TEN

THE helicopter roared in low over the mountain at ten o'clock. Grandmother Lee was already impatiently waiting on the porch, her bag packed, her rebellious granddaughter not quite in hand.

'But we only got to the int'restin' part,' Nora objected. 'I wanna stay around and see the ending.'

'Your papa will take care of the ending,' her grandmother insisted.

'He'll make an awful mess,' Nora said stubbornly. 'You got any idea how many floozies he brought home and almost got married to, only I wouldn't let him?'

'Floozies?' Grandmother frowned her most regal frown, and then a tiny smile formed. 'Some of them were very far-out, were they not, child?'

'He's probably the smartest lawyer in the world,' Nora continued, 'but he don't know from nothin' about women. He needs a—a keeper.'

'There may be something in what you say,' Grandmother mused.

'And I like this one,' Nora insisted.

'To tell the truth, so do I.' The grey eyes blinked at the blue ones, and two smiles appeared. 'You have just got a terrible headache,' the matriarch said. 'The helicopter noises will make it worse. You will probably be sick.'

'I do? It will? I would?'

'Yes,' her grandmother said. The machine made one more pass over the front yard. Bits of stick and grass and debris were vacuumed up and spread over the adjacent quarter-acre. Grandmother Lee stood up, with one hand on Nora's shoulder to provide balance. And at that moment, hurrying from opposite ends of the house, Kate and Jack put in an appearance. The jet engine was throttled back, and the rotor sounds dropped to conversational level. 'There is nothing better,' the matriarch said, 'than having a child who understands without a great deal of explanation.'

'I thought I'd be too late to say goodbye,' Kate said. 'I was upstairs—cleaning the bathroom——' Oh, what a lie, she told herself. I was upstairs crying, that's what. What am I going to do about the Lee family? If the Washington football team had a runner as shifty as Jack Lee they'd be national champions every year. If I give this pirate an inch he'll take a mile. And if I *don't* give him an inch he might just walk off and find someone else! Kate was startled when Grandmother Lee rambled on.

'Lenora has a headache,' the matriarch announced. 'A very bad headache.' Her granddaughter dropped her chin and tried to look miserable. 'All of which can only be made worse by a trip in a noisy helicopter.' Nora, a consummate actress, like most little girls, managed to winkle out a tear and cover her ears with both hands. 'Therefore it will be better for her to remain here. When a girl is feeling sickly there is nothing better for her than the attention of a loving father.' Nora, overplaying her part, gagged very realistically, and only stopped when the hand on her shoulder squeezed a little too hard. 'Kiss me, child.'

Nora stretched, Grandmother Lee bent over slightly, and the deed was done. But it was the regal grandmother who turned to Kate and said, 'You too, child. You may kiss me.' The conversion from Grandmother to royalty was a little too much for common Kate, but she rubbed

her lips with her wisp of a handkerchief, bent over the
tiny woman, and complied.

And while her ear was still close to the royal cheek
she heard a whisper. 'Go get 'im,' royalty said in a very
plebeian aside.

Jack Lee was a very subdued man as he came back
from escorting his grandmother to the chopper. Nora
stood on the porch beside Kate, holding her hand and
brushing as close as possible to her side.

During the course of the elderly lady's trip to the
helicopter, her arm solidly entwined in her grandson's
arm, the pair on the porch could see much emphasis
with the fingers, the hand, the arm—all from the
matriarch. From time to time Jack would nod, but it
was obvious that he was not being given time to respond.

'Getting his marching orders,' Nora giggled. 'There
are times my dad thinks he's in charge of the family.'

'And he's not?'

'Depends on who he's talkin' to,' the girl answered.
'But when Grandmother cracks the whip—well!'

'How interesting,' Kate reflected as she stowed that
tidbit away in the corner of her mind marked 'Him'.
Maybe that's the way to handle him—the imperial way
that his grandmother uses!

And then a little touch of ceremony over at the helicopter stairs brought a trace of a tear to Kate's eye. The
matriarch extended her hand, her grandson took it,
bowed to kiss it, and then stepped back, backbone
straight as steel, watching as the crew helped the old lady
into the machine. At which he proffered a stiff quarter-
bow, and stepped away. 'And that,' Kate said, dabbing
at her eye, 'is one of the fine little ceremonies we've lost
in passing through the years. It might be nice being a
princess, pet.'

'Don't you believe it,' Nora replied. 'For a minute, maybe, but not for life. Grandma had many a scare, many a threat during her life. Revolutions aren't just ice-cream and cake. Once I heard her tell my dad about the time in 1916 when the rebels had her and her mother lined up against a wall. Uncle Vanya saved her. No, Europe is still cluttered with ex-royalty, scraping to keep body and soul alive. And you have no idea how many poor noblemen still turn to Grandma for help! Nope. They don't have no pension plan for royalty after the revolution. I'm gladder to be Nora than Lenora.'

'I hadn't thought of it that way,' Kate said, brought down from her dream-trip in a hurry. 'Glad, not gladder,' she corrected.

'Whatever you say,' Nora agreed, and squeezed the hand she was holding. Across the field the helicopter coughed, worked up some enthusiasm, and went roaring away into the brilliant morning sun.

'Thank the lord,' Jack said as he came up the porch steps, wiping perspiration off his brow. 'My grand-mother is——'

'Your oldest relative,' his daughter interrupted, with a scathing look. He glanced down at her, surprised, and mulled over the comment for a moment.

'Yes,' he said solemnly. 'My oldest relative. Now then, ladies, except for a few court cases—and that damn clock—I suppose we can get down to routine living.'

'Don't you lay a finger on my clock,' Kate threatened.

'Oh, Papa,' Nora said, dismayed. 'My headache's getting worser.' Neither one of the adults, looking at her disgruntled face, dared to offer a correction.

Not until the child had gone upstairs did he dare to say a word. 'A fine little lady,' he commented. 'Just a few more lessons and she'll turn out to be one of the cheekiest ladies on the east coast.'

It was just enough to set off Kate's temper. 'And who,' she declaimed pompously, 'do you know who's smart enough to teach her?'

He recognised the danger-line and stepped over it jauntily. 'My grandmother, for one. And my wife for another.'

'Ha! A likely story that is. Who do you know that's fool enough to marry a Croatian bandit?'

He held up his left hand, as if exclaiming his finger-nails. 'Besides you, you mean?'

'Don't give me that guff,' she roared at him. But it was only a half-hearted roar. Behind her beautiful high forehead gears were running at full speed. Besides you?

'Now that *is* a laugh,' she retorted weakly, but even *she* could hear the quaver in her voice. He was wearing a lazy sort of smile as he moved closer to her, and dropped a heavy hand on each of her shoulders. One gentle little shake followed.

'Now listen up,' he said. 'My grandmother gets away with that stuff because I admire and respect her. She's had seventy-five years of——'

'Eighty-five,' Kate corrected. Which earned herself another little shake.

'And that's another thing,' he muttered. 'All that "I know everything" stuff is just right for my daughter, but from my wife—that is something, lady, up with which I will not put!'

'Winston Churchill said it first,' she interjected, and earned herself two more little shakes. Well, perhaps they weren't all that little. He *was* a very big man.

'I can see I have to take you firmly in hand, Kate Lovewell. They were almost nose to nose, but Kate found herself unable to leave it alone. 'You and how many brothers will that take?' she demanded.

'Oh, I think I can manage to work my way through the thickets, as we say in Virginia.'

'As *we* say in Virginia? Why, you darn carpetbagger!' She had meant to say something nasty about his parentage, but by the time she had chosen the right words his lips were on hers, the seal was complete, and although she struggled for a second or two they both knew the battle was lost.

Kate closed her eyes, and relaxed within the circle of his arms as his tongue pursued her back into the cave of her mind. He relented long enough to say, 'Repeat after me. I love you.' And a single little shake.

'Repeat after me. I love you,' she murmured, and the warm moist pressure of his lips were back on hers again. It lasted until she had run out of air, until her feet were tingling, until her breasts had snapped to attention and her mind was playing tag on some far pink cloud. And then he stopped again.

'Always a smart-aleck,' he said softly. 'Fight until the last drop of blood. Right?'

'Right. We Lovewells fight on, even after the Confederacy surrendered! It's a wonder there are any of us left.'

'I wish I could have known your father.' He cuddled her up against his shoulder, using one hand to lock her in place, and the other to course up and down from her hip to her breast. She shuddered in anticipation. 'I'm sure there was a lot I could have learned from him.' Another kiss, that sent her mind reeling. When he released her her knees could not hold her up. She dropped on to the nearby rocking-chair. It took a moment or two for her to work up a facsimile of a frown.

'If you think all this sweet-talking is going to get you all my land to building a gas station on you've got another thought coming, John Lee.'

'A-ha! That's the mouse nibbling at the cheese, huh?'
He leaned down and picked her up, hugging her closely.
'You are indeed a hostile witness,' he said, sighing.
'Answer yes or no. No buts. No equivocation. Got that?'

'I'll——'

He lifted her a little higher, and gently bit the lobe of
her ear. 'Yes or no,' he repeated as he tossed her up in
the air.

'I get seasick easy...'

'Yes or no. Got it.' He faked another toss up into the
air. She gasped and clung more closely to him.

'Yes,' she whispered.

'That's better. Now. You're going to marry me.'

'I have a choice? No! Don't——'

'You're going to marry me?'

'Yes.'

'You can't help yourself because you love me?'

'Yes.'

'And if I want to dig a coal mine in front of this house
you'll smile sweetly and applaud?'

A little silence. Not very much of one. He was too
close, the pattern had been set, the truth had been
paraded up in front of the whole world, and besides he
smelled so magnificently male, and, she told herself, I
wouldn't mind at all finding out what the next act is!
He jogged her gently. 'Yes,' she said hurriedly. 'Yes!'

'I guess that's enough for the first lesson,' he said.
'Why are you looking so disappointed?'

Not me, she told herself firmly. You don't get a
statement out of me on that score. I wasn't born
yesterday. I know all about male-female relationships.
Well, I know *some* things about relationships. Lift up
the banner of women's rights!

'Put me down,' she insisted, and was totally surprised
when he did just that. 'When I get married I don't expect

to become a house-slave,' she said. 'I believe in women's rights, and I mean to have some! Women are the equal of man any time!'

'I *knew* there'd be trouble,' he said, shaking his head dolefully. 'In the old Croatian system I'd end up beating you for saying things like that.'

'Well you'd better not try,' she snapped. 'You're too old a Croatian to get away with it. I'm a big girl!'

'Indeed you are,' he said, chuckling. 'And I wouldn't know what to do with a subservient woman. No, lady, a marriage is shared. But remember this, in marriage men and women are complementary to each other, not identical. You get to run the house, balance the budget, order the children around——'

'What house?'

'*This* house. I've decided not to open a coal mine on the front lawn. The kids might fall in. We're going to live here. You and I and Nora and John Junior and Harry and Katie...'

He was too close to miss. She kissed the end of his nose, and got into the spirit of things. 'But after our son Vanya is born,' she said, 'we're going to buy a television, or maybe go to the movies more often.'

'I knew you'd get the hang of it!' He laughed as he threw her up in the air again—and missed catching her!

'Oh, Lord!' she gasped. 'We're not even married yet, and you've broken my back!'

'Yeah, well,' he sighed. 'The spirit was willing—you weigh an awful lot, love.' He knelt down beside her, all commiseration, running his hands up and down her body from ankle to nose—and back again. And again.

'I don't feel anything broken,' he muttered as he worked his way up from her hip and stopped halfway. 'How do you get this thing off?'

'There's a zipper in the back,' she teased. He fumbled for another moment or two, and then muttered something that sounded like 'Oh, hell!'.

So very suddenly that Kate could not understand the change, she was panting for breath, perspiring like mad, trembling in all her joints, wishing...!

He seemed to snatch at her frantically, as if unable to wait another moment. Back in his arms again, still shuddering, she ducked her head into his shoulder as he strode up the stairs, stomped down the hall, and kicked the door of her bedroom open. Despite her own desperation, her own tension, Kate spared one loving look at the man—her man. He was puffing under her weight, and the steepness of the stairs, but he was not about to quit—until he came to the side of her big four-poster bed, where his breath ran out, making a whistling noise the way an emptying tea kettle might do, and he dropped her right in the middle of the bed.

The bed was old but well-sprung. Kate felt herself bounce a time or two, and could not keep from laughing. Her skirt had gone awry, and he had managed to find the zip on her blouse. He stood at the side of the bed, hands on hips, and glared at her as he rocked back and forth on the soles of his feet.

'Woman,' he said fiercely, 'don't you ever laugh at your husband.'

'I'll remember that, just in case we might get married,' she giggled.

He had rocked too far. His bulk toppled over on her. He managed to get his hands out just enough so that he didn't squash her, but he did effectively pin her down.

'Just in case? Damn. What you need is a good lesson! I'm going to——'

'I wish you would,' she giggled.

'What's going on here?' A squeaky little voice from the doorway. Nora, standing just inside the room, hands on hips, her face red with anger. 'Don't you dare hurt Kate. I need her!' A moment of absolute silence, and then a brilliant smile flashed across the little face.

'Oh! I know what you're doing. You're making a baby!'

'Where in the world did you learn something like that?' her father spluttered.

'I know lots of things,' Nora replied. 'Susie Sandson's in the sixth grade—for the second time—and she told me that when her mother and father fight on the bed that's what they're doing. Isn't that wonderful?' With which she sparkled a kiss at each of them, and turned and walked out of the room, carefully closing the door behind her.

Kate rolled over on her side to face him. 'My goodness,' Kate murmured as her fingers began to struggle with the buttons on his shirt. 'What a clever child you have.'

'*We* have,' he grumbled. 'But if she gets on the telephone to tell her grandmother my name will be mud.'

'She might do that?' Kate's face was as red as her rambling roses. Red but determined.

'She might just do that,' Jack Lee said. 'Well, as long as I've already got that name, Mrs Mud, why don't we——?'

'I thought you'd never ask,' Kate moaned. 'Hurry up! We have direct-distance dialling in this county!'

# THE DEVIL YOU KNOW
*by*
## HELEN BROOKS

# CHAPTER ONE

'YOU'RE not hiding again, Carina! What's the matter with you? Can't you stand a little fun and excitement for just a few hours?' As her stepmother's high, strident voice cut into the book she was reading, curled up on the large window-seat behind the heavy concealing velvet curtain, Nina's heart sank still further.

'Come on!' Isobel's thin red-tipped hand pulled roughly at her arm. 'There's someone who is just dying to meet you, though goodness knows why!'

'Please, Isobel.' Nina stopped dead as her stepmother jerked her back towards the large drawing-room, where the main host of loud, objectionable revellers were screaming riotously. 'I'm not going back in there.'

'Why ever not, you stupid child?' Isobel's slanted green eyes were cold. 'This whole thing is for you—you aren't sixteen every day! This party has cost us a fortune.'

'I said I didn't want it.' Nina's voice was desperate. 'I told you I didn't want any fuss, but you had to have your own way. I don't know any of these people and neither does Dad.'

'Where is your father?' Isobel's voice dripped ice.

'He's in his studio.'

'Well, you aren't escaping so easily.' Her stepmother's voice was as relentless as was her grip. 'There's a friend of your father's in there who could do us a great deal of good if you are nice to him, and you haven't even said hello yet. You're so gauche.'

'No!' As Isobel dragged her back into the main room Nina's wide violet eyes sprang immediately to the huge window at the far end. He was still there! She tried to disentangle herself from the other woman's tight grip but Isobel's hands dug spitefully into her arms as she felt her resistance.

'For crying out loud, Carina! I'm only asking you to talk to someone for a few minutes, and then you can go to hell as far as I care.'

'All right.' All the fight fled from Nina's slight form as the party surged around them, hiding the tall dark figure in the distance from her nervous gaze. 'It's just that someone has been looking at me all night and he scares me.'

'The cat would scare you!' Her stepmother's voice was vicious as the emerald eyes swept scornfully over Nina's pale face. 'You ought to be pleased someone's noticed you.' She looked disparagingly at Nina's slim form in the loose white cotton dress she had insisted on wearing, smoothing her own tight black dress over her hips contentedly. 'That dress is more suitable for a Sunday-school picnic than a party.'

They had been moving slowly through the crowd as they spoke, and the crescendo of sound was deafening. As a strong gust of whisky-laden breath from a fat balding man to one side of her hit Nina full in the face she closed her eyes briefly, fighting back the tears. These awful people! They had invaded her home, dropped cigarette ash over her father's beautiful antiques, so lovingly collected, slopped drink over all the carpets and eaten voraciously all weekend. Just one man was different, the stranger who had arrived earlier that day. He had remained cool and aloof from the rest of Isobel's friends, but he frightened her more than the rest of them together. His dark burning eyes had never left her face for a moment, and she could feel his rapier gaze slicing into her brain even when she was lost from his sight.

'Carina.' She opened her eyes again as Isobel's sharp elbow nudged her painfully in the ribs.

'Here's the party-girl, Steed,' the shrill, affected voice continued. 'I've brought her specially to meet you.'

As she raised her head and met those piercing dark eyes that had been haunting her all night her whole being jolted with scorching shock.

'At last.' His voice ran over her taut nerves like fire, deep, cool and sardonic, its timbre as hard as steel. Now she was so close to him that she was conscious of his great height and the leashed power emanating from the big, relaxed body. 'You must be Carina?'

Adolescent shyness combined with inexplicable alarm, and, as she looked up into the dark face towering above her, ripples of apprehension flooded down her spine.

'How do you do?' she answered automatically, holding out one small, slim hand, and as he took it in his own large brown one she shivered instinctively, her deep blue eyes glued to his face. He raised her hand slowly to his lips in gentle laughing salute, and as she felt his warm, firm mouth on her cool flesh she snatched it away sharply, stepping backwards, large eyes clouded with fear.

'Carina!' She had landed on Isobel's foot, and her stepmother pushed her forward again irritably, her voice shrill.

He put out a hand to steady her, and she noticed his smile had died, leaving his face still and cold, his eyes narrowed into grey slits. 'Would you like to go into the garden for a few minutes, away from all this?' His hand had encompassed the swarming crowd disdainfully and she had the impression he liked them no more than she did.

'No!' She answered more instinctively than politely, and the austere face went a shade colder at the promptness of her refusal.

'Of course she does, Steed,' Isobel cut in cloyingly, one bony finger digging Nina sharply in the back. 'She's been complaining all night about the noise and smoke, and what girl could resist making every other woman in the room wildly jealous?' Nina could imagine the flirtatious smile on the red-painted lips.

'I think Nina is old enough to answer for herself.' The soft words had carried a warning that Isobel was not slow to miss, and she took the rebuke badly, swinging round and disappearing into the screeching herd with a flick of her head.

'I'll come outside for a while,' Nina said quickly as he looked down at her again, his expression indiscernible. That poke in her back had reminded her that this was an influential friend of her father's; she couldn't offend him.

He took her hand without speaking and it took all her will-power not to pull away as he led her through the crowd that parted magically before the big, solid figure, and out through the open french doors into the darkness beyond. The cool night air was wonderfully fresh after the heavy stickiness of the house, and she breathed in its sweetness, scented with the rich perfume of roses. 'Better?' He didn't look at her as he spoke, wandering with seeming casualness away from the light and noise across the smooth green lawns, into the more dense blackness beyond.

'If I remember rightly there's a seat somewhere over here.' His voice was cool and friendly, but for the life of her she couldn't reply, and it wasn't until they were seated under one of the huge old oak trees that scattered the grounds that she ventured a glance at him in the dim shadowed light.

He caught the look and the grim mouth turned up at one corner in cynical amusement. 'You make me feel like the wolf in Red Riding Hood,' he said softly, his eyes gleaming strangely in the half-light.

'I'm sorry.' She didn't know quite how to reply, and he chuckled softly as she lowered her head so that the soft gold of her hair covered her face.

'I like that.' He touched a silken strand lightly, and she felt a trembling in the pit of her stomach as his arm rested loosely along the back of the old wooden seat close to her body.

'You're a friend of Isobel's and Dad's, then?' she said nervously, wondering how quickly she could engineer returning to the house without making it too obvious. The faint salty breeze drifting in from the sea below the cliffs that bordered the house lifted a soft tendril of hair and drew it lazily across her flushed face, and before she could lift her hand his finger had brushed it back into place, leaving a burning sensation on her cheek where it had touched her flesh.

'Your father and I share the same club in London and we often have a meal together when he is in town. I think you could say we are friends, yes,' he answered slowly. Nina noticed he didn't mention Isobel. 'He's a wonderful artist,' he continued quietly, 'you must be very proud of him.'

'Oh, I am.' She turned warm, enthusiastic eyes up to his impulsively, thrilled as usual by any mention of her father's talent. 'Did you go to his latest exhibition?'

'No, I was abroad on business at the time.' His cool voice held a thread of laughter that she felt was directed at her, although not in an unkind way. 'You enjoyed it?'

'It was wonderful.' He was making her feel naïve and very childish, and she didn't like it. Her voice quivered into silence and he looked at her consideringly.

'You're very young for sixteen.'

'Not really.' She was annoyed at the overt criticism in the gently mocking voice.

'No?' His voice was soft and thick, sending a flicker of fear across her face. 'Have you ever been kissed?'

'What?' She stared at his face in the darkness, and his teeth gleamed white as he smiled easily, noting her confusion.

'Has a boy ever kissed you?' The trembling in her stomach increased to a slow churning, and she gulped deep in her throat as the slumberous eyes fastened on her mouth. 'Sweet sixteen and never been kissed.' He laughed softly deep in his throat. 'We can't have that, can we?'

Before she was aware of what was happening he had moved closer to her side, lifting her slightly with experienced ease and pulling her into his arms so she was half lying across his lap, imprisoned by his hard body.

'So innocent and pure.' The words were a whisper against her face as she stared, mesmerised, into the burning eyes. 'Is it for real, or are you just a figment of my imagination?' His clean breath was warm against her skin, and the smell of his aftershave was sending goose-pimples all over her body. She felt frightened and excited at the same time, but his gentleness was reassuring and she relaxed slightly as he kissed her forehead with warm, firm lips.

'This is madness.' His voice was husky as he lowered his mouth to hers, but the kiss was incredibly sweet and her lips quivered softly beneath his as he tangled his fingers in the soft silk of her hair. 'Like honey...' The words were a groan against her mouth, and suddenly the tempo of the kiss changed, his lips becoming more demanding as they opened hers with slight force. He pulled her closer to him so she was moulded into his body as the blood began to pound in her ears.

The intimacy of the darkness was like a warm veil, hiding them from the rest of the world, and she began to tremble helplessly as he swept her face with hard burning kisses, returning again to her half-open lips and plundering the warm interior of her mouth greedily. She was lost in a whirlwind of shattering sensation; his touch was triggering a response that she was quite unable to hide. She raised her hands shyly to the dark, crisp hair at the base of his neck, and as he felt her fingers, warm on his skin, he groaned in his throat, his body hardening in answer to her response.

As she felt his body stirring against hers the fear she had first felt began to overshadow the bewildering excitement his kiss had aroused. 'No.' She struggled slightly against his broad chest, but her voice was lost against the fierce pounding of his heart and her cry went unheard. His hands stroked down her body caressingly, touching the budding curves through the soft fabric of her dress, and, thoroughly frightened now, she jerked violently in his arms, her head colliding with his in a sharp crack as she struggled to sit up. 'Don't!'

There was no mistaking the panic in her voice, and this time Steed heard it as he raised his head in surprised enquiry. 'Steady; that hurt.' His voice was full of laughter, but she edged away from him swiftly, her breath coming in shaky little sobs.

'I'm going back to the house.' She rose so quickly that she almost fell, and as his hand went out to save her she shrank from his touch.

'That's a good little girl.' His piercing eyes swept over her teasingly, but she flinched as she sensed the mockery in his deep voice. 'Back to your party.'

She turned to leave, but as she did so he picked a small glittering object from his suit jacket and handed it to her with a dry little bow. 'Yours, I take it.' She took the earring with hands that shook, feeling the laughter he was trying to keep in check, a red tide of humiliation staining her pale cheeks.

'Thank you.' Her voice was low.

'My pleasure. All my pleasure?' The last three words were a question, and as she looked at him his big body began to shake with laughter. She started to run back to the house, but as she did so his laughter followed her, ringing in her ears, pounding in her brain, until the whole world seemed full of taunting, cruel hilarity and she felt more alone than she had ever felt before in her whole life.

'It's time, Carina. Everyone's here.' Isobel's smooth, cold voice couldn't quite hide the excitement that was turning her face red under the heavy powder.

Nina turned from her bedroom window, where the harsh icy rain was beating an insistent tattoo against the glass. She was glad it was raining. Since her father's sudden death from a massive heart attack five days before, the weather, at least, had been in sympathy with her, the small funeral that day a muddy nightmare.

'Steed's here.' Isobel's voice was callously eager. 'He's just flown in from Germany and didn't know the funeral was today. I wonder why Tom made him executor of the will?'

Nina shuddered in spite of the central heating. Why had her gentle, unworldly father entrusted his wishes to that man, of all people? She couldn't believe it. He had known how she hated Steed, although not the reason for it.

In a flash her mind had winged back five years to that fateful birthday party, and her soft lips pulled into a straight line as she remembered the torment she had felt then. She had hidden in her room the rest of the evening and all the next day, ignoring Isobel's furious rantings and not leaving her sanctuary until she was sure all the guests had left. A note had been slipped under her door as she had heard the visitors leaving, but after opening it and seeing Steed's bold scrawling signature at the bottom of the page she had ripped it up unread, dropping the pieces as though they had burnt her. It had taken her a long time to come to terms with the fact that she must forget the incident, but with it had come a semblance of peace.

When she had heard her father had invited him down for the weekend some months later she had run like a terror-stricken animal before its hunter, spending the weekend with friends, and only returning after she had telephoned to make sure the coast was clear. She had confided in her father after that, telling him of her dislike of his friend and asking him not to invite him to the house again. He had been perturbed and upset by what he had considered her unreasonable and inexplicable hatred, but had agreed immediately. He loved her too much to do anything to hurt her.

'Don't stand there dreaming today, of all days.' Isobel's hard voice cut into the memories like a sword-thrust. 'You get more like your father every day.'

Nina stared at her, her huge violet eyes blind with grief. 'How my father ever came to marry a woman like you I will never know,' she said in a low, throbbing voice, a look of disgust sweeping over her white face.

'Don't look at me like that,' Isobel screeched, her green cat's eyes narrowing furiously. 'It was no picnic being married to that miserable old fool, I can assure you. I might have got a few pounds from this marriage to live the way I wanted to in the last few years, but that's all I did get from it. It was "Nina, Nina, Nina", from the day I walked in this place. The pair of you made me sick.'

'You've bled my father dry from the first day you met him.' Nina's voice was raw with misery. 'He loved you in the beginning, but you only wanted his money, didn't you? Nothing could satisfy you.'

'He certainly couldn't, that's for sure.' Isobel's grating voice stopped suddenly as Nina's hand smacked her face with a loud crack.

'Don't you ever talk about him like that again,' Nina whispered shakily as Isobel lifted one beringed hand to her scarlet cheek in horror. 'He's dead now and you can't hurt him any more. There's no reason for me to have to listen to you now, and I won't. You'll get what you ask for.'

'You'll pay for that!' Isobel was shaking with rage. 'You might still think you're lady of the manor, but you are in for a shock, my girl. You can't stay at home with Daddy painting your pretty little pictures any more now, can you? It's a big, bad world out there, and they eat little girls like you for breakfast. Now, are you coming to hear this will read or shall I tell them you feel too consumed with grief?' Her lip curled on the last words and she looked remarkably like an old painting of a medieval witch, no vestige of beauty left in the cruel painted face.

'I'm coming.' Nina's voice was weary as the fight drained out of her. What did it all matter now anyway? Her beloved father was dead, but at least she still had Grayfields, the home they had both loved so much.

All she had to do was to get through the next hour or so and then they would leave her in peace. She knew her father would have left the beautiful, rambling old house to her. It had been in their family for generations, succeeding families having added their own touch to its splendour, an annexe here and a complete wing there, until it roamed across the grounds in untidy picturesque beauty.

The tall man standing immobile in the dimly lit hall, dark in the stormy afternoon, watched her expressionlessly as she slowly descended the winding staircase in front of Isobel. He noted her immediate recoil as she caught sight of him in the shadows, and the harsh mouth tightened fractionally as she recovered herself in an instant, her smooth skin turning a shade paler and then flushing as Isobel brushed past her, arms open wide.

'Steed, darling, what are you out here for? You'll freeze to death. You know how awful these old houses are.' She turned to Nina, her eyes poisonous. 'I think you met Carina before. At her sixteenth party, wasn't it?' The middle-aged face was as hard as iron, malicious satisfaction in every feature. Isobel was no fool and she had always wondered exactly what had transpired that night, drawing her own conclusions eventually, which weren't too far removed from the truth.

'Good afternoon, Mr Charlton,' Nina said coldly but with a slight quiver in her voice she couldn't quite control, forcing herself to look up into the dark face staring down at her unsmilingly. The dark grey eyes flicked over her briefly, taking in the long high-necked dress of soft mauve material that highlighted the unusual hue of her thickly lashed eyes but protectively covered all her smooth honey-coloured skin from probing eyes, and the long silky hair that gleamed like molten gold in the artificial light.

'I was very sorry to hear about your father, Carina, I know how close you were. It must have been a great shock.' The deep, cruel voice she remembered was warm with sympathy, the formal words coloured with genuine concern. Surprised at the difference, she blinked her fear away, and as she stared deep into the shadowed face watching her so carefully she saw with relief that he wasn't the black devil her imagination had painted over the years. His grey eyes were gentle, as though he understood her pain, and the handsome, austere face held no mockery in its depths.

'My friends call me Nina,' she said stiffly, dropping her eyes shyly with a quick glance at Isobel's grim face. Her stepmother had refused to call her anything but Carina, using her name as a subtle insult most of the time.

'Then I hope you will allow me to call you Nina,' he replied slowly, his velvet voice lingering over her name. As before, the timbre of his voice sent tiny shivers down her spine, and she flushed in confusion, feeling suddenly threatened. As though sensing her agitation and the reason for it, he turned away abruptly towards the drawing-room, where the sweet smell of burning pine logs flavoured the air. 'Everyone is waiting,' he said expressionlessly over his shoulder. 'I wondered if something was wrong.'

Besides Mr Atkinson, their solicitor, there was only Steed, Isobel and two distant old aunties in the room as she entered. As the solicitor's dry formal voice began to read slowly she felt her mind beginning to wander, her eyes drawn against her will to the big dark man listening so intently across the other side of the room. He still had a strange effect on her emotions. The hard profile could have been etched in granite and he was undeniably handsome, but there was something more, a compelling magnetism that both attracted and repelled her. His expensive clothes were worn with casual nonchalance, sitting comfortably on the powerful body, and even when he was sitting perfectly still, as now, there was a commanding force generating from the big frame, a live energy that was undeniably sensual.

The cool, penetrating gaze suddenly veered towards her and she flushed involuntarily, lowering her eyes swiftly and longing to return to the safety of her room. She wished all this were finished.

'Nina?' Mr Atkinson's dry voice suddenly pierced her thoughts, and she looked at him with wide, startled eyes. 'Do you understand what I've just been saying?'

'Yes,' she answered dully. She didn't, but what did it matter?

'Now, although your father left Grayfields to you, there is a severe complication.' She looked at him in surprise and glanced across to where Isobel was sitting, rigid with fury.

'Didn't he leave anything for me?' Her stepmother's voice was burning with hate. 'I'll contest it all; I'm not having this; he can't——'

'Please, Mrs Kirkton.' The solicitor's voice was weary. 'Wait until I've finished.'

Isobel sank back down in her seat with an expression of venomous anger twisting her face. 'You're not getting it all, my girl,' she spat at Nina, her eyes blazing.

'I'm afraid, Mrs Kirkton, that nobody is getting anything.' Mr Atkinson was obviously losing patience. 'It would seem that Mr Kirkton was put to a lot of expense in the last ten years.' Nina glanced swiftly at her stepmother, and Isobel flicked her head defiantly. 'Totally against my advice he mortgaged and remortgaged Grayfields to pay mounting debts, which were still never fully covered.'

'What do you mean?' Nina whispered as the bent old man looked at her sorrowfully.

'There's nothing, child.' He was obviously finding this very difficult. 'To satisfy your creditors you are going to have to sell Grayfields for whatever you can get for it, and quickly, but even then I doubt if all the debts can be met.'

'You knew!' Isobel had risen slowly like a wild, demented goblin, her hands clawing the air like talons. 'You must have known!' Her voice was rising slowly as she approached Nina's chair. 'He told you everything.'

'We never discussed finances,' Nina replied stiffly, heartsore and shocked beyond measure at Isobel's reaction.

Steed was by her side in an instant as Isobel lifted her hand to strike, grasping the thin wrist tightly and jerking the crouched figure round to face him with vicious force. Nina had shrunk deep into her chair at Isobel's approach; the ageing face had been positively fiendish, but the raging fury in Steed's face quelled even Isobel's madness.

'Touch her and I'll kill you.' His voice was deadly. 'I want you out of this house and out of her life as soon as you can pack.'

'You're crazy,' Isobel whispered, glancing to the assembled company for support, but they all sat, stunned, in their seats, the two old aunties looking as though they were going to collapse any moment.

'You killed Tom just as surely as if you'd put a gun to his head and fired the trigger.' His voice was relentless. 'You took everything, and when that was all used up you made him part with Grayfields to satisfy your flamboyant lifestyle and constant greed. You broke him, Isobel; you turned him into a caricature of the man he once was. You used the fact that he was one of life's natural gentlemen to full advantage, didn't you? Didn't you?' He shook her slightly, his lips curling back from his strong white teeth in a contemptuous snarl.

'Well, no more! It's all gone. You've had your pound of flesh, and if I ever see your face in these parts again I won't be responsible for my actions. I mean it, Isobel.' As he let go of her wrists she backed towards the door, her face ashen. 'Get out and stay out.' His voice was savage, and Isobel made no attempt to reply, her green eyes glassy with shock and her face white under the heavy rouge and powder.

As the door closed behind her stepmother's stumbling form Nina shook with tremors she couldn't control, one thought only burning in her brain. She had lost Grayfields; there was nothing. Oh, Dad, she asked silently into the empty void stretching out before her, why didn't you tell me? But she knew the answer even as the question formed in her mind. Her father had had the ability to shut unpleasant things out of his consciousness most of the time, ruthlessly blocking their in-

trusion into his inner sanctuary. She remembered finding
him once, hunched over his easel, his face torn with
worry and anguish, but at her approach it was as though
a veil had come down over his emotions, and within
seconds he'd been his old self again, chatting to her easily
while they had painted.

Now Grayfields would have to be sold and strangers
would own the old mellow stone and gaze out of the
leaded windows at a wild, furious sea on a stormy winter's afternoon. She couldn't bear it.

She looked around the room dazedly, her tormented
eyes drinking in the familiar objects, the heavy antique
furniture her own mother had lovingly collected, the
thick Persian carpet covering the floor, and the glittering old chandelier overhead. She pictured the grounds
outside, the well-kept lawns surrounding the house and
the unruly wilderness near the cliffs where the rabbits
played uninterrupted on balmy summer evenings.

'Help me, somebody.' The words were a whispered
plea, so faint that they were like a sigh leaving her
bloodless lips.

'Nina.' She became aware that Steed was kneeling at
her side and the room was empty.

'They've gone?' Her voice was tiny, like a child's.

'Yes, they've all gone. Mr Atkinson is taking the aunts
home.' His voice was indescribably tender. 'Drink this.'
He formed her nerveless fingers round a balloon glass
half full of brandy.

'I don't drink.'

'You do today.' His voice was authoritative and she
obeyed him without thinking, choking and spluttering
on the first mouthful as the hot, burning liquid fired
her throat.

'It's disgusting!'

He smiled wryly as he watched her silently, his eyes tight on her face. 'One more mouthful.' She grimaced and swallowed again. She had to admit that the brandy was steadying her nerves.

'Did you know?' She looked him full in the face and he straightened from her side, moving across to the chair opposite and sitting down with a heavy sigh.

'Not exactly.' His voice was sad. 'I'd got a good idea and I'd tried to question Tom once or twice, but he wouldn't discuss it. He knew I would have helped him and he was a proud man.'

'I know.' Her eyes filled with tears. 'I still love him, you know, in spite of all this.'

'Of course you do.' He smiled gently. 'He's your father.' She was so glad he hadn't said 'was'.

'What shall I do?' Strangely it didn't seem wrong to be asking him for advice, and she suddenly had the feeling that that was why her father had made Steed his executor, to help her in the first aftermath. 'I know Dad would have wanted to pay everyone he owes, but what shall I do if there's not enough when Grayfields is sold?' She gulped on the last words and her voice was high with pain. 'How long do people wait?'

He looked at her for a long moment without replying. Outside a harsh wind had blown up, whistling over the vast cliffs, its whining voice melancholy and haunting as it rattled the old windows and caused Nina to shiver deep in her soul. 'Steed?' Her voice was a question mark; there was something burning deep in his eyes she didn't understand.

Still he didn't speak, and Nina suddenly had the feeling that he was troubled, deeply troubled, but that was ridiculous. She brushed the thought aside swiftly. Her problems were of no real concern to him—they had only met once, when all was said and done.

He spoke at last, his voice deep and mellow in the quiet of the room. 'There is a way you can keep Grayfields and pay off the debts.'

She looked at him in amazement. 'Don't play games with me, Steed.' Her voice was infinitely weary. 'I might not be much of a businesswoman, but even I know that is impossible.' Her voice cracked slightly as she spoke, and he winced as though her pain was his pain.

'There is a way, but I don't know if you could bring yourself to take it.' His face was curiously tight and the dark slate eyes burnt into her wide blue ones.

'I'll do anything.' Her voice was eager. 'Tell me.'

'You could marry me.' The words hung in the air, stark and brittle, and for a moment Nina thought she had misheard him.

'What?' She stared at him blankly.

'I said you could marry me, become my wife and live here.' Their eyes clashed, hers naked with undisguised horror, and his coldly challenging.

'You're mad,' she breathed as a distant rushing in her ears began to grow into a dark flood and a faint feeling of nausea gripped her stomach.

'I've never been more sane in my life.' As she stared at him his eyes became black pools that were drawing her inwards, and just before she lost consciousness she was aware of a bitter tormented anguish twisting the dark face into a devil's mask.

# CHAPTER TWO

NINA came round to find herself lying on the sofa which had been drawn close to the bright red flames of the crackling fire, a light blanket covering her body. Steed was crouching by her side, his dark face unreadable and his big body tense and still.

'I'm sorry.' He spoke as she gazed at him blankly for a second, trying to remember where she was. As realisation rushed in on her she struggled to sit up, but he pushed her down firmly and he stood up slowly, his eyes cold. 'I shouldn't have sprung it on you like that after what you've been through today. It was stupid.'

'Was it a joke?' Her voice was hopeful and he smiled ironically, his eyes mocking.

'No, it wasn't a joke.' He sat down at the end of the sofa and she moved her feet quickly into a corner, fearing any contact with his warm flesh. If he noticed the gesture he made no comment, his stony face implacable.

'In my youth, when I imagined my first proposal to a woman, I always had the vision of her falling into my arms.' His voice was wry. 'You certainly fell, all right, but not quite in the way I had imagined.'

She looked at him doubtfully, unable to gauge his mood. Steed gazed across at her, a tiny muscle working in his jaw. 'That was my way of telling you I have never honoured another woman by asking her to change her name to mine,' he said slowly, self-mockery dripping from his words.

'Oh.' The word was flat and that was how she felt, as though all this were unreal and she would wake up soon and everything would be normal again.

'You sure aren't making this any easier.' He moved restlessly, standing up in one fluid movement and pausing to look down into the fire, his back towards her and his strong arms resting on the ornate mantelpiece.

'I know this probably seems a nightmare to you, but will you just try and forget all that has gone before and listen to me a minute while I explain a few things to you?' He turned as he spoke, and she saw with surprise that although his face was cold with pride there was a strange pleading in the grey eyes that he couldn't quite hide.

'Yes, I'll listen,' she said quietly, her eyes wide with curiosity and apprehension.

'Three years ago my brother and his wife were killed in a boating accident and I became the guardian of their two boys.' Nina looked at him, perplexed. What had all this got to do with her situation?

'Unfortunately my lifestyle is not conducive to children,' he continued drily, 'but the twins were happy, well-adjusted boys and they were already settled at an excellent boarding-school when the tragedy occurred. I saw no reason to change what they were accustomed to, and they have continued at the same school for the last few years, holidaying with me when my business commitments have allowed it, which has been less frequently than I would have liked.' He ran his hand through his crisp dark hair abruptly, his face harsh.

'Due to some sort of virus infection, Jason has been ill recently; it affected his blood quite badly, but that has all been regulated now. Unfortunately the illness has left him both weak and depressed, and what affects one twin affects the other. They are very close, you see.' His face softened, and Nina nodded sympathetically, her eyes glued to his.

'The specialist has been quite specific about what Jason needs now: no more medicines and drugs, but a settled family life and a long, easy convalescence, possibly a private tutor for some months, but certainly as little pressure as possible. They are eleven years old and have been at boarding-school since they were six.' He sighed deeply. 'It won't be easy to integrate them into a normal home, and virtually impossible for me, living alone. I have a flat in London, an apartment in America and two villas abroad, but absolutely nowhere I can take two young children and feel confident they are in the right environment.'

He paused, his grey eyes searching her small face intently. 'Until now, that is. I would like to buy Grayfields, Nina, and make it their home.'

She looked at him in bewilderment. 'I still don't see how that concerns me...'

He held up his hand, checking her voice abruptly, his dark face impassive. 'I would be prepared to buy Grayfields at a price which will enable you to clear all your financial burdens and leave you with a totally clean slate if you would live here and oversee the twins' well-being for the immediate future. Furthermore, I would make you an allowance of several hundred pounds a month, with a written contract promising a lump sum at the end of that time which will make you financially independent for the rest of your life.'

She stared at him, mesmerised by the expressionless voice. 'Your part of the arrangement would be to provide the constant stability that has been missing in my nephews' life so far, a warm family background that they can learn to feel secure in.'

'But I don't have to marry you for that,' she murmured in a dazed voice, her head reeling.

'Yes, you do.' His voice was grim. 'I'm not talking about a few months, Nina. If I buy Grayfields you stay here with me for the next seven years until the boys are eighteen. At that time you would be free to terminate all commitments, and Grayfields would be made over to you to do with what you would.'

'Seven years?' She stared at him, fear and dread leaping out of her eyes.

'You will still be a young woman at the end of that time,' he said coldly. 'Twenty-eight, by my calculations. You will own Grayfields lock, stock and barrel, and be extremely wealthy into the bargain. Not something to be dismissed without careful consideration.'

'Can't I just promise to stay here and work for you?' Her voice was desperate. 'I wouldn't——'

'Not good enough.' There was no mercy in the frosty face. 'You need my money, I need your services. I've met many women in my life, Nina, but there is no one I would rather trust my nephews to than you. If you agree to my conditions I know you will fulfil them to the best of your ability. What the twins need is a normal, natural companion, someone who is unworldly and innocent.' That strange expression she had caught once before flickered across his face, swiftly gone, and his harsh features softened as his eyes noted her white face and clenched hands. Her heart stood still as he took one small fist and gently smoothed out the long fingers in the palm of his hand.

'If you chose to remain purely housekeeper and mother-figure to the twins within the marriage I would accept that.' His eyes were tight on her face. 'I wouldn't particularly like it, but I would accept it.'

Her face burnt with hot colour and she lowered her eyes swiftly.

He stretched out his long muscular legs towards the fire, still holding on to her hand that quivered slightly in his grasp like a small trapped bird.

'You're frightened of me; why?' The question was gentle, and she looked at him in confusion.

'This is all so sudden,' she said weakly, her voice dying away as he shook his black head slowly.

'It's nothing to do with that. I have a vivid memory of a beautiful young girl in a pure white dress with fresh flowers wound through her hair. She stood out from the other...' he paused sardonically '...ladies present like a dove among ravens. I spoilt her birthday.'

Nina looked at him sharply, her face crimson. 'Please, that was a long time ago; I don't want to discuss it.'

He nodded, seeing the withdrawal in her huge violet eyes. 'OK, Nina, subject closed. It was just that I'd hoped you might have mellowed a little towards me during the last few years.' He smiled wearily. 'It doesn't matter anyway; I'm a big boy now.'

He looked at her as she lay huddled at the end of the sofa, pale cheeks turned pink by the heat of the fire and her gleaming hair spread out beneath her shoulders like a silky pillow. 'I've taken the liberty of calling you Nina and I'm not sure if you consider I have the right. Can we try and be friends?'

She nodded slowly. 'Yes, of course.'

'And you'll think about my proposition?' She nodded again. 'I meant what I said about the more...personal side of the arrangement.' His mouth twisted slightly. 'I've never understood the need for human sacrifices.'

Her breath caught in her throat as she looked back at the handsome austere face watching her so closely. He was so near that she could smell the delicious tang of expensive aftershave, and even when he was relaxed, as now, the muscled power of his big male body was faintly threatening and strangely exciting.

'Steed, I don't think this could work——' she began suddenly, but he stopped her, putting a finger to her lips.

'Don't decide now. It's something you must consider very carefully. I'm leaving for Germany in the morning for five days on business. On my return I will expect a decision, and whatever you decide I shall treat it as irrevocable.' He looked at her thoughtfully. 'Think hard before you refuse my offer; you have nothing to lose and everything to gain.'

'But you, what do you gain? It doesn't seem fair.' Her voice was earnest, and he looked at her searchingly for a long moment before shaking his head slowly in amused incredulity. 'I don't know if there is another woman on this earth who would be concerned for my welfare in these circumstances,' he said ruefully. 'I know what I am doing, Nina. Things are clearer to me today than they have been in a long, long time.'

Nina gazed at his face, so near to her own, puzzled and troubled. He was talking in riddles again.

He moved along the sofa until he was bending over her slightly and put out a gentle hand to her hair as though driven by some inner compulsion, talking as if to himself. 'So silky and soft, like sunlight playing on clear water.' He ran the gleaming gold through his fingers slowly, his hand continuing down the nape of her smooth neck, his touch sending electric ripples down her spine.

She forced herself not to flinch, although her senses were screaming as his hand caressed her throat quietly. His fingers burnt her skin and he cupped her small chin in his hand suddenly, looking deep into her dark blue eyes. She could see the tiny white laughter-lines winging away from his eyes, and noticed a few strands of silver in his thick black hair.

'I've never seen true violet eyes before,' he murmured thickly, and as his narrowed gaze dropped to her mouth she jerked away abruptly, totally panic-stricken.

He sat perfectly still for a full minute and then stood up, moving over to the fire and warming his hands in front of the glowing embers. Her pulses slowly stopped racing and she took a few deep, calming breaths as he kept his broad back to her, beginning to feel ridiculously foolish. He must think I've got the personality of a frightened rabbit, she thought miserably as the long seconds ticked away in the silent room.

'I'll be here at eight on Wednesday evening,' he said blandly at last without turning his head. 'Try and get plenty of sleep and eat sensibly in the meantime; it's easy to neglect your health at a time like this.'

She nodded to his back. 'Yes, all right.'

'Do you need any cash?'

'What?' The question took her completely by surprise.

'I said, do you need any cash?' he said patiently, turning to face her, his face cool and closed.

'No! No, thank you.' She answered instinctively, wanting him to go, and he walked across to the door slowly, making no move to touch her.

'I will see Isobel before I leave.' His voice turned into ice. 'I shall expect her to be gone by the time I return on Wednesday. Have you a friend you can ask to stay with you?'

'Yes; yes, I have,' she answered quickly, although no one sprang to mind. She didn't want anyone anyway; she needed to be alone for a time.

'Goodbye, Nina, till Wednesday.' The door shut firmly, and for a crazy moment she had the impulse to call him back, to ask him to stay. He had the ability to turn her emotions upside-down and round about in a matter of seconds, and she had never felt so confused in all her life.

Isobel left early the next morning, her vitriolic hatred spilling over as she waited in the large hall for the taxi to arrive. 'Goodbye, Isobel.' Nina had held out her hand in farewell but the older woman turned on her like a demented virago.

'Don't you "goodbye, Isobel" me, Miss Pure and Innocent.' The painted mouth had fairly spat the words in Nina's white face. 'Going to marry him, are you, then?' The green eyes narrowed into feline slits. 'Oh, yes, he told me.' She nodded as Nina stared at her, horrified. 'I've got to remove my contaminating presence from his dear bride-to-be. How you managed to pull that off I shall never know—half the women I know have been after him for years.' The thin lips pulled back from her mouth in a bitter sneer. 'They say the quiet ones are the worst, and all the time I thought you were so chaste and untouched.'

Her voice was rising shrilly with each word, and as she screamed out the last sentence the doorbell announcing the arrival of the taxi cut into her anger. She gave Nina one last look of pure venom and then she was gone, the taxi speeding her away to who knew where.

Nina stood leaning against the solid wood of the front door and let out a sigh of enormous relief as her legs began to stop shaking. She was gone. She hadn't realised how the other woman's presence had oppressed her for years.

The little daily had come as usual, clucking like a fat mother hen on finding Nina all alone in the great house. She was owed three months' wages, which constituted a small fortune to the middle-aged Cornishwoman, but she had never even mentioned the fact to Nina before the reading of the will and didn't do so now. 'You can't clean this big house by yourself, my pet,' she admonished Nina firmly. 'Your dear father would never forgive me if I didn't keep an eye on you, especially now that one has gone.' It occurred to Nina that in all the time she had known Mrs Finch she had never heard her refer to Isobel by her name. She kissed the small woman's plump poppy-red cheek gratefully, warmed by her friendship.

The morning of the fifth day dawned grey and misty, an intermittent icy drizzle coating the bleak landscape in a wet shroud. Nina spent a miserable few hours wandering along the cold seashore, the swirling fog turning the coastline into a hazy grey and the small rock-pools into slippy traps. She returned home at lunchtime, soaked to the skin, her stomach a mass of knots as she contemplated the evening ahead.

By mid-afternoon a bitingly cold wind had risen, scattering the swirling fingers of mist and creating a melancholy whispering down the chimney that made Nina shiver. 'Looks as though we're in for a storm,' Mrs Finch said cheerfully, looking up into the leaden sky as she left in the early afternoon's dim light. 'It's cold enough for snow and I thought we'd had it all for this year. I don't like leaving you here by yourself, Miss Nina. Why don't you come home with me for the night?'

'It's OK,' Nina said quietly, squeezing the work-worn hand gently. 'I'm expecting a visitor this evening.'

The little woman nodded, reassured, and disappeared down the long drive where the bare branches of the great trees were bending and creaking in the gathering force of the gale.

By teatime the first fat snowflakes had begun to fall from a dark windy sky, blown in great gusts against the old window-panes. Far from abating, the storm was gathering strength with each passing hour, and Nina found herself peering anxiously into the swirling blackness as she prepared dinner for two in the large warm kitchen.

The lights were flickering ominously now and again, causing her heart to rise into her mouth, and she kept glancing nervously around, hearing strange unfamiliar sounds as the great house steeled itself for the on-slaught. 'Don't be so stupid,' she admonished herself firmly as she pushed the roast lamb into the oven with shaking hands. 'Keep busy.'

Leaving the meat to cook slowly, she sped upstairs, showered and slipped into a loose wool dress in a soft grey, applying the same colour to her eyelids with a light touch of mascara on her thick dark lashes. Her flawless skin needed no cream or powder, and after brushing her hair into a high loose knot on the top of her head she gave a cursory glance in the mirror before returning to check the food.

By nine p.m. she was convinced Steed wasn't coming. A veritable blizzard was raging outside and already great drifts of gleaming snow were piling up against the house, reaching halfway up the huge studded front door.

At ten-thirty p.m. she threw what was left of the charred meat into the bin with the dried-up vegetables and sat down with a weary plop at the kitchen table, bursting into angry, disappointed tears. 'Why didn't you get here, Steed?' she asked the empty room irrationally. Until this moment she hadn't realised how much she had counted on his coming; subconsciously she had accepted his offer the minute he had made it, the logical part of her brain recognising a means of escape from impossible circumstances.

It's just the storm that's prevented him tonight, she told herself firmly, but another part of her mind was asking why he hadn't phoned to let her know he couldn't make it, and she began to feel terribly afraid that he had changed his mind. He had very little to gain from the arrangement, after all—a large, rambling old house he was paying nearly double for, a wife who would not be a wife, and an inexperienced companion for his wards whose salary was exorbitant. For the first time the generosity of his offer really hit home.

When the lights went out Nina knew real, stomach-wrenching fear. 'Come back on; please, please come back on,' she begged out loud into the blackness as slow terror numbed her limbs and her blood sang in her ears. She was incapable of moving from the safety of the kitchen where at least some light from the pure white landscape outside was reflected through the large picture window. Her father had once explained that her inordinate fear of the dark had begun on the night her mother had died, but that was of no comfort now. She felt her flesh begin to crawl and reached for the bottle of wine she had bought specially for this evening. It might give her some sort of courage to get through what was going to be a very long night.

After the first two glasses the darkness didn't seem so bad; in fact, the dim light cast a pleasant glow over the familiar objects in the room. Nina had never liked the taste of alcohol, preferring soft drinks normally, but by the third glass she was wondering why she had never tried it before. The rich, mellow red wine was warming the empty place in her stomach where the spoiled dinner should have been, and she was just thinking she might face the dark, draughty hall after all when a light scratching sound caused her to freeze.

She stared fixedly at the closed kitchen door, and as a muffled bump shook the silence her heart began to pound. As she pulled herself to her feet she was surprised to find her head swimming alarmingly and she nearly fell, but as the dizziness passed she listened intently, relaxing slightly as the only sound she heard was the whining of the wind through the nooks and crannies of the old building.

'It's all right,' she told herself shakily, 'it's only the storm.' For some reason she couldn't seem to get the words past her tongue and a slight feeling of nausea gripped her stomach, but as a distinct creak from the hall rent the silence she stumbled across to the old dresser and fumbled in the drawer for the carving knife, its steel blade bright and sharp. Armed with the vicious-looking knife, she crept over to the door, shrinking against the wall in terrified dread as it slowly began to open.

She remembered reading in a martial-arts journal of her father's that a savage yell as one attacked demoralised the opponent, so as the door swung to one side she gave a blood-curdling shriek and lunged forward at the same time with the rapier-sharp blade.

The tall, dark figure in the doorway leapt two feet in the air, the knife missing his broad chest by a hair's breadth. Swearing fluently, Steed wrenched the weapon from her suddenly nerveless fingers, pulling her back into the kitchen and pushing her limp body down on to a chair. 'What the hell do you think you're playing at?' he snarled, his face contorted in the faint light.

She shook her blonde head helplessly, golden strands falling down about her chalk-white face. 'I'm sorry, I...' Her voice broke and tears flooded down her face, her soft mouth quivering with relief and bewilderment.

Steed gave a muttered exclamation, bending down and drawing her up into his arms, cradling her shaking body against his hard chest. 'You little idiot,' he whispered against the shine of her hair, 'what on earth were you trying to do?'

'Frighten off a burglar,' she sniffed, her sobs subsiding against the rough tweed of his coat, feeling immensely comforted by the big masculine body as a sudden hiccup caught in her throat.

'You did an excellent job,' he replied wryly. 'Who needs a Dobermann if they've got you?' She looked up at him nervously. He was looking down at her with a small smile pulling at the side of his mouth, his eyes tender.

'I think it must have been the wine,' she stammered feebly, slowly becoming aware of his strong arms holding her close and that familiar delicious smell of aftershave on the brown skin. 'I thought you weren't coming, and the lights all went off...' Her voice trailed away as her aching head began to swim again.

He set her back down in the seat abruptly, glancing at the practically empty bottle with narrowed eyes. 'I think a stiff black coffee is in order,' he said drily, 'I know I could do with one.'

'Oh, I'm sorry,' said Nina shakily, trying to gather her wits. 'I'll see to it. You've been out in this awful weather and——'

'Please, just do us both a favour and sit still.' The words were final and she sank back thankfully, her legs peculiarly weak. 'You're going to feel great in the morning.' It didn't sound as if he expected a reply and she couldn't think of one anyway.

'Did Isobel vacate the premises?' His voice was cool as he poured hot water into two porcelain mugs.

'Yes, she went the next day.'

'Who did you get to stay with you, then? Couldn't you have woken them tonight if you were nervous?'

She looked at him warily, taking the mug he offered and sipping the hot liquid gratefully before she replied. He wasn't going to like this and she was suddenly apprehensive of his reaction.

'There's not anyone here.' Her voice faltered as the full glare of the dark eyes was directed straight at her.

'Why not?' His voice was tight.

'I couldn't think of anyone to ask and I wanted some time to think anyway. I'm perfectly all right here and——'

'You don't mean to tell me that you have been living here alone for the last few days?' He shook his black head in disgust. 'You stupid girl. Don't you ever read the newspapers? I could spank you.'

She stared at him, eyes wide with fear as she realised he was furiously angry, his face cold with smouldering rage. 'I specifically told you to contact someone, anyone, and arrange for them to stay. If it comes to that, you could have had one of those aunts round. Anyone is better than no one.' He took a big gulp of hot coffee, holding his hands round the cup. 'Don't you ever disobey me again, Nina. You are allowed one mistake, but only one.' She glanced at him under her eyelashes to see if he was joking, but was disconcerted to see he was deadly serious.

'Look, I'm not a child...' Her protest died as he moved a pace towards her.

'Then stop acting like one. I don't give orders unless they are absolutely necessary, but when I do I expect them to be obeyed—instantly! Do you understand me?' She nodded sulkily. All this fuss!

'You are far too young to be living alone in an isolated house in the middle of nowhere. The village is a good ten minutes' walk away. I know——' his voice was wry '—I've just walked it.' Nina looked at him enquiringly. 'All the roads are blocked for miles. I've left the car in a lay-by somewhere; they'll have to dig it out in the morning.'

He shrugged his coat off wearily, white lines of exhaustion carved deep in his face. 'I seem to be wet through. Is there an old dressing-gown or something I could wear?'

'Of course.' Nina felt guilty she hadn't noticed the state his clothes were in. Her dress felt damp from being pressed against his coat, and she saw now that he was shaking with cold, his face grey and tired.

'We'll have to feel our way upstairs,' she warned as, reeling slightly from the effects of the wine, she led the way to one of the guest bedrooms which had its own *en suite*. The alien blackness didn't seem so unfriendly now Steed was there to share it, although, on her leaving the room after gesturing to the bathrobe and pyjamas she had laid on the bed, tiny prickles of fear trickled down her spine, causing the hairs on the back of her neck to rise. Halfway down the stairs she lost her nerve and sped back up the curving steps, her head thick and muzzy and her legs trembling.

She could hear Steed splashing about in the bathroom when she gingerly peered in the semi-dark room, the brilliance outside causing an eerie glow, familiar objects taking on weird connotations.

'I'm going to wait for you out here,' she called shyly, opening the bathroom door a fraction and dropping the dry clothes through. 'I'll get us both a snack when you've finished.'

The splashing stopped and his deep voice murmured something in reply, but her head was aching painfully and her eyelids were too heavy to hold open any longer. She lay down on the soft bed, dragging the thick, warm quilt round her until she was enmeshed in a cosy cocoon and dropping instantly into a deep sleep.

'Nina, Nina.' She was dragged up from layers of dreamless sleep by someone whispering her name, and became conscious of a warm hand restlessly shaking her back and forth. 'Come on, wake up, woman! How many glasses of that damn stuff did you drink anyway?'

'Don't. Leave me alone.' Her sleepy voice was muffled in the bedclothes and she felt herself being rolled out of the warmth into the stark chill of the night air.

'Come on, Nina, show me your room and then you can get to bed properly and sleep it off.'

As the words sank into her dazed mind she gave a protesting little moan and tried to sit up, but the dizziness swamped her again and she fell back on to the bed with a little giggle. 'I feel funny.'

Steed muttered something under his breath and lifted her into a sitting position, one arm supporting her back as he knelt by the side of the bed. 'Listen to me. I'm going to take you to your room and then you can go to sleep. Which is your room, Nina? Are you listening to me?'

She opened heavy eyes to find his dark face inches away from her own. 'Don't want to go to my room,' she muttered defiantly. 'I want to stay with you.'

'For crying out loud!' He tried to haul her to her feet, but she moved sharply and caught him off balance, causing him to fall beside her on the wide bed.

'Please.' She caught hold of the towelling robe with both hands. 'I don't like the dark. I don't want to be by myself.' She moved closer to him as she spoke, and he stiffened, his deep voice a low growl.

'You don't know what you're asking.'

'Please, Steed.' She rolled to face him in the velvet darkness, her small hands still clutching the front of his robe tightly, bringing her face into line with his. As though in spite of himself, he moved one large hand into the soft fragrance of her tangled hair, coiling the silky strands round his long fingers, while the other pressed into her back, straining her closer to his long shape.

She watched his face breathlessly with clouded eyes, her limbs relaxed and lethargic. His brown skin smelt fresh and soapy-clean from the bath, and with a tingling shock she realised he wasn't wearing the pyjamas as her wandering fingers tangled in the small curling tendrils of hair covering his broad chest. He groaned deep in his throat at her touch and his voice was thick. 'Stop it, Nina. Stop it now, before it's too late.'

She heard him as if in a dream, his low words barely registering in her languorous stupor. 'Please, Steed,' she whispered imploringly, 'don't make me go.'

As his warm lips found her soft mouth she felt small tremors of pleasure begin to shudder down her body, the kiss growing more demanding as he felt her reaction.

Her hands moved involuntarily across the bare chest and his arms tightened, drawing her softness against his hard muscular thighs. He explored her mouth intimately, his scorching lips moving down to kiss the pulse throbbing wildly in her throat.

'Nina.' Her name was a groan on his lips and as his hands slid over the warm rounded curves of her trembling body she moved against him, her heart pounding so hard that she thought it would burst. She felt small ripples in the hard limbs pressed so close to hers and with a small shock of excitement realised he couldn't hide his need of her, his body hardening against hers as he drew her still closer into his rigid shape.

As she felt his hand on the zip of her dress she wriggled against him, her voice a little lost sound in the depths of the bed. 'Steed?'

He suddenly froze, and then his arms pushed her away in quick rejection as he swung his legs over the side of the bed and sat, silently hunched, holding his head in shaking hands.

'Steed?' As she repeated his name he gave a muttered exclamation and moved violently away, his movements stiff and angry, striding across the room and flinging open the wide leaded windows so the icy air flooded in, dispelling any warmth with its cold breath. He stood there for some minutes, starry snowflakes settling on his dark head and shoulders and drifting on to the carpeted floor, before he turned at last to face her.

She had buried deep under the covers again and lay, sick with hot humiliation, horrified at her lack of control. How could she have behaved like that? She writhed under the quilt in twisting mortification, her head swimming and a small lost sob escaping her lips.

'Don't cry.' His voice cracked. 'I'm sorry; it was my fault. Forget about it.' Embarrassment made her dumb as he continued, 'It won't happen again. You have my word on that.' She closed her eyes, sick at heart. It hadn't been his fault; she had to admit the blame was well and truly at her door. The alcohol had anaesthetised her senses until she hadn't had any control over what she was doing. Thank goodness he had stopped.

His voice was stronger as he came over to where she lay, curled into a tight little heap under the quilt. He smoothed back the hair from her hot, wet face, his lean outline in the short robe silhouetted against the grey light. The enormity of what had nearly happened washed over her in a burning wave and she sat up suddenly, pulling the covers tightly round her.

'It's all right, Nina; no harm done.' It was as though he could read her mind.

'I don't know what came over me,' she whispered huskily. 'I've never done anything like that before in my life.'

'Do you think I don't know that?' he said roughly, reaching out to take her hand in a gesture of comfort. She flinched sharply away before she could stop herself, her flushed face tensing as he drove one fist tightly into the palm of his other hand in bitter self-anger.

'Get some rest now.' He stood up and looked down at her, his mouth a tight white line. 'I'll find a few blankets and sleep in the chair.'

'No, I'll go——'

He interrupted her viciously, his tone brutal. 'You are frightened to be alone. There is one bed. I will sleep in the chair. Now, for the sake of my sanity, damn well shut your eyes and go to sleep.'

She said no more, snuggling down under the covers like a scared child, feeling the warmth begin to relax her stiff limbs as he closed the window and prepared a makeshift bed on the big easy chair in the corner of the room. Within minutes she was asleep, her breathing even and regular, but the big figure in the chair sat for hours with his piercing eyes on the small curled body under the mound of covers in the middle of the bed, his cold face a harsh, unreadable mask of pain.

# CHAPTER THREE

NINA awoke early next morning as the deep blackness grew paler and dawn crept stealthily into the room, the birds in the silver birch just beyond the bedroom window singing their welcome to the pale still world outside. A shaft of weak sunlight fell on to her upturned face and she stretched sleepily to find herself entwined in the quilt, her eyes snapping open as the events of the previous night rushed in on her with sickening clarity.

She glanced across the room to the far corner, where Steed was swathed in blankets like an Egyptian mummy, sitting slumped awkwardly, fast asleep in the chair, the heap of blankets making him appear curiously vulnerable. The austere grim features were softened in slumber, and already his face was dark with stubble.

She felt a small pang in her heart region as she looked at him. How could she face him after last night? He could have taken her then and he knew it, and yet he had pulled back before things had gone too far. Why? Her smooth brow wrinkled. She had only had two other boyfriends since that first encounter with Steed at sixteen, two fresh-faced lads from the village who had both driven her mad with their constant desire to kiss and touch her. Neither had lasted beyond a month, and she had never met anyone who remotely stirred her blood, except... She looked again at the silent figure in the chair. What was it about him? Just seeing his face caused her breath to catch in her throat.

She hated him. The silent voice in her head was determined. He had used her and hurt her all those years ago, mocking her innocence and making scars that had taken a long time to heal.

She carefully climbed out of the bed and crept over to the door cautiously; she desperately needed to have a shower and wash her hair before she spoke to him again. She needed to feel in control.

'That smells absolutely delicious.' Steed's voice was warm with approval, causing her to jump away from the kitchen window, where she had been gazing into the white fairyland outside that the tiny snowflakes had created, while the rashers of bacon spluttered merrily under the grill and three large eggs cooked in the frying-pan. 'You aren't just a pretty face, then?'

Nina flushed nervously, aware he was teasing her but uncertain of how to respond to this big, intimate stranger. 'I love cooking,' she said quietly. 'I've done most of the meals here since I was about ten. Isobel hated it so I just carried on after she came.' She didn't raise her eyes to his, keeping them fixed on the view just outside the window, where the stately trees were clothed in pure bridal splendour, their branches illuminated against the pearly grey sky.

'It hasn't been easy for you, has it?' Steed remarked gently as he seated himself at the kitchen table. Even in her father's old pyjamas and dressing-gown, and with his face unshaven, he was still the most devastating man she had ever seen.

'I'm fine. Dad was wonderful to me and I didn't really need anyone else,' Nina said quickly, her tone defensive. 'He enabled me to do what I really wanted most of the time, which is to paint. The housekeeping just fitted in.'

Steed looked at her consideringly. 'I know how Tom felt about you, Nina. He thought he was acting for the best, keeping you from the big, bad world out there. He knew I thought he had overdone the protective-father bit, so I'm not telling you anything I haven't told him in the past.'

She flushed miserably. Isobel's cruel gibes over the years had made her super-sensitive to any criticism of her father, however oblique.

'I liked things the way they were,' she repeated stubbornly.

'Sure, you did.' His voice was conciliatory. 'Nevertheless, you never had anything else to compare it to except this tiny corner of the world.'

His brooding presence seemed to fill the room as she served him breakfast, his dark face making her all fingers and thumbs. Sitting down opposite him with her own plate, she became excruciatingly aware of the intimacy of the moment, her throat constricting until she was unable to eat, simply moving the food around on her plate, hoping he wouldn't notice.

'I'm not going to jump on you.' His voice was grim, all tenderness gone, and as she glanced up sharply she met his taciturn gaze, his grey eyes stormy.

'I'm just not hungry,' she lied unsteadily, and he smiled mockingly, standing up and moving to the door.

'You're a poor liar, Nina, unlike most of the other women I know.' His face was tight. 'We've got a few things to sort out this morning, so while I get dressed you can make us another pot of coffee, and for crying out loud try and relax.' He glanced at her white face. 'You're making this whole thing a lot harder for both of us.'

She reflected on his words as she deftly cleared away the breakfast dishes and put the coffee on to percolate, her actions mechanical. She had to admit Steed was right. Her nerves felt like jangled wires, stretched so tight that they could snap at any moment. 'It's understandable,' she said to the bright-eyed robin who had come for his usual breakfast crusts from the kitchen window. 'Dad dying like that and the shock of all the debts...what does he expect?' And yet she knew it was more than that. Her whole being seemed to be waiting for something, but what, she didn't know.

She badly needed some time in her father's studio, where she could lose herself in her work. The big untidy room at the top of the house had been a haven in the past from which to escape Isobel's sharp tongue, its magnificent full-length windows giving a panoramic view over the smooth lawns and wild unkempt garden beyond, stretching down to the cliff's edge and the beautiful Cornish coastline in the distance.

'Coffee ready?' The firm male footsteps on the polished wooden floor of the hall had made her stomach turn over, and as she turned to face Steed, who was standing in the doorway, she felt suddenly light-headed, whether from emotion or lack of food she wasn't sure.

His face was still dark with unshaven stubble but glowing from a vigorous wash, his curling black hair damp from the shower. He was casually dressed in a thick Aran jumper and dark trousers, the latter stained at the bottom with a tide-mark of damp. 'Oh, I'm sorry.' Nina flushed. 'I should have dried your clothes properly, or found you some of Dad's.'

'I don't think Tom's clothes would fit me,' he said in his deep voice, and as Nina's eyes swept down the powerful muscled body she flushed still deeper, remembering how his hardness had felt against her soft flesh.

'I'd appreciate the use of a razor, though,' he continued, touching his chin thoughtfully. 'I grow a beard overnight but I didn't like to touch your father's personal possessions without permission.'

Nina nodded, amazed at his sensitivity. It didn't fit in with her memories. Some of her surprise must have shown in her face because he moved swiftly to where she stood like a sleek jungle cat, placing his hands on her slim shoulders, his face dark with anger.

'OK, let's have it, Nina. You seem to think I'm some sort of monster. Has Isobel been telling stories about me? Is that it?'

She shook her head defensively, her face troubled. 'No. I don't know anything about you—that's half the trouble.' What the other half was even she couldn't define.

He nodded slowly, his taut face relaxing and the grey eyes losing their chill. 'Yes, I can accept that. Well, we've got some catching up to do, it would seem, but before that I want to know the answer to the proposition I put to you the last time I was here. Have you reached a decision?'

Now the fateful moment was here it seemed remarkably simple. 'Yes,' she said calmly, her large liquid eyes fixed on his tense face, feeling an enormous sense of relief and a sudden instinctive assurance that her answer was the only one possible. She knew beyond doubt it would have been what her father had wanted.

His face was cold, his expression blank as though he was holding himself in check with iron resolve. 'Yes, you have reached a decision, or yes, you have agreed to my suggestion?' he asked smoothly.

'Yes, I would like to marry you,' she replied softly, intimidated by his coolness, and as his face remained a remote mask she added politely, 'Thank you for asking me.'

For a swift transient moment the mask slipped and something gleamed in the heavy-lidded eyes that frightened her, a burning raw hunger that was all-encompassing, but then it was gone so quickly that, she told herself afterwards, she must have imagined it. He seemed quite unaffected by her reply after all, moving away immediately to stand staring out of the window at the frozen still world outside for long minutes before turning slowly and casually reaching for his coffee-cup, still quite silent.

'So,' he said tersely when the silence was beginning to scream, 'it's up to me now to make sure you don't regret your decision. We will take it from here.'

As Nina padded along the soft white sands towards the small secluded cove she had found the previous day the fierce Spanish sun beat down, its brilliance reflected in a myriad dancing tiny waves that rolled gently on to the sun-baked shore. Stooping to pick up a particularly large and beautiful shell that lay in her path, its luminous mother-of-pearl interior gleaming in the light, she reflected for the tenth time that day on Steed's generosity and the power of his wealth that had placed her in this enchanted corner of the world.

Events had happened with breathtaking swiftness from the moment she had accepted his offer. His private helicopter had landed in the grounds that same day, and within hours Nina was installed in an elegantly furnished suite at a wildly expensive hotel in the heart of London. The deep, thick white carpet, dusky pink silk lamps and ornate furniture had taken her breath away as she nervously entered the penthouse accompanied by Steed and the manager of the hotel, who was almost falling over himself in his efforts to please. 'It meets with your approval?' Steed's voice was suave and unimpressed.

'It's lovely.' With a tremendous effort she made her voice firm and unemotional, and a spark of approval flared briefly in the hard grey eyes watching her every move.

'My flat is just round the corner and I eat most of my meals in the excellent restaurant downstairs. It would be convenient for you to stay here while the arrangements are completed, but if it is not to your liking...?'

'It's fine.' She just wanted to be left alone. The speed and efficiency with which Steed was controlling her life had left her weak and trembling, with a faint sense of rebellion beginning to stir deep inside. He remained coldly distant all day, his face steely whenever he had met her troubled gaze as though he was already regretting his amazing proposition.

The next few days consisted of numerous shopping trips. Steed insisted on a complete new wardrobe and even a gruelling session with a top beautician, who crisply assured her that a short bob was just what madam's hair needed. She asserted herself more vigorously than tactfully at this point, leaving the beautician mortally offended and Steed shaking with silent laughter all the way back to the hotel, where he gravely informed her he wouldn't have let her hair be cut anyway.

'What do you mean, *you* wouldn't let it be cut?' Her small chin stuck out angrily. 'I decide how I want my hair. You might be buying all these clothes and things, but you aren't buying me.' The words hung in the air, stark and ugly, and she turned away rebelliously, suddenly sick at heart.

He strolled over slowly to where she stood, a strange expression in the steel-grey eyes, and gently turned her to face him. 'If I want your hair left long it will be left long—make no mistake about that.' His voice was splinter-cold. 'You have entered into this agreement entirely of your own volition, and until such time as it is completed you will consider my opinion in every small thing that affects you, as I will do with you. It's a two-way thing. Do you understand me, Nina? I don't want to have to repeat myself.'

She stared up into the handsome, menacing face, her hair turned into spun gold in the bright artificial light, her violet eyes shadowed with anger and exhaustion, and nodded wearily.

That night over dinner in the quiet candle-lit restaurant he silently slipped a heavy antique ring on to the third finger of her left hand, his touch sending needle-sharp tremors up her arm. The ring felt too heavy for her small hand and as she gazed in wonderment at the intricate design, heavily encrusted with tiny rubies, pearls and diamonds, he briefly explained it was a family heirloom. 'But it's too valuable,' she protested, her eyes wide with shock and the growing realisation that she was really committed to this volatile, bewildering man. 'You've done so much for me already, I can't wear this. I don't need a ring——'

He interrupted her violently, his voice biting as he read the panic in her eyes. 'To all intents and purposes, you will be my wife shortly. It will be expected that you wear the Charlton ring, and wear it you will. Most women would jump at the chance to flaunt such a trophy.'

'I'm not most women.'

'That you certainly aren't, my little sleeping beauty. Who is going to be the prince who wakes you, I wonder? Whoever he is, he's going to have a long wait for the next seven years.' His voice was savage.

'W-what have I done?' she asked unsteadily, feeling time in his company was like walking blind through a minefield.

He muttered something under his breath, his dark face bitter. 'You haven't done anything,' he said at last, taking a deep breath and running a hand distractedly through his crisp hair. 'I'm not renowned for my patience, and it's been wearing thin over the last few years.'

'I don't understand.'

'Maybe it's just as well you don't,' he replied grimly, changing the subject and letting the moment pass.

Later that evening as they shared a pot of coffee in the quietness of her suite Steed talked of his family and business interests, the two intrinsically linked through the chain of shops first his grandfather and then his father had opened. As he described the extent of his empire Nina felt herself grow cold. She had had no idea he was so wealthy or moved in such exalted circles as he was portraying. How was she going to cope with all this?

She rubbed trembling fingers across her pale face and, seeing her distress, he caught her hands in his own, his hard face tender. 'Don't worry. It will all work out. You won't meet anyone until I feel you can handle it.'

'I don't know if you can wait that long.' She tried a wobbly smile, tears of exhaustion and fear held at bay by sheer will-power.

'I can wait.' The smile had gone and his face was deadly serious. 'I've had a lot of practice.' He was talking in riddles again, but somehow it didn't matter, as time seemed to stop and the room took on an expectant stillness. She gazed uneasily into the hard-boned face inches from her own, and when the kiss came it was gentle and light, his arms protecting rather than possessive. Her soft lips quivered under his and warm pleasure invaded her tired body as the kiss deepened, his mouth more intent, parting her lips and sending shivers of delight trembling down her spine.

'So fresh and beautiful.' His voice was a murmur against her soft skin and she sighed fleetingly, her eyes closed, wanting the moment to go on forever, feeling wonderfully comforted and safe. His hands wandered caressingly over her back, drawing her gently closer into his hard body until she could feel every inch of him against the softness of her shape.

'This is driving me mad...' His voice was such a deep whisper that she couldn't quite catch what he had muttered into the hollow of her throat, but he straightened suddenly, moving her carefully away, stroking her hair lightly as he did so.

'You're exhausted. I've worn you out with all the excursions over the last few days.' His voice was rueful.

'I'm fine.' She raised dazed eyes to his, aware she hadn't wanted the embrace to finish, amazed at the security and peace she had felt in his arms.

'You're more tired than you know. I've been a fool to press you so hard on top of all the emotional upheaval of the last few weeks. Get some rest now, and we'll have to think about a short break in the sun before you meet the twins.'

After he had left she undressed and climbed into bed, asleep the moment her head touched the pillow, unaware that it was the first night thoughts of her father and her old life hadn't pulled at her heartstrings in the last moments before sleep.

The shrill persistence of the telephone awoke her late the next morning and as she padded swiftly into the lounge area she noticed with surprise that it was snowing heavily outside, tiny patterned stars crystallising the huge glass window that looked out on to half of London.

'Miss Kirkton?' The cool, superior voice of Steed's private secretary flowed down the line, well-modulated and expressionless. Nina had met her briefly on the day she had arrived in London when Carol had brought some important papers to the hotel for Steed to sign, and had felt immediately intimidated by the other woman's cold, immaculate blonde beauty. She had been the epitome of the well-dressed, cool businesswoman, beautifully turned out and perfectly in control.

'Mr Charlton asked me to call you this morning. He would have spoken to you himself but he was called away to Germany urgently in the early hours. A project he has been handling for some time has developed a few teething troubles.' The clear voice was smooth and bland, but Nina sensed, as she had done when they had met, that the secretary didn't like her much, that she resented her sudden arrival in Steed's life.

'He has asked me to arrange for you to be flown to his villa in Spain this afternoon. A taxi will call for you at three p.m. to take you to the airport with your tickets, Spanish currency and other information, and you will be met at the other end by one of Mr Charlton's employees, a man called Lopaz.' The voice was slightly tighter as she continued, 'Mr Charlton will telephone you at the villa tonight, and hopes to join you direct from Germany in a few days.'

By nightfall that same day she was transported into a different world...

* * *

The white heat began to penetrate the enormous straw hat Nina had pulled on as protection against the sun's powerful rays, and she straightened up slowly, dropping the large conical shell into the striped beach-bag slung across her shoulder. Shading her eyes with one hand, she gazed along the deserted stretch of pale white sand, the sapphire-blue sea and brilliantly clear sky like a picture postcard, beautifully unreal.

Once established in the tiny cove cut into the cliff face, she spread out the huge, thick beach-towel and methodically stroked sun-cream on to every inch of visible flesh, determined to make the most of the unusual heat wave that had started the day after her arrival. The heat was bouncing off the warm rocks behind her and creating a perfect sun-trap.

'This is the life,' she muttered lazily to herself, the attraction of basking in warm sunshine after the snow and storms she had left behind in England too good to resist. It was just a minute's walk from Steed's villa down a winding cliff path to the vast empty beach below.

Yawning sleepily, Nina rolled languidly over on to her stomach, shutting her eyes, her wandering mind reviewing the events of the last few days. She had been met at the busy airport by Lopaz as arranged, and he had explained on the ride back to the villa that he and his wife Maria kept house for Steed, his wife taking care of the housekeeping and cooking, while he was employed as gardener and odd-job man. 'Is very good,' he said smilingly, showing all the gaps in his discoloured teeth. 'The *señor*, he treat us like his family. Is very good.'

After leaving the noisy, hot confines of the terminal the low powerful car that Lopaz drove with such childish pride ate up the miles in quiet luxury. They passed tiny, sun-baked villages and small bustling towns, carefully tended olive groves and sprawling orchards, and then Lopaz turned into the slumbering hills where only the occasional large house, shuttered behind great stone walls and leafy trees, could be glimpsed.

Dusk fell as they finally drove up the short drive to the villa, and Nina's first glimpse of the house was masked by the velvet scented darkness. She was aware of thick stone walls, whitewashed in the inevitable Spanish tradition, and wide latticed windows surrounded by foliage, but was too mentally and physically tired to do more than pay lip-service to the delicious meal Maria had waiting, falling into the wide, soft bed that was waiting for her with her mind a mass of confused vivid images and colours.

The next day the full beauty of this occasional home of Steed's overwhelmed her with its natural grace. 'You come and see it all,' Maria encouraged after she had finished serving breakfast. 'I show you everything.'

She realised she had subconsciously been expecting a brash modern villa, but the huge old house set in a slight hollow in the hills was at least a hundred years old, surrounded by tall whispering pines that trailed their way right down the cliff path a hundred yards away on to the magnificent silky white sands of the deserted beach.

The interior was in keeping with the wonderful timelessness of the place. Marble floors covered with soft hand-woven rugs, ornate and delicate furniture with deep buttoned silken upholstery and white walls covered with exquisite paintings of such variety that Nina was awestruck. 'The *señor*, he like to have beautiful things,' Maria said proudly as she saw Nina's wide eyes. 'He collect the paintings for many years now.' With a sudden jolt of shock Nina saw one of her father's pictures in a prominent alcove, then another, then another. A sketch here, a portrait there—she recognised more of her father's work as she wandered from room to room, her eyes filling with tears as she realised Steed had valued her father highly.

The scents of summer permeated the high sunlit rooms; besides the terracotta pots holding a profusion of sweet-smelling flowers, Nina noticed intricately carved wooden bowls placed strategically in small nooks and crannies, their contents of dried flowers and herbs expelling a rich perfume into the warm air.

'This is all so lovely, Maria,' she breathed to the little plump woman who was red with pride, obviously delighted by Nina's enthusiasm.

'You know Señor Steed was born here? That this is his first home?'

'No, I didn't,' Nina replied in amazement, and Maria went on to explain that Steed's Spanish mother and American father had been visiting her parents on holiday when his mother had unexpectedly gone into labour, producing Steed in one of the bedrooms upstairs. Nina listened, spellbound, as the small woman rambled on, her wandering tongue giving Nina a rare insight into the complicated character of the new master of Grayfields...

'Well, and what juicy morsel do we have here?' The light, mocking male voice brought Nina abruptly out of the semi-doze she had fallen into and she sat up sharply, momentarily disorientated. Her blonde head collided with that of the tall, lean man kneeling at her side, and he collapsed on the hot sand, rubbing his nose ruefully.

'Steed said you knocked 'em for six, but I didn't realise he meant literally.'

'You know Steed?' She observed the young man warily, her head ringing where it had hit his. He was incredibly handsome, his fair straight hair cut long and sleek into his neck, and the blue eyes that were holding her own in an amused inspection were a deep dark azure, their brilliance breathtaking.

'I'm James.' As her expression remained blank he grimaced slightly. 'James, Steed's cousin. Don't tell me my big cousin hasn't told you all about wicked old me?'

'I don't think he's mentioned you,' Nina said uncertainly, not wishing to offend this smiling stranger.

He threw back his smooth blond head and laughed, his tanned skin reflecting the golden glare of the sun. 'Oh, you'd remember if he'd mentioned me. I'm what's known as the black sheep in the estimable Charlton family.' His full mouth curved into a hard smile. 'I prefer to spend money rather than make it.'

'There's nothing wrong with that as long as it's your own money you're spending,' Nina said drily as their blue eyes met and held. His glance narrowed and his eyes swept over her slim form again with growing respect.

'I wondered what the female would be like who finally managed to bag old Steed. You haven't disappointed me.'

'I can rest content, then.' Her voice was mildly sarcastic.

He laughed again but without taking his vivid blue eyes from her face. 'Or did *he* bag *you*, I wonder? What makes me think you just might be different from all the rest?'

'I've no idea.' Nina felt hot anger permeating her body, and turned from his mocking gaze to pull on the cotton top she had discarded earlier. The insolent blue gaze had seemed to undress her.

'I've upset you.' His voice was faintly apologetic. At twenty-two, James Kent was hopelessly spoilt, used to unquestioning devotion from a succession of eager young women attracted as much by his easy wealth as the unusual good looks. Not particularly bright, he found it simpler to enjoy life with an ever-ready stream of companions than to make any effort to work. His doting mother idolised his every action, and his father had long since washed his hands of his wayward son, concentrating on James's older brother to take over the family business that Steed's father had helped to launch before his death. It suited James admirably; he expected little of life beyond amusement and adulation.

'Yes, you have upset me, as it happens.' Nina looked him straight in the eye, her face straight. 'I'm not used to your particular brand of rudeness.'

He straightened up, his mouth falling open in amazement, incredulity written all over the classical features. He clearly wasn't used to plain talking, especially from the opposite sex.

'I think I've been severely reprimanded.' His voice held a note of childish surprise. 'I apologise if I've spoken out of turn.'

'Forget it.'

'No.' He caught hold of her arm with his hand as she turned away, her face aloof. 'I meant it. I really am sorry if I hurt your feelings. My tongue runs away with me at times; it doesn't mean anything.'

Her heart-shaped face lit up in a warm smile, causing the man sitting by her side to catch his breath suddenly. 'Shall we start again, then? I'm Nina.' She stretched out her hand.

'How do you do, Nina? I'm James.' He gravely shook the small hand, surveying her through his thick golden lashes, his expression indiscernible.

The next day Nina awoke with a strange sense of expectancy and lay for a moment in the wide, soft bed, trying to marshall her thoughts. She had enjoyed James's company yesterday during the remainder of the day, and it had been pleasant to have someone to share the evening meal with instead of sitting in remote splendour at the huge polished dining table. He was an amusing companion, his easy charm and quick wit causing the hours to fly by, and he had seemed boyishly determined to remain in her good graces. And yet... She paused in her reflections. There was something... something she couldn't quite put her finger on.

He had begged to take her sightseeing today, and she stretched lazily under the pale silk covers, the shadowed room already warm in the morning light. Bright rays of sunlight slanted in through the wooden shutters, dancing over her sleepy face and causing her to bury her head in the deep scented pillows.

She didn't hear the soft knock at the door and started violently as a warm, hard hand touched her shoulder. 'Nina? I've brought you a cup of tea. We were going to make an early start, remember?'

James looked down at the slim shape partially hidden under the thin covers, his eyes licking over her body swiftly as she pulled the sheet up to her chin.

'James, get out.' Her voice was tight and her eyes were blazing. 'This is my bedroom, for goodness' sake. Maria brings me a cup of tea in the mornings, as you well know. What will she think?'

'Does it matter?' His eyes were narrowed.

'Yes, it does. I'll be downstairs in a few minutes. Please, James.' He didn't move, his face stubborn.

'If you don't get out in thirty seconds flat you can forget the sightseeing.' Her voice was as cold as ice and he seemed to realise at last that she meant what she said. He left the room reluctantly, and as soon as the heavy oak door closed behind him Nina flew across and pushed the stiff old bolt into place. Perhaps this sightseeing trip wasn't such a good idea after all, she mused under the shower as the warm water washed the last traces of weariness from her golden-brown limbs. She hadn't missed the predatory gleam in his eyes as his glance had swept over her. Still, it must be all right. Steed had allowed him to come here, knowing she was alone. He must have known he could trust his cousin?

She still felt faintly uneasy as she dressed quickly in a thin blue cotton sundress, the deep hue of the material turning her eyes into dark pools. It seemed strange that Steed had encouraged James to entertain her in his absence, but James had been adamant last night. 'Steed's coming later in the week, as you know,' he had smiled cheerfully at dinner. 'He says we can use the Mercedes so I can show you a bit of the real Spain. It'll be a nice day out.'

He was waiting for her as she came downstairs, a picnic hamper already prepared by a frowning Maria, which James went to load in the car.

'Is anything wrong, Maria?' Nina asked as the small woman merely nodded a cool reply to her 'good morning' and made to disappear into the kitchen at the back of the house.

'Is not right, *señorita*. Is not right.'

'What isn't right?' Nina could feel the agitation coming off the little woman in waves; her plump red cheeks were fairly quivering with indignation.

'For you to go out with Señor James like this. Señor Steed, he would not like it. His cousin is a...a plaything, I think it is?'

'A playboy.' Nina's voice was flat.

'*Si*, *si*, a playboy. He does not have the respect in his heart that makes him a suitable escort for you.'

'But, Maria,' Nina said gently, 'Steed knows that James is here. If he were at all concerned he would come himself, wouldn't he? I'm sure it's all right. We are just going for a day's sightseeing, and we'll be back well before dark.'

'I wouldn't bank on that.' James's voice sounded from the open doorway. 'I was thinking of rounding off with dinner at a nice little place I know down by the waterfront at Lambardia.'

'We'll be back before dark,' Nina repeated firmly, throwing him a warning glance. He really was strikingly handsome as he stood nonchalantly, framed in the arched doorway, his smooth blond head turned into a white halo in the sun's light and his dark blue eyes insolent as he glared at Maria. How much of their conversation he had heard, Nina wasn't sure.

They prepared to leave immediately after a light breakfast. The sun was a white ball in the clear blue sky and already it was warm enough to sunbathe, Nina thought longingly. The scent of pine trees mingled with the sweet heavy perfume of the dog roses entwined on the old stone wall which formed part of the garages at the back of the house, and as Nina waited for James to bring the car out she breathed in the rich warm air appreciatively, her eyes closed and head uplifted to the glare of the sun.

'You look like one of the vestal virgins with your eyes closed and your hair hanging down your back like that,' James remarked as he drew up by her side, the dark blue Mercedes purring gently. 'It's incredibly erotic.'

'Really?' She folded herself gracefully into the plush leather seat, her voice coldly dismissive.

'Are you, then, or has Steed already claimed the prize?'

'What?' She had lost the thread of the conversation and glanced enquiringly at his eager face, the vivid blue eyes bright and sharp and his tongue licking his lower lip.

'Are you a virgin?' He gestured insultingly.

'Right, James, that is it!' She unbuckled her seatbelt and opened the car door in one movement, furiously angry. 'I don't know what sort of company you are used to keeping and I care even less, but I am not used to this sort of conversation and I won't tolerate what I don't have to.' She glared at him through the open window, slamming the door with unnecessary force. 'You are a total pain.'

She marched back into the house, crossly ignoring his angry voice calling her name. How dared he? Jumped-up little upstart! Just because he was used to every female he met falling at his feet—well, he left her stone-cold! She stopped abruptly in the doorway, amazed at her train of thought crystallised by her fury. She really did find him totally unattractive; he was so different from his cousin.

Steed's image swam before her eyes and she felt suddenly hungry for his presence, the dark, cold face and big masculine body vivid in her imagination. What was the matter with her? Her cheeks burnt with hot colour. She didn't even like him, did she? It was a business arrangement they were entering into. He needed the house as a secure base for his wards, and she needed financial solvency. He wasn't even interested in her as a wife. James had intimated last night several times that Steed had had many women friends, preferring uncomplicated relationships, with no animosity on either side when they burnt themselves out. No doubt countless women found him irresistible—he would be able to take his pick. 'Stop it, Nina.' She spoke out loud, her thoughts racing.

The harsh screech of burning tyres brought her back to the present as James flashed past her in the Mercedes, driving far too fast down the short tree-lined drive. She caught a glimpse of his face, dark with anger, and then he was gone in a swirl of red dust and blue metal.

Her father would have disliked that young man intensely. Her eyes shadowed with grief as she walked back into the house, pausing in the wide square hall as Maria caught hold of her arm excitedly. She had been rattling away in rapid Spanish on the telephone and now passed the receiver over to Nina with a delighted expression on her perspiring face.

'Is Señor Steed.'

'Hello, Nina?' To her surprise she felt her legs shaking as the familiar deep, rich voice came down the line.

'Hello, Steed; I nearly missed you.' Her voice sounded squeaky.

'So I gather.' His voice was cool and guarded. 'I understand James is there with you?'

'Well, you knew that already, didn't you?' Nina replied. 'He said he's spoken to you.'

'He did speak to me.' The tone was dry in the extreme. 'As far as I was aware, we had arranged to meet up together at the weekend and travel down then. He knew I'd got delayed here. He was going to spend the weekend with us and then meet some friends next week.'

'Oh.' Nina's voice was small. Maria had been right.

'Maria tells me you are going out for the day.'

'Not exactly.' Now Nina's voice was guarded. She had the distinct impression Steed was holding his temper at bay with some considerable effort.

'What do you mean, not exactly? Are you going out for the day with my cousin or not?'

'Not.'

'Look, Nina,' his voice was getting frostier and more irritated by the moment, 'this is one hell of an expensive phone call, I'm in the middle of a million-pound take-over that has developed a headache, and I haven't got time to play games. What's going on? Let me speak to James—perhaps he'll make sense.'

'You can't.'

The silence at the other end of the phone was deafening. 'He's not here,' Nina rushed on. 'We had a slight disagreement and he's gone off in the car.'

'My car?' This was getting worse every second. She said nothing.

'What did you argue about?'

'We didn't exactly argue.'

'Nina!' The word was a pistol shot and she nearly dropped the telephone in fright, glancing in helpless appeal at Maria, who was standing to one side of the hall, her brown face troubled.

'He just made a remark I didn't like, that's all. It didn't mean anything.' Her voice was shaking.

'Which was?' His voice brooked no dissent.

'He asked me if I was a virgin.' There was fluent and volatile swearing, and then she heard him apologising to someone in the background, his voice muted.

'Nina?' His voice was sharp. 'When my cousin returns from his jaunt in *my* car—which, incidentally, he is not insured for—you will ask him to leave immediately. Do you understand me?'

'I can't, Steed.' Her voice was weak. 'This is not my home and he's your cousin. I can't——'

'Nina!' Her name was barked down the line and echoed in her ear. 'I'm not suggesting that you do it, I'm telling you! You order him to go.'

'I can't.' Her voice was flat. 'How can I——?'

'Put Maria on.'

Nina handed the telephone to Maria, who took it gingerly, as though it were going to bite her. Although their conversation was conducted in Maria's native tongue, it didn't need a genius to interpret Steed's instructions to his housekeeper, whose round face became more and more upset. By the time the call was finished both women felt weak at the knees and Maria was nearly crying, her plump cheeks wobbling with agitation.

Lopaz wandered in from the garden behind the garages, where he had been tending the flowerbeds, and Maria collapsed on his small stocky frame, her voice growing shriller and shriller as she explained the morning's events. He took them both through to the kitchen, poured two mugs of strong coffee and then disappeared into the garden again, almost at a run.

They drank the strong liquorice-tasting coffee in subdued silence, each lost in her own thoughts, and then Maria leant across the spotlessly scrubbed wooden table and took Nina by the hand, her face warm with understanding.

'The *señor*, he is missing you. It is not nice for Señor James to come here. He is not a good boy.'

Nina nodded in quiet agreement—he certainly was not a good boy.

'I will make it OK.' Maria's black head bobbed reassuringly as she spoke. 'You spend the day here, in the garden?'

Nina nodded again, hugging the small Spanish woman impulsively as she left the shining kitchen. Wandering upstairs, she collected a book from her bedroom and returned downstairs to find Maria already busy at work, her capable brown hands deftly rolling paper-thin pastry.

'Go, go.' The housekeeper gestured smilingly to the garden door. 'You sit in the sun.' As Nina stepped into the white sunlight the heat settled on her like a warm blanket. The large gardens were meticulously well kept, the regimented flowerbeds and smooth green lawns beautifully tended under the tall, still pine trees.

Further away from the house in a small incline out of the wind, a tiny orchard sat drowsing in the warmth, surrounded by thick stone walls mellowed with age. The wiry grass was long and unkempt under the bent old trees, threaded with tiny forget-me-nots and perky little daisies, and it was here Nina made for, spreading out the old rug she had brought with her and lying back with a contented little sigh in the perfumed golden air. She could hear the distant whisper of the sea and a slight murmur in the pines, the odd lazy insect droning from flower to flower; otherwise it was blissfully quiet and peaceful.

She spent the day alternately reading and drowsing under the shady trees, returning briefly to the house to eat the cold lunch Maria had prepared, carrying the dessert of fresh black grapes and juicy red cherries back to her little hidey-hole. The air was growing cooler, although it was still pleasantly warm, and Maria informed her a storm was expected to end the unusual hot spell. The few days in the sun had tinted her silky skin a rich honey-brown, lightening her blonde hair and smoothing away the constant look of anxiety on her face.

She was awakened from deep slumber in the late afternoon by a light kiss on her mouth, and opened heavy eyes to see James's carefully smiling face a few inches from her own. Mauve shadows were lengthening under the trees, and birds were beginning to call evensong in the cypresses and pines preparing for the velvet night ahead.

'Sorry, Nina.' He spoke before she could order her thoughts, his face watchful. 'I keep forgetting you aren't one of Steed's normal little "friends".' There it was again, that subtle spiteful innuendo regarding Steed's love-life.

'Leave Steed out of this, please.' His eyes narrowed at her tone as she sat up, smoothing her dress over her knees. 'Has Maria spoken to you?'

'I haven't seen Maria. Why?'

She looked into the confident young face before her, seeing the weakness and vanity normally concealed by the classically fine features. 'Steed phoned after you'd gone this morning. He isn't too thrilled with you.'

James shrugged, but not before she had noticed the look of fear flash over his face, swiftly masked. 'So, tell me something new!'

'Why did you tell me he knew you were here when it wasn't true? What was the point?'

'Maybe I couldn't wait to see the wonder-woman who had snared my dear cousin.' His voice was still playful but with an underlying nastiness that made Nina suddenly realise the orchard was a long way from the house.

'Don't you like Steed?' She tried to keep her voice neutral. She had been right when she'd felt something was wrong with this handsome young man; there was something quite menacing in those bright blue eyes. A tiny shiver trickled down her spine. An original human chameleon.

'Not particularly.' His gaze wandered away from hers and he stood looking out towards the darkening coastline, just visible through a break in the pines, his profile like that of a magnificent Greek statue. 'But then there are very few people I do have any affection for.' A slight breeze ruffled the pale hair.

'Why not? What's happened to make you feel like that?'

He brought his eyes back to her with visible effort, his thoughts lost in a cloudy past that made his face alarmingly hard. 'Happened?' He laughed coldly. 'Nothing much has happened to me. If you're looking for a dramatic story, forget it. My life has been a succession of nannies, tutors and then boarding-school. What you see before you now has been shaped and moulded by people paid to look after me. Some of them were kind, and some not so kind.' He shrugged. 'It didn't do my brother any harm, so why should I complain? I can look after myself. I take what I want now.'

'All children are different,' Nina said quietly, her heart swamped with pity for the mixed-up young man in front of her. He was like a blighted fruit, beautiful on the outside but marred within.

He intuitively sensed her sympathy and was quick to capitalise on it. Kneeling quickly by her side in one fluid movement, he took her hands in his own before she realised what was happening. 'Don't shut me out,' he said softly, his blue eyes beguiling. 'Let's be friends.'

'I don't want to shut you out, James.' Nina kept her voice calm and cool. 'Of course we can be friends, but let's go back to the house for now and have some dinner.' The swiftly encroaching dusk had enfolded them in intimate solitude, and Nina felt a prickle of panic shiver down her spine. She should have moved away while they were talking.

'You do like me, don't you?' He sounded like a small boy, and with a dart of fear Nina realised the playboy exterior housed a disturbed soul within. A glint of red glowed deep in his eyes, and although his expression hadn't changed he suddenly seemed like a different person.

'Of course I like you.' She struggled to stand, but he was holding her arms in a vice-like grip.

'Prove it, then.' They both knew what he meant. He ran his tongue over his lips, his eyes unblinking.

'Don't be silly, James. Let me go. Steed won't like this.' It was the wrong approach. At the mention of his cousin's name he flushed scarlet, then paled, his eyes running like live things over her body. With one deft movement he flung himself on top of her, still holding her arms in a steel grip, toppling her backwards on to the rug. She began to kick and twist against his superior weight, jerking her head from side to side as his wet lips sought her mouth.

'Don't fight it. You know you want me really; they all do.' As his mouth found hers she felt a wave of hot revulsion cause her stomach to clench, and lashed out with her legs wildly. They found their mark. He gasped deep in his throat and his grip lessened for a fraction of time, his face falling away from hers.

'Steed!' Her despairing cry rang out into the still night, causing a mad fluttering of wings in the branches around them, and then James's hand came across her mouth and nose, stopping her air supply.

'Bitch.' The flat tone was venomous, all the more chilling in its quietness. Her struggles were weaker now, a hazy blackness from her aching lungs causing her head to spin and her dazed eyes to dilate. He was going to show her no mercy; his weight was crushing her.

There was a sharp explosion by her face, and then the bruising weight was gone. She drew breath desperately into her burning chest, gasping with pain. As the darkness receded she was vaguely aware of being lifted, and tried to fight the arms holding her limp body.

'You're all right, Nina. It's me. Everything's all right.' It sounded like Steed's voice, and although she knew it was impossible she stopped her struggles and let herself fall into the rushing blackness coming to meet her, drowning in its consuming silence.

# CHAPTER FOUR

NINA came out of the swirling confusion of unconsciousness to find herself lying on her bed. She lay for
a moment, her head swimming with a thousand images
and her eyes heavy and aching, trying to collect her
thoughts. Maria was fluttering around her, stroking her
forehead and murmuring incomprehensible words of
comfort in rapid Spanish.

As she moved her head slowly she was aware of a tall
dark shadow by the window, and raised herself slightly
to see Steed watching her in cold silence.

'Well?' The air was electric and she saw he was furiously angry, his grey eyes glittering dangerously.

'What happened?' Her voice was weak and he barked
a sharp laugh.

'That's my line.'

'I don't understand.'

'You and me both.' His voice was shaking with rage.
'I gave express orders that James was to get his marching
orders this morning, and instead——' His voice cracked
and he turned sharply to gaze out into the darkness, his
broad back rigid.

'He was away all day,' Nina protested, her voice quivering. 'I was reading in the garden when he came back
and——'

'I can work out the rest,' he interrupted scathingly. 'I
just want to know one thing and I want the truth, Nina.
Did you give him any encouragement?'

71

'Encouragement?' She stared at him blankly, and then as realisation swept over her she turned scarlet, her whole body trembling. 'No, I didn't encourage him. How can you ask me that?'

'How can I ask?' The words were Arctic-cold. 'I'll tell you how I can ask. James is an attractive man, more your age than I am. I understand women like him, and you were alone together in a romantic setting. Do I have to spell it out? I want the truth.'

'I told you the truth.' Her eyes were blinded with tears. 'Perhaps some women do like him, but I don't.' She shivered helplessly. 'I really don't like him, Steed.' Her voice ended on a plea, and her face was deathly white.

He shook himself suddenly and strode over to the bed, pushing Maria roughly away and gathering her up into his arms. 'OK, baby, OK,' he whispered into her shining hair as sobs began to tear her body apart. 'I had to ask, sweetheart. Cry it out.' He held her tightly against his chest until the tears subsided, his face taut and grey. Maria reappeared, holding a large brandy goblet.

'Drink it,' Steed ordered, feeling tiny tremors of shock still shaking her body. 'All of it.' Protesting weakly, she forced down a little of the fiery liquid, gasping as it burnt its way into her stomach. 'Come on, there wasn't much there; drain the glass, and then Maria will help you undress and bring you something to eat in bed.'

'Where are you going?' Nina asked miserably, panic rising in her voice as he walked purposefully towards the door.

'To finish something I started,' he replied harshly, his face grim.

'Please, Steed.' She half rose in the bed and then, as the combination of shock, exhaustion and neat alcohol overwhelmed her, she sank back against the pillows with a small bewildered cry. He was back by her side again in an instant, his face savage.

'Will you do as you are told, you little fool? Just lie still. Maria will give you a sedative when you've eaten, and it will all seem different in the morning. He didn't hurt you, did he?' His face suddenly drained of colour. 'It looked as though I was in time. He didn't...?'

'No.' Nina dropped her eyes shyly, her eyelashes fluttering on her hot cheeks. 'He just scared me, that's all.'

'I'll kill him.'

'No, please...' Fear for him and the consequences of what he might do caused her voice to rise shrilly, and he met her glance directly, his expression freezing.

'I thought you didn't like him.'

'I don't.' Wearily she brushed a strand of golden hair from her face. 'But if you hurt him...'

'I've already done that.' The words carried immense satisfaction as his hands clenched into fists by his side and she remembered the violent crack she had heard, and saw the knuckles on his right hand were dripping blood.

'You're hurt.' Horrified, she gazed up at him, her violet eyes huge.

'You ought to see the other fella,' said Steed with grim humour. 'You needn't try and stop me—he's had this coming for a long time. When I think if I hadn't come back today...'

He was gone before she could say anything else, and she stared in helpless appeal at Maria, who shook her head slowly and shrugged in typical Latin style. 'He is your man; what do you expect?' the housekeeper said philosophically, opening the door to Nina's bathroom and turning on the shower.

Much to Nina's embarrassment the housekeeper insisted on remaining with her while she showered, tucking her up in bed afterwards as though she were a tiny child. Her thoughts were churning wildly as Maria left to fetch her a snack, and by sheer will-power she put all thoughts of James's groping hands and hot mouth out of her mind, concentrating instead on her anxiety for Steed. He had been so coldly determined.

She was struggling to eat the feather-light omelette Maria had cooked when he returned, the huge lump in her throat threatening to choke her with every mouthful.

She looked up as he entered the bedroom, her damp hair brushed to demure order and the high-necked buttoned nightdress she wore adding to the overall impression of a young schoolgirl.

'You can sleep in peace. He's taken the Mercedes and vanished. No doubt I shall have a phone call telling me where the car is eventually.'

'I'm sorry, Steed.'

'Don't apologise when it's not necessary.' His voice was brusque.

'But the business deal and everything. You shouldn't have come back.' She pushed the tray away dispiritedly.

He stood leaning against the open door, his arms crossed and with a strange expression on his taciturn face. 'I damn well should have. I've followed my instincts all my life and they haven't let me down yet.' He moved restlessly. 'I should never have sent you here by yourself in the first place, but you seemed so exhausted in London. I thought Maria and Lopaz could take care of you until I arrived. It was a mistake that you nearly had to pay for.' His eyes glinted. 'I hadn't reckoned on James's reptilian ability for ferreting out anything new.'

'He isn't normal, Steed . . . not to behave like that.'

'He'll be even less normal by the time I've finished with him,' he said grimly. Nina shivered in spite of the warm room.

'No, I mean it. I think he needs help.'

'I'll help him, all right.' His voice was pure steel. 'I intend to whip that young man until his back is raw. He was born with a silver spoon in his mouth, which he has used to his advantage ever since he could toddle. How his mother and mine were born of the same parents I will never know. She is a bit of candy-floss without an idea in her pretty little head, and James has always run rings around her. Unfortunately my uncle worships the ground she walks on, and consequently the pair of them have got away with murder.'

With a slight nod in her direction he stepped backwards. 'I shall deal with James as I see fit, Nina. This time he pays for his fun.' He closed the door with a firm click.

She had made him even more angry. She swallowed the two white pills Maria had placed on the tray with a sip of water and slid under the covers, convinced she would lie awake most of the night, reliving the nightmare, sick at heart.

She awoke late the next morning after a deep, refreshing sleep to find the room filled with soft grey light, and lay in a dazed stupor. A steady rhythmic drumming slowly infiltrated her consciousness and she looked towards the leaded windows, where fat raindrops were leaving shining trails down the smooth glass like a million bright diamonds.

It was raining, here! She sat up slowly, bruised muscles crying out in protest, amazed to find she must have fallen asleep immediately the night before. A chair had been placed close to the bed and a newspaper lay across its cane seat, the Spanish words indecipherable. Maria must have sat with her for part of the night. She felt a warm rush of gratitude towards the small Spanish woman for her thoughtfulness.

She showered slowly, washing her hair under the warm water, rubbing it vigorously as though to erase all memory of the night before. She dressed in jeans and a warm sweater—the air had a definite bite after the sultry warmth of the last few days—and was brushing her damp hair into a high, sleek pony-tail when a gentle tap sounded at the bedroom door.

'Come in,' she called brightly, expecting to see Maria's small, plump shape as the door opened, but instead Steed's tall, lean body stood in the doorway, his dark face relaxed and heavy-lidded eyes cool. She looked down hastily, her pulse beating fast, the unexpected sight of him causing her breath to catch in her throat.

'How are you feeling this morning?' he asked lazily, his deep velvet voice sending shivers over her skin. She mumbled a reply, keeping her eyes lowered, horrified to feel warm colour staining her cheeks. What was the matter with her? She was acting like a girl on her first date.

He came swiftly across to where she sat in front of the small ornate dressing-table and gently lifted her chin, his grey gaze searching her eyes seriously. 'Don't be embarrassed, not with me.' He smiled tenderly. 'This is a new day, yesterday is a forgotten dream, and tomorrow is what you make it. Live for today.'

She nodded mistily, thankful he had mistaken her confusion for shyness over yesterday's episode with James. She saw the strong jaw stiffen as his fingers left her chin to trace the blue marks staining her lower arms left by James's cruel grip, but he said nothing, merely tightening his mouth into a thin line.

'Some old friends of mine have asked us to call by,' he said lightly after a long moment. 'I would like you to meet them.' There were times when a certain inflexion in his perfect English hinted at the Spanish heritage Maria had outlined, and she longed to ask him more about his family and upbringing, but held back, concerned he would think she was merely being nosy.

'That would be lovely,' she replied, trying to match his carefree tone. 'Do you want me to change?'

His narrowed eyes swept over her slim body appreciatively and he shook his black head slowly. 'You look good enough to eat.' Their linked gaze held and intensified, and deep in the pit of her stomach she felt a slow ache begin to throb in time with her heartbeat.

'Would it be in order for me to kiss my fiancée good morning?' he asked as his eyes fell to her mouth, and she nodded slowly as he raised her to her feet. Bending over, he brushed her mouth fleetingly with his cool lips, his touch gentle. She noticed a tiny muscle working in his hard jaw as he straightened and stood looking down at her, his expression slightly satirical. 'You are causing me to exercise a self-discipline I never knew I had,' he drawled mockingly after a moment. 'It feels so bad that I'm sure it must be good for me.'

She looked at him in bewilderment and he laughed quietly, his grey eyes bright with self-derision. 'You haven't a clue what I'm talking about, have you?' She shook her head doubtfully as he raised his hand and traced a path down her soft cheek.

'Isobel did have a point after all, you know. Your father did rather keep you like the princess in the ivory tower.'

'He didn't,' she returned quickly, her eyes flashing, and he laughed again, his dark gaze more intent.

'Can I kiss you as I would like to, then?' he asked lazily, and she stared at him uncertainly without replying. This time his mouth moulded and parted her lips in sweetly searching arousal, his arms pulling her against his hard-muscled body until she could feel his outline against hers. Pleasure flooded tiny goose-pimples along her limbs, and as his mouth worked its subtle magic on hers she began to feel a heavy, languid warmth spread through her veins. All memory of James's violent assault was washed from her mind as Steed's slow lovemaking cleaned and healed the wound, drawing tiny flickering flames of desire from deep inside her body. As she began to respond to his kiss her arms tightened round his strong neck, and without realising it she pressed closer into his body, fitting against him like the last piece of a jigsaw.

It was Steed who drew away a few seconds later with a small sound deep in his throat. 'Hoist with my own petard,' he said thickly. 'You certainly are an apt pupil, sweetheart.' It was the second time he had used that endearment and, although she realised it probably didn't mean anything to him, it sounded good.

'Nina, I want to take it nice and slowly, but there's something I must know. You aren't still frightened of me, are you?' He moved back a pace and thrust his hands into his pockets as he kept his eyes tight on her face. 'I know things went too fast for you that night at the party and——'

She interrupted him quickly; after last night she didn't feel up to any soul-searching. 'I'm not frightened of you.' Her brow wrinkled. 'I don't know if I ever was, not really. I can't explain. I felt somehow that you threatened everything I knew, all the ordinary things...' Her voice trailed away and they stood looking at each other, his expression sardonic and faintly amused.

'And now?'

'You've been marvellous, Steed. I'm very grateful,' she said quickly, and his face darkened ominously.

'I don't want your thanks,' he growled softly, his face menacing. 'I want to know how you feel about me.'

She looked at him nervously through her lashes. 'I like you, Steed; you've been so good to me. I'm sorry...I don't know what else to say,' she finished weakly as his expression didn't change. James's words had flashed through her brain like lightning. Steed never wanted romantic involvement. He chose his women for their sophisticated awareness, their ability to play the love-game and then move on with no rancour to the next beau. She couldn't play that game; she didn't know the rules and she didn't want to learn them. If she gave her heart to Steed it would be forever, and he would look on that as a millstone around his neck.

She looked into his cold grey eyes. He would expect a light affair from her and nothing more, a mere blending of bodies. Maybe, in spite of all he had said that night at Grayfields, he looked upon his proposal as the right to a full marriage and all that that entailed. She looked up abruptly, her thoughts written plainly on her face. 'Steed, if you've changed your mind I understand. It's not too late to call everything off...' Her voice faltered to a halt as his jaw ground slowly.

'You don't look on me as a father-figure, do you?' he asked suddenly, his expression horrified. It was obvious that complication hadn't dawned on him before.

She smiled at the look on his face in spite of herself. 'No, I can promise you that idea has never crossed my

mind,' she said slowly as his face relaxed slightly. If only
he had said one word of love to her since they had met.
He made it plain he found her desirable, and his reaction to James's presence showed he valued her as a
possession, but she wanted more than that from him.
As her thoughts led her into areas she had tried to shut
down in her consciousness her agitation increased. She
didn't want to be one link in a long chain, and a pretty
weak link, at that. She knew none of the tricks women
played to dazzle a man of the world like him, and he
would tire of her immediately he won the chase. She
mustn't let him suspect what she now acknowledged was
the truth: that she loved him, had always loved him.
Even at sixteen, all those years ago, in the midst of his
mockery, she had known he was the one man who could
turn her safe little world upside-down.

Some vestige of her thoughts must have shown in her
face, as Steed sighed deeply, his face wry. 'I think you've
been sent to keep me humble,' he muttered to himself
as he walked to the door. 'No one could accuse you of
bolstering my ego, that's for sure. In my world of
sycophants and charlatans you stick out like the prov-
erbial sore thumb.'

She looked searchingly at his sombre face but could
read nothing there to encourage her to tell him the truth.
He was his old self again, heart-wrenchingly handsome,
cool and aloof, his dark masculinity vibrant and
dangerous. 'And don't say it,' he warned ferociously as
he paused in the doorway, his hair gleaming blue-black.

'Don't say what?' She looked at him, thankful he
didn't have the ability to read her mind.

'That you're sorry. I really couldn't take it.' With that
he bowed slightly and was gone, leaving an electric
tension in the air so real that it almost crackled.

A weak sun was struggling to surface behind dove-grey clouds as they left the house an hour later. The torrential rain had stopped, leaving a fresh new world gleaming with bright colour, the clean air heavy with the rich perfume of bountiful vegetation. Deep salmon rose blossoms, pink hibiscus and a riot of trailing honey-suckle fought for supremacy on the old stone walls sur-rounding the house, vying with pale pink dog roses and vivid orange trumpet-like flowers that clung to every crevice in the aged walls.

'It's all so beautiful,' Nina breathed as she settled herself into the small jeep Steed was driving.

He looked at her, his fine, chiselled face warm and relaxed, showing no signs of their earlier conversation. 'You're seeing it at its best before the heat of summer dries everything up,' he said slowly, 'but there is no place on earth quite like this for me.' His eyes flicked away and she realised he was revealing a small part of himself to her. 'I was born here and I will be content to die here.'

'Don't say that,' said Nina quickly, touching his muscled arm hesitantly with the tips of her fingers.

'I didn't mean in the foreseeable future,' he returned, smiling slightly at her nervous expression and patting her hand casually, although the grey eyes were tight on her face. 'I'd like to leave my sons in residence first to carry on the illustrious Charlton name. Any suggestions how quickly you think that might be accomplished?' Her cheeks burned and he chuckled softly to himself, mut-tering something quietly in Spanish that sounded almost like an endearment.

'I apologise for the somewhat basic mode of transport,' he said after a time as the small jeep bumped along the rough-hewn road travelling even further into the low, rolling hills. 'Lopaz looks on Gina as his own,' he continued, patting the dashboard fondly, 'but with my dear cousin absconding with the Mercedes I'm afraid she's all we've got for today.'

'I don't mind,' Nina protested stoutly. 'I like this better than the Mercedes anyway—it's more friendly.'

He looked at her in amazed incredulity and then burst out laughing, the deep, rich tones echoing round the confined space. 'You're going to be an easy wife to please,' he said, controlling his amusement with visible effort. 'No other woman of my acquaintance could honestly say she preferred this old heap to my beautiful Mercedes.'

'Perhaps you haven't been mixing with the right women, then,' Nina replied tartly, causing the heavy black eyebrows to rise in nodding assent, his face suddenly serious as he glanced at her pure profile.

'Now, you could be right there,' he agreed slowly, swerving violently to avoid a wandering goat strolling lazily across the tufted road with a small necklace of bells round its white neck. 'I always knew my little kitten had sharp claws,' he continued as though to himself, slanting a sly glance at her face, which was turning a vivid shade of pink. He laughed softly as she flounced round in her seat, pretending an intense interest in the scenery flashing past the open window.

It was lunchtime when they reached their destination. Steed parked in a small curve in the road, and after helping her out of the jeep pointed down the valley to where a small stone house was just visible through the foliage of a large olive grove. There was no other habitation for miles around, just a battered old truck to one side of the dusty dirt track. 'Pedro and his family live down there,' Steed said shortly, watching her face closely.

'Oh, Steed, it's lovely,' she said in surprised pleasure, 'what a gorgeous place to live.' She had expected his friends to be high-fliers in the social whirl, mentally preparing herself for barbed innuendoes and veiled searching questions as to her suitability to be his consort. This tiny whitewashed house, hidden among the olive trees and cacti with its brown thatched roof of dried turf, was not at all what she had pictured.

He appeared satisfied at her reaction, taking her arm firmly and guiding her among the low branches as they walked towards the cottage. As they neared the building she noticed a large pen holding several fat well-fed goats, which were bleating noisily at their approach.

'Pedro and Carmel are my oldest friends,' he explained softly as they approached the small wooden front door. 'We grew up together until I was eight, when my father took me to America for my education, but he always allowed my mother and me to come home here to my grandparents' home for the holidays. Then the three of us, along with some other children from the village school, would run riot all summer. The others tended to draw away from me after a time——' his face didn't change, but something in the low voice told Nina the childrens' defection had hurt the boy Steed deeply '—but Pedro and Carmel were always the same. I danced at their wedding ten years ago, and they have six children now.' She glanced at him in open amazement and he chuckled quietly. 'The Spanish are a virile lot.' He shot a wicked glance at her. 'I'm half-Spanish.'

The door of the small cottage suddenly burst open and a veritable stream of chanting, laughing children descended on Steed in an overwhelming flood. Moving hastily to one side against the protection of a bent old tree, Nina watched in rapt fascination as they climbed all over the big, lean frame, calling his name shrilly and shouting in rapid Spanish. With a bright-eyed toddler in his arms and two curly black-haired urchins clinging to his back, Steed stumbled towards the cottage door, where a small, stocky dark man was shouting instructions to the children, which they patently ignored.

A tall, slim woman joined the throng, waving her arms and pulling one child from Steed's back, whereupon another immediately took its place. It was a good five minutes before some sort of order was restored, by which time a form of introduction had taken place and Nina and Steed were settled in two battered easy chairs, the latter groaning under the weight of Steed and four toddlers of assorted ages. Two older children stood at the side of his chair, stroking his arm now and then: a young dark-eyed girl as pretty as her mother, and a small boy who was the very image of Pedro.

'The babies, they adore him!' explained Carmel laughingly to Nina as she gestured towards Steed lovingly, and as he smiled back at the slim Spanish woman, his face open and all wariness gone from his eyes, something pierced Nina's heart like a sword. He never smiled at her like that. She winced visibly.

'What is it?' He was by her side instantly as children scattered in all directions, and she smiled shakily as she shrugged an answer.

'You're tired and bruised after yesterday,' he said grimly, 'it's to be expected.' He spoke swiftly in his native tongue to Pedro and Carmel, and as the concern on their faces changed to deep anger Carmel knelt by her chair, her long black hair sweeping Nina's arm.

'That James, he is a pig,' she said slowly and distinctly, and Nina looked questioningly at Steed, her pale face flushing with embarrassment.

'I just explained he had pushed his luck,' Steed said shortly. 'We're with friends, Nina; you can relax here. No questions or reprisals.' She stared at him wordlessly, her violet eyes huge with reproach, and he stood up abruptly, clearly irritated by her censure.

Carmel's brown gaze darted from one to another and she too stood up, her lithe full-breasted figure so different from that of her small plump husband. 'Come and see upstairs, Nina,' she invited, turning with a swift meaningful glance to Pedro and nodding at Steed, who was standing with his back to them, looking out through the open doorway.

Nina found the house fascinating. It was larger than she had first thought, and spotlessly clean, but still incredibly tiny to house a family of eight with no running water or normal amenities. A crystal-clear stream ran in a slight hollow a few yards from the cottage, its sparkling water pure and clean, and a small outhouse at the side of the main building held a large wood-burning stove and cooking utensils, with strings of onions and various cuts of meat hanging from its smoke-blackened ceiling.

'I can understand it must be good here in the summer when the weather's fine, but how do you all manage in the winter months?' Nina asked Carmel as they sat on the big window-seat in one of the two bedrooms looking out over the rolling hills and blue sky.

The tall Spanishwoman burst into laughter. 'I don't!' She grimaced slightly. 'We only come here when it is warm; we go back to Panthoss before winter.' She explained they spent the cold winter months in the huge town house they shared with Pedro's parents and assorted brothers and sisters and their respective families. 'We are very many,' Carmel said carefully, holding ten fingers up several times in front of Nina's face. 'Steed, he buy us this for just Pedro and me. It was, how you say, the wedding present?' Nina nodded her understanding, glimpsing another facet of the complex personality of the man she had promised to marry. It must have been wonderful through the years for Steed's friends to know they could spend their summers alone with their family.

They ate lunch sitting by the pebbled stream on thick coarse rugs spread over the damp grass, the children splashing with shouts of glee in the icy shallow water. The air was warm again and faintly perfumed by the tiny flowers dotted in the meadow on the other side of the stream. There was a sweet restfulness in being with the young family that Nina found very soothing.

The meal was a simple one of pungent tasty goat's cheese, cold smoked bacon and garlic bread, washed down with goat's milk for the children and a spicy red wine for the adults which made Nina cough helplessly at the first sip.

'Would you prefer milk?' Steed asked gravely with a small smile twitching at the side of his firm mouth as he noticed her streaming eyes.

'Yes, please,' Nina said gratefully, turning to Pedro and Carmel as he poured her a glass of the frothy white liquid and explaining she wasn't used to wine.

'No, I can vouch for that,' Steed affirmed with a wicked look in his eyes as he handed her the glass of foaming milk. 'Wine has the strangest effect on her.' Nina blushed hotly and the Spanish couple exchanged an intimate smile, changing the subject adroitly.

The four younger children were becoming truculent as they finished the impromptu picnic, flicking handfuls of water on to the watching adults and running screaming through the long grass on the other side of the stream.

'Come on, you little monkeys,' Pedro said firmly, giving two wriggling bodies to Carmel and whisking two more into his muscled brown arms. 'Time for a nap.'

'Would you like to go for a walk?' Steed suggested as the family made their way back to the cottage with much cajoling and threatening by the harassed parents. 'It will give the children a chance to go to sleep. I tend to have a distracting influence on them.'

'I had noticed!' Nina laughed as she gazed up into his face. 'They adore you, though, don't they?' And who wouldn't? she thought to herself as she stood up slowly, watching him through her lashes as he gazed across the sparkling water to the sunlit hills beyond. The sun was directly overhead now, but the harsh heat of the last few days had vanished with the night's storm to be replaced by a soft, languid warmth, reminiscent of an English summer.

He swung her gently across the narrow brook on to the wiry grass beyond, calling their intention to Pedro, who replied with a raised hand and a huge grin. Among the sturdy blades of grass the meadow had a carpet of tiny white and blue flowers, their starry faces turned up to the deep blue sky above. Nina knelt to look more closely at their fragile beauty. 'It seems such a shame to walk on them,' she murmured sadly, noticing small sprigs of thyme peeping out from the grey rocks scattered here and there.

'I'll carry you if you like,' Steed offered immediately, his grey eyes mocking, and she shook her head in laughing refusal, picking a few green leaves of thyme and inhaling the aromatic perfume of the tiny herb.

'Come on, let's walk,' he said impatiently, pulling her up by her hand, which he then kept in his own large fist, nonchalantly matching his superior stride to hers. Her small hand trembled slightly in his grasp but he appeared not to notice, pointing out the majestic circular sweep of the hills in the distance, their outline black against the foreign sky.

'You were a great hit back there,' he said casually as they wandered through the meadow, reaching the uneven hillside that stretched as far as the eye could see. 'If I didn't know better I would have thought you'd met them years ago.'

'It felt like that,' Nina agreed, sensing warm approval in his deep voice. 'They are good people.'

'The best,' Steed agreed, looking down at her with grey eyes crinkled against the sun. 'Pedro makes enough on the family fishing boat to get by, and Carmel works in some of the big hotels cleaning in the summer months to get them through the winter. They're as poor as church mice, but rich in everything that matters.'

'I'm surprised——' Nina began but stopped abruptly, suddenly aware she had been about to be very tactless.

'Yes?' Steed had let go of her hand and positioned himself on a large grey rock, its surface smooth and warm, and his eyes flicked over her intently, noticing the expression on her face. 'What were you going to say?'

'Nothing really.' She flushed slightly. 'I was just going to ask you how you have kept in contact with them through the years.'

'No, you weren't.' His voice was barbed. 'You were going to say you were *surprised* I have kept contact with them during the years. I asked you once before and I'm asking you again, what exactly do you think of me? I have the strangest feeling that I'm neatly tagged and labelled in that little computer in your brain, put in a tidy slot marked "untouchable, danger—may contaminate". Does that about sum it up?'

'No,' she answered indignantly, amazed he could misjudge her so totally, while being secretly relieved he didn't suspect her true feelings for him.

'Why were you surprised, then? Explain.'

She looked at him miserably. 'Well, you're a successful travelled businessman and everything. You're so wealthy, whereas they...' Her voice trailed into silence.

He listened to her stammering without moving, his black head tilted to one side and his eyes shooting steel darts. 'Charming. You have a lot to learn about me, my dear,' he said frostily. 'I do not abandon my friends or compromise my principles to fit in with my lifestyle. I may be rich, but if all my wealth were gone tomorrow I would still survive because of what's in here.' He banged his chest with a clenched hand. 'I somehow thought you were the same.'

'I am.' Her drooping head snapped up at his last words. 'I do live by my own standards. I don't go from affair to affair like some people...' She stopped. She had said more than she'd intended.

His face was livid. 'Meaning I do? And who has been telling you all these wonderful fairy-stories about the big, bad wolf?'

She flinched at the contempt in his voice. 'James said that you had lots of women friends, that you liked to keep things free and light——'

'And you believed every word, of course.' His voice dripped ice. 'James is such a reliable source of information, isn't he? You didn't consider it necessary to ask me about it or wait a little before you made a judgement? But of course not; how silly of me. His tales fitted perfectly into the picture you've always had of me, didn't they? You've always considered me on the same level as something that's crawled out from under a stone, and now it would seem I have risen to the dizzy heights of a worthless Romeo and shallow speculator. Delightful.'

Fear trickled down her spine at the red fury in his eyes. 'As it happens, my dear cousin is partly right,' he continued, fixing her with his gaze like a hunter with its prey. 'I do have many women friends. Some of them are merely friends and others have been something more.' Her stomach somersaulted. 'That is in the past. I was foolish enough to think it could remain there. However, you have at last made your opinion of me very plain, for which I thank you.' He rose, clicking his heels together in a small bow, his foreign blood suddenly very obvious. 'I think it is time we return and make our farewells.' He strode away.

She stumbled after him, stricken with remorse but quite at a loss to know what to do or say to put matters right. 'Please, I'm sorry...'

'I'm sick to death of hearing you say that!' He swung round at her words, his face savage and black with anger. 'I'm running rapidly out of patience with this whole ridiculous farce, so just give it a rest, Nina, if you know what's good for you.'

She followed him down the narrow hill path and on to the rough surface of the meadow at a run, his large strides in no way allowing for her small steps. His words had left her numb; her only intention now was to keep up with him and return to the villa and the safety of her bedroom as soon as possible.

The sharp triangle of rock that caused her to stumble also cut through her sandal like a hot knife through butter, and as she fell the breath was knocked out of her body in a screaming gasp. She landed in a curled heap,

her chest burning and her throat rasping for air, unaware that blood was pumping furiously from the deep
gash in her foot, staining her cotton dress with red drop-
lets and splattering her bent arms and legs crimson.

# CHAPTER FIVE

STEED was kneeling beside her as her lungs stopped their labouring, his face grey with shock. 'Nina?' He smoothed back the loose golden hair that had fallen round her face, wiping a smudge of brick-red dirt from her cheek. 'Where are you hurt?'

He lifted her into a sitting position carefully, laying her back against his chest, and her dazed eyes widened at the sight of all the blood. 'It's just my foot, I think,' she murmured huskily, feeling better now she could breathe easily again.

'Thank goodness.' His warm fingers touched the gaping wound, causing her to wince. 'I thought you'd hurt your head.' He took off his short-sleeved shirt and wrapped it hastily around her foot in a giant bandage. 'It will need stitching, I'm afraid.'

He lifted her carefully, cradling her in his arms, her face pressed against his broad bare chest. 'All right? Do you feel faint?'

'No,' she whispered softly, the sensation of being held in his arms next to his warm skin driving all lucid thought from her head. 'It doesn't even hurt.'

'It will,' he said grimly, walking back to the cottage almost at a run, holding her as lightly as though she were a child. She could feel his heart beating madly, and the curly black hairs covering his chest were wiry against her soft cheeks; she felt light-headed with the longing to run her hands through their dark mass.

\* \* \*

The next day her foot throbbed with hot needles of pain, and she was glad to spend the day resting in bed as the doctor had suggested. Steed had driven straight to the nearest hospital after rushed farewells to a stunned Pedro and Carmel, whereupon the smiling young doctor had put four stitches into the cut, which had seemed to affect Steed more than her, causing his face to blanch and beads of sweat break out on his forehead.

Once back at the villa, he had called Maria to help her wash and get into bed, and then had almost fed her the tempting evening meal that Maria had brought to her room, giving her the sedative the doctor had prescribed immediately she had finished. She had been asleep almost as he'd left the room, waking once in the night as a sharp stab of pain had cut into her drugged dreams, but then falling back into deep slumber at once.

'I'm sorry to be such a nuisance,' she apologised to Maria as the housekeeper brought her lunch on a tray. The lobster salad looked delicious and she was surprised to find she was ravenously hungry, having slept through breakfast. 'Thank you for sitting with me the other night,' she continued as the little woman bustled round the room, straightening her pillows and smoothing the fine silk sheets.

'Sitting?' The plump face was puzzled, and then as comprehension dawned Maria smiled slowly, clucking her tongue and shaking her black head. 'No, no.' She settled Nina back on the fluffy pillows placing the tray carefully on her lap. 'The *señor*, he sit with you.'

'Steed?' Nina flushed scarlet.

'The *señor* thought maybe you would have the bad dreams. He sit with you all night. Now you eat.' After Maria had gone Nina sat quietly, absorbing what the small woman had told her. He had cared enough to stay with her all night until he was sure James's rough handling had not caused her to suffer any ill effects. A small smile played at the corner of her mouth. It was a start, a small ray of hope that she was more to him than just a passing fancy.

She waited all afternoon for Steed to visit her, but dusk was casting cool mauve shadows into the darkening room when he popped his black head round the half-open door. 'How's the invalid?' His voice was friendly but there was a withdrawn expression on his handsome face as he stood just inside the room, the dying light from the window throwing his high cheekbones into sharp relief.

'Fine, thank you.' It wasn't true. The ache in her foot had magnified through the long afternoon of waiting for his footsteps. 'Maria said you sat with me the night James left.' She smiled warmly, her mouth straightening slightly as he turned his head from her glance.

'Think nothing of it.' There was a definite coolness in his tone. 'The doctor said the stitches can come out in a few days. Once you are recovered I would like to bring the boys out for a short holiday to meet you. Would that be convenient?' It was as though he was talking to a difficult employee, and with a start of misery Nina realised that in a way that was exactly what she was.

'Perfectly.' She matched her tone to his.

'Once that is accomplished and we return to England I can see no reason for any delay with the arrangements.' The cool voice was hurting her more than she would have thought possible. 'I suggested the middle of May to the caterers as a good time for the wedding. If you agree we can send the invitations out as soon as we get back. Carol has already ordered a supply.' His voice was clinical—they could have been discussing a television programme rather than the joining together of two lives.

'Yes, May is all right. It doesn't really matter, does it?' Her voice was listless, and he glanced sharply at her in the dim light.

'Doesn't it?' Just for a moment there was a spark of something in his voice, but then he turned away, his face sombre. 'I have to go back to England tonight. I've checked with my uncle, and James is back home again. I explained the situation and you will have no more trouble from that quarter.' His voice was dismissive. He obviously couldn't wait to leave. 'I shall bring Jason and Peter out with me on my return unless you inform me to the contrary.'

She felt hot tears pricking at the backs of her eyes and kept her head lowered, the blonde curtain of hair hiding her face in a shimmering veil. He clearly had meant what he'd said yesterday: he considered their marriage a ridiculous farce. She heard him move across the room and kiss the top of her head lightly, and then he was gone, the door shutting with a final-sounding click.

The next few days dragged by. Her foot was more comfortable the next morning and she could hobble about the villa carefully, although the winding cliff path to the gently shelving beach was beyond her.

On the fourth day Maria looked at her face as she served her breakfast on the sunny patio. 'Today you have a ride,' she said firmly as her sharp gaze took in Nina's pallor and empty eyes. 'Lopaz and me, we show you our Spain. The *señor*, he will be glad for us to take you.'

Nina looked at her miserably. 'Oh, he'd be glad for anyone to take me,' she said softly, her voice heavy with a double meaning that escaped the small housekeeper.

The Mercedes had been returned, so they rode in
comfort, and despite her heavy heart Nina had to admit
she thoroughly enjoyed the day. The middle-aged couple
were inordinately proud of their homeland and were determined to show her its many faces that the average
tourist never saw.

They passed ancient stone reminders of where Stone
Age inhabitants used to live, the small stone huts dank
and cold after the cool Spanish winter. She marvelled at
sheltered fjords and idyllic pine-fringed bays of white
sand protected by rocky cliffs, the sparkling azure sea a
gently shimmering carpet. After a time Lopaz turned
the powerful car inland, where lush pastures and brick-
red fields were being worked by black-clad peasants in
a manner as old as time, their backs bent in the warm
sunshine, whitewashed farmhouses visible in the distance.

'We stop now,' Maria informed her at midday. 'You
will eat the *conejo al ajillo*.'

'I will?' asked Nina nervously, waiting with some
trepidation for the meal to arrive. She was relieved to
find it was nothing more adventurous than rabbit with
garlic, served with a delicious creamy mayonnaise and
perfectly complemented by the light dry red wine Lopaz
had chosen.

The food and wine relaxed her and they spent a couple
of hours sitting outside the homely rural tavern, finishing with rich black coffee as thick as syrup, served in
tiny heavy glasses. Nina felt the tension flowing from
her body in great waves and, shutting her eyes against
the glare of the afternoon sun, she leant back against
the mellowed old stone wall with a small contented sigh.
Maria and Lopaz exchanged a satisfied smile, their
brown faces shiny in the heat.

The sun was beginning to throw mauve-blue shadows on the dusty red fields as they drove homewards, passing pretty walled gardens and small white cottages where black-dressed old women gossiped on scrubbed door-steps, their lined faces suspicious of the big car.

Nina felt pleasantly tired for the first time in days after the long hours in the fresh air and slept deeply, waking refreshed the next morning with her mind more at ease. That lasted until Steed's telephone call in the evening to Maria. She stood waiting in the hall while the little woman rattled on, and as their conversation drew to a close the housekeeper handed her the phone silently.

'Hello, Steed,' she said nervously. It was the first time she had spoken to him since their last conversation in her bedroom.

'Good evening, Nina.' The cool, deep voice flowed down the line, doing crazy things to her nerves. 'I trust your foot is healing? I understand from Maria that Lopaz is taking you to have the stitches removed tomorrow morning.' There was still that note of careful reserve in his voice that grated on her.

It was clear that their heated conversation in the meadow that day was still to the forefront of his mind; he had erected barriers that she had no experience in dismantling.

'Yes, I can walk OK now.' Why couldn't she think of something to say to let him know that his assumption of her feelings for him was all wrong? She took a deep breath; she had to clear the air.

'Steed, darling, come on.' The female voice in the background was faint but just discernible as she went to speak, and the words of explanation died in her throat. He had a woman there with him! How dared he phone her when he was with someone else? Shock froze the blood in her veins.

'I'm sorry, I seem to be keeping you,' she said coldly as she heard his low muffled voice talking urgently to someone—he obviously had his hand over the receiver.

'That's OK.' His voice was bland and cool: he clearly had no idea he had just torn her heart out by the roots. 'I'm in a restaurant, so it's a little difficult. We've been working all day and decided to finish negotiations over a meal.'

I bet! Nina thought viciously, unknown white-hot needles of jealousy piercing her chest; she would never have believed that love could produce actual physical pain, but she was experiencing it now. 'You had better return to the...others, then, hadn't you?' she said brightly, forcing herself with a strength she never knew she possessed to make her voice light and uncaring. He would never know how much he had hurt her.

'Nina? Are you all right?' Obviously her acting ability wasn't quite as good as she would have liked.

'Me? Oh, yes, I'm fine, absolutely fine. Why shouldn't I be?'

'You tell me.' His voice was irritated now, she could tell, and if she didn't finish this conversation soon the tears that were streaming down her face would sound in her voice.

'See you soon, then.'

'In a couple of days, actually. I phoned to tell Maria to get a room ready for the boys. I'm bringing them out Tuesday.' He hadn't even intended to talk to her, then; she could see it all now. She was so stupid. Her breath caught in her throat and she heard someone laugh shrilly in the background. It certainly wasn't a male who was laughing like that, unless he had severe problems.

'Bye, then.' She put the phone down before he even had time to reply and stood quite still for a moment, her world falling apart around her for the second time in as many months. She had thought the death of her father and the resulting tortuous days of misery were the worst things that had ever happened to her. They were child's play compared to the grief that was twisting her insides into knots now. She should have known. All the signs were there; James had tried to tell her. She brushed the tears angrily from her face with the back of her hand. They had all been right: her father had kept her too sheltered. She had no weapons at her disposal to fight for her survival in this hard, strange world into which she had been plunged, where all the values and ideals she had learnt since babyhood seemed invalid. A sob caught in her throat. Well, she didn't care. However much she loved him—and she admitted now life would be empty without him—the battle would be won or lost on her terms. She would not compromise her soul.

She had her emotions very much under control by Tuesday when Lopaz drew up in the Mercedes, with Steed's dark head and two smaller ones visible in the back of the car. Her stomach fluttered slightly, but her face was calm and smiling as the door opened and two small dark-haired boys walked slowly on either side of Steed to greet her.

'How do you do?' They spoke in unison with a quick nervous glance at their stern-faced uncle, and held out little thin hands to be shaken.

As she looked down at their strained, tired faces so ridiculously alike, with melting brown eyes and mouths stained from the hours of travel, she knelt down on the warm cobbles and gathered the small, slight bodies into her arms, muttering their names against their heads.

'Hello, you two,' she said warmly. 'I've been longing to meet you.'

For a moment both boys were stiff and unyielding, as though unused to any form of contact, and then they relaxed against her soft shape, their small arms reaching up to hug her neck in a tight grip.

She looked up, her eyes bright with unshed tears, to see Steed looking down at her with a similar expression contorting his handsome features. She smiled weakly, and as the boys' grip lessened, stood up, taking each twin by the hand and drawing them with her into the house.

'Now you must tell me who is who,' she said when they were all seated in the lounge, the bright afternoon sun showing up the unnatural pallor of the childrens' complexions.

'I'm Peter and he's Jason,' said the slightly larger of the two boys, his brown eyes watchful. 'You can tell us apart because I'm two inches taller than him and my hair's curlier.' He had moved protectively closer to his twin as he'd talked, and Nina noticed Jason's small hand slip into that of his brother's. 'He's been ill, but he's better now,' he added firmly, squeezing the thin hand resting in his.

'Yes, I know.' Nina's heart went out to them. 'Your uncle and I thought it would be nice for you both to have a holiday and get to know me at the same time. Is that all right with you?'

They looked at her in amazement, patently surprised at having their opinion asked for. Steed looked equally surprised.

'I suppose so.' Peter spoke again, his face wary. 'How long will it be before you send us away?'

She looked at him intently and spoke carefully, realising intuitively that there was hurt here that no one had recognised. 'We aren't going to send you away, Peter. Uncle Steed will have to go back to work after the holiday, of course, but I shall stay with you all the time. When we've finished our holiday here we will go home to England to a lovely old house by the sea where I grew up. Your uncle has just bought it.' She glanced fleetingly at Steed. 'If you don't want to go back to boarding-school no one is going to make you, I promise.' She avoided looking at Steed now, sensing him stiffening in his chair. 'You can either go to a school near by, where I used to go, or have lessons at home.'

They sat with their mouths wide open, their small faces so shocked and stunned that Nina wanted to laugh and cry at the same time. She did neither.

'Really?' Peter turned to Steed, sitting slightly behind him, for confirmation, his expression frankly disbelieving.

'Nina's in charge,' Steed said drily, his eyes meeting hers. 'What she says goes.'

'Wow!' The two little faces lit up with pure delight. 'No more rotten old Radstowe.'

'I thought you liked your school.' Steed addressed Peter as spokesman. 'You've never complained.'

'We hate it.' The low voice was flat. 'They always tease us because we're small for our age and because we haven't got a proper mum and dad and have to spend some of the holidays at school.' He looked quickly up at his uncle, suddenly realising his last words could be taken as a criticism, his brown eyes apprehensive.

'Well, you've got a proper aunt and uncle now, and that's nearly as good,' Nina said firmly into the silence, sensing that Steed was out of his depth. 'You'll each have your own room and your own toys at Grayfields, and when you want your friends to tea it will be *your* home that you invite them to. Right?' She looked at them gently.

They stared back at her incredulously, looking as though all their Christmases had arrived in one giant parcel.

'Uncle Steed says you are getting married soon.' Peter was already speaking with more confidence. 'Can we come and see?'

'Come and see?' Her voice was playfully chiding. 'He wants you both to be his best men. You are the most important people in his life, so he would hardly leave you out, would he?'

Steed was sitting in what appeared to be a trance, his grey eyes slightly glazed. When the twins ran over to him and flung themselves round his neck he gazed over their brown heads to Nina, his expression comically dumbfounded.

Later that night when the twins were tucked up in the big double bed in the room next to Nina's, their small bodies curled tightly together and their breathing slow and even, she wandered downstairs to find Steed waiting for her, a glass of wine in hand.

'Are they asleep?' His deep voice was gentle.

'Yes, after three stories and a description of every room in Grayfields!' She took the crystal goblet he proffered and gulped at the sparkling white liquid nervously. She suddenly became horribly aware of all the promises she had made to the two small boys without consulting their uncle first. Still, there hadn't been time—it had needed to be done there and then. She raised her chin defiantly at the thought, her blue eyes cloudy.

'Now what's going on in that razor-sharp mind of yours?' He had been looking at her intently. 'Why do I get the familiar feeling that I've done something wrong?'

She looked at him in surprise, a slow flush staining her sun-tinted skin. 'You haven't done anything wrong. I was worried you would think *I* had.'

'My dear girl,' his voice held that note of labouring patience, 'why should I think that?'

'I didn't ask you whether the twins could leave school or about their being your best men or anything...' she finished haltingly as he gave a small dry laugh, totally lacking in humour.

'Do you really think I would disapprove after seeing such a transformation in them in just a couple of hours in your company,' he asked coldly, 'just because you didn't ask my permission to put their minds at ease? I'm not some sort of dictator, whatever you may think to the contrary, but that's another story.' The full, well-shaped mouth thinned. 'I am more than happy for you to have a free hand with the boys. You clearly understand them far better than I do. I had no idea they were unhappy at school. Besides,' his voice was wry, 'you are the one who will have all the work if they stay at Grayfields.'

'I don't mind that.' Her voice was eager. 'They so need a secure base, Steed. It must have hurt them dreadfully when their parents were killed so suddenly, and they've kept it all in through the years.'

'They had each other.'

'That's not enough; they need other people as well. It's not healthy for them to rely totally on each other. They need adults they are close to and can trust to be there for them, besides friends of their own age. Surely you can see that?'

He smiled slowly, his eyes lazy. 'I can see I made the right choice for them.' Somehow his words saddened her still more. Was that what she was to him? Just a good choice for the children?

She stiffened slightly and put down the half-empty glass with a shaking hand. 'I'm very tired; it's been a long day. Is it all right if I go to bed?'

'Of course it's all right!' The harsh, irritated note was back in his voice. 'You can do what you want, for goodness' sake!'

Oh, but I can't, my love, Nina thought as she wearily climbed the stairs to her room. What I want to do is tell you how much I love you, ask that we have a real marriage and make a proper home for the twins. Instead it will all be play-acting, make-believe. Except for the children. Her thoughts turned to the two little figures curled in sleep. She would at least do her best to make them happy, be everything they needed.

The first blood-curdling scream brought her out of a light, restless sleep with a violent start. She was out of bed in one rapid movement as the next one rent the air with piercing clarity, reaching the boys' room and flicking on the light-switch seconds before Steed threw himself through the door, black stubble standing out in vivid contrast to his shocked white face.

Jason was sitting up in the vast bed, shaking his brother's shoulder, his face fearful, but Peter was still enmeshed in the nightmare, his brown curls wet with perspiration and his face twisted. His dilated eyes held an expression of such dread that Nina's blood ran cold, and she was across the room in a second, gathering the small threshing body in her arms and rocking him back and forth comfortingly while muttering words of endearment against the hot, wet face.

It was a full minute before he relaxed against her, quiet sobs taking over from the frantic gasps that had followed the screams. Steed joined her on the bed, taking Jason on to his lap, their eyes glued to the small body in her arms.

'It's all right, my love, it's all right...' Nina continued to murmur as the small shaking figure in her hold buried his sticky face against her neck. 'It's all over now; just calm down.'

'You won't punish him, will you?' Jason's urgent voice cut into the silence that had fallen on them, punctuated by Peter's gasps. 'He can't help it; he doesn't do it on purpose.'

'What?' Steed's voice was gently questioning. 'Why should we punish him, Jason?'

'Well, Matron at school used to make him write out lines when he had woken the dormitory like tonight. That's why they moved him to the sick-bay with me, but he still used to have the dreams, and then she said he was a baby and he had to have his meals on a little table separate from everyone else.'

Steed's face was blazing with fury, his lips a thin white line, and he carefully put Jason to one side and went to the window with his back towards them. 'What else did she do?' His voice was amazingly controlled.

'Nothing really,' said Jason miserably, looking over to where Nina was still holding his brother tight. 'But when she made him sit on his own the other boys started teasing him all the time, and nobody stopped them. If anyone got into trouble it was always Peter.'

Peter raised his small face to Nina, his long lashes wet with tiny drops of moisture. 'I tried not to go to sleep so it wouldn't happen again, but I got so tired.'

'Of course you did.' She hugged him tightly, her stomach contracting with anger. 'Can you remember what the dreams are about?'

'Yes.' His voice was reluctant. 'It's only ever one dream and it's always the same.'

'Tell me,' she asked coaxingly, stroking the damp hair from his brow.

'It was when Jason was first ill. I'm walking by myself through a sort of desert place with snakes and scorpions everywhere, and there are big black birds that keep swooping at me.'

'Yes?' she encouraged as he wavered, his voice trembling.

'Then Mum and Dad would be on this green grassy hill in front of me and Jason is with them. They're sitting in lots of flowers and Jason is always making a daisy chain. They call me to come and join them, but however much I try I can't get near them. I run and run but I get further away, and then they start laughing and wave goodbye, and I scream and scream at them not to go...' His voice faltered. 'That's when I wake up.'

Steed groaned deep in his throat, his back stiff and tense. Nina shot a quick glance at the tall figure as she reached across and gathered Jason in her other arm, hugging both boys to her.

'Look, Peter, would it help if I explained why you have this dream?'

'I think so.' His voice was doubtful.

'It might help you not to dream it if you know what's causing it, you see? You can sort of face it better, bring it out into the open.'

He looked up at her, his face trusting. 'If you think so.'

'Well, when you lost your parents three years ago I expect everyone told you and Jason you had to be brave, didn't they?' He nodded slowly. 'Did you cry much?'

'We did when we were by ourselves,' Jason proffered, 'but most of the time we were with the other boys and they said we were babies if we cried in front of them. Then Matron and some of the teachers said we hadn't got to talk about Mum and Dad because we only got upset.' The sheer insensitivity of the adults in charge of these young minds took Nina's breath away, and she saw Steed clench his fists against the window.

'Now, I know you had to be very grown-up and you were very brave,' Nina continued, 'but when something like that happens and you can't talk and cry about it it kind of buries itself deep in your mind. It makes you sad even when you're happy.' Both boys nodded vigorously, obviously understanding this strange logic.

'When Jason got poorly you began to worry about him, which is only right,' she said gently, looking at Peter's intent face, 'but instead of being able to let your worry and fear out you had to keep it all hidden again, and that wasn't good for your head.' She tapped the soft curls playfully. 'So your mind cleverly decided to get rid of all that concern by making a play in your head with your parents and Jason and you as actors. You were frightened he would die and leave you too, weren't you?' Peter nodded, his lips shaking. Steed moved restlessly by the window, turning and sitting on an easy chair close by, his dark face grim.

'He is perfectly well again, Peter.' Violet eyes held brown ones in an unwavering grip. 'The illness made him tired and he hasn't grown as quickly as you, but we are going to put all that right. Aren't we, Jason?' Jason nodded enthusiastically. 'Jason is not going to leave you,' she emphasised firmly. 'Uncle Steed and I are not going to leave you. You and Jason are going to be together with us in your own home. You can have a pet too, if you like,' she finished with inspiration. Peter's face broke into a big grin.

Jason looked at her quickly. 'What about me?'

'One for you too,' she agreed softly, tucking the boys under the covers again and stroking their hair from faces so comically alike.

'Now sleep,' she said firmly. 'And if the dream comes again—although it probably won't now you know what's causing it—you can say to yourself, "This is just a stupid dream and it can't hurt me." OK?'

'OK.' She kissed each small face as Steed walked towards the door, his big shoulders hunched.

'Uncle Steed!' Jason's small voice stopped his uncle in mid-stride.

'Yes?' Steed turned and looked towards the three of them, his expression unfathomable.

'You didn't kiss us goodnight.'

'Now, how could I forget that?' Looking inordinately pleased, Steed hugged each child to him, kissing them tenderly as Nina switched off the main light, leaving a small lamp to keep the room in semi-darkness.

'I think we need to have a talk, and if you aren't too tired I'd prefer it to be now, without the kids around.' Steed's voice was abrupt, and Nina looked at him enquiringly, shivering slightly in the cool night air on the wide landing.

'Go and get your robe.' His eyes swept over her and Nina was suddenly embarrassingly aware that all she had on was a wafer-thin silk nightie. Her body gleamed through the soft material with a translucent paleness, and she noticed a small muscle working in his tanned cheek as his eyes met hers.

'Oh!' With a startled exclamation she covered herself with her arms in a protective hug, hot colour flooding her body until her skin glowed, and turned quickly into her room, hearing his low, dry chuckle as the door closed.

'You pig!' she muttered as she shrugged on the fluffy white towelling robe he had bought her in London, pulling the belt unnecessarily tight around her slim body, her movements jerky with humiliation. 'I suppose he thinks I ought to have got dressed before I saw to Peter,' she said into the empty room. She would have to stop this—she talked to herself far too much when he was around.

Pushing her feet into matching white slippers, she made her way downstairs to where Steed was waiting in the darkened lounge, a single lamp flickering in the corner, casting a desultory glow over his still face.

'That's better—or not, depending, of course, on which way one looks at it,' he said softly, his eyes gleaming in the shadows.

'I'm sorry,' said Nina sharply, her face red. 'The only thing on my mind was Peter.'

'Just as well all reason didn't leave me,' he said drily, and as her eyebrows rose he continued lazily, 'I've never indulged in the English fondness for pyjamas.'

The mental picture that flashed into her mind caused her cheeks to burn and she blessed the concealing darkness in the room. 'Really?' Her voice was carefully bland.

He laughed softly again, walking over to the drinks cabinet and pouring two small measures of *paliofi*, an excellent home-brewed gin he bought locally, topping Nina's glass with a generous measure of orange juice.

'Drink that. I think we both need something to calm us down.'

'Yes, Peter's distress was very upsetting.' She ignored the double meaning heavy in his words.

He sat down with a sigh in one of the chintz easy chairs, his dark face suddenly becoming deadly serious. 'I shall close that damn school. I've never heard of such cruelty.'

'I can imagine there's far worse.'

'Not for a member of my family, there isn't.' He downed his drink in one gulp, fetching the bottle and placing it near his seat. 'Their father was my baby brother, you know. He was only twenty-seven when he died.' He poured another measure, filling the glass this time, and settled back in the chair, stretching out his long, lean legs wearily. 'He wouldn't have believed I could let his sons down so badly.'

'You thought they were happy at school. How could you know?' She meant her words to be comforting, but he wasn't in the mood for consolation.

'I didn't *think* at all. I've been too wrapped up in my own life to worry unduly about them. They seemed OK, and I never delved any deeper, and all the time this has been going on.' He poured himself another drink. 'John was a good man, just a bit too vulnerable for the cut and thrust of this world.' His words were still crystal-clear but the big body was relaxing more in the chair as the alcohol anaesthetised his raw emotions.

'He was more like our mother.' He shot her a quick glance. 'You would have liked *him*.' The inflexion on his words was unmistakable.

'I like you.'

'Sure you do.' He laughed in the back of his throat, his face austere in the lamplight.

'Why do you want to talk to me?'

Her calm tone seemed to draw him out of the self-destructive melancholy, and he straightened in his seat, clasping his large hands between muscled knees.

'I thought Jason was the one with the problems, but it seems Peter is more ill in a different way.' He paused and continued painfully, 'Do you think he needs to see a psychiatrist?'

'No, I do not!' She shot up, spilling the orange liquid in her glass. 'Don't be so ridiculous...he'll be fine. There's no need for that.' Her eyes softened as she took in his tormented face. 'He'll be OK in a few weeks, Steed, you have my word on that. He's on the mend already.'

'You're incredibly comforting.' The grey eyes focused on her soft mouth. 'You're so nice to have around. Why don't we get on, Nina? Why don't you give me a chance?'

She sat mesmerised by this new soft Steed, looking up nervously as he moved to where she sat on the wide flowered sofa. He sat down, pulling her roughly on to his lap as he did so, covering her face with quick hungry kisses before she could move. His lips moved to her throat, gently brushing her ear-lobes until her heart was thudding against her breast and she began to melt against him, wanting his arms to hold her forever. She turned her head so his hard mouth met hers and he growled softly, sensing her submission as she tangled her fingers in his hair. She had so longed to feel his arms round her once more, uncertain after his recent coldness if he cared enough to try again.

'We'll be married soon. Will you let me show you how I can love you then?' His voice was a soft groan as he untied the belt of her robe, gently sliding his hands up the smooth skin of her arms and down over the swell of her breasts, their points hardening at his touch under the thin silk of her nightie.

She knew she would hate herself if she didn't stop this now, but the pleasure of having him close after all the heartache and bitter pain of the last few days was driving all rational thought from her head. He doesn't love you; you're his bought possession, a trinket he'll soon tire of. The thoughts were thudding in her head but his hard body was warm against hers and his heartbeat was alive and vital under her hand pressed against his chest.

'You're so lovely.' His voice was trembling as he lowered his black head down against her throat, his lips leaving fire wherever they touched. His mouth moved still lower, creating an exquisite need that was threatening to overwhelm her, her limbs shaking uncontrollably against his hard flesh.

'I need you, Nina.' The deep whisper throbbed with emotion. Maybe he could learn to love her? Learn to be content with one woman? She couldn't answer him; his lips were taking her own again in wild, sensuous exploration that made even her fingertips alive with hot feeling.

'Don't...' Her voice was a little whisper against his mouth, lost in the heated sweetness that was consuming her from head to toe. She felt his hands on her body but had lost the will to understand or think any more...

'No!' She caught hold of his hands as they peeled the thin silk from her flesh. 'Don't, Steed, please.'

He raised his head quizzically, his face tender. 'Why not? You know you want me to make love to you.'

'I don't.' She shivered as his hands continued to work their magic, almost swooning under their expert touch.

'You might be telling me one thing, but your body is telling me another.' His eyes were gentle. 'I won't hurt you, Nina. Don't you know——?'

She stopped his words abruptly as she jerked away from his body. 'I said no!' She stumbled shakily to her feet, pulling the robe tightly around her. 'It's got to be more than just a physical thing for me; can't you understand? It might not be the done thing in your world, but I want to know that the man I give myself to loves me, really loves me.'

He went to speak, his face still tender and warm, but she silenced him with a distraught gesture, her eyes swimming with tears. 'We don't love each other, Steed, and I don't want second best. I'd rather have nothing at all than that.' In her agitation she was speaking straight from the heart and her words were stark with honesty. The man staring at her went suddenly grey, as though he had been punched in the stomach.

His eyes turned into cold slits as he stood up slowly, his mouth a thin, tight gash in his pale face. 'I see; then there's nothing more to be said. I promise you I won't inflict my unwelcome attentions on you again. I had no idea they were so distasteful to you.' He waved a hand towards the stairs. 'It will be necessary to cultivate a courteous and believable relationship in front of the boys, and I regret the difficulties that have arisen in that quarter. I did not know your job with them would prove so harrowing.' His words were clipped and formal with a steel edge to them that cut into her heart like a knife.

She raised her eyes momentarily to his face and caught a look of such bitter contempt and agony on the harsh face that it appalled her. What had she said to cause that?

'Go to bed, Nina.' His voice held a dead note, and she escaped from the room in an instant, almost falling up the stairs in her haste to leave the tall dark figure standing so still in the silence.

'Second best.' The words were ground out through clenched teeth. 'Second best!' With a cold, savage violence he threw his glass towards the wall, where it smashed into a thousand glittering pieces.

# CHAPTER SIX

SUBDUED laughter and muffled thuds awoke Nina the next day to a room filled with bright sunlight. She had fallen asleep as dawn had crept over the night sky, and her heavy eyes were still red-rimmed from weeping. She lay for a moment, her limbs languid and her mind blissfully numb.

A sudden sharp crash brought her fully awake, and after pulling on her robe she padded next door to the twins' room. A pillow fight had obviously been in progress seconds before her arrival, culminating in a cascade of floating white feathers and a broken picture.

Two pairs of brown eyes watched nervously as she began to pick up the sharp fragments of glass without speaking. 'Sorry, Nina.' They spoke as one.

'You will be by the time you've cleared every single feather from this room,' she said lightly. 'It should take you until breakfast if you work hard,' she added, looking at the small alarm clock on the chest of drawers by the bed, 'and I'd hurry if I were you. It's bacon and eggs this morning. Nine o'clock prompt.'

Their faces were crestfallen but resigned as she left the room, and she heard helpless giggles a few minutes later as she dressed, her own lips curving in response to the infectious sound. They clearly hadn't been crushed by her actions, but she knew it was necessary to set some sort of discipline from the start.

Fifteen minutes later, her golden hair coiled into a French plait, and wearing a white top and shorts, she entered the dining-room, where Steed was already sitting eating breakfast, hidden behind a newspaper.

'Good morning.' She kept her voice neutral as she helped herself from the covered dishes on the long sideboard which stretched down the length of one wall, glad her back was to Steed and he couldn't see her hands trembling.

He answered her briefly, clearly disinclined to talk, and within minutes the noisy arrival of the lively twins broke into the charged atmosphere, dispelling any awkwardness with their excited chatter.

'The boys would like to spend the day on the beach if that is OK with you?' His voice was cool and polite as he left the dining-room and she nodded in agreement, looking deep into his eyes for the first time that morning and seeing nothing in their depths but a remote coldness that sent a chill down her spine.

They spent the day under a huge striped umbrella, Nina alternately dozing and paddling while Steed and the twins swam and explored the myriad small paths leading down from the rugged cliffs. The day was pleasantly warm, the tranquil sea reflecting the azure blue of the clear sky, and the white sandy beach was totally theirs apart from the odd curious bird flapping down in search for crumbs from their picnic lunch.

'This could have been heaven on earth,' Nina murmured to herself as she watched Steed laughingly splashing water on the screaming twins, her face shaded by her hand. As it was, her stomach muscles bunched every time that dark glance flicked her way and nervous tension was causing a painful ache in the back of her head that was getting worse with every passing hour.

She was desperately aware of Steed's powerful bronzed body in the brief swimming trunks he wore, firm muscles rippling under brown skin and tiny drops of water glistening in the tightly curled hair covering his chest. His nearness was a bitter-sweet agony that was driving her mad.

The afternoon sun was casting golden shadows across the pale sand when she was woken from a light doze by Steed flinging himself down beside her under the umbrella, his long legs wet and sandy. 'Come and swim.'

'I don't think so. The water looks freezing.'

He smiled that slow, lazy smile. 'It is, but the twins would love you to—they don't like to be separated from you for long.' His eyes narrowed on her face and there was a strange expression burning in their grey depths.

She shrugged lightly. 'I suppose I could stand a few minutes.'

'Brave girl.' His voice was dry, and she flushed, sensing the criticism it contained. 'They didn't take long to wrap you round their little fingers, did they? I'll have to ask them the secret.'

He was gone before she could reply, running swiftly down the beach like a sleek black panther to join the two small figures waving at the water's edge.

That day set the pattern for the next two weeks. Nina discovered she thoroughly enjoyed the twins' company, and they responded to her affection with an unswerving and immediate devotion that brought many a wry comment from Steed. They were serious, well-behaved little boys, but with a highly developed sense of humour that led them into mischief more than once.

As they grew in confidence so their personalities blossomed, and the two adults discovered they were quite different in many respects. Peter gave the impression of being the leader in their close relationship, but Nina swiftly found that he was more shy and sensitive than his brother, often holding back for fear of ridicule.

Jason, on the other hand, was quite fearless, as his name suggested, and provided the solid support and encouragement his brother so often needed. She found them quite fascinating, and already the warmth of the Spanish climate had tanned their white skin a light brown and brought a healthy colour into pale cheeks.

As their holiday drew to a close Steed explained that on their return to England they would spend a few days in London before travelling down to Cornwall and their new home. 'Nina and I have some arrangements to make,' he told the twins gravely, his eyes cool as they flicked over her still face.

'Oh, no, can't we go straight to Grayfields?' Jason asked disappointedly, and Steed's face settled into its usual austere lines, his expression sardonic.

'We all have to do things we don't like, Jason,' he replied softly to his small nephew, ruffling the dark curls as he turned to Nina. 'Don't we, my dear?' His eyes flashed a message only she understood, and she shivered at the bitter mockery in his face.

London was cold and damp as they stepped off the plane at Heathrow, a chill mist entering the taxi with them and coating the grimy windows, through which the children peered uninterestedly. The warmth and colour of the foreign land they had left three hours before seemed light-years away, and as the boys had one of their rare squabbles, their tired faces mutinous and fretful, Nina realised with a sinking heart that the wedding was only a few weeks away. This was cold reality.

As the taxi ground to a halt at the address Steed had given, its windscreen wipers methodically clearing the thin icy drizzle from the cold glass, Nina realised with alarm that they were outside Steed's London flat. The street lights were shining weakly in the grey dusk, casting a faint glow over the quiet tree-lined avenue.

'We can't all stay here.' She spoke without thinking, clutching hold of Steed's coat sleeve urgently.

'We can't?' His voice was impersonal and cold. 'Why not?'

She looked at him, her eyes wide with apprehension. He was playing with her like a cat with a mouse. 'You said it only had two bedrooms...'

He smiled caustically. 'Which is why I shall be taking up residence at my club for the duration of your stay in London. It would be more suitable for the twins to be in an apartment than confined to a hotel room.'

She relaxed, a faint pink staining her cheeks.

'That meets with your approval?' The words were cutting.

He took her arm as they ushered the twins through the wide swing doors into the large air-conditioned lobby beyond, nodding briefly to the security guard on duty. 'Hi, Jim. No problems?'

'None, Mr Charlton.' The middle-aged man snapped to attention as though on inspection. 'Your apartment is all ready, sir. The groceries you ordered have been delivered, and Mrs Pearce has been in all morning to see to things.'

'Thanks, Jim.'

As the carpeted lift took them swiftly upstairs Steed looked at her beneath his black lashes, his eyes mocking. 'I trust it's OK if I stay long enough to see the boys settled?' She flushed miserably and he turned away, his eyes hard.

As the lift doors slid open her eyes widened in amazement. The wide hushed corridor screamed elegance, the deep-piled white carpet and champagne walls talking pure luxury. Even the twins were awed, their shrill voices dying to a murmur as their feet sank into the soft, thick wool.

Inside the flat the rooms were large and fashionably furnished, if somewhat impersonal. It had two enormous bedrooms, a huge reception-room with a quiet tasteful colour scheme in gold and cream, a small study, crammed full with official-looking papers and books, and a luxuriously fitted pale grey kitchen and bathroom. The overall effect was one of understated opulence.

'You'd better sleep in my room,' Steed told her, opening a door to reveal pale oak fitted wardrobes and a magnificent four-poster bed covered with black sheets. She glanced at him in dismay. His powerful presence was stamped all over the vitally masculine room, a small oak desk in the corner holding all his personal toiletries, perfuming the still air with the expensive aftershave peculiar to him.

He caught the look but said nothing, showing the twins the other bedroom, holding two large three-quarter beds with a panoramic view from the large picture window of a silent London shrouded in thick mist.

'I would have thought you would have preferred this room,' Nina commented absently as she peered through the window. 'The view is wonderful.'

'As I'm sure you are aware, I am usually otherwise occupied in the early hours.' The huge bed swam into her vision and she turned sharply away from his taunting gaze, almost knocking Jason over in her haste to escape. 'I might as well be hung for a sheep as a lamb,' Steed commented into the air, his face bland. 'If you can't beat 'em, join 'em.' She feigned deafness.

After the twins had bathed and changed into their pyjamas, looking impossibly angelic with big brown eyes drooping in tiredness and damp curls plastered tight to their heads, Nina prepared them a sandwich and a glass of milk, which they consumed in record speed.

'I've sent out for a meal for us,' Steed said quietly when she rejoined him in the lounge after settling the twins in their room. They had been asleep almost as their heads touched the pillows, thick lashes curled on warm, flushed skin.

'That would be lovely,' Nina murmured gratefully, suddenly realising how exhausted she felt. There was a dull throb in the old wound on her foot, and a stiffening in the back of her neck that spoke of an approaching headache.

'Come and have a drink and unwind,' Steed offered, pouring pale cream sherry into a crystal glass and gesturing to the deep-cushioned sofa beside him. She looked at him uncertainly; there were times like now when he was enigmatically foreign, the mixture of Spanish and American cultures producing a dark attractiveness that made her skin tingle.

'I'm not going to eat you,' he said irritably, noting her hesitation, 'but we need to go over the wedding lists tonight, and you'll need something to fortify you, believe me.'

They spent the next half-hour discussing mundane details until the delivery man rang the doorbell, loaded down with bulging carrier-bags. 'Good grief, Steed, there's enough here for an army,' Nina commented after the young lad had left, his eyes wide at the generous tip Steed had given him. She tipped the contents of the foil dishes on to the plates that had been warming, and Steed carried them over to the huge coffee-table he had pulled in front of the settee by the fire. 'It's cosier than the dining table,' he said briefly as he caught her eyes.

'It looks wonderful,' Nina smiled, her breath catching as he turned away swiftly as though fearing the intimacy of the moment. The plates were steaming with the delicious aroma of Chinese food, and by the time they had eaten their fill there was very little left.

'I'd better be going.' Steed stretched as he stood up, his long, lean body uncoiling with natural animal grace, and he smiled a casual farewell as he shrugged into his big, heavy overcoat. 'I've arranged a sitter for the twins tomorrow,' he informed her as he walked towards the door. 'Get a good night's sleep because we've got quite a schedule over the next few days.'

It was a typical male understatement. In between dashes to the office and long, often irate, telephone calls to his business colleagues, Steed kept to a relentless timetable which astounded and exhausted Nina, but at the end of five days all the wedding arrangements were complete.

She was thrilled with her dress, a soft, frothy creation in ivory silk, the bodice covered with tiny hand-sewn pearls that were matched on the edge of the filmy lace veil and again on the skirt, where it flounced at the hem and was caught with tiny pale-pink bows. Steed had given her a free rein in choosing her finery, dropping her at the wildly exclusive salon first thing in the morning and picking her up at lunchtime. She had been childishly adamant that he couldn't see the wedding dress before the marriage and he had indulgently conceded, his cold face slightly amused at her vehemence.

They drove down to Grayfields on the Sunday morning in the inevitable fine damp drizzle that had persisted since their arrival back in England, but after stopping for lunch at a small country inn Nina was pleased to see a weak yellow sun breaking through the dove-grey clouds. She wanted the twins' first sight of her beloved home to be in the best possible circumstances.

'Don't worry, they'll love it.' Steed clasped her hand for a brief moment in a tiny gesture of comfort as they neared home, reading her anxious face accurately.

'I hope so,' she whispered back, touched at the spontaneous action. It was the first time he had touched her voluntarily since the twins' first night in Spain.

'How could they fail to?' he answered simply. 'It's got you written all over it.' She looked at him quickly, but the hard face was closed and shuttered against her eyes.

They reached the small sleepy village that held so many precious childhood memories by mid-afternoon, the slate roofs of the old stone cottages in the main street dark against the blue-grey sky. The narrow winding lane that led on to Grayfields was full of large, deep puddles and sharp, jutting rocks, but the big car negotiated the obstacles with consummate ease, disdainfully picking its way upwards into the clear Cornish air.

The twins were immediately enchanted with Grayfields, running madly through every room and calling shrilly to each other with every new discovery. The pleasure Nina got from their rapturous approval was spoilt by Steed's obvious impatience to leave within minutes of their arrival.

Since her adamant refusal of him he had firmly kept her at arm's length, his dark face polite but remote, showing a marked lack of interest in her company. It was humiliating to recognise that he was regretting his involvement in her life, but she had slowly come to the conclusion that his brief desire for her had vanished, leaving him impersonally friendly and gently courteous.

'Can't you stay for tea?' she asked stiffly after he had carried the mountain of luggage through to various rooms, staggering under the weight of the boxes of toys and games they had purchased for the twins.

'Do you want me to?' He looked down at her, his face serious.

'Of course I do. There'll only be the boys to talk to once you've gone, and it will be two weeks before you come down again, won't it?'

The strangely expectant look died in his eyes as he smiled wryly. 'I see. Any port in a storm. Yes, Nina, I'll stay for tea, but I must leave immediately afterwards. There's an important meeting tomorrow morning that I need to prepare for.'

She looked at him uncertainly. 'Well, if you want to go now...'

'I said I'll stay.' He gave a bark of laughter. 'As you so rightly reminded me, I shan't be down for another two weeks.' His voice sounded bitter and she got the impression she had offended him somehow, but couldn't think how. It had been his suggestion that he concentrate on business commitments over the next few weeks in order to enjoy a month's honeymoon after the wedding.

His grey eyes searched her small face intently, seeming to seek something in the violet depths of hers, and after a long moment he turned away with a weary sigh. 'You'll have time to show me the grounds again before tea. I shall be living here some of the time in a few weeks, so I suppose I ought to become familiar with them.' He sounded as if he didn't really care one way or the other.

'I'll call the boys.' As she moved to the door she froze in her tracks, his deep voice a snarl in the quiet of the room.

'Can't you do anything without them?' Shock made her face white as she turned to face him, and he came towards her like a menacing jungle beast, his eyes bright and glittering in his angry face. 'You would try the patience of a saint and, as I'm sure you are aware, I'm no saint.' He was taut with rage and she looked at him in bewilderment, her wide eyes fastened on his.

'For crying out loud, don't look at me like that.' As he spoke his body relaxed, and he ran his hand distractedly through his hair. 'I'm sorry, Nina. We're both under a lot of strain and it's beginning to tell. Forget it.'

Taking her arm, he walked out into the panelled hall, calling the boys sharply, his face grim. She had the impression he was keeping his temper in check with iron resolve, and stood quietly at his side, her face troubled.

Peter bounded down the stairs like a young gazelle, closely followed by Jason, and the next hour was spent showing them the gardens and high cliff walks, the wild sea-swept beach and harsh coastline.

'Nina?' They were sitting in uncomfortable silence in a sheltered spot on the deserted beach underneath the overhanging cliff, watching the twins, close to the water's edge, exploring the myriad small rock-pools the retreating sea was uncovering.

'Yes?' She turned to look him full in the face as she spoke, surprising a curiously vulnerable softness in the grey eyes as they looked at her, which was gone in an instant.

'It's not too late to change your mind.' His voice was flat. 'It's not really working out, is it?' He held up his hand as she went to reply. 'I know you aren't happy. How much that is due to your father's death I don't know. He was a good man, far too good to find himself with a wife like Isobel.'

She moved restlessly, her heart exploding with pain. It was true, then. He wanted to get rid of her.

'Don't worry about Grayfields.' His voice was sombre. 'I'll make it over to you legally. I owe that to Tom's memory. The same applies to the debts; you can forget about them. I would have cleared them for him when he was alive if he had let me.'

Jason gave a sudden shriek of laughter as Peter stepped unheedingly into a small, deep hole filled with icy salty water, losing his balance and almost disappearing under the little crested waves as he hopped madly from foot to foot, trying to empty his rubber boots of cold liquid.

'What about them?' Her voice was numb. 'We can't let them down after all our promises.' Hot humiliation swept through her as she spoke and she let the golden fall of hair swing over her face, her eyes burning.

'They're young. They'll get over it.' She glimpsed a glimmer of uncertainty in the cold voice.

'They won't.' With tremendous effort she kept her voice calm. He mustn't suspect he was tearing her apart. 'We owe it to the boys to go through with the wedding as arranged. You don't have to live here afterwards.'

'Don't be ridiculous.' His voice was angry. 'If we do it we do it properly. If the whole point of this sacrifice is to make a home for the twins that's what we shall have to do.'

He looked on their marriage as a sacrifice. The pain and misery she had suffered in the past was nothing to the hot agony that rent her body now. The hope she had cherished that he would learn to love her in the years ahead turned to ashes in her heart, and she was suddenly overwhelmed with the desire to hurt him, to drag her nails over the calm, handsome face and to feel the blood run sticky under her fingers. She balled her hands into her pockets swiftly, horrified at the primitive animal instinct to attack and destroy. What was happening to her?

'That was the original plan, wasn't it?' Her voice sounded amazingly normal.

'Yes,' he agreed wearily, his voice a sigh, 'that was the original plan.'

A wailing scream followed by a huge splash announced the end of the conversation, and as Nina rushed to lift Peter out of the surprisingly deep rock-pool he had fallen into she didn't know if she blessed the appearance of the two small boys in her life or resented it. One thing was certain: but for their presence in their uncle's life her own destiny would have been very different. She would have been struggling under a mountain of debts and very possibly homeless, but her heart would have been her own.

Later that night, when Steed had driven off into the darkness, his stony face a harsh mask, she stood for hours in the huge studio at the top of the house, staring out of the windows into the swirling windy blackness. The bare old oak trees groaned and howled in the gale, wildly thrashing their outstretched branches, and somewhere in the distance a lonely melancholy owl called to the moon, its white light hidden behind scudding grey clouds.

A sick weariness gripped her bruised mind as his stiff, hard words ran through her aching head again: 'a sacrifice'. Well, a sacrifice it would be on both sides. He would be forced to spend time with her and his nephews in this crumbling old house far from the bright lights, and she would have to wave him goodbye each time he left without betraying the fact that he was taking a little bit of her heart with him. But she would be his wife. A quiver shook her slight frame as the thought darted into her mind, and she hugged her arms tightly round her body, the chill of the night creeping into her bones. And she still had Grayfields.

The next morning a small hand shook her gently awake to a room filled with bright sunlight. 'We've brought your breakfast.' Two endearing identical faces looked earnestly into her sleepy eyes as she blinked awake, her head muzzy. 'There's cereal and toast, and we made some coffee. We did it all ourselves,' Peter finished proudly, his head on one side like that of a satisfied parrot.

'It took us ages to find everything,' Jason added, his brown eyes alight. 'It's an enormous kitchen, isn't it?'

'Gigantic!' Nina agreed lightly as she steadied the loaded tray on her knees. There was a mountain of heavily buttered toast, which the twins were eyeing expectantly, swiftly joining her on the bed as she patted the coverlet and demolishing the pile with rapturous enjoyment. Nina leant back and watched them as they ate; already their pinched faces had filled out and the subtle pallor of illness was just a memory on Jason's.

'I do believe you've grown in the last three weeks,' Nina congratulated Jason as the three of them finished eating and the twins prepared to take the empty tray downstairs. He flushed with pleasure and Peter agreed enthusiastically, his face beaming. 'It'll be even harder to tell you apart now,' Nina laughed as they marched to the door. 'No tricks, mind!'

'You always know who we are,' Peter said seriously as he opened the door for his brother, his large eyes intent on her face. 'Mum always knew too.'

His words left a warm glow that remained all day. The twins had a wonderful time exploring every nook and cranny of the rambling old house, unpacking the numerous boxes filled with toys and games and ar-

ranging them in the large sunny room they had chosen
as their playroom. They had decided to share a bedroom
rather than separate, so Nina gave them the huge room
next to their playroom which had an interconnecting
door and *en suite* bathroom.

Late afternoon, hot, dusty and tired, she introduced
them to her father's studio, the aching void his death
had caused beginning to close slightly as she drew
comfort from the twins' affection. They wandered slowly
around the massive room smelling of turpentine and
paint, fingering the stacked canvases and rolls of paper,
the countless tubes of paint and stained easels.

'Do you think I could do some painting?' Peter asked
hesitantly, his voice diffident.

'Of course you can,' Nina agreed immediately, looking
at his bent head sharply. 'Do you like art?'

'He loves it,' Jason volunteered. 'He used to do some
smashing drawings at school before I got ill.'

'Would you like to paint too?' Nina asked Jason, but
he shook his brown curls firmly.

'No, thanks. It's boring. I'd rather read, if that's all
right.'

The next few days settled themselves into a
comfortable pattern. Peter was a surprisingly gifted
artist, having an acute eye for detail that Nina envied.
While Jason read contentedly curled up in an easy chair
in a corner by the window, Nina and Peter worked
silently behind their easels, conferring occasionally over
their palettes as they mixed colours.

The twins were thrilled with the quick portraits she
did of them one rainy afternoon at the end of the first
week, pinning the charcoal drawings over their beds
proudly. She had drawn as she always did, using her
heart as well as her eyes, and consequently the boys'

portraits were subtly different, the turn of a head and a fleeting expression making them two distinct individuals.

'You're really very good,' Peter said consideringly that evening as she cleaned her brushes in the deep old sink at the back of the studio. 'You could sell some of your work, you know.'

She hugged him tightly. 'Not yet, Peter, but perhaps one day. I'm not good enough yet.'

'Well, I think you're great,' he replied staunchly, his face earnest. 'Can you teach me?'

'Of course, but you've already got something no amount of technique can improve upon,' Nina said gently, looking down into the small face lifted up to her. 'You've got a real talent, Peter. It would be a pleasure to teach you.'

His face flushed with pleasure and his skinny arms clasped her waist in a swift hug before he ran off to find Jason. She knew a piercing moment of heart-wrenching love for the two small pieces of humanity given into her care, and her thoughts turned immediately to Steed, wishing she could share this time with him. His harsh face flashed into her mind and her breath caught raggedly in her throat. In spite of the twins' companionship, the week had seemed endless, and it would be another seven days before she saw him again.

Later that evening, as the three of them sat at the kitchen table eating the delicious beef casserole that Mrs Finch had prepared earlier, she heard the scrunch of footsteps outside the window seconds before Steed's dark head appeared silhouetted against the light from the house.

'Steed!' In her haste to rise she almost knocked over the large earthenware pot that was Mrs Finch's pride and joy, and as she steadied it Peter and Jason leapt to the kitchen door, sliding the bolt and springing at their uncle's tall, lean form like two baby monkeys.

'Hey, hey!' As the familiar deep voice grated in the darkness Nina's heart did a double somersault, and she licked suddenly dry lips nervously. He appeared in the doorway with the boys balanced on either hip, his powerful body encased in tightly fitting jeans and a cream leather jacket, black hair ruffled by the icy wind. 'Hi.' His voice was laconic, grey eyes lazy and cool.

Nina felt a sudden sharp stab of anger that he should be so unaffected at seeing her, while she was shaken and trembling, and her voice was unintentionally cool as she returned his greeting, her head downcast.

He sat down at the table without a word, catching her eyes silently, the excited chatter of the twins paling into the background as their linked glance held and deepened, desire flashing between them like a bolt of lightning. His strong, sensual face filled her mind and took over her senses until she wrenched her eyes away with a small whimper of panic, covering the sound in a flurry of movement as she fetched a warmed plate from the huge old stove.

'I didn't think you were coming down this weekend,' she said hoarsely, her breath catching in her throat, ladling the rich meaty stew on to his plate until his firm warm hand covered hers, holding the spoon.

'That's enough, thanks.' His voice was rich with amusement. 'I didn't bring an army with me.'

She flushed as he stared at her, his burning gaze travelling over the slender body, taking in the paint-smeared smock and softly ruffled hair. 'I'm sorry I look such a mess,' she said weakly, pushing back her heavy fall of hair nervously. 'If I'd known you were coming——'

'You would have changed and been neat and tidy to welcome the weekend guest,' he finished brusquely, his jaw tightening.

'I didn't mean it like that,' she said slowly. 'It's just that we've been working all day and I feel so sticky and dirty.'

His face softened. 'You've been up in the studio?'

'We all have.' The twins had decided they had been out of the conversation long enough. 'I've been reading, and Peter and Nina have done some painting,' Jason continued. 'They're pretty good really,' he added reflectively, bringing a quick smile to Steed's face.

'I'm glad they meet your high standards,' he said drily, softening his words with a warm grin at his small nephew.

'Is there anything wrong?' Nina asked as he finished his meal with the twins. His sudden arrival had taken away her appetite and she had merely moved her food round on her plate.

'Does there have to be anything wrong for me to spend some time with you all?' His expression was taciturn. He seemed intent on misunderstanding everything she said, his sharp eyes on her full plate as she carried the dishes to the sink after sending the twins to get ready for bed.

'No, of course not.' She kept her back to him as she spoke. 'The twins have settled in fine,' she added brightly. 'I think they feel it's their home now. Of course, we can't replace their mother and father, but I think they'll learn to love us in time.'

The silence was deafening and she turned to see if he had left. He was looking at her with that strange expression in his eyes, turned as if to stone. 'Love is a strange thing.' He shook his head slightly. 'It's frightening to be in its clutches.'

She stared at him, not knowing how to respond. 'Have you ever been in love?' The words left her mouth against her better judgement, a small knife twisting in her ribs.

'Once.' His voice was grim.

'What happened?'

'I'd rather not discuss it,' he said thickly, a dark flush staining his brown skin as he stretched his long legs restlessly under the kitchen table.

'You aren't still in love, are you?' Nina asked recklessly with a note of horror in her voice. Why hadn't she considered that possibility before? How could she have been so blind? There was clearly someone else; it was written all over his dark face.

Steed swore violently under his breath as he noticed the shocked amazement on her face, moving swiftly to her side in one fluid movement. 'Is your opinion of me so low that you imagine I can't love?' His voice was a snarl, his teeth gleaming white in his furious face. 'You think I'm some sort of machine, don't you? A robot with no natural feelings or desires.'

'No.' She tried to back away but he followed her, pinning her against the wall with his long body, his arms outstretched on either side of her slim form.

'Damn you!' The words were ground out through clenched teeth. 'For some reason you branded me as untouchable the first time we met and it's been the same ever since. Well, I bleed when I'm cut and I feel pain. I've been in love. I've loved so badly that it's torn me apart night after night until I thought I would lose my mind.' His voice lowered to a husky murmur, his face stark with loss. 'But you can't get it out of your system that easily.' He was talking as if to himself now, his voice hoarse with longing. 'It eats away at you minute by minute, hour by hour, and somehow you learn to live with pain. You get by.'

'Steed.' Her soft murmur focused his haunted eyes back on to her white face and he jerked away, his body rigid.

'I hope by all that's holy that you never love like that.' His voice was bitter and strangely defeated. 'I wish you were right, Nina; I wish I were just a shell.'

'I never said...' Her voice trailed away before the savagery in his eyes.

'Get out of here now, before I do something we'll both regret.'

'Please, Steed, you must let me explain. I didn't mean——'

'You didn't mean? But you never mean, do you? One minute I feel you're playing some sort of game with me, and then I look into those damn great eyes of yours and I don't know where I am.'

'I'm not playing games.' Her voice was a whisper.

'Maybe it would be better if you were,' he said wearily. 'I feel you're like a chameleon; I start to get a little close and you change again. Or maybe a will-o'-the-wisp would be a better description,' he added thickly, lifting up a tendril of pale golden hair and letting it slip silkily through his fingers.

She shivered, her face wary. What did he want from her? He had as good as told her there was someone else— how did he expect her to act? She watched his dark face come closer, his large hands reaching up into the shining mass of her hair and tightening either side of her pale face.

'I want to brand you as mine, do you know that?' he muttered huskily. 'To clothe you from head to foot in veils so no other man can look at you, to keep you wholly to myself.'

She listened, mesmerised, his glittering eyes boring into hers until his mouth clamped down in cruel subjection. She jerked her head away violently, catching him by surprise. 'I'm not your possession, Steed. I'm me; I'm a person.'

His face changed, grim anger replacing the passion. 'I sure as hell know that.'

'You act as though you've bought me,' she whispered unsteadily, a pleading note in her voice.

'Well, haven't I?' he asked cruelly, his face tightening. 'You asked me once what was in this deal for me. Perhaps I've changed my mind about that.' His mouth was drawn back in a bitter sneer and his eyes were like slate; his whole body seemed poised to pounce.

She stared at him in anguish. What was driving him to make him so devilish?

'Stop looking at me like that. Can't you look at me as if I'm a normal man for once?' His voice was shaking with rage and some other emotion she couldn't place. She went to turn away, sick at heart, but he pulled her forward roughly, his grip bruising her arms, until her body was against his hard chest. She made no effort to escape; her mind felt dull and her limbs dead.

'I want you, you know that.' He lowered his mouth and claimed her lips again, crushing her against his muscular body until she could hardly breathe.

She wrenched her face away from his, horrified to find her treacherous body responding to his nearness in spite of all he had said. 'Don't...' It was a faint whisper.

'Why?' There was granite in his voice. 'You know you want me. I can at least awaken that sleeping body.'

She flushed painfully, her eyes wild. 'Animals mate with more tenderness.'

It was as though she had thrown cold water over him. He pushed her away so sharply that she stumbled and would have fallen but for the dresser behind her. There was a look on his face of such deep hurt that for a moment she wondered if she had misunderstood all that had gone before. But no, he had made it plain he desired her body, nothing more.

'There are times, Nina, when I regret the day I ever saw you.' He slammed the kitchen door viciously as he left to go upstairs, the sound jarring her bones until she felt she would break into a million tiny pieces, hot tears running in a flood down her cheeks, and an agony in her heart that was tearing her in two.

# CHAPTER SEVEN

'GOOD morning.' Nina opened dazed eyes to find Steed standing by her bed with a cup of tea in his hand and a slightly apologetic expression on his arrogant face.

'Good morning,' she answered softly, looking at him uncertainly as she pulled the bedclothes more tightly round her.

'Did you sleep well?' His voice was uncomfortable, and as she returned his gaze, her face eloquent, he flushed slightly and handed her the steaming cup. 'If it's any consolation, neither did I.'

'It isn't,' she answered simply with the ghost of a smile.

'I'm sorry about last night, Nina.' He walked over to the window, where he stood gazing out into the garden below with his back to her, the sunlight turning his black hair midnight-blue. 'Believe it or not, I have a reputation for my ability never to lose my cool. It's one of my greatest assets in business, but somehow, where you are concerned...' He paused. 'You always seem to manage to hit the fire button.'

'I do?'

'You do,' he said grimly, swinging round and walking over to the bed. 'Nevertheless the fault last night was completely mine and I wouldn't like it to spoil the weekend for everyone concerned. The twins are like cats on a hot tin roof as it is. Can we start again?'

'Of course,' she said immediately, and as his mouth softened into a smile she added hesitantly, 'I'm sorry too, Steed. You have done so much for me and I am grateful, even if it doesn't seem like it.'

'Don't be grateful.' His voice was firm. 'Whatever you do, don't be grateful—that would be the last straw. I only ever do what I want to.'

'I'm not sure if I believe that.'

'Believe it,' he said adamantly. 'You owe me absolutely nothing, if that's the thought that was running through your beautiful head. Your agreement to take the twins on has more than paid the debt in full. We are equal, Nina. We can meet on equal terms.'

She looked up at him, her eyes misty in the early-morning light, and something in their deep blue depths caused a muscle to jerk convulsively in his tanned cheek. 'Hell, Nina, don't look at me like that, not when it's not for real.'

He was gone before she could reply, and as she sat quietly drinking the tea she could hear the twins calling him to their room and wished she had the same freedom. If only things could be different; if only he loved her... She pushed the self-pitying thoughts away sharply. This weekend would not be spoilt. He was here, wasn't he? That was something at least, even if it was probably only to see the twins.

'I wondered if you'd like to come up to London for a meal tonight?' She looked at him in amazement as they sat having breakfast; he spoke about the long journey as though it were a mere five minutes.

'But you've just driven down,' she protested. 'Surely you want a rest?'

'Not particularly.' His eyes were warm as they rested on her wide-eyed face. 'As it happens, some old friends are in London for the night and I've told them a lot about you. They'd like to meet you if you're willing.'

She nodded uncertainly. 'They have just made some important concessions on a particular deal I've been struggling with for some time, so I feel I had to at least ask you. Are you sure?'

She nodded again. 'Of course, if you'd like to. What about the boys, though?'

'Same arrangements as before. You can all stay at the flat and I'll go to my club. Mrs Pearce will be happy to babysit again—she was OK last time, wasn't she? The twins got on well with her, I understand. It'll just be overnight; I can bring you back tomorrow.'

'Fine.' Nina felt the familiar feeling of bemusement creep over her that Steed's lifestyle always managed to produce. He spoke about a four- or five-hour journey in the same way other people discussed a visit to the local supermarket.

The drive up to London was easier than she had expected, the twins' chattering dispelling any embarrassment, although she was vitally aware of Steed's lean body close to hers as he controlled the big car with effortless ease, his large hands resting lightly on the steering-wheel.

She was dreading the evening ahead, although she thought she had managed to keep her fears hidden from him. The prospect of meeting his friends was bad enough, but the fact that they were business colleagues as well caused a nervous fluttering of panic in her stomach every time she considered it. How would she know what to talk about? She was no female tycoon or astute career woman; seeing her in his world, he would realise how totally unsuited she was to become his wife. She sighed deeply; perhaps it was all for the best.

'Don't worry, you'll be fine. I promise I won't let them eat you for the main course.' His hand covered hers for a brief second.

She smiled wanly; she should have known he would sense her unease. 'But do they know that?'

'That's the girl.' He flashed her a quick smile of approval that lit up his cold face so her breath caught shockingly in her throat. 'Don't let it get to you. You're more than a match for anyone I know.'

Later that evening she stared at her reflection in the big oval mirror in Steed's bedroom with something akin to awe. She was wearing a dress Steed had chosen for her on one of their recent shopping sprees, a madly expensive creation in soft silk that she would never have contemplated buying herself.

The style was deceptively simple, its smooth classic lines a perfect setting for her ethereal beauty, the soft gold of the material reflected in her hair, which she had swept up into a loose knot on the top of her head. A single diamond looped on a fine gold chain and her engagement ring were her only jewellery, and the whole impression was one of gentle glowing innocence and radiant beauty. She hardly recognised herself, but the dress had given her the lift she needed to face the evening ahead.

She walked out to answer Steed's knock at the front door as though in a dream, and he caught his breath sharply at his first sight of her, his eyes narrowing as a small flame flared in their dark depths. 'You've never looked lovelier,' he said quietly, putting a small box in her hands as he lightly placed his lips on the top of her head before moving away to sit watching her as she lifted the lid slowly.

'How beautiful,' she breathed, staring at the tiny golden comb covered in fresh flowers of a deep velvet blue.

'To match your eyes,' Steed said as he fixed the comb at the base of her coiled hair. 'Orchids just weren't right somehow.'

'What are the flowers called?' she asked as she raised her eyes to his penetrating gaze.

'Love-in-a-mist,' Steed replied drily, moving to sit on the sofa again. 'Appropriate, do you think?'

'They're gorgeous.' She smiled at him warmly.

'That's not quite what I meant.'

The boisterous arrival of the twins with Mrs Pearce in tow, fresh from choosing a video for the evening from the huge shop a street away, dispelled the question mark that had arisen in Nina's mind at his enigmatic words.

'The things they have in that shop!' Mrs Pearce rolled her grandmotherly eyes in horror. 'They only wanted *The Night of the Living Dead*, a horror movie or some such rubbish! I told 'em, you have *Mary Poppins* or nothing, my lads. I have to go home to an empty flat, and some of those films would scare a body out of her mind!' She turned as she spoke and winked conspiratorially at Nina.

'Thank you, Mrs Pearce,' said Nina gratefully.

'I bought 'em a few sweets to eat while we watch, if that's all right, lovey?' she continued, fetching two enormous bulging paper bags out of her old shopping bag as she spoke.

The twins' eyes lit up and Nina nodded smilingly. The woman really was a treasure. Her handling of the twins was masterly, their lost choice quite forgotten at the sight of those bags.

They arrived half an hour early at the cocktail lounge where they were to meet Steed's friends due to the traffic's being far less congested than Steed had thought. She felt the old panic rise in her throat as Steed ordered two drinks from the attentive waitress. He was so perfectly at home in this environment, while she felt like a very ordinary fish out of water.

'You're going to knock them dead.' His voice was calm and soothing on her tight nerves. 'Just look round you, Nina. Who else do you see who has your natural poise and dignity?'

She looked around and could see quite a few, but a certain intonation in the lazy voice told her he had not said his words lightly. He meant it. He thought she was as good as all these beautiful women who wore their exquisite finery so casually. The thought stiffened her back and put a sparkle into her deep blue eyes.

'I was wondering, would you like me to keep the destination of our honeymoon secret or would you prefer to choose where we go?' At his quiet voice she looked up, startled, from her surreptitious contemplation of a famous actress and her entourage in the middle of the room, to find his eyes on her face.

'I don't know,' she stammered, blushing furiously. 'What do you normally... I mean, what is usual...?'

His face hardened into dark steel even as he spoke, his words deceptively soft. 'Are you asking what I normally do when I take my women away somewhere?' The silk in his voice didn't fool her for a moment. She recognised his anger.

'No, not exactly...' Her voice trailed away. 'It's just I don't know anything about this sort of thing.'

'And I do?'

She looked at him suddenly, her face defiant. 'Well, don't you?'

They glared at each other for a few seconds and then his face softened as he sighed deeply, leaning back in his chair and crossing one muscled leg over another. 'Nina, Nina, Nina. What am I going to do with you?' She held his glance miserably. 'I never pretended I was a monk, sweetheart, but you seem to rate me between Don Juan and Casanova.' His eyes were dark and glittering as he looked deep into her troubled face. 'Just for the record, I have never taken anyone else on honeymoon before, and although I hate to disappoint that extremely vivid imagination of yours I am not into dirty weekends or "business trips" abroad either. I have to admit that, as I have reached the age of thirty-five without taking a vow of celibacy, there have been ladies who have been more than friends, but you knew that already.' He twisted in his seat and leaned forward again. 'Well, which is it? A surprise, or have you somewhere in mind?'

'No, you choose—a surprise.' A tight sensation was restricting her breathing and she knew she was blushing again but was quite unable to stop the hot colour staining her cheeks. She looked down at her hands resting in her lap, twisting the heavy engagement ring on the third finger of her left hand.

'We aren't taking the twins with us, you know.' Her head shot up in surprise at his words. The thought was entirely new to her and he clearly read her amazement in her wide violet eyes as they searched his face.

'I never thought for a moment we would,' she said indignantly, 'not on our honeymoon.' There was a wealth of shock in her voice and he smiled mockingly, his hand reaching out to enclose one of hers in a soft caress as he turned her fingers over gently in his big palm and stroked the pulse at the base of her wrist with a knowing finger.

'Didn't you? Well, maybe there's hope for me yet, then, but I thought I'd make sure. After all, it won't be the normal sort of honeymoon, will it? Will it?' There was a deep heat in the last words that frightened and thrilled her at the same time. She looked at him wordlessly as every cell in her body quivered in answer to the throbbing need in that dark, rich voice.

'I've dreamed of that time alone with you.' His voice was thick and there was a burning hunger in his narrowed eyes that was met and understood by something deep inside her own flesh.

'Have you?' It was a faint whisper.

'I've thought of nothing else lately; I've eaten, drunk and slept it. Just the two of us together, alone in our private world, with no one to interrupt us, no business commitments, no twins...' His eyes trailed fire over her skin wherever his gaze rested and it was as if he was already making love to her, a shiver of pleasure flooding her body and a flush of desire making her violet eyes liquid.

'Yes, it will be very nice,' she agreed weakly, her voice shaking, disconcerted when he gave a bark of laughter, his eyes wicked.

'Oh, Nina, you're unique! Absolutely unique! I hope the world doesn't change you with its hard cynicism.'

She looked at him under her eyelashes, uncertain if he was mocking her, but there was a wealth of tenderness in the handsome dark face. 'There's a sweet agony in being with you. Have you any idea at all what I'm talking about?' His words were a soft, low growl, and as she nodded slowly his breath shuddered in his throat. 'Let's get out of here now. Go somewhere where we can be alone and talk, just talk. I want to know what's going on in that head of yours.' She looked at him silently, her eyes huge in her flushed face.

'Steed, darling!' The light female voice was familiar somehow, but Nina couldn't place it.

Steed shut his eyes briefly for a second and then opened them to look at Nina with a sigh of resignation. 'Marcia, Paul. Nice to see you. I don't think you've met Nina before.' He turned and rose as he spoke, swiftly pulling out a chair for the slim, beautifully dressed woman who had just reached their sides and shaking her tall smiling husband by the hand.

'We might not have met you before, but I feel we know you already,' Marcia said warmly as she took Nina's hand in a firm clasp, dropping a light kiss on her cheek. 'Steed has talked of little else over the last few weeks. I feel this last contract would have been more difficult if he hadn't got his heart set on getting back to you as soon as he could.'

'Marcia!' Her husband was laughing but his expression carried a warning as he looked at his beaming wife. He had noticed the slight tightening of his friend's firm mouth.

'It's true!' She spared him a swift glance and then turned back to Nina, her brown eyes merry. 'We have never received so many concessions on delivery dates and distribution before. Normally Steed is a hard man to deal with, even if we have been friends for years. I've been dying to meet you.' She smiled in unaffected friendship. 'I can see why he's so captivated—you're everything he said and more.'

'Marcia.' This time the note in her husband's voice made contact and Marcia tossed her dark glossy curls as, introductions completed, the men seated themselves after ordering another round of drinks.

By the time they wandered through to the quiet sumptuous restaurant half an hour later Nina's head was spinning with the effort of following Marcia's quick tongue. She barely noticed the grandeur of her surroundings as Marcia related one witty anecdote after another, often directed against the fast sophisticated world in which they lived, always careful to draw Nina into the conversation and explain anything that could be misunderstood. The two men were clearly used to her volatile enthusiasm, indulgently putting in a word here and there but leaving the thrust of the conversation to the beautiful brunette.

They had just ordered coffee after their excellent meal and were sitting chatting quietly when Marcia turned to Nina with a quick gesture of apology. 'Oh, I meant to ask your forgiveness for my blunder the other day.' Her face was wry. 'As you have no doubt gathered from this evening, I do have a tendency for rushing in where angels fear to tread.'

'And how!' Her husband's voice was a groan of agreement and she flashed him a quick laughing grimace before turning back to Nina, who was looking at her, puzzled.

'I'm sorry, Marcia. I don't know what you mean.'

'When Steed phoned you the other week, you know.' She flicked Nina's arm lightly. 'I had no idea he was calling you. I thought it was the office yet again, and we had been working all day on the contract and had gone out for something to eat. We were all starving.'

'It was you!' Nina suddenly recognised where she had heard the laughing warm voice before. It was the day

Steed had called from England before he had brought the twins out to Spain.

'Afraid so.' Marcia pulled a face. 'I bet you thought he was badgered by business all the time. Can't even make a telephone call in peace.'

'No, not at all.' Nina spoke without thinking, unaware of a lull in the men's conversation and Steed's eyes tight on her flushed face. 'I'm glad you told me it was you. I thought...' She stopped suddenly, aware that she couldn't voice what she had thought.

'What did you think?' The gentle loving companion of the evening had vanished, leaving in its place a cold bleak stranger. Steed's eyes were the only live things in his rigid face, glowing with menacing fury. He had half risen from his seat as though unaware of his surroundings, his burning gaze held fast to Nina's pale face. 'What did you think?' He repeated the words in a low expressionless voice.

'Steed, it's just something Nina's clearly misunderstood.' Marcia was trying to defuse something she didn't understand. 'I'd just told her that——'

'I heard what you said, and my fiancée's reply.' His voice was Arctic-cold, and Marcia cast a helpless glance at her husband, who replied with a shake of his head and a 'what have you done now?' look on his worried face.

'I'm sorry.' Steed stood up slowly, moving round to Nina's chair and pulling it out carefully as he took her arm in a steel grip. 'We're going to have to leave. I'll settle the bill on my way out, Paul.'

'Steed, please...what have I done?' Marcia's voice was frightened and he looked at her briefly, his hand going out to pat her arm reassuringly.

'Nothing, Marcia; you haven't done anything wrong. Relax.' He turned to his friend, who had risen, and held out his hand. 'I'm sorry, Paul, but this can't wait. I've enjoyed the evening.'

Nina made her farewells while Steed settled the bill, her face white and drawn. There was a deathly grimness about his eyes that warned her this was no passing tiff; there was a rage in his face that had gone beyond mere anger.

'Get in the car.' An attentive doorman had brought the car round to the entrance of the hotel and Steed helped her in, tight control in all of his movements. He was as white as a sheet.

He drove without speaking to a dark secluded street, cutting the engine with a swift savage jerk at the keys and turning to her slowly, his eyes gleaming in the dim light from the street lamps.

'Well?' She was almost fainting with fear, her face a white mask in the stillness, but there was no compassion in his taut face as his eyes searched hers. 'I want you to tell me what you thought when I phoned that night. I want it all.' The last words were a bark and she visibly started, her hands going to her mouth. 'I'm waiting, Nina.' The iron voice was relentless.

'I thought...' Her voice quivered, but his face didn't move. 'I thought you were with someone.'

'I *was* with someone.' He was merciless. 'I was with Marcia and her husband.' He stressed the last two words slightly. 'I don't understand. Explain further.' He was going to extract the last drop of blood.

'It sounded as if...' She stopped, and for a moment the stillness was complete. 'I thought you had taken another woman to dinner.' There; it was said. She looked at his face and it was dangerous, his eyes dark and furious and his jaw clenched.

'Let's get this right.' He paused. 'You thought I had made a telephone call to you while I was entertaining another woman for the night? Did this entertainment include the inevitable in your busy little mind?' She stared at him miserably. 'Did it?' There was a pain in his eyes that matched her own.

'It just sounded as if...' She stopped. 'I'm sorry.'

'You're sorry.' His voice was amazingly even and cool. 'You assume that I would insult you by first of all taking another woman out for the evening and maybe into my bed, and follow that up with such a total disregard to your feelings and status as my fiancée that I would actually telephone you while in her company? Is there nothing you think me incapable of? No depth to which I would not sink?'

'You must see how it sounded to me?'

'No!' The word was a whiplash of hate. 'I do not see at all. If a man insulted me the way you have tonight he would not live to see the morning light.'

She was too frightened for tears, panic filling her mind at his implacable fury. She couldn't reach him; it was as though he had been turned into stone. 'I thought something like that wouldn't mean much to you...' She was trying to explain, but her faltering words were the last straw in his iron control.

'You dare to say that!' His eyes tore into hers. 'You credit me with all the finer feelings of a cockerel in a farmyard! Have you no idea...?' His voice died as he pulled her violently across the seat into his arms. 'To hell with it! If that is how you see me, why should I bother?' She struggled madly in his arms, conscious that a brake that had been holding him in all their embraces before had suddenly gone.

'You have pushed me too far, Nina. Tonight you become a woman...' His mouth devoured hers even as she tried to kick and struggle against the big, solid body, and as he felt her resistance he turned her slightly in his arms so now she was lying cushioned between the seat and his body with her legs trapped beneath his and her arms held tightly in a cruel, biting grip. 'There's no escape. I will prove I'm everything you have thought of me.' The throbbing anger and pain in his voice replaced all desire and his kiss was a punishment, a dark, savage, primitive punishment.

'No, please, not like this...' She wrenched her head away as he followed the line of her throat with his lips, and he laughed softly, his breathing harsh.

'But why not? This is what you imagine I like, is it not? A quick, sordid mating with no care or love on either side, a joining together of two bodies in animal passion?'

His lips found hers again as his weight moulded her into the hard outline of his body, his thighs like steel against her softness and his male power obvious against her shape.

She hadn't known she was crying until she felt him suddenly stiffen against her, his hand releasing one of her arms to brush her face with the tips of his fingers. 'I'm going mad.' There was a strained incredulity in his thick husky voice that reached through her fear and terror and brought her eyes up to the wild glitter in his. 'I'm losing my mind.' He released her slowly, taking his weight off her and lifting her shaking body into her own seat, where she curled in a small, crushed heap, drawing the torn silk round her legs where it had caught on the controls of the car.

He reached in his pocket and gently wiped her face with a linen handkerchief, not taking his eyes from hers for a moment. She quivered as his hand touched her face but he continued in his task, reaching over to the back seat and pulling the car rug over and around her, his eyes bleak.

They drove back in silence, and later that night, when Steed had driven Mrs Pearce home and she was alone, she wandered into the twins' room, sitting by the window while they slept and peering through the slatted blind at the bright lights of London. She couldn't sleep, although her mind was numb and beyond thought, her empty eyes watching the cars crawling about below like tiny glow-worms as the city went about its business.

Dawn came slowly in a soft pink greyness, a light mist subduing the sharp outlines of the night. Wearily Nina crawled into bed to lie in the warm darkness, waiting for the twins to awake.

She was pale and heavy-eyed when Steed arrived mid-morning to drive them home, his face hollow and cold in the weak sunlight, his eyes hard. His mood intimidated even the twins, who lapsed into an obedient silence as they left the apartment, causing the drive back to be a silent affair. Steed was immersed in his own thoughts and far away from them all; he had withdrawn into himself to the point where Nina felt he was oblivious of her presence, although she was vitally aware of every small movement he made.

'It's been a long weekend.' There was no warmth in the cool grey eyes watching her as they neared the village. 'You'll be glad to get home.' It wasn't a question and Nina didn't reply, his face chilling her blood.

It was mid-afternoon when Steed's Mercedes drew into the tree-lined drive and they saw Grayfields's dark roof illuminated against the mauve-blue sky. The timeless call of a wood-pigeon rang out in the clear air, scented with the first tender blossom from a bent old lilac tree at the side of the house.

Nina breathed in the cool fresh air as she stepped from the car, lifting her face thankfully to the familiar land-scape, unaware of the sombre haunted gaze of the still figure behind the wheel.

The twins piled out in a mad scramble of jeans and trainers as soon as Steed cut the engine, disappearing with wild whoops behind the house in a noisy game of tag.

'I won't come in.' His voice was tight, the sound jarring on the soft Cornish air, causing her to turn and meet his dark gaze. 'You are very tired and the twins need to bathe and eat.'

'Can I make you a cup of coffee before you drive back?' Nina offered hesitantly, her stomach twisting as she met his eyes. What a disaster the weekend had been.

'You're very kind.' His mouth twisted mockingly. 'However, we are both aware you can't wait to see the back of me, and I can't say I blame you.'

'That's not true.'

'No?' He sighed deeply. 'You really care for the twins, don't you?' Something in his voice disturbed her further, a strange inflexion she couldn't name. Was he going to take them away from her? Her eyes flared in panic but she kept her voice calm.

'Yes, they're great kids. A credit to you.'

His mouth twisted as though in contempt. 'Let's face facts. If it had been left to me my brother's children would still be struggling in an impossible situation, without their guardian and protector having the faintest idea anything was wrong.'

'It wasn't your fault.' Her voice was gentle as she looked at him through the car window. 'How could you have known? Anyway, you arranged this whole thing for them, didn't you—me, Grayfields, everything? You have nothing to reproach yourself for.'

There was complete silence. 'You really don't see, do you?' His voice was thick. 'You really don't have any concept...?' She stared at him as his voice ground to a halt and his eyes met hers with a deep haunted bitterness in their grey depths. 'We don't speak the same language.'

He turned the key so that the big machine sprang into life, his face weary and his voice hard. 'I think it would be best if I don't come down again until the weekend before the wedding. I shall be busy, and the boys don't need me as long as they have you.' She made an involuntary gesture of denial but he stopped any words with a quick shake of his head. 'I've had all I can take, Nina. I'll be seeing you.'

As she stepped back from the car he ground round her in a scream of burning tyres, roaring down the drive without looking to left or right. She was walking up the crumbling stone steps to go and find the twins when she heard the squeal of laboured brakes, and as she turned the big car was backing furiously towards her in a flurry of silver metal. A cloud of birds rose from their perches in the old trees, calling their shrill disapproval of the crazy behaviour of humans in grating cries.

'Steed?' He was out of the car as she spoke, taking the steps two at a time, pausing before her with an almost satanic expression sharpening the rugged features. His dark masculinity reached out to overpower her, and for a moment she felt breathlessly afraid as his icy grey eyes swept over her slender face.

'I forgot to say goodbye.' He pulled her roughly into his arms before she realised his intention, his grip inexorable.

'Don't.' She gasped in shocked surprise at his abruptness as he stared down at her, his teeth gleaming in a bitter sneer.

'Don't? Don't what? Don't kiss my loving fiancée farewell? Is my touch so repulsive to you? I seem to remember that on other occasions I can get you to forget your inhibitions. That is, of course, when I use a little finesse.' She twisted in his grasp, alarmed by the wild savagery on his face, the cruel compelling line of his jaw as he lowered his ebony head to hers.

She had expected the kiss to be brutal, but as his firm, warm lips parted hers his touch was gentle, probing the intimacy of her mouth in a sweetly passionate need that drew her into his body until she felt as though they were one, so closely were they entwined. He was murmuring incoherently in his throat, his hands stroking her soft body under her coat until she felt hot desire leap into play, catching the breath in her chest and causing her own hands to explore in turn.

He groaned convulsively at her touch, his ragged heartbeat in tune with hers, his lips scorching her flesh as his mouth moved down her face and into the hollow of her throat where the pulse was fluttering like a live thing. Her helpless trembling was feeding his desire and he raised his head shakily, looking down into her flushed face, searching her eyes with a sudden curious longing.

'Nina?' She gazed up at him, lost in a shivering whirlwind of desire. 'Nina.' He shook her slightly, his face torn with a hungry pain, a shadow of self-contempt pulling at his mouth. 'It isn't enough, is it?'

'What?' She could scarcely hear him, but he pushed her away from him slightly so the cold air was icy on her face.

'You are so young, so innocent, so very pliable.' She gazed at him in confused perplexity, her eyes still clouded with passion. 'It would be so easy to take you and damn the consequences, but you would end up hating me more than you do now.' She shuddered, this time with foreboding, and his hand went out to her to stop midway, a groan wrenched from the very heart of him. 'Second best.' He turned away slowly, his big shoulders bent. 'You're right, sweetheart—you deserve better than that.'

This time he didn't come back. As the car disappeared in a swirl of grey dust the night's approaching quietness settled on the garden. A bird twittered briefly in one of the vast oak trees lining the drive, and then all was silent again.

Nina stood quite still, her heart and body frozen. Somewhere behind the house she could hear the twins shouting, but the sound hardly registered as a heavy sick weariness invaded the ice round her heart. In those last few seconds after he had pushed her away his face had been rent by pain, humiliation and a bitter, cold misery so deep that she felt he was drowning. He still loved the other woman that much. What had he said? She wrinkled her brow as she tried to remember his muttered words; oh, yes: 'It isn't enough'.

'Why, Steed?' she whispered into the cool air. 'Why did you have to come into my life and make me love you? Why couldn't you have just left me alone?'

Later, after the boys were asleep, she sat in quiet reflection on the old stone steps in the dark of the night.

'Help me, Dad,' she prayed into the blackness. 'I need you. I don't know which way to go any more.' As she spoke the night's velvet darkness was lifted into light and the moon sailed out in full splendour from behind dense clouds, shafts of white moonlight illuminating the hushed garden and giving a stark beauty to the tall ancient oak trees, their vast limbs naked and cold, silhouetted against the soft glow of the night sky.

'Nothing worth having comes easy.' Her father's words spoke into her head with sharp clarity, his voice so real in her mind that she almost expected him to be standing by her side. It had been one of his favourite sayings when things went wrong. Steed was worth having. In the past few weeks she had seen so many facets of his personality, each more endearing than the last: his tenderness with the boys, his strength and determination, his intrinsic compassion. Even the lasting love he had for this other woman spoke of his intensity of spirit.

She had been handling this all wrong. How could he begin to care for her as something other than her father's daughter and an attractive woman if she held him at arm's length? She would fight this woman on equal grounds. What did pride or self-preservation matter when her whole future was at stake? Because she suddenly knew one thing with shocking truth: if she couldn't have Steed she would never have anyone else.

'I'll tell him how I feel,' she breathed softly. 'I'll tell him I don't expect anything, that I know he loves someone else but I'll be there for him.' A solitary bat curved down towards her in swift flight, turning at the last moment and disappearing into the motionless trees.

She shivered in the silence. Could she do it? What if he rejected her still further when confronted with her love, with the bonds of commitment he so abhorred? She raised her small chin unconsciously, her eyes gleaming as she looked into the dark future. She had to try. Without him she had nothing.

# CHAPTER EIGHT

'I'M SO sorry, Miss Kirkton, I'm afraid Mr Charlton still isn't available.' Carol's cool, superior voice didn't sound at all sorry. It was the third time Nina had called and she was beginning to despair that Steed would ever talk to her again.

She had slept surprisingly late that morning after a restless night, tossing and turning into the early hours, going over her proposed conversation with Steed, longing to talk to him now the decision had been made. By the time she had called London Steed had been in conference, and, after ascertaining it wasn't a matter of life or death, Carol had tightly informed her in clipped tones that he had left orders he wasn't to be disturbed.

'Do try later, Miss Kirkton,' she had suggested firmly, and it was now three hours and two more phone calls later, and Nina's teeth gritted in impotent fury. The secretary's voice was just bordering on complacency, her attitude proprietorial.

'I see, Carol.' Nina's voice was as cold as the other girl's. 'Please tell him I rang when he's free, and ask him to call me this evening. I shall be busy for the rest of the day.'

Now why had she been goaded into saying that? Nina thought crossly as she put down the receiver with unnecessary force. Cutting off her nose to spite her face. The afternoon stretched endlessly before her, an animal restlessness pervading her agitated mind. It was the twins' first day at the village school and they had woken her that morning with a goodbye kiss as they had left. She had intended to take them herself and settle them in, and consequently had felt mildly guilty all morning.

After preparing and eating a light lunch she wandered upstairs to the studio. The large room was full of light, and as always the comforting smell of paint and turpentine soothed and calmed her. All her life she had run to this room with her troubles. It was here she had really got to know her father, their shared interest in art forging bonds that had proved unbreakable in the traumatic years following Isobel's arrival.

A sudden burst of adrenalin fired her senses as she gazed at a half-finished portrait her father had been working on before his death. The laughing face of the young schoolteacher from the village stared back at her, the contours blurred and muted. Her father had been painting from a photograph, which was still propped to one side of the easel, slightly curled at the edges. She remembered vaguely the finished work was to have been a surprise birthday present for his elderly mother.

She worked on the canvas all afternoon, so absorbed that she was unaware of the twins' return until they burst exuberantly into the room in a flurry of cold air and school disinfectant. 'That's very good.' Peter moved his head to one side as he considered the portrait, his face serious.

'Good? It's terrific!' Jason said warmly, his face alive with admiration. 'Why don't you paint a picture of Uncle Steed, Nina? You did one of Peter and me.'

'They aren't pictures, silly,' said Peter condescendingly, giving his brother a light punch on the arm. 'They're called portraits.'

'I don't care what they're called,' Jason returned smartly. 'I know Uncle Steed would like one.' His usual good humour was quite unruffled by his twin's superior air.

'Come and tell me how you got on at school,' Nina interrupted firmly, guiding them out of the room hurriedly, recognising the possibility of an argument. They both spoke at once as they went downstairs, the big old kitchen enveloping them in its homely warmth as they opened the heavy door, the enticing smell of fresh bread rich in the air.

'Mmmm…' They lifted noses in unison, sniffing madly as she pushed them towards the worn oak table.

'The Bisto twins,' Nina laughed gently, a sudden surge of maternal love lifting her heart as she looked at the flushed, grubby little faces as they devoured great chunks of Mrs Finch's delicious bread.

It was eleven o'clock when Steed finally rang. She had just finished checking the doors and windows prior to going to bed, and was in the kitchen making a cup of cocoa, having long since resigned herself to the fact that he wasn't going to call.

'Hello, Nina, is that you?' She licked dry lips nervously, her stomach fluttering madly.

'Yes, it's me; thank you for calling back.' The sound of his deep, gravelly voice was doing bizarre things to her insides, and in her agitation her voice came out in a breathless squeak.

'Carol left a message to say you wanted to talk to me. When did you ring?'

'This morning.' Three times, she added silently in her head. 'She said you were tied up in conference.'

'Stupid woman!' For a startled moment Nina thought he was referring to her. 'She knew I would be away all day—she had a number where she could reach me. It's only by chance that I called back here tonight to pick up some papers I need to work on.'

'I did say it wasn't important.' Now why am I trying to smooth things over? Nina thought in exasperation.

'Nevertheless, she knows better than that.' From the sharpness of his tone Nina gathered he wasn't to be placated. 'Well, what do you want?' He sounded faintly harassed and extremely tired, and Nina stood staring at the dove-grey wall silently, her mind blank.

'Nina?' His voice was irritable. 'Are you still there?'

'Yes, I'm here,' she stuttered into the receiver, feeling shivers of panic run down her spine. She didn't know where to start.

'Why is it a telephone conversation with you always resembles twenty questions?' His voice was carefully patient, as though talking to a very young child.

She pictured the big, lean body relaxed at his desk, the cold handsome face tight with exhaustion, and felt her breath constrict. 'I don't really know where to start.'

There was a pregnant pause and then, 'I'm not going to like this, right?' Steed asked grimly. 'Does it have anything to do with this weekend?'

'Yes and no,' Nina replied miserably, and heard the sharply indrawn breath on the other end of the line with a beating heart.

'Nina, I've been in a hell of a meeting since eight this morning and we're no nearer to a settlement now. I've got to work half the night preparing some figures and be back in there with all guns firing first thing tomorrow morning. I'm tired, I'm hungry and I need a shower. Now spit it out.'

'I can't discuss it over the phone, Steed; I just can't.' The silence was deafening. Long seconds ticked by.

'Damn you, woman; you'll be the death of me yet,' the deep voice drawled with wry humour. 'Do you mean to tell me you called to say you can't talk to me?'

Nina giggled nervously—he must think she was completely crazy. 'Sort of.'

'Look, sweetheart——' her heart leapt into her throat at the casual endearment '—I've got too many people relying on me to let this deal slip. There are a lot of people's jobs on the line and we need to come out on top. It's maybe going to take another couple of days' intensive negotiating before I can leave. If you need me there now I'll come, but can it wait?'

'Yes, it can wait,' she agreed immediately. 'I don't want you racing down here in the night and then driving back to London.'

'Am I allowed a clue to what this is all about?' he asked abruptly. 'The twins are OK, aren't they?'

'It's nothing to do with the boys,' she replied swiftly, her voice apologetic. 'It's us, Steed. We need to get things straight between us.'

'I see,' he said flatly. 'You sure as hell pick your moments. Are you trying to tell me you don't want to go through with it?'

'No!' The word shot out before she had time to think. 'That's the last thing I'm trying to say.'

'It is?' His voice was thick. 'Well, you've lost me.'

'I hope not.' Her voice was no more than a whisper and the silence at the other end of the phone was complete. A full minute ticked by and still he didn't speak, although she could hear him breathing. She struggled for words. 'We haven't been honest with each other, Steed, and I can't go on as we are. I want to tell you how I feel and you must do the same. It won't alter anything, I know; we'll still go ahead with the wedding and everything...' Her voice trailed away.

'It's a dangerous game you're playing.' His voice was husky. 'You might not like what you hear. Better the devil you know...'

'I'll take that chance.' Her voice was firm.

'Will you?' There was dark amusement in his voice. 'I don't know if I want to.'

'Please, Steed.'

'Thursday evening.' He spoke as if pronouncing a death sentence. 'I'll be with you Thursday evening. I'll call before I leave to say what time to expect me.'

'Thank you,' she answered quietly, and heard him mutter something under his breath as he replaced the receiver.

She awoke early the next morning from a deep dreamless sleep to find her mind clear and at peace for the first time in days. She found herself humming quietly as she prepared the twins' breakfast in the sunny kitchen. It was a beautiful spring morning, one of those rare English days when the sweet scent of life was heavy on golden air, a promise of lazy summer days ahead. A slight breeze stirred the flowering honeysuckle hanging precariously over the kitchen window, and a solitary bee droned by on its early quest for nectar. 'The drink of the gods,' Nina murmured dreamily to herself.

'You're happy this morning,' Mrs Finch beamed approvingly as she bustled in the kitchen door as the twins were leaving in a mad scramble of textbooks, gym kits and packed lunches. 'About time I heard you singing again—I've missed it.'

'Do you need any help?' Nina asked the small woman smilingly. 'If not, I thought I'd work in the studio today.'

'Go on with you,' Mrs Finch replied firmly. 'You know I like my kitchen to myself, Miss Nina. I'll bring you elevenses later.'

As she opened the creaking door to the studio she stood for a moment framed in the doorway, drinking in the familiar objects gilded in the sunlight streaming in through the huge windows. The room was already pleasantly warm, the massive panes of glass acting as giant radiators, and she opened one of the small windows at the side of the room, letting the cool breeze play over her hair, teasing the feather-light tendrils falling round her face.

'Right, Steed,' she muttered to the blank canvas before her. 'I'm going to capture you on paper, even if I can't in the flesh.'

By the time Mrs Finch waddled up the stairs, puffing and blowing, with her coffee and biscuits, the old varnished floorboards were strewn with discarded sketches, and Nina greeted the old woman's entrance with a huge sigh.

'What's the matter, lovey, can't you get it right?' The small daily bent and picked up several pieces of paper, exclaiming in wonder as she flicked them over, revealing Steed's dark face in a number of different views. They were all quite different in expression, but each one captured the vibrant and magnetic quality of the subject.

'I just can't decide which one I want to make a portrait of,' Nina said despairingly, gathering the pencilled sketches into a pile and looking through them again. 'Every time I decide on one something else just springs out.'

'My word, Miss Nina, you've come on,' Mrs Finch murmured admiringly. 'This is your young man, isn't it?' She gave a little shiver and plumped up her ample

bosom with her forearms as she stared at the enigmatic
face on the paper in front of her. 'I can see why you've
fallen for him,' she continued slowly. 'Like a film star,
isn't he?'

Nina smiled indulgently. 'I don't think he would appreciate that description, but I know what you mean,'
she agreed.

'You've certainly made him seem alive,' the little
woman continued thoughtfully. 'I've never met him, but
I feel I know him from all these different pictures. I hope
he loves you as much as you do him,' she added as she
walked towards the open door.

'What do you mean?' Nina asked, flushing scarlet.

'Oh, don't mind me, Miss Nina,' Mrs Finch chided,
seeing her stricken expression, 'you know how I ramble
on. It's just that you've drawn him so... Oh, there, I
don't know what the word is.' She closed the door
quietly, leaving Nina standing in the middle of the room,
dumbfounded.

She riffled through the sketches again, trying in vain
to see what the little Cornishwoman had meant. She had
drawn Steed as her heart's eye saw him—it was the only
way she could work. Her father had always approved
her unusual style, but now she wondered if maybe this
whole idea was a mistake.

'No,' she said out loud to the big room as she sipped
her hot coffee thoughtfully, 'I'm not ashamed of how I
feel, and if it comes through in the portrait, well, so be
it.' The frown which had wrinkled her brow at Mrs
Finch's words cleared as she glanced through the sheets
of paper again; it was only Steed's face that stared back
up at her.

By mid-afternoon she had put paint to canvas, returning again to the darkened room once the twins were

asleep and working on into the early hours, totally absorbed.

She found it surprisingly easy to wake the next morning, dressed and downstairs long before the twins stirred. The warm spell seemed to have ended, and a cold wet mist had stroked its damp tentacles round the house during the night, swathing the garden in heavy moisture and banishing the sun behind heavy grey clouds.

She drove the twins to school in spite of their combined and vehement protests, and a low growl of thunder rolled across the darkening sky as she parked the car in the large double garage at the back of the house.

Following an impulse, she walked across the lawns, the young spring grass wet and slippery underfoot, and followed the narrow path that led through the wild tangle of trailing bushes and stunted trees to emerge on the crumbling cliff path that straggled perilously down to the sea. Far below, menacing dark grey water was hurling foam-crested waves viciously on to the deserted beach, and a few wind-blown despondent seagulls called their lonely haunting cry into the dark void.

'I will get through this.' She sat down on a smooth polished rock, drawing her knees into her chin and gazing into the vast expanse of sky and ocean, revelling in the primitive power the elements were displaying. 'I will make him love me.' The wind snatched her words away, the mystic, savage majesty both thrilling and comforting her, touching some hidden chord deep in her soul that encouraged her to fight.

Eventually the piercingly cold wind chilled her bones through the thick red duffel coat she was wearing, forcing her to stretch stiffly and seek the sanctuary of the house.

Once inside, the call of the studio proved irresistible and, leaving the breakfast dishes soaking in hot soapy water, she hurried to the attic room, looking afresh with critical, probing eyes at the outline she had begun the day before. 'Not quite the right angle,' she muttered to herself, and after a few moments the room had worked its spell, drawing her into her work until she was totally absorbed. Mrs Finch came and went, the storm spent its fury, but she was blind to everything but the strong dark face taking shape on the canvas.

When the telephone rang she wriggled briefly in annoyance and then glanced at her watch, noting with surprise that the twins would be home soon. Taking the stairs two at a time, she skidded into the shadowed hall in seconds, whisking up the receiver as she jumped the last step and speaking the number breathlessly.

'Nina? Is anything wrong?' Just hearing that voice sent her heart into her mouth.

'I'm just out of breath,' she answered quickly. 'I was painting in the studio and I didn't want the phone to stop.'

'I've finished earlier than I expected,' he said brusquely. 'I can come down tonight if you haven't changed your mind.'

'I haven't changed my mind,' she affirmed quietly, intuitively recognising the tension the abrupt tone was endeavouring to hide. 'Are you sure you feel like driving down after working so hard? The weather isn't too good.'

'Damn the weather.' Nina smiled to herself—that sounded more like Steed. 'You're right, by the way,' he continued.

'I'm right?' He read the confusion in her voice.

'We do need to have a talk. I've been doing some thinking of my own over the last couple of days, and I think you can handle what I want to say.'

'I'm not a child, Steed.' Her voice was reproachful.

She heard a strained chuckle at the end of the line. 'Now that I am aware of, believe me. You're the only woman I've ever met who is a complete and utter puzzle to me in every way, and I don't like it.' His voice softened. 'I want to understand you, and I can't even get to know you.'

Her stomach churned but she forced herself to speak the words in her heart. 'I want you to get to know me, Steed, and I want to understand you, I really do.'

'Do you?' His voice was thick and husky. 'Hell, Nina, why are we having this conversation with half the country separating us? I'm coming down tonight. I'll take the chopper and land on the main lawn.'

'I'll be waiting for you.' There was a small tremor in her voice.

'You will?' She flushed at the question in the velvet tones. 'I wish I could see you now, face to face. There are things I need to know. Do you realise that, in all the time we've known each other, this is the first conversation where you have really talked to me?' There was a faint note of male triumph in his voice. 'I began to think you were never going to let me in; you've no idea what——' His voice stopped suddenly. 'Sorry, don't back off; I'm not going to rush you. It's just that I've been treading on eggshells for so long...'

'Eggshells?' She had the old feeling creep across her that they were talking at cross purposes again.

'Just stay there,' he said. 'Don't move; don't even breathe. I'll be with you as soon as I can.'

She heard the kitchen door flung open and Jason's shrill voice calling seconds before the twins came bursting into the hall. 'I shall have to go, Steed; the boys are home.'

'OK, just make it four for dinner. And Nina...'

'Yes?' she breathed, sensing his hesitation as his voice faltered.

'Remember I told you I'd been in love once?' Did she remember? It had haunted her ever since. 'The girl in question wore a white dress and had fresh flowers in her hair. I'd never seen anything so beautiful in my life. I couldn't take my eyes off her all evening but she was so young, just sixteen, and I frightened her badly. It all went wrong, and although I wrote her a letter to explain and tried to see her again she wouldn't let me near.' The letter he had written on the night of the party—she had ripped it up without reading it!

'What did the letter say?' Her voice was a tiny whisper, but he heard it.

'Didn't you get it?'

'I tore it up. I was feeling so hurt...'

'Don't.' His voice was a groan, and there was a moment of agonised silence. 'It only said I realised that night I had just made the biggest mistake in my life. I humiliated you without meaning to; I just wasn't used to dealing with such innocence. It begged for a second chance and asked your forgiveness. It said...'

'Yes?' Her legs were shaking so much that she could hardly stand.

'I'll tell you when I see you.' His voice was a deep throb. 'There's never been anyone before or since who has remotely touched my heart, Nina.' Something burst inside her with an incredible sweetness. 'I probably shouldn't be telling you now, but things couldn't be much worse than they have been for the last few weeks. I've felt I was going crazy, wanting, loving you so much...' She heard him breathe deeply. 'I'll settle for friendship from you if that's all you can give; I understand, but I need something…' His voice faltered and the phone went dead as he replaced the receiver at the other end.

'Steed!' She shook the receiver dazedly, unable to believe he had rung off without giving her a chance to reply. 'Steed, you idiot!' She felt suddenly light-headed, a million words cascading around her head causing her ears to throb and her chest to constrict tightly. He loved her! He had always loved her… Why hadn't he told her? But she knew the answer even as her mind posed it. He had thought he would frighten her still further away, and perhaps he would have been right, at the beginning. But what heartache they could have saved each other from.

'Nina?' Jason's small hand touched her arm gently. 'What's the matter?'

She focused her eyes with difficulty on the two small concerned faces in front of her; they kept swimming alarmingly in and out of her line of vision. 'Nothing's the matter—everything's wonderful,' she answered shakily and then promptly burst into a flood of tears, trembling with the force of her relief.

It was the sight of Jason's quivering lower lip and Peter's frightened red face that restored sanity. Gathering the children in her arms, she hugged them close, laughing through her tears as she tried to explain the madness of grown-ups.

'Didn't you know Uncle Steed loves you, then?' asked Peter incredulously, his face stretched in amazement. 'You should have asked me and Jason; we knew.'

She nodded solemnly. 'I'll remember that in the future, but everything is going to be all right now.' She was to remember those words a short while later and wonder what demon had been listening in the quiet of the dying day.

# CHAPTER NINE

AN HOUR had ticked by painfully slowly since Steed's call and the twins were feeling the overt pressure as much as Nina. Alternating between sharp bursts of rough play and sulky silences, the tension grew until Nina horrified herself by slapping Jason on his arm and shouting at Peter until the boy's small face was scarlet. Mortified, she pulled them both into her arms again, muttering her apologies and asking their forgiveness.

'Let's go down to the beach,' Jason suggested when calm had been restored over milk and biscuits. 'The rain's stopped and it's not so windy.'

Nina looked out of the kitchen window. Angry black clouds were scudding across a wild darkening sky, and the kitchen's soft warmth seemed temptingly cosy.

'I don't think so; it will be dark soon,' she said doubtfully.

'Oh, please, Nina,' Peter begged, adding his plea to his brother's. 'It won't be really dark for ages yet, and the wind is keeping the fog away. You always say the mist is the dangerous thing round here.'

They looked hopefully at her, brown eyes spaniel-like, and she capitulated suddenly, shooing them into thick coats and wellington boots. 'We're only going for a few minutes, mind,' she cautioned them as the boys ran, screaming, past her as she closed the kitchen door. 'Uncle Steed will arrive soon and we must be here to greet him.' Her heart pounded at the thought.

The tide was coming in fast as they reached the big beach of firm sand, the twins immediately disappearing behind a small cove hidden between rocky fingers where three or four of their school-friends were busy fishing in a massive rock-pool. Fierce Atlantic rollers were crashing tiny pieces of debris up the beach, and Nina wandered along the shoreline, idly sorting shells with the toe of her old beach shoes, breathing in the strong salty air as it whipped her long golden hair into wild disorder.

'He loves me, he loves me,' she said out loud to the wind and sky, the wonder of it causing her heart to palpitate madly. There was nothing stopping them now. She pictured Steed's strong, stern face as she told him what he had longed for years to hear.

A large grey wave swept vigorously up to her feet, causing her to leap backwards with a giggle of surprise. She turned and looked down the beach, checking on the boys, and was relieved to see they had left the hidden cove and were trailing along behind her, darting here and there as some particular morsel was unearthed by the encroaching sea.

She had lectured them again and again on the dangers of the fast incoming tide in these parts; the shores of Cornwall could be treacherously deceptive with their labyrinths of rocks and caverns. The enchanting rock-pools that were such a delight in the day could swiftly become murky graves by night.

We can be really married now, she thought as she gazed with unseeing eyes at the wind-tossed sea. Have children, make a life together. The thought of Steed as her husband in every sense of the word brought a thrill of pleasure shooting through her body. 'I'm so lucky,' she murmured into the charcoal sky, and it was at that point that the world as she knew it stopped existing.

The first inkling she had that something was terribly wrong was as Peter caught hold of her sleeve, his small face white and panic-stricken.

'Nina, we've been calling and calling!'

'The wind takes the sound away,' she answered automatically, arrested by the horror in his staring eyes. 'What's wrong?'

'It's Mary Finch.' Mrs Finch's granddaughter and the apple of her grandmother's eye. The small girl had been premature at birth and it had been touch and go for three months, and her mother was unable to have any more children.

'What about her?'

'We thought she'd follow us, Nina, really we did. Bob and Kelly said they'd wait for her but they got fed up and went home. Jason heard her calling; she's stuck on the rocks...' Nina was running now, her stomach turning over with fear. Peter was sobbing quietly as he ran, his small legs manfully keeping stride with hers. A stormy grey dusk was settling swiftly on to the shadowed sands, dark clouds obscuring the moon's faint light and plunging the beach into night.

'Where is she?' Nina reached Jason, who was jumping up and down in his anguish, tears coursing unheeded down his white cheeks.

'Over there.' He pointed into the distance where the children had been playing such a short time before, and Nina's heart sank with despair. The cove was completely submerged in angry foaming water, the waves already splashing halfway up the razor-sharp rocks.

'Are you sure she's there?' Nina began to ask, but then she saw her, a stiff little figure clinging desperately to the rock face in a small cleft in the cliff. The waves were breaking viciously near her thin body and it appeared that any moment she would be swept into the icy water and against the shingle-covered rocks.

'What are we going to do?' Peter whimpered faintly, echoing the question in her own heart. She glanced round frantically but the empty beach was bleak and cold. There was no one to help.

Her racing mind went into automatic and she found herself speaking calmly to the two boys, issuing orders quickly and firmly. 'Jason, you go up to the house and use the telephone. Ring the coastguard, ambulance... they'll tell you if anyone else needs to know. Go on now.' She gave him a little push and he sped off into the darkness as though he had wings on his feet.

'Peter, you take the short cut to the village. Go straight to Mary's house and tell her parents what's happened. Tell them to bring a rope, blankets, anything else they can think of.' He was running before she'd finished speaking and she called after him into the enveloping blackness, 'Be careful, Peter—mind the cliff path!'

Left alone, she looked back towards the small girl. Even as she had been speaking to the twins the sea had advanced another few feet, washing over her shoes as she stood on the shoreline. Mary would never hang on until help arrived. Fear and the biting cold water would cause those small hands to lose their weak grip and she would plunge into the black water. Even if she could swim, the fury of the sea would dash her against the rocks in seconds. She had to try and reach her; together they might both survive.

The shock as the icy water reached her middle caused her to gasp. She had discarded her shoes and coat at the water's edge, wading into the murky depths without a backward glance. The sea was like a silent enemy, powerful and relentless. She soon had to swim, the crashing waves trying to force her back to the shore, their magnetic pull insidious.

'Please, God, let me reach her...' she prayed out loud into the unfriendly sky, the bitter cold making her legs numb and her limbs heavy. She felt hard contact as the sea drove her slight frame against a submerged rock, but the fierce cold had anaesthetised her body and she was unaware that her legs were torn and bleeding. She was tiring; she wasn't going to make it...

She began to talk in her mind to Steed, telling him all the things she had left unsaid, making him promises she would not now be able to keep. It was as if he were here in the water beside her, encouraging her, forcing her to go on. She remembered his last pleading words, 'I need something...' The salt was stinging her eyes and filling her ears; her clothes were lead weights that were dragging her down. She didn't feel cold now; she didn't feel anything. 'Please, God, don't let me die...'

She was close enough now to see Mary's face. The small girl was blind with fear, her mouth drawn back in a contorted soundless scream, her wet hair plastered to her skull.

Nina had no more strength left to swim, and she was battling just to stay afloat. Time and time again the huge waves threw her close enough to the shining, slippery cliff face for her to feel the cold rock, but each time the relentless pull of the sea dragged her back into the foaming depths. The deep was claiming her for its own, reluctant to give up its prey.

She never knew how she managed to find the foothold. One minute she was totally submerged under the raging black water, the next she was clinging to the cliff surface with both feet wedged into a cleft and her hands scrabbling for a grip on the rough stone. Mary was a few inches above her but the waves were sweeping against her tiny body with enormous strength. It was a miracle that she had held on for this long.

Slowly Nina pulled herself up the cliff face an inch at a time. Twice she nearly fell back into the boiling water beneath her, but finally she was beside Mary, moving protectively against her small body.

It was some moments before the little girl became aware of her presence, and her tenacious grip on the rock surface didn't lessen. She might have been a small barnacle, so tight was her hold. She came from generations of fisherman stock; fear and respect of the sea was as natural to her as breathing. She knew what would happen if she should weaken for one second.

'Mary?' Nina whispered, worried the child had lapsed into shock. That would be deadly.

The small girl blinked twice, her wet salty face stiff. 'Hello, miss.'

'Everything is going to be all right,' Nina said reassuringly. 'All we've got to do is hang on tight and wait for them to come and find us.' She shifted slightly on the precariously narrow ledge.

'I'm scared.' The small voice was a whisper.

'You're doing wonderfully. Your mum and dad will be proud of you.'

'Me ma'll go mad.' The tiny body swayed as she flexed the small fingers of one blue hand. 'I can't hold on much longer, miss.'

'Do you think you can get up there if I help you?' Nina flicked her head upwards. She had noticed an area of rock where the spray disappeared. There was obviously an opening of some kind and it might be large enough to protect them from the pounding surf. They had to try. The water was still rising.

'I want to stay here.'

Nina looked into the terror-stricken eyes. It was imperative they move and soon. Quietly she began to talk, her low voice steady and confident, explaining the need for their ascent, calmly instilling trust into the trembling child.

Mary was immobile for a moment, staring down into the churning water, and then she nodded carefully. 'If you think we should, then, miss.'

'Good girl.' There was no time to lose. 'I'll go first and then reach down for you. We'll do it bit by bit. When I tell you, reach up one hand and hold on tight with the other one.'

Her body felt strange as she tried to move. She was shaking with cold and yet her legs had no feeling; a dangerous numbness was making her clumsy. Her heart pounded with fear as she strained for a hand-hold; the misty spray made the cliff treacherously slippy.

They struggled, inch by inch, up the solid wall. Her breath was hot in her throat and her muscles screamed in protest as she hauled the child bodily from one tiny ledge to another. Mary's slight little frame would normally have been as light as a feather, but her thick sodden clothes were weighing her down, making her seem as heavy as lead.

Exhaustion was making Nina's head swim, and as she jerked Mary the last few inches she sobbed with relief, falling backwards into the small wet cave thankfully.

The cave was, in fact, no more than a long narrow indentation in the stark cliff face, going back a mere five feet or so into the solid rock, but to Nina's sore, blurred eyes it was the most beautiful little room in the world.

Without its protection they could only have survived a few more minutes.

'When will they come for us?' Mary's cracked voice was trembling and her large brown eyes brimming with tears.

'Soon, darling, very soon.' Nina forced the panic from her voice. 'The thing now is to try and keep as warm as we can. I know you're wet through, but if we cuddle together as tight as we can it will make us feel better.' Hypothermia was a dark spectre at their side. She pulled the child into her arms, lying with her back to the opening, where drops of salt water fluttered, cradling Mary tightly against her chest.

They lay quietly for a time, their frozen limbs slowly relaxing. Her whole body ached with cold and sick exhaustion, and now that the blood was beginning to flow through her legs again the pain was excruciating. She became aware that her jeans were in tatters and it felt as though her left foot was broken.

'Tell me about school, Mary—do you like it?' Her teeth were chattering so much that she could hardly get the words out, but she felt they must keep talking; she was terrified they would fall asleep and never wake up.

They spent the next few hours weakly talking and dozing, stretching their cramped limbs every few minutes to keep them awake, although any movement now caused Nina acute agony. At one point icy water flooded round their chilled bodies, causing them to crouch upright in helpless fear, but after a few minutes it didn't happen again. They were clearly right at tide level. Nina breathed a quick prayer of thankfulness.

In the midst of the dark weary night Nina thought she heard voices shouting somewhere near by, but her throat was too sore and cracked to reply and she was sure it was just her imagination anyway. Mary had long since stopped asking about their rescue; she lay in the curve of Nina's body, quietly sleeping, and Nina didn't have the strength to waken her any more.

She felt herself slipping into unconsciousness, her efforts to fight it growing weaker each time. Gradually her swollen eyelids closed and her tormented mind raced menacingly down long water-filled corridors in wild dark dreams.

'They're here—we've found them!' She was vaguely aware of disjointed voices bouncing round her head, but her limbs were too heavy to move and this sweet sleep that had eased the pain from her body was too precious to lose.

She felt a warm hand touch her cheek and her eyelids fluttered slightly; beside her she was aware of Mary stirring in her sleep.

'They're still alive but they're in a bad way. Get those bags lowered down on the harness and tell the men we're bringing them up.' She wished all this shouting would stop; it was breaking into her head and making the pain come back. Why didn't they just leave her alone and let her sleep?

She felt herself being gently pulled over the cold wet rock and the pain was too intense to ignore any more. A voice was groaning and calling out in agony, but she didn't recognise it as hers.

'What the hell are you doing to her? Give her to me.'

'Look, mate, with all due respect, I'm trained for this sort of thing; let me——'

'I said give her to me.' She recognised that deep authoritative voice.

'Steed?' She tried to speak his name but there was no sound, and she forced her eyelids open. 'Steed?' This time a cracked murmur emerged from her white lips, causing the iron-hard arms that were holding her to stiffen. She could just make out his blurred outline against the dim early-morning light and was aware of his urgent voice talking as she lost consciousness again.

She came round once in the ambulance as it sped through the quiet sleeping streets, its siren screaming, fighting against the heavy material that cocooned her in its folds.

'It's all right, my love, it's all right. We've got to keep you warm. You're going to hospital.' Steed was by her side and the animal panic lessened, her white face relaxing as he stroked her cheek gently. 'You were so cold, my darling.'

'Mary?' He bent low to hear the whisper and she could see his face clearly, the dark unshaven skin and ruffled hair.

'She's fine.' His voice cracked. 'No bones broken; just shock and exhaustion, as far as they know.'

'I hurt.' He made a sound deep in his throat, a muscle tightening in his dark cheek. 'You need a shave...' She drifted off again into that welcoming abyss.

'Good morning.' The bright, cheerful voice and opening door registered in Nina's brain at the same time. She opened bleary, sore eyes slowly. 'It's a beautiful day and you've been asleep for nearly twenty-four hours. We're calling you the Sleeping Beauty.'

The young nurse was fresh-faced and glowing with energy. 'Come on, pet, let's have you sitting up, and then you can drink a nice cup of tea.' She helped Nina to rise in the smooth white hospital bed, plumping up the hard pillows vigorously as she spoke.

'Thank you.' Nina's voice was faint; all this boundless efficiency first thing in the morning was a little hard to take.

'Frightened everyone to death, you did,' said the nurse happily as she passed Nina the steaming cup of tea with two biscuits in the saucer. 'Still, as I always say, all's well that ends well.'

Realisation came bursting in as Nina glanced round the small pale green room, bright sunlight lighting up the tiled floor and turning the yellow daffodils on her bedside locker into shining gold.

'How's Mary?' she asked quietly, taking a small sip of the scalding-hot tea.

'The little girl who came in with you? Oh, she's fine—you know what children are. Down one minute and up the next; they're more resilient than us. She only stayed in for the day to be checked over. The doctor let her go home last night, more to put her poor mother's mind at rest, I think.'

'How long have I been in here?' Nina asked, grimacing as she shifted her aching legs slightly on the hard mattress.

'You were admitted early yesterday morning,' the nurse replied blandly, straightening the already immaculate bed. 'Caused quite a stir—it was all stations go for a while.'

The door opened again and a middle-aged sister beckoned urgently to the nurse. 'Bedpans on ward six, please, Nurse, and you'll have to help Mr Larkin down to the toilet. He flatly refuses to use a bedpan. And check Mr Swinton's dressing.' The nurse disappeared immediately in a flurry of activity, her big black shoes squeaking on the white tiles.

'Sister!' Nina called to the woman as she was closing the door again. 'Can I have a word, please?'

'Certainly.' The sister's smile was warm.

'What exactly is wrong with me?'

'The doctor will be round soon and he will explain,' the sister said politely, her expression softening as she saw Nina's troubled face. 'Nothing to worry about,' she confided softly. 'You were suffering from shock and cold, and lacerations to your legs and arms. I'm afraid your left ankle is broken, but you're healing nicely and there are no other complications. A few weeks and you'll be as good as new, my dear.'

The elderly doctor later confirmed the sister's words. 'You'll need plenty of rest for a day or two, but you're young and healthy and there's no need to treat yourself like an invalid.' His voice was clinically cool; she was clearly just another number to him. 'I see no reason why you can't go home later today. I understand your fiancé has made arrangements for you to be cared for.'

'Has he?' Nina asked eagerly, her face lighting up. The sister had told her Steed had had to be almost forcibly removed from her room late last night, where he had kept a vigil by the side of her bed until the staff had persuaded him to go home and take some rest.

'I must say you have been a lot less trouble than him,' the doctor added wryly, his thin, austere face breaking into a small smile as he saw the surprise on Nina's face. 'One would have thought you were the only patient in the hospital.'

'I'm sorry,' Nina said contritely, but the doctor gave a dry chuckle.

'Don't be. Reminds me of when I first met my wife. She died three years ago, but we had thirty happy years together and I wouldn't have missed a day. Oh, and by the way,' he patted her gently on the hand, 'that little girl owes her life to you. That was a very brave thing you did, young lady; very brave.' He patted her hand again and left the room, leaving Nina in a warm daze, her eyes full of tears. She had misjudged him; he wasn't such a dry old stick after all; just lonely. She sank back against the pillows and closed her eyes.

She heard Steed coming long before he reached her room. He was obviously arguing with someone in authority, his deep voice reaching her ears as he neared the door. 'I'd left strict instructions for you to call me the minute she was awake.'

'But there was no need, Mr Charlton.' The doctor's voice was painfully patient. 'You had told me you were calling back here first thing, several times,' the voice was mildly sarcastic, 'and she has only been awake a couple of hours.'

'A couple of hours!' The door was nearly swung off its hinges as Steed strode into the room, coming to an abrupt halt as he saw Nina sitting up in bed. The doctor who had spoken to her earlier cannoned into his broad back and an entourage of nurses and junior doctors came to a standstill in the corridor, their expressions ranging from outrage to delighted amusement.

'See what I mean?' the doctor mouthed silently as he backed quietly out of the room, closing the door gently behind him.

Steed stood rooted to the spot, the expression in his eyes causing hot colour to flood her pale cheeks. 'My precious love,' he muttered thickly, 'my beautiful, precious love.' He was by her side in an instant, almost lifting her out of the bed in his passion. His mouth was on hers, desperate hungry kisses covering her face until she could hardly breathe and her head began to swim.

'I'm never going to let you out of my sight again,' he said softly, his grey eyes dark with pain. 'I want you by my side every minute of every day.'

She looked up at him, her love glowing like stars in her eyes. 'Oh, Steed, I realised there was so much I wanted to say to you and I didn't think I was going to get the chance.'

'Don't.' His mouth straightened in anguish. 'I can't bear to think of it. I nearly went mad when I got home and there was no one there. I saw lights on the beach and went down...' He stopped and ran his hand through his hair. 'I think they must have thought I was crazy. The whole village seemed to be there and the police and ambulance arrived just as I did. When I found out it was you who was missing I think I really must have lost my mind for a while.'

He looked at her ruefully. 'It took three of them to hold me when I tried to go in the water. I'm afraid I was a little rough on them.'

'Oh, Steed,' she said weakly, her eyes soft.

'When it was decided by the sea-rescue that we had to wait until first light I'm afraid I totally disgraced myself. I doubt whether there's one person in the village left who doesn't think you must be mad to marry me.'

He stopped suddenly. 'You are marrying me, aren't you?' There was a trace of a smile at the corner of his mouth.

She opened her arms in reply, drawing him down beside her on the narrow high bed. They clung together tightly, their warm breath mingling as they drank their fill of each other's faces. 'You would have killed me too, you know,' Steed said softly as he stroked the soft golden hair from her flushed face. 'If you had been lost I wouldn't have wanted to go on. I love you more than life itself, Nina; I always have.'

He took her face in his hands as he looked deep into the dark violet eyes. 'Say it, Nina. Tell me I wasn't wrong yesterday when I went up to the studio and saw your work. Tell me what those pictures told me.'

'I love you,' she said simply, her heart in her eyes.

'I've dreamed for years of hearing you say that. I've waited so long for you that I'd almost given up.' His face was both tender and wistful with a deep throb of possessive victory in his voice that thrilled her heart. He kissed her again, long and deeply, drawing away to run a shaky hand through his hair. 'My ego's taken a bit of a hammering, I can tell you.'

She smiled at the mocking reproach in his voice. 'Well, from what I've heard, it was about time.'

He looked at her through narrowed eyes. 'James?' She nodded slowly as his face straightened. 'I could whip that young man for all the trouble he causes.' There was a trace of the furious anger he had displayed at the villa. 'One thing I promise you, Nina: from the first day I saw you there has been no one else in my life who matters that much.' He snapped his fingers sharply. 'It's to my eternal discredit that I first had the idea regarding the twins because it seemed a feasible proposition to put to you when your father died. I was worried if I just arrived on your doorstep offering to buy the house for you and settle the debts you would think I had an ulterior motive.'

'Well, didn't you?' she teased gently.

He grinned wickedly. 'You can bet your sweet life I did. I've never been as nervous in my life as I was that day.'

She remembered vividly her fear of the cold hard stranger he had seemed that evening so many weeks ago. 'You didn't appear nervous.'

He drew her to him again, turning her gently against him so she was pressed slightly backwards, looking up into his hot dark eyes. 'You've got a lot to learn about me, woman, and I'm sure going to enjoy teaching you. I've practised so much restraint over the last few weeks that I think I'm going to eat you alive. You can't imagine how much I've wanted you, how many times I nearly took you, regardless of how you felt about me.'

'I knew you wanted to make love to me,' she said, flushing as his eyes devoured her mouth. 'But I thought it was just a physical thing, that you loved someone else.'

'Someone else?' His voice was incredulous. 'Who on earth...?'

'I hadn't decided that,' she replied demurely.

He laughed softly, his face wryly amused. 'For such an innocent little thing, you can be as hard as iron when you want to be, can't you? Didn't you know you were putting me through hell on earth?'

'But you were always so angry, so overpowering...'

He grinned sardonically. 'I'd have preferred "charismatic" or "irresistible", but I can live with "overpowering".' She leant against his hard body, soaking up the male smell of him.

'I think I knew even at sixteen you were the one man I could love for the rest of my life.'

His mouth twisted cynically. 'Well, you sure fooled me. To have the goods displayed so temptingly and be unable to touch...'

She punched him lightly in the chest. 'You did a certain amount of touching, if I remember rightly.'

He grimaced mockingly. 'I never was very good at resisting temptation. I was always the one caught with my hand in the candy jar. However, I think you'll realise once we're married just how much restraint I've had to exercise...' His eyes glowed with desire. 'How I shall survive the next three weeks I can't imagine. You'll have to lock your bedroom door each night or put the twins on guard duty.'

She looked down at the stiff cotton bedspread, her fair hair falling round her face. 'You don't have to wait,' she whispered slowly. 'I want to belong to you and——'

He interrupted her, lifting her chin and looking into her shy eyes. 'I'll wait.' His voice was grimly determined. 'Nothing is going to spoil that day for us. It might be old-fashioned, but when you walk down the aisle and make those vows you become my wife in the eyes of the world. I'm going to make that night a night you'll remember all your life. Get plenty of sleep before the big day——' his eyes glittered teasingly '—you're going to need it—you won't get much thereafter.'

'Steed?' She panicked suddenly. 'My ankle. What if I can't walk by then? We'll have to postpone it.'

'Oh, no, we won't,' he said thickly. 'I'll carry you if need be. My patience only runs so far.' He smiled at her, his eyes burning. 'I still can't believe this is for real; I need to know you're mine.' His voice was a low groan as he pulled her tightly against him, his hands moving over her body in a slow caress while she drowned in the heat of his kiss. She shivered when she felt his touch on her breasts, their points hardening in answer to his gentle fingers as a wild excitement had her pressing still closer to his body, the breath shuddering in his throat.

'I want to set you on fire, make you gasp my name again and again as you ask for more...' He slid his hands down to the curve of her thighs, pulling her into his hardness, his voice harsh with longing.

'I love you...' Her own voice was soft with desire, an exquisite yearning to belong to him completely leaving her trembling and unresisting in his arms.

It was Steed who pulled away at last, running a shaking hand over his face as he pulled her close with his other arm. 'I'm sorry,' he said gruffly, 'I don't want to frighten you.'

'You don't.' Her voice was shy.

'Well, you sure scare the hell out of me,' he said with grim humour. 'Maybe it's me who's going to need the guards on the door until D-Day.' She laughed tremulously, her body still hungry for his touch.

'We've got all the time in the world.' He looked at her lovingly. 'As long as I have you, nothing else matters. Nothing will part us again; I'll never let you go. You are mine now and forever.' As his voice rang out in ecstatic triumph he drew her against him, lifting her chin and claiming her lips in possessive mastery.

The old doctor opened the door and smiled gently, shutting it again quietly and hanging the 'Do Not Disturb' sign on the handle with a soft sigh. 'Love calms the savage breast,' he muttered to himself as he walked down the silent corridor, his watery eyes seeing back down the years, with a lightness to his step that had been missing for many a long day.

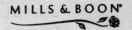

MILLS & BOON®

# Christmas Treats

### A sparkling new anthology
### —the perfect Christmas gift!

Celebrate the season with a taste of love in this delightful collection of brand-new short stories combining the pleasures of food and love.

**Figgy Pudding**
by PENNY JORDAN
**All the Trimmings**
by LINDSAY ARMSTRONG
**A Man For All Seasonings**
by DAY LECLAIRE

And, as an extra treat, we've included the authors' own recipe ideas in this collection—because no yuletide would be complete without...Christmas Dinner!

# MILLS & BOON®

---

> ## Season's Greetings
> ## To all our readers!

The Season's Greetings Gift Pack brings you four fabulous romances from star-studded authors including Betty Neels.

And as an extra special Christmas treat we're offering the pack at a discounted price of just £6.60--that's 4 books for the price of 3.

The Mistletoe Kiss  by Betty Neels
Merry Christmas  by Emma Darcy
The Faithful Wife  by Diana Hamilton
Home for Christmas  by Ellen James

Available: November 1997

*New York Times* **Bestselling Author**

# REBECCA BRANDEWYNE

## *Glory Seekers*

Broadcast journalist Claire Connelly is reunited with
her ex-lover, homicide detective Jake Seringo, as they
both investigate the death of a US senator's wife.
Up against corruption, lies and murder, they race to
untangle a web of secrets that could topple a dynasty.

*"Like fine wines, some writers seem to get better and
better. Rebecca Brandewyne belongs to this vintage
group"*—**Romantic Times**

1-55166-276-0
**AVAILABLE FROM DECEMBER 1997**

# LYNN ERICKSON

## *Night Whispers*

**Someone is watching her every move...**

Anna Dunning is living a nightmare. A stalker
is on the prowl and her only hope is a tough
ex-cop—but can she trust him?

*"...shadowy and suspenseful, leaving the reader with
a creepy, unsettled feeling of
expectation."*—Publishers Weekly

MIRA®

1-55166-178-0
**AVAILABLE FROM DECEMBER 1997**